POUND OF FLESH

ARCANE CASEBOOK 10

DAN WILLIS

Print Edition – 2023

This version copyright © 2023 by Dan Willis.

All rights reserved. No part of this book may be reproduced or transmitted in any form or by any electronic or mechanical means, including photocopying, recording or by any information storage and retrieval system, without the express written permission of the copyright holder, except where permitted by law.

This novel is a work of fiction. Names, characters, places and incidents are either the product of the author's imagination, or, if real, used fictitiously.

Edited by Stephanie Osborn
Supplemental Edits by Barbara Davis

Cover by Mihaela Voicu

Published by

Runeblade Entertainment
Spanish Fork, Utah.

1

DISENCHANTED

Something was wrong.

Alex couldn't figure out what it was, but something was definitely amiss. He could feel himself drifting back to consciousness and, any moment now, the massive headache that always accompanied Limelight use would hit him. That was never fun, so he reveled in the nothingness of his semi-awareness.

Yesterday he'd been shot right through his linked shield by a German with a machine gun. It happened because the runes he linked to his body took a fraction of a second to recharge. The Limelight was supposed to give him the insight to fix that problem, and he had a deep feeling that it had done just that.

He'd have to wake up and wait for the headache to subside, but once it had, he'd check the typewriter.

The thought of his typewriter pulled another memory from the depths of his mind. For some reason he'd imagined speaking to Iggy in his vault. The man had berated him for using Limelight but Alex couldn't remember anything else. His drifting mind reminded him that since it was a dream, there might not be anything else to the thought.

Gradually, Alex began to perceive light, then the ceiling of his vault. Several things were immediately wrong with this, and a surge of adrenalin pushed his mind into a semblance of focus. First, the debilitating headache he was expecting hadn't come. The light hurt his eyes a bit, but it was more like the feeling of being in a dark room when someone turned on a bright light, not the agonizing spasm of sunlight with a hangover.

Second, the prickling sensation that always accompanied his connection to his magic wasn't there. It was like the few times he'd been in the country and was suddenly aware of the quiet, the absence of the background noise of the city.

Last, the ceiling above him was high, arched, and not made of gray vault stone.

"Wharugh," he mumbled, trying to force his body to sit up.

This brought another out-of-place fact to his consciousness...he was in a bed.

He tried to speak again, to call out to whoever owned the strange room, but only a rough gasp came out.

When no one responded, he tried to move again, slowly forcing his head to turn. He still wasn't able to raise it, but at least he had a better view of the room. White wallpaper with blue accents covered the walls interrupted by a large, arched window casing that let in the pale light of morning. A door of whitewashed wood occupied the wall that faced the foot of the bed, but Alex could only see that out of the corner of his eye.

Beside the bed was an end table that held a shiny silver lamp with a cream-colored shade, a book with a dark cover, and a glass of water on top of a cork coaster.

As soon as he saw the water, Alex became aware of the dryness in his mouth. His tongue felt like it was swollen to twice its normal size.

No wonder you can't talk, he thought.

"So," Sorsha's voice greeted him. "You're finally awake."

Alex shifted his gaze to the door where the sorceress now stood, leaning on the frame. She wore a white dress that clung to her slim frame in all the right places, and her black cigarette holder hung from her fingertips. Where Alex expected an affectionate grin, or maybe a subtle smile, he found her lips in a tight line and her eyes were hard and cold.

Uh-oh, Alex thought, his mind finally starting to put the pieces of what he'd seen into place. The decor meant he could only be in one of Sorsha's guest rooms in her flying castle. If Alex was here, that meant he'd been found in his vault, where the Limelight had been sitting out, in plain view, on his rollaway table. Logically, the only person who could have found him was Iggy, since only he had a rune key that would allow him to pass Alex's cover doors. Sorsha could blast one down, of course, but Iggy was far more likely.

If Iggy found me, he thought, *then I should be at the brownstone. The only reason for me to be here is if I've been asleep for a long time.*

That thought gave him chills, even under the heavy blanket on the bed.

"Water," he managed in a broken rasp.

Sorsha walked around the bed to the side table, vanishing her cigarette holder as she went. Her heels clacked on the stone floor until she drew even with the bed and stepped onto the large rug beneath it.

"You'll need to sit up first," she said, her face still a mask of anger.

She waved her hands and the covers withdrew, folding themselves out of the way. With another gesture, Alex felt himself pulled up so that he was leaning against the pillow and the headboard in a sitting position.

"Drink this slowly," she said, picking up the water glass and pressing it to his lips.

Alex resisted the urge to gulp down the cool liquid, and sipped instead. After half a minute of this, he pulled his head back and Sorsha withdrew the glass.

"Thanks," he managed. "How long..."

His voice gave out and he swallowed.

"Five weeks," Sorsha said, her eyes no longer cold, but flashing with anger. "Five weeks," she said again. "Five weeks where I didn't know if you were going to live or die; well, make that four weeks because that Limy doctor wouldn't tell me anything for the first week." She was pacing by the bed, but she suddenly rounded on him. "Explain yourself."

"Uh," Alex stammered, his still-sluggish brain struggling to catch up. "Well, you remember the Limelight powder?"

"Of course I do," Sorsha sputtered. "I'm not a simpleton. I also remember how dangerous it is, and I remember how practitioners who use it go insane. How could you be so stupid as to expose yourself to it?"

"You were dying," he said. It wasn't the only reason he'd used the drug, but it was certainly the one that mattered most to him.

Sorsha raised her hand and slapped him.

"Don't you dare blame this on me!" she shrieked at him.

"I'm not," Alex managed, unable to move his arm enough to rub his sore jaw. "You were in trouble and I had a way to help you; besides, I took precautions. I don't have an overwhelming need for the drug."

Sorsha's look softened.

"Well, that's good," she said, "because Iggy poured your stash down the sink in the brownstone's kitchen."

Alex's muscles surged and his heart beat faster at that news. He liked to pretend he wasn't addicted to Limelight, but his body disagreed.

"I'm not sorry," Alex said once his racing heart calmed down. "You're alive."

The anger bled out of Sorsha's eyes, and she sat down on the bed next to him.

"So, it seems, are you," she said, taking his hand. "And I am glad."

Alex smiled at her but that only brought back her hard eyes.

"If you ever do anything like this again," she scolded him, "I'll make you suffer for it the way I've suffered for the last month."

"Yes ma'am," he said, in his most serious voice.

Then Sorsha leaned in and kissed him. It was a gentle kiss where she pressed her lips slowly and deliberately to his.

"I'm relieved," she said as they broke apart. "Iggy didn't know if you'd ever wake up."

Alex found that he could move his arm and held it up to cup Sorsha's cheek.

"Thanks for looking out for me," he said.

Sorsha leaned in quickly and planted another kiss on him, this time on his forehead.

"Drink your water, then get dressed. Your clothes are in the wardrobe."

She pointed to a large, white cabinet on the other side of the bed, then stood.

"I'll call Ignatius and inform him that you're awake."

With that, and a wink, Sorsha left the room, summoning her cigarette holder, with its still-lit cigarette, as she went. Alex watched her go, noting the sway of her hips in the form-fitting dress. Lots of people called Sorsha the Ice Queen, partly for her business and partly for her demeanor, but Alex liked her warm, playful side, even though she didn't show it much.

Once the door was closed, Alex picked up the cup and sipped the water till it was gone. By then, his hand wasn't trembling as much and he felt like he could stand. Swinging his legs over the side of the bed, he tried to get to his feet and fell back onto the mattress.

Mustering his will, he tried again and managed to get upright. The more he moved, the more confident he felt in his ability to control his limbs, and he made it to the wardrobe with only a few wobbles. He meant to get dressed right then, but the act of standing made him seek out the bathroom urgently.

Once he finished in there, it took him almost fifteen minutes to dress himself, but he managed it, and he was just tightening his tie when Iggy arrived.

"Well, you're a sight for sore eyes," he said. "Standing up, I mean."

"Sorsha said you've been taking care of me," Alex said. "Sorry about that, and thank you."

Iggy set his medical bag down on the bed, then opened it. Instead of just the two halves of the lid opening opposite each other, the bag sagged open as if the sides weren't connected. Alex could see that the long sides had a hinge on the bottom and they were attached to the short sides by the lining of the bag. When the lid was closed, the two halves kept the sides in place, but once they opened, the entire bag sagged open like some sea monster's great maw.

"That's new," Alex said.

"I'm getting too old to dig around in my bag for things," his mentor replied.

Alex didn't bother to hold back the smile that was forming on his face. He was grateful to see the old man, despite the circumstances. Sorsha had said he'd been unconscious for over a month, but it didn't feel that way to Alex. He felt like he'd just woken up from a long sleep. Paradoxically, it did feel like it had been a long time since he'd seen his friend and mentor.

Iggy didn't appear changed by the time that had passed; in fact, he seemed invigorated, with a bristling mustache and eyes that shone with vigor.

"Sit on the bed," Iggy said, as he finished selecting things from his bag.

As Alex complied with his instructions, Iggy went around the bed to the side table and retrieved the empty water glass. Taking it to the bathroom, he filled it halfway with water from the tap, then returned to his bag and began adding liquid and powders from several containers.

"Drink," he said, pushing the glass into Alex's hands.

Steeling himself, Alex put the glass to his lips and downed it in one go. Alchemical draughts were usually vile, and he made a point of drinking them quickly. This one did not disappoint.

Once Alex finished the disgusting concoction, Iggy listened to his heart with a stethoscope, took his blood pressure, and then looked him over with one of Andrea Kellin's True Seeing lenses.

"Well," he said at last, slipping the lens back into its velvet case. "The good news is that you're in excellent physical health, despite your long convalescence."

"I chalk it up to clean living," Alex joked.

"You may attribute that to me," Iggy said with no trace of humor. "I kept you well dosed with alchemical substances that would maintain your organs and your muscle tone while you slept."

"Speaking of sleeping," Alex said, his tone turning serious, "why did you keep me out for so long? I'm assuming you used dream syrup."

"Of course I did," Iggy replied, annoyance in his voice. "The reason is a bit complicated, and I promised to share it with Sorsha once you were awake." He began packing up his bag, then pulled a cord that retracted the sagging sides. Shutting the lid and fixing the clip to keep it closed, he picked up the bag, turning to Alex. "She's expecting us for tea in her winter parlor."

With that, Iggy turned and headed for the door. Alex started after him and found that whatever the doctor had put in his water, it had eliminated the fog in his mind. As far as he could tell, his arms and legs worked just like they always had, and he had no trouble keeping up with his mentor.

Iggy led the way through the hall and around the curved edge of the flying castle to an ornate balcony. Below was Sorsha's massive foyer, and Alex could see the cover door he'd installed when Sorsha had been under the Legion's withering spell. Down on the main level, an ornately carved door led to a solarium with large windows, several bookshelves, and elegant couches.

Sorsha sat on the largest couch in the center of the room, with her cigarette holder clenched in her teeth. A low table stood in front of the couch, and a maid had just finished setting down a silver serving tray with a teapot, cups, milk, and sugar.

"Right on time," Sorsha said, motioning for them to sit. She vanished her cigarette, then poured out the tea, being careful to make it to each person's taste. Once she'd handed both Iggy and Alex a saucer with a teacup on it, she picked up her own and sat back in the couch.

"Now," she said, ignoring her tea, "I've waited a full month for an explanation and I am finished waiting." When she said this, the pale blue of her eyes flashed, lit from within by her magic. "So, out with it."

"You remember his little problem with transfer toxicity," Iggy said once he'd sampled the tea.

"Of course I remember," Sorsha scolded. "I'm not a simpleton."

Iggy dared to give her a patronizing look.

"Then explain it to me," he challenged her.

Sorsha blew out an exasperated breath, giving Alex a hard look that clearly communicated that this was all his fault.

"Alex used too much magic," Sorsha began, "or rather he channeled too much power into and out of his physical body. Like a bricklayer trying to lift too many bricks, he injured himself, but instead of just hurting his back, he made his body excessively sensitive to the flow of magical energy."

Iggy raised an eyebrow at Sorsha's explanation, but he quickly followed it with a smile.

"Quite right, my dear," he said. "In Alex's case, it means that he can't use runes that cause large amounts of magic to flow into or out of his body—runes such as escape runes or the life restoration construct."

"What does that have to do with me being asleep for a month?" Alex asked.

Iggy turned to face him, giving Alex a serious look.

"Because Limelight floods your brain with magical energy," he said. "That's why it feels like you understand all of magic's secrets when you use it."

"But the strain on the mind is just like transfer toxicity," Sorsha guessed. "That's why everyone who used it went insane."

Iggy turned to her and nodded.

"Yes," he said, turning back to Alex. "I'm afraid that the Limelight damaged your mind and body further."

"How much further?" Alex asked.

"Far enough that any use of magic could overwhelm you," he said. "It might even kill you outright."

Alex just sat there, letting the silence grow. He'd known, of course, that he wouldn't be able to use any escape runes until his body had a chance to heal itself, but this seemed a bit extreme.

"No magic at all?" he asked.

"Nothing," Iggy said. "Even writing a mending rune could damage you."

Alex thought about that, turning it over in his mind. There was only one conclusion, but he simply refused to accept it.

"You'll have to swear off magic," Sorsha said, naming his most desperate fear. "At least until you're well again."

"Isn't there a potion I can take to speed this up?" Alex asked.

Instead of answering, Iggy looked at the floor.

"What is it?" Sorsha prompted him.

"From now on, Alex can't do any magic," he said.

"I won't," Alex assured him. "I can handle myself."

"If that were true, lad, you wouldn't have used the Limelight. No, when I said you can't use magic, I meant exactly that. I think you'll also find that only extremely minor potions will work on you, and even they might not be fully effective."

Alex felt the hair on his arms stand up as he remembered waking up in Sorsha's guest bed. He hadn't been able to feel his magic then and, as he searched inwardly with his mind, he couldn't feel it now.

"What have you done?" Sorsha demanded, clearly reading the growing panic on Alex's face.

"Iggy?" Alex said, his voice teetering on the brink of fear.

"I've sealed your magic away," the doctor said, "until I believe your body is healed enough for you to continue being a runewright."

"You can't do that," Alex gasped. "It's not possi..." His voice faded off to nothing as an image flooded into his mind. The image of a vibrant and complex rune worked right into the skin.

"Alex," Sorsha said, raising her voice in alarm. "What is it?"

Alex didn't answer. Instead he grabbed at the buttons of his shirt and began undoing them as quickly as he could. There hadn't been a mirror in the wardrobe in his sick room, so he hadn't seen himself when he dressed, and now he wondered if that was on purpose.

Pulling his shirt open, Alex gasped.

"What...is...that?" Sorsha demanded, rising partially from her seat.

To Alex it sounded like her voice was coming from someplace far away. All across his chest, from his left shoulder running diagonally down to his right hip was an incredibly complex rune. It glowed with jewel-like colors but at a subdued level, like it was low on magical energy. He knew what the rune was, he'd seen it before, once on Paschal Randolph and once on Moriarty. The Immortals used it to enforce whatever strange covenants their member runewrights pledged to uphold. If they broke their oaths, the rune would activate and cut them off from their magic.

"A damnation rune," he said, answering Sorsha's question.

2

RETURN TO NORMALCY

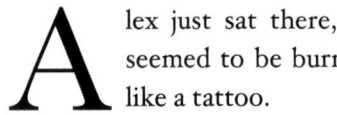

Alex just sat there, staring down at the complex rune that seemed to be burned into his chest, existing under his skin like a tattoo.

"You can't do this," he said again, his voice hoarse.

Iggy harrumphed at that, puffing his cigar.

"The evidence of your own eyes would seem to differ."

"What...is...that?" Sorsha repeated her question, tension blooming in her voice.

"No," Alex said, his astonishment fading. "I don't mean that it can't be done, I mean that *you* can't do it. Not unless your rune lore has taken a substantial leap." He looked up, staring hard at Iggy. "Did you use the Limelight?"

Anger flowed over the doctor's face, but he mastered himself almost instantly.

"Tosh," he sneered. "I don't mean to sound callous, but I wouldn't have used that stuff if your life was in the balance."

Alex's guts seemed to twist inside him. He didn't know whether to be relieved or insulted. After a moment's consideration, he settled on relieved. No sooner had he decided on that, than the inevitable conclusion of that answer blossomed in his mind.

"That means you involved Moriarty," he said, a bit stunned by the conclusion. "How?"

To his surprise, Iggy's face seemed to sag, and he rubbed his forehead.

"Thank God," he said in a soft voice.

"If someone doesn't tell me what's going on right now," Sorsha growled, her voice shifting dangerously close to her sorceress voice, "I'm going to start freezing body parts."

Iggy raised his hand in a defensive motion.

"Easy, my dear," he said, "give me a moment, please, and I'll explain everything."

Her drawn-on brows threatened to knit together, but after a moment she sat back in her chair and folded her arms.

"First of all," Iggy said, puffing on his cigar again. "Alex just figured out how that rune got on his chest, something that would have required deduction skills. That makes me think he hasn't lost his mental faculties."

Alex looked to Sorsha as Iggy explained, and she seemed to visibly relax at his conclusion.

"I found Alex passed out in his vault several months ago," Iggy went on. "I suspected he was using some kind of magical drug, but I didn't suspect Limelight because I was under the mistaken presumption that it had all been destroyed."

"We all were," Sorsha said, giving Alex a hard look through narrowed eyes.

"Anyway," Iggy said, clearly attempting to keep the conversation from fracturing, "I took the glass Alex used the night I found him passed out and gave it to Moriarty."

"How?" Alex demanded.

"Why?" Sorsha said.

"To answer your question in reverse order, I sought out Moriarty because the rune lore he and his immortals possess is well beyond even my own knowledge. I needed him to analyze the residue in Alex's glass."

"What did he find out?" Alex asked.

"Unfortunately, all he could tell me about the substance was that it was alchemical, and that it was saturated with magic. I wasn't sure it was Limelight until I found Alex's stash of the stuff five weeks ago."

"But how did you contact Moriarty in the first place?" Alex demanded.

"I knew he was keeping an eye on you somehow, and that he'd penetrated the brownstone's defenses in the past, so I simply knocked on the wall where you said his vault door appeared."

"And what?" Alex asked, "he just appeared?"

"Apparently, he believed your life was worth saving," Iggy replied.

"And you had him put a damnation rune on me why?'

"Obviously, to deprive you of your magic," Iggy said, as if that were the most normal thing in the world. "Your body has suffered extensive magical damage," he went on, looking Alex in the eyes. "I know you'd be tempted to use your magic whenever anyone was in trouble, and when you did that, it would kill you, little by little."

Alex wanted to refute that statement, but deep down, he knew his mentor was right. Still, that should have been his decision to make.

"So you forced me into convalescence."

"If he hadn't, I would have," Sorsha said, her pale blue eyes flashing. "So, count yourself lucky that you get to work while you heal, instead of lying in one of my many freezers."

Alex wanted to be mad, but he could hear the anxiety underlying her voice. Of all the people he'd let down by using the Limelight, Sorsha clearly felt it the most.

Of course, she'd be dead if you hadn't used the Limelight, he reminded himself.

Out loud, he said, "How long is it going to take my body to heal?"

Iggy gave him a sympathetic look and shrugged.

"No way to know," he said. "As far as I know, no one has ever attained this level of transfer toxicity. We're in uncharted waters, my boy."

"So it could be months or it could be years?" Alex said, his voice rising in anger.

Iggy shrugged again.

"How am I supposed to do my job?" he demanded.

"The same way I do," Sorsha said. "My work with the FBI is mostly about my intellect and what I know; my magic rarely comes into it."

Alex thought about arguing, but Sorsha had a point.

"Fear not," Iggy said, crushing out the remains of his cigar. "I've been working with your apprentice, Michael, in your absence, and his rune writing has come along nicely. Between him and myself, we should be able to keep your rune book stocked with what you'll need in your detective work."

Alex didn't like that, but his rational mind told him it would work out fine. The good thing about runes was that you didn't have to have a scrap of magical talent to use them; you only needed magic to write them.

Still, it didn't feel right, not that he had much of a choice.

He looked down at the rune on his chest again, then began buttoning up his shirt.

"I don't know that I like this," Sorsha said. "Alex has an annoying tendency to get himself shot. You said only minor potions will work on him now, so how will he use that fancy shield rune of his?"

"He'll have to wear a pendant like the one he gave you," Iggy said. "Even then, the proximity to the damnation rune might affect its usefulness."

The expression on Sorsha's face showed Alex that she didn't like that one bit. To be fair, he had been shot a bit more than what statistics would say was average.

"I'll be careful," he offered.

"Liar," Sorsha and Iggy said together.

"Cross my heart," Alex protested. "If anything gets hairy, I'll bring in Mike, or Danny."

"If anything gets, as you call it, hairy, you'll call me," Sorsha insisted, her eyes glowing again.

"Or you," Alex amended hastily.

Iggy sighed heavily, then leaned down to grab his bag.

"Well, that's all the bad news," he said, standing. "On the plus side, your body is physically fit and, sooner or later, it will heal enough for you to access your magic again. For now, you can return to work. I can attest that Sherry, Michael, and Daniel are all eager to see you."

Alex started to stand, but Sorsha gave him a look that dared him to leave, and he sat back down.

"I'll be along in a bit," he said.

If Iggy caught Sorsha's look, he ignored it. He simply nodded politely to Sorsha, then turned and headed back out into her foyer where Alex's vault door was located.

Alex and Sorsha sat in silence until the sound of the vault door closing reached them, then Alex spoke.

"I'm sorry," he said.

Sorsha stood up and crossed to him as he stood as well. He wasn't sure how she was going to react, but he was pleasantly surprised when she threw her arms around him and buried her face in his chest.

"No," she said, "I'm sorry. You had to use Limelight because you wanted to save me. Thank you."

Alex held her tightly, running his hands up and down her back.

"So, we're both sorry," he said.

She pushed on his chest, freeing herself from his grasp.

"Don't think that means I'm not upset with you," she said, looking up at him with a half-smirk playing across her lips. "You've got a long road ahead of you before I'm going to forgive you."

Alex chuckled.

"I suppose I deserve that. How can I make it up to you?"

"You're going to have dinner with me tonight."

"Somewhere special; I can make reservations."

She shook her head.

"We'll eat here," she said. "Six o'clock sharp. After that I want to hear about your day, and maybe we can do some reading."

"Reading?"

She smiled sweetly at him.

"I'm sure you have many files to catch up on. And, if you get tired of that, bring some of Dr. Bell's pulp novels."

Alex laughed.

"You wouldn't like anything like that," he said.

"I have my own reading material," she said, smirking. "This is about spending time together. And," she went on, arching one eyebrow, "once we're tired of reading, we'll go to bed."

For the first time since he woke up, Alex's face split into a genuine smile. It wasn't the first time he'd stayed over with Sorsha, and she'd even been to his vault bedroom a time or two, but it seemed like a very long time. He enveloped her in his arms again, smelling the fresh scent of her platinum blonde hair.

"I don't need to go to work today," he said, nuzzling her hair. "I'm sure everything can wait for tomorrow."

Sorsha pushed him away again, giving him a smirk.

"Your friends have been worried about you," she said, stepping back. "Go to work and let them know you're fine. I'll see you tonight."

Alex leaned in and kissed her briefly, then followed Iggy out to the foyer and into his vault. He figured someone had been keeping him clean while he was unconscious, but the idea that he hadn't showered for a month made him feel dirty, so he stopped off at the brownstone for a shower.

Once he felt sufficiently clean, he ignored the rune on his chest as he shaved, then got dressed and headed for his office.

"Boss!" Sherry shrieked the moment he opened the vault door into his office.

Alex didn't have time to even register what was going on before his secretary slammed into him, wrapping her arms around him in a fierce hug. He didn't have to ask how she knew he was coming, but it still surprised him.

"Easy," he said, trying to catch his balance.

"I was so worried about you," Sherry said, still holding on to him. "Dr. Bell wouldn't tell me anything. No one would tell me anything, even my cards."

Her voice was shifting from happy to weepy, so Alex returned her hug then pushed her to arm's length.

"I'm sorry I scared you," he said. "I was hurt pretty bad, but I'm okay now. Let's just put it behind us and get back to work."

Sherry looked at him with a raised eyebrow, but when Alex didn't elaborate, she smiled.

"I'm just glad you're back."

"Is Mike here?"

Sherry shook her head.

"He's out on a case, but he'll be back this afternoon."

"Are there case files on my desk?"

"Put them there this morning," Sherry said.

"Good," Alex said, grabbing the handle of his office door. "When Mike gets in, tell him to come see me."

"Will do," Sherry said, giving him a second hug before heading back toward the front room.

Alex smiled as she went, feeling like his life was starting to fall back into place. When he opened his office, there were at least a dozen folders in his 'in' box. That made him smile even wider, and he rounded his desk, sat down, and picked up the topmost one.

An hour later, Alex had gone through most of the files. While he'd been out, Mike had been taking on the cases Sherry picked for him; the cases on his desk, however, would need someone with more experience. None of them seemed too complex, but it would keep him busy for the rest of the week at least.

Alex sat up suddenly as he realized something. Keying the intercom, he waited for Sherry to respond.

"What's the date?" he asked, consulting his desk calendar.

"November thirteenth," she responded, which would make it Tuesday.

So I've still got time to get some cases done before Saturday, Alex thought.

"Boss," Sherry went on, "I've got a Mrs. Hannover here, and I think you should speak to her."

Alex keyed the microphone again.

"Bring her back."

A moment later, Sherry opened his door and ushered a middle-aged woman into his office. She was broad of shoulder, with rough hands and thick arms, the kind of frame that belonged to a woman who'd done hard work. Her plain face bore the ghost of youthful beauty, but her eyes were hard and dark. She wore a modest dress, but it was of a newer fashion, which told Alex that her fortunes had come up since the days of her hard labor, and her lips and fingernails were tastefully painted.

"How do you do, Mrs. Hannover," Alex said, rising. "Please have a seat."

The woman took one of the overstuffed chairs on the far side of Alex's desk, clutching a well-made handbag in both hands.

She's new to money, Alex thought. *She's protecting her handbag so no one can grab it.*

"Now," he said, sitting back down while Sherry withdrew, "how can I help you?"

"I'm being haunted," she said without a trace of humor.

Alex hesitated only a moment. Magic existed in the world and people were used to that, but as far as he knew there wasn't any evidence that ghosts existed.

"Okay," he replied, keeping his voice even. "Tell me what's been happening."

Mrs. Hannover gave him a hard look, as if she was looking for any sign Alex was mocking her. After a moment, she continued.

"I recently bought a home in the inner-ring," she began. "Everything was fine for the first month, but after that, things began to happen."

"What kind of things?"

"There were sounds in the night, bangs and thumps, then it escalated to glass breaking and wood cracking."

Alex noted that in his book.

"Was there any actual damage?" he asked.

Again, Mrs. Hannover hesitated.

"No," she admitted at last. "I was too afraid to go downstairs at night, and when I went down in the morning, nothing was out of place."

Alex considered what he'd heard. It was strange enough, but it didn't sound like ghosts, assuming ghosts existed in the first place. It sounded more like someone doing construction or demolition work.

"Are there any homes in your neighborhood that are being worked on, Mrs. Hannover?"

"Not that I know of," she replied. "You think I'm hearing noises from a neighbor's house then?"

"It's a possibility," Alex said. "Sometimes when the city puts in the water lines, they don't cap them off properly. Metal pipes carry sound very well."

"It's a vengeful spirit, I tell you," Mrs. Hannover insisted.

"If it's a vengeful spirit, what is it seeking revenge for?"

"It doesn't want me in that house," she said. "It says the most horrible things about me and my son, uses the most vile language."

"You hear it speaking?"

"Obviously."

Alex leaned back and consulted his notes. He was sure it wasn't a ghost, but he was also certain it wasn't nothing. The only thing that was clear was that Mrs. Hannover needed help.

"Would it be possible for me to go through the house later today?" he asked.

"Nothing happens during the day," Mrs. Hannover insisted.

"I understand, but I'd like to look around anyway. If this is someone trying to scare you, I'll have a better chance of finding it during the day when the light's good."

"And if you don't find anything?" Mrs. Hannover challenged him with a raised eyebrow.

"Then I'll come back after dark and see if I can find your ghost," Alex assured her. "I can't come tonight," he cautioned. "I have a previous engagement, but if I need to, I'll come by tomorrow night. Whoever this ghost of yours is, I'll find him."

Mrs. Hannover's expression almost cracked. Alex could tell she was relieved to find someone who took her seriously.

"Thank you," she said at last.

"I'll need a key to your house," he said, "and it will take me at least an hour to examine the property, probably two. Is that all right?"

She reached into her handbag and pulled out a heavy ring with three keys on it.

"One is to the front door, one to the attic, and one for the shed in the back of the property."

She dropped the ring on the desk, and Alex passed her a pencil and his notepad.

"Put the address down there," he said. "I charge thirty dollars a day plus expenses," he went on. "Is that okay with you?"

Mrs. Hannover reached into her purse again and dropped a twenty and a ten on the desk, along with Alex's notepad.

"Thank you, Mr. Lockerby," she said, standing up. "I haven't had a good night's sleep in a week."

"Call me Alex," he said, "and I'll find your ghost for you, and make sure he finds a different place to haunt."

With that, Mrs. Hannover bade him good day and showed herself out. Alex waited until she was gone before picking up the cash and dropping it in his suit coat pocket. The address she had given him was inner-ring and fairly close to Empire Tower. He wanted to make calls on a few of the case files Sherry had given him, then swing by the Hannover residence in time to be finished before his dinner with Sorsha. That would give Sherry some time to go over to the hall of records and learn as much as she could about the house itself.

As he gathered up the folders he wanted to work on, however, the phone on his desk began to ring.

"Alex?" Danny's voice greeted him once he picked up the receiver. "Sherry said you were back."

"I am," he replied. "I was going to swing by later and see you."

"Can you make it right now?" his friend said.

"Sure," Alex replied, dropping the case files he'd intended to visit. "What's going on?"

"I've got a man in here who's covered in blood but it's not his," Danny said.

"That's ominous. Whose blood is it?"

"That's just it," Danny said. "He was brought in by a patrolman who found him wandering in the street over in Alphabet City. He claims not to know who he is or how he got there. I thought maybe something in your bag of tricks could help us find out who he is."

Alex felt a rush of adrenalin. He didn't want to tell Danny, or anyone for that matter, about the damnation rune, and if he didn't have a rune in his kit, he'd have to make some excuse to go get one. He didn't like lying to his friends; he'd done enough of that for a lifetime.

To Danny, he said, "I'll be right over."

3

LOST & FOUND

Alex stepped out of his cab in front of the Central Office of Police, pausing for a moment to look up at the ten-story structure. It felt like he'd been here just yesterday, but in reality it had been weeks. As he crossed the sidewalk to the glass doors, he felt a bit guilty that Danny had to hear of his return from Sherry instead of from him.

I should have called him as soon as I got in, he chided himself.

Three minutes later, Alex got off on the fourth floor where the interrogation rooms were located.

"Alex," Danny's voice greeted him.

His friend stood by the check-in desk with a big smile on his face.

"Welcome back," he went on, stepping forward and offering Alex his hand. "You don't look like someone who was sick for six weeks."

Alex took his hand and shook it.

"That's because it was only five weeks," he said. He tried to retrieve his hand, but Danny held on.

"You know Iggy wouldn't tell me what happened to you," he said, leaning in so he couldn't be overheard. "So, whatever happened, it was bad. It's good to see you on your feet."

"It's good to see you too," Alex said. "I'll tell you all about it, just not today."

Danny let go of Alex's hand and stepped back.

"Fair enough," he said.

"So where's your mystery man?"

"This way."

Danny turned and headed down the hallway opposite the elevator. He led Alex down to the end of the hall and turned into a room with the number 'six' on the door.

Alex had been in the Central Office's interrogation rooms before, but room six was different. The standard interrogation room was small, just big enough for a table and a few chairs. Beside each room was an observation room, separated from the interrogation room by a sheet of one-way glass.

Room six was as big as both rooms together with a conference table in the center of the room and chairs all round. Across the table from the door sat a man with tired eyes. He sat slumped to the side, leaning on the arm of his chair, and didn't react when Alex and Danny came in. Alex could see the remnants of blood that hadn't been completely washed from his face or from under his fingernails and the man was dressed in ill-fitting clothes.

"Is he injured?" Alex whispered.

"No," Danny said, causing the man to stir.

"Then whose blood is all over his clothes?"

"That's what I want to know," the man said, his voice hoarse.

"I'm Alex," Alex introduced himself. "Can I ask you what happened?"

"You can ask all you want," the man said with a sad smile, "but I don't know any more about it than you do."

Alex set his kit bag on the table and sat down opposite the unknown man.

"A patrolman in Alphabet City found him wandering the street covered in blood, so naturally, they brought him in."

"And you don't remember who you are?" Alex asked.

The man just shook his head.

"No identity card or bankbook," Danny said, "No store labels in his clothes or jeweler's marks on his watch."

"Well done," Alex admitted. Some of those were the kind of tricks only he used, but over the years, Danny had picked up a lot from him. Of course, he'd learned that stuff from Iggy, so Alex couldn't be territorial about it.

"Yeah, I'm not just a pretty face," Danny said.

"What did he have on him?"

Danny opened the door and picked something off a shelf in the hall. A moment later he was back with a box that he placed on the table.

"This is everything," Danny said, reaching inside. "In addition to his clothing, he had a ring of keys," Danny put the ring on the table, then pulled out a round leather pouch. "A change purse containing two dollars and thirty-two cents, a jackknife," he added a short, thick folding knife to the row, "and lastly, a pocket watch."

Alex looked over the four items. The change purse wasn't likely to be of much use, but he dumped the coins out on his hand and examined them just to be sure. Setting them aside, he picked up the watch. It was heavy, sturdily built, with the cover release built into the crown.

"What are you thinking?" Danny asked.

"Not yet," Alex said, replacing the watch on the table. "Let's go through the rest."

"If you figure out who I am, don't forget to tell me," the mystery man said.

"Sorry," Alex said, as he picked up the jackknife, "this must be strange to you."

The man chuckled but there was no humor in it.

"You say that stuff is mine, but...I've never seen any of it before."

"Don't worry—," Alex began. "What do we call you?"

The mystery man shrugged again and just shook his head.

Alex looked at Danny, who shrugged as well.

"Well, you're a new man," Alex said, "born fully grown, so how about Adam?"

"It doesn't feel right," the man said, "but I guess it's as good as anything."

"Well, Adam," Alex said, examining the blade of the jackknife, "you definitely know how to sharpen a knife; I could shave with this."

"Is that important?" Adam asked.

Alex refolded the knife and picked up the pocket watch, turning it over before popping the cover open.

"By itself, a sharp knife is just a sharp knife," Alex said, "but you seem to like your things in good order." He held up the watch by its chain while he consulted his own watch. "This watch is polished, the hinge is tight, and it's set exactly on time. It may not be much, but I can tell you're a man who takes care of his things."

"Apparently I don't think that well of my clothes," Adam said, nodding at the box.

Alex reached into the box and pulled out a white shirt smeared with blood. He smelled it, but the blood was dark and dry with very little of the iron tang common with fresh blood. Turning the shirt, Alex found a bloody smear on the back of the left shoulder but other than that it was free of blood.

"Was it raining earlier today?" he asked.

"I don't know," Danny admitted. "Why?"

Alex held the shirt up, into the light.

"There are water stains here," he said.

"Why is that important?" Adam asked.

Alex gave him a half-smile and held up the garment.

"A man of your apparent habits would never go out in a stained shirt," he said, "so if there was rain somewhere in the city today, that could narrow down our search for your identity."

"I'll call the *Times* office," Danny said, making a note in his book. "Their weatherman keeps track of things like that."

"Did you clean Adam's knife before I got here?" Alex asked.

"Of course not," Danny said, a bit of irritation in his voice. "Why?"

"This blood here," Alex said, pointing to the smear on the back of the shoulder. "It looks to me like someone with blood on their hands grabbed him."

"I don't know how that got there," Adam protested, "but I know I'm not a killer."

"Actually you don't know that," Alex said with no accusation in his voice. "I live with a doctor, and I gave him a call before I came over

Pound of Flesh

here. He said that if you actually have amnesia, you'll have no memory of your past, no sense of who you are."

Adam started to speak but hesitated.

"For how long?" he managed after a second attempt.

Alex shrugged.

"He said that your memory could come back if you're exposed to people or places you're familiar with, so it's important that we figure out where you come from."

"What happens...what happens if I don't remember anything?" Adam asked.

"In that case," Alex said, "you get the chance to become whatever, or whoever, you want."

"Assuming you're not responsible for all this blood, that is," Danny said, indicating the shirt.

"I'm not," Adam insisted, but he looked suddenly hopeless.

"Well, let's take a look at the rest," Alex said. He pulled the trousers out of the box and checked the pockets. He knew Danny and the police had already checked, but old habits died hard. The pockets were empty, so he laid the trousers out on the table. Like the shirt, the trousers were smeared with blood, but unlike the shirt there was blood on the backs of the legs, right where the calves should be.

"Anything?" Adam asked when Alex didn't speak.

"Don't worry," Danny said. "He does this all the time, you just have to be patient." He reached into his pocket and pulled out a cigarette pack. Shaking it, Danny offered a cigarette to Adam, then placed his lighter on the table.

Moving without hesitation, Adam tapped the cigarette on the table, then slipped it into his mouth and lit it with the lighter.

"Well, you definitely smoke," Danny said, picking up the lighter.

Adam looked at the cigarette, then shrugged and put it back in his mouth.

"Interesting," Alex said, pulling the shoes from the box.

"What?" Danny and Adam said in unison.

"There's blood on the outside edges of the shoes, but not on the insides."

Both men waited expectantly for Alex to explain, but he only set the shoes aside and withdrew the last item, a leather belt, from the box. The buckle and the pin were worn, but made of heavy-duty material and the leather of the strap was supple and recently oiled.

"This is expertly made," Alex said. "There's no maker's mark or stamp."

"Well, that's everything," Danny said as Alex set the belt next to the shoes on the table. "Is it time to make with the magic?"

"Not just yet," Alex said, picking up his bag. "I'm a bit tired. Let's get a cup of coffee first and I'll pick this up after that."

Danny hesitated, covering it by puffing on his cigarette.

"There's a pot up in the bullpen," he said at last. "Do you need anything, Adam?"

"I could use some coffee, too," the mystery man said, "and maybe a sandwich."

"How does that work?" Danny said. "You can't remember who you are, but you know what coffee and a sandwich are."

Adam seemed to think about it, then just shook his head.

"Well, sit tight," Danny said, "I'll send someone down with coffee and something to eat."

With that, Danny opened the door and ushered Alex out, locking it behind them. They walked down the hall to the little lobby by the elevator in silence. When they reached it, Danny turned to the desk sergeant and instructed him to call someone for coffee and a sandwich for Adam.

"Okay," Danny demanded once he finished with the sergeant, "what's all that about?"

Alex chuckled at that.

"What makes you think I don't want coffee?"

"First off, I've seen you work when you're dead on your feet," Danny said. "You look a bit tired, but you're not that tired."

Alex laughed and gave Danny a side-eyed look.

"What's the second reason?"

"You've had Marnie's coffee," Danny said. "You'd rather die than drink the swill that passes for coffee around here, so spill it. What have you figured out?"

"Well," Alex began, "I don't know who Adam is, but I'm pretty sure he's not a murderer."

Danny offered Alex a cigarette and then a light.

"Why?"

"There's no blood on his extremely sharp jackknife," Alex said.

Danny thought about that for a moment.

"You mean that if he wanted to kill someone, he'd have used the knife. Why not a gun?"

"There was an awful lot of blood on Adam's clothes," Alex said. "Gunshots don't bleed like that, not even two or three."

"So whoever that blood belongs to, they were stabbed," Danny agreed.

"Repeatedly."

"And Adam's jackknife is clean, but it is possible for a man to own more than one knife."

"Sure," Alex admitted, "but the blood on Adam's clothes tell a strange story, don't you think?"

Danny took a long drag on his cigarette, then crushed it out in the ashtray on the floor sergeant's desk.

"Blood on the shirtfront," he said, ticking it off on his fingers, "a blood smear on the back of one shoulder, as if someone grabbed him."

"Then there are the trousers," Alex said. "There's blood on the front until you reach the knees, then it switches to the back, or rather the inseam and the back."

"And blood on the outside edge of the shoes," Danny added. "He was sitting with his legs crossed when he picked up the blood."

"I suppose it's possible he was trying to strangle someone in that position," Alex said, "but it's much more likely he was holding someone, someone who was bleeding a lot."

"Lover's quarrel?" Danny suggested.

Alex shrugged.

"Could be," he said.

"Maybe someone he just stumbled upon?"

"Iggy told me that amnesia is usually brought on by one of two things," Alex said, "a blow to the head, or overwhelming trauma."

"I'll have the police doctor check for a head wound, but I didn't see one. That just leaves trauma."

"That was a lot of blood on his clothes," Alex pointed out. "Whoever he was holding, they were pretty messed up. Maybe it was too much for him."

"It's useless to speculate at this point," Danny said. "If we're finished with your coffee break, maybe you can do some of your magic and find out where Adam came from."

"I'm not sure that's an option," Alex said. "Finding runes have to link to something."

"What about that knife," Danny offered. "You said it was well cared for, it's obviously important to him."

"I *could* use that," Alex admitted, "if I wanted to find Adam. With his link to it, it would lead me right to him."

"How about amberlight?" Danny suggested. "Like how you found that missing truck in the museum business."

"That would only work if he kept his knife in the same place day after day. He carries it with him, in his pocket, so it's in motion all day, same with the rest of his gear."

"What about the keys? You've used keys to find locks before."

Alex shrugged.

"It's possible," he said, "but my magic is…it's a bit weak at the moment."

When Danny didn't respond, Alex turned to face him.

"You've either said too much or too little," his friend said, giving him a hard look.

"Too much," Alex said. "It's a subject for another time…another place."

Danny held his gaze, then gave him a terse nod.

"All right, I'll drop it," he said. "Now, can you help me any more with Adam or not?"

"I think I might be able to conjure up a trick or two," Alex said, adding his cigarette to the ashtray on the desk. "Go get Adam's things and we'll go up to your office."

Danny gave him another side-eyed glance, then headed down the hall. Alex watched until he disappeared into interrogation room six, then he patted the outside left pocket of his suit coat, feeling the piece of chalk inside.

Ten minutes later Alex led Danny through the vault door to his office and down to the map room. His map of the city was right where he expected it, laid out across the large conference table. The only evidence of use were the few wooden markers laid out to reference the cases Mike had been working.

Danny dropped the box of evidence from Adam on the table with a thunk, then gave Alex a direct look.

"Are you going to tell me what happened to you now?" he demanded.

Alex sighed and looked at his shoes. It wasn't right to keep his best friend in the dark, but there was too much to do.

"Tonight," he said, then remembered his date with Sorsha. "No, tomorrow. Come by the brownstone for dinner with Iggy and me. I'll give you the whole story then."

"All right," Danny replied, "but I thought we were good enough friends to just talk about things, but being invited to one of Iggy's dinners takes the sting out. Just a bit," he added with a grin.

Alex nodded, grateful Danny didn't press the issue. He didn't want to admit to using Limelight to his friend, but it was something that needed to be done. Turning to the sideboard where they kept the tin compasses and the box of finding runes, Alex withdrew one of each. "Give me Adam's shirt."

Danny dug into the box and withdrew the bloodstained garment, then passed it over.

"What are you going to do?" he asked. "You've told me before that once someone dies, they lose the connections to the world."

"That takes time," Alex said, laying out the shirt, the compass, and the rune. "You said a patrolman picked up Adam wandering sometime around noon. That means the owner of the blood died sometime this morning."

"Maybe they were already dead when Adam found them?"

Alex shook his head.

"Too much blood," he said. "With this much it means their heart was still pumping. With a little bit of luck, the bonds between the blood and the body are still there."

He fished the gold lighter Sorsha had given him out of his pocket and lit the rune. It exploded into an orange facsimile of itself that spun above the compass and the shirt. Alex held his breath as it began to spin, then slowly wound down until it burst into a shower of sparks.

"Did it work?" Danny asked, his voice barely above a whisper.

Because the shirt was on top of the compass, Alex couldn't be sure. Being careful not to break the compass' contact with the table, Alex lifted the shirt and set it aside. The rune had behaved the same way it would when a connection was made, but when he looked at the compass, its needle was pointed steadfastly north.

He felt his stomach churn. Runes should work whether he had his magic or not.

Maybe the blood is too old, he told himself. Even his inside voice sounded doubtful.

"Don't give up yet," he whispered.

Taking hold of the compass, he slid it along the map. As it went, the needle moved, pointing slightly east of north.

"It worked," Alex said, still sliding the compass. "Whoever donated all this blood, you'll find them right..." he kept moving the compass until the needle began to spin, "here."

Lifting the compass, Alex and Danny squinted at the map.

"Outer ring," Danny said.

"Near Alphabet City," Alex added, "Right where your patrolman picked up Adam."

He straightened up and handed Danny the compass.

"I've got a haunted house to go look at," he said. "This should lead you to the victim. With any luck, knowing them will let you find out who Adam really is."

Danny accepted the compass and fixed Alex with a stern look.

"Thanks for your help," he said. "I'm glad you're back, but I'm not going to be easy about it until I hear the whole story."

"Tomorrow," Alex said.

"Tomorrow," Danny agreed, then turned and headed out the door.

4

INTANGIBLES

Alex stepped out of a cab in front of a large, three-story Victorian house. Based on the notes Sherry had given him before he left the office, the building had been built in nineteen twenty-five. During that time, the neighborhood had been nothing but little homes and the occasional acre or two of farmland. Empire Tower wouldn't be built for another five years, so the houses in this area had larger lawns than most of their neighbors, as much as a quarter of an acre.

Mrs. Hannover's house occupied a corner lot and sat on a hill, looking down on the road. The house itself was in good repair, with white painted gingerbread accents on the eaves of the roof, white shutters and trim, and a dark wood front door complete with a heavy brass knocker. All the boards were straight and Alex couldn't see any areas where the peach-colored paint was peeling. A long, curving stone stair led up from the curb to the front door and the wide porch that disappeared around the far side of the building.

Because of the hill on which the house sat, even its front porch would have an excellent view of the city, to say nothing of the view from the single tower that stuck up above the main roof. Those rooms were usually small, but would serve well as an office or reading room.

Alex whistled, his breath steaming in the November air. The steam reminded him of the temperature and he shivered, pulling his overcoat closed. Iggy and Mike had been making the runes that would keep Alex's business running, but no one had bothered with his climate runes. To be fair, they were a bit too complex for Mike, although Iggy could make them in his sleep. Alex had resolved not to ask his mentor to make runes that only existed for his convenience, but in the dead of winter, he had to admit that he missed his climate rune.

Fishing into his pocket, Alex withdrew the heavy key ring Mrs. Hannover had given him, then he opened the wrought iron gate at the bottom of the stone stair and began to climb. Despite the look of the steps, they were actually longer than he thought. By the time he reached the top, he could actually see over the smaller homes nearby.

Looking up, Alex judged that the view from the little tower must be fantastic. He had no idea what Mrs. Hannover paid for her new home, but ghost or no ghost, the view was worth it.

Stepping onto the porch, Alex put down his crime scene kit and examined the front door. Since he was fairly certain ghosts didn't exist, it was much more likely someone simply broke into the house during the night. The fact that Mrs. Hannover hadn't found anything missing was a problem with that theory, but maybe she missed something.

Alex bent close to the brass plate that surrounded the front door's keyhole. It was made of antiqued brass and any scratch would stand out against the dark finish. There were a few minor scratches on the rim of the keyhole, but that was to be expected from normal use. Three long scratches showed that someone had missed the mark in the past, but these scratches were dull, almost hidden by the action of rain and soot from the air. The lack of any new scratches or marks, where a tension tool would have been used on the lock, made it unlikely an intruder entered by the front door.

Sighing to himself, Alex slotted the key into the lock, turned it smartly, and walked in. The foyer beyond was sparsely furnished with a simple mirror on the wall with hat pegs all around protruding from its frame, and a coat rack in the corner. A long carpet ran down the hall to the left with a set of steep stairs climbing up to the next floor on the right. Before the bottom of the stairs, an open door led to a parlor that looked out onto the wraparound porch.

The wallpaper had been washed recently and only had a light coating of dust. As Alex took the long hallway toward the back of the house, he found a neat study, a solarium that served as a dining room, and a large kitchen. There were signs that the house was recently occupied, including several boxes of household items that hadn't yet been unpacked. Other than that, however, everything was clean and neat.

If something went missing, it might be hard to find with the unpacked boxes, he thought. *Still, if someone came through here looking for something, they didn't make much of a mess.*

Usually people who broke in to conduct a search in the middle of the night wanted to get out as quickly as possible. They tended not to be careful or delicate.

"Maybe there's something upstairs," he said out loud.

"Stand your ground!" a high-pitched male voice called out behind him.

Alex put his empty hands up so whoever was behind him could see them, then he looked over his shoulder. A boy of about fourteen stood in the hallway, just out of reach, holding a baseball bat on his shoulder.

"Easy, kid," Alex said, turning slowly. "Why aren't you in school?"

"Don't call me kid," he spat, raising the bat. "Who are you? What are you doing here?"

"I'm Alex Lockerby. I'm a private detective. Mrs. Hannover, the owner of this house, asked me to take a look around for her."

"Prove it," the boy said, but there was doubt in his eyes.

"She gave me the key to the front door," Alex said, "that's how I got in. I'm going to reach into my pocket now to get the key, so don't try to brain me with that Louisville Slugger."

Moving slowly, Alex pulled out the key and set it on the nearby kitchen counter. The boy stared at it, but it was clear that, to him, it was just a key.

"Is Mrs. Hannover your mother?" he asked.

"Uh, yeah," he said, shifting his gaze nervously from Alex to the key and back.

"She said there was some kind of disturbance here the other night,"

Alex said, lowering his hands and clasping them in front. "She thought a ghost was rattling chains or something like that. You hear anything?"

"No," he admitted at last. "By the time Mom woke me up, whatever it was had stopped."

"She said that she searched the house and that nothing was missing." Alex nodded at the bat. "Did you and your slugger accompany her?"

"Of course," he said, offended that Alex would question his youthful chivalry.

"And nothing was disturbed, nothing missing?"

The boy shook his head.

"Put that bat down and show me," Alex said.

The young man hesitated, then lowered the bat, tucking it under his arm.

"What's your name?" Alex asked.

"Rick," he said. "What's yours?"

"I already told you, it's Alex."

Rick hesitated, then seemed to relax.

"The upstairs is this way," he said, nodding back toward the stairs.

"Is there a basement?"

"No," Rick said, heading down the hall.

That wasn't really a surprise; Manhattan was an island after all, and most houses didn't have basements because the water table was too high.

Alex followed Rick up the stairs to the second floor. Three bedrooms and a water closet occupied the floor and none of them looked like they'd been meddled with. Moving up, the third floor contained the large main bedroom along with a south-facing reading room. Like the floors before, there was nothing that seemed amiss.

"Well, I don't see anything that looks like it's been disturbed," Alex was forced to admit. "Do you think your mother had a bad dream?"

"I don't know," Rick said, "but I don't want anything to happen to her."

"Fair enough," Alex said, heading for the stairs. "Would you do me a favor and pull the curtains on the ground floor? I'm going to use some special tools to look around. If anyone was in here, I'll find out."

As Rick moved to comply, Alex picked up his kit from the foyer and moved to the dining room. His hands shook a little when he removed his multi-lamp from the repurposed doctor's bag. He knew that runes didn't require any magical talent to use, but the damnation rune on his chest seemed to burn as he thought about the lamp.

He set the lamp down and rubbed his hands together until they stopped trembling.

"Get ahold of yourself," he admonished his traitorous hands. "It's like riding a bike."

Taking a deep breath, Alex took out the silverlight burner and lit it with his lighter. Once the wick burned steadily, he clipped it into the bottom of the lamp and closed the crystal shutter. Setting the lamp aside, Alex reached back into the bag and pulled out a flat wallet made of silk. Opening the top flap revealed four compartments, each with a pair of pince-nez spectacles inside. Selecting the first pair in line, Alex pulled them out, revealing deeply blue lenses, and clipped them on the bridge of his nose.

Picking up the lamp again, Alex pointed it at the front door. In the semi-darkness afforded by the closed curtains, he saw fingerprints exactly where he expected them. Checking the floor, he didn't find anything out of the ordinary, mostly the residue of dirt and oil tracked in on shoes.

Moving to the parlor, Alex swept the room, finding only fingerprints and some old stains.

"Nothing out of place," he said when he finished. He was starting to get the feeling that whatever Mrs. Hannover heard, it wasn't an intruder. "Maybe he climbed in a window upstairs," he said.

"The windows are all locked," Rick said. "After Mom woke me up, she had me check."

It sounded like the boy was telling the truth, but Alex would have to check anyway. Iggy had drummed into him the idea that you only trust the evidence you verified yourself. Before he checked all the windows, however, he had the rest of the downstairs to sweep.

Two hours later, Alex blew out the burner in his multi-lamp and set it aside. He'd been up and down the house twice, first with silverlight, then with ghostlight. There was plenty of evidence the house was occupied, but no hint whatsoever of anything criminal or magical going on.

"Did you find anything?" Rick asked.

During Alex's investigation, he'd mostly kept quiet, watching as Alex moved through the house and only asking a few questions.

"No," Alex admitted. "I don't know what your mother heard, but it didn't happen in this house."

"Could it have come from outside?" Rick asked.

"It's possible. Maybe a truck full of scrap hit a bump." He didn't believe it, but unless he was willing to start believing in ghosts, it was the best explanation he could come up with.

"I'll write up a report for your mother," he went on, packing up his gear. "Let her know that I'll come back tomorrow night as we discussed and, in the meantime, keep the doors and windows locked."

Rick promised that he would, and Alex handed him the borrowed house key.

"What if we hear something tonight?" Rick asked as Alex headed for the door.

Alex wanted to tell him that everything would be fine, but there was a note of unease in the boy's voice that made him hesitate.

"If anything happens," he said, reaching into his shirt pocket for one of his business cards, "call me at this number right away."

Alex had guessed right, and by the time he'd finished up at the Hannover house, it was too late to visit any of the other potential clients. There was enough time to make a few phone calls, however, so he stopped in Empire Station for a cup of Marnie's coffee, then headed directly up to his office.

"There you are," Sherry said when he came in. She was waiting behind her desk, busily making notes in several case files. "Danny's been calling for you every half hour since you left." She looked up and gave him a warm smile. "It's good to have you back," she added.

"Thanks. Did Danny leave a number?"

Sherry picked up a paper torn from a notebook and held it up.

"Is Mike in?" he asked, crossing the front room to take the paper.

"He's at the library researching the provenance of a marble statue of the Venus de Milo."

"Sounds like an interesting case," Alex said, intrigued. "If he gets back while I'm still here, tell him I want to see him."

"Will do, Boss," Sherry said with a smile.

Alex headed down the hall to his office, then called the number Danny had left. He knew from experience that it wasn't the police exchange, so it must be some shop near that crime scene in Alphabet City.

"Hardman Five and Dime," a gruff male voice answered.

"Is there a police lieutenant there name of Pak?"

"Yeah," the man on the other end of the line said, a sneer in his voice.

"Get him," Alex growled, "and keep your opinions to yourself."

Danny had been such a part of Alex's life for the last decade or so that it always surprised Alex when someone reacted to Danny's being of Japanese descent.

"Alex?" Danny came on after a two-minute wait.

"Yeah. Don't tell me you couldn't find your crime scene."

"Oh, we found it," Danny said, a strange tone in his voice. "I really need you to take a look."

"That bad?"

"Worse," his friend admitted. "I couldn't hold the body any longer. It's with the coroner now, but there's still plenty to see here."

Alex glanced at the clock. He had to be at Sorsha's at six, and it was almost five.

"I can't stay long, but I'll come take a look. Where, exactly, is Hardman Five and Dime?"

It only took fifteen minutes for Alex to take a cab from Empire Tower to the grubby little five and dime on the outskirts of Alphabet City. Danny was waiting outside the building, negating the need for Alex to meet the proprietor of Hardman's, something that put a smile on his face.

"This way," Danny said as Alex hefted his kit bag out of the cab.

He led Alex down to the end of the block and around the corner to an alley behind a cooper shop. Before they even reached it, Alex could smell the iron tang of blood. When he turned the corner into the alley, it became obvious why Danny wanted him there.

About fifteen feet along the alley, Alex could see copious amounts of blood.

It was pooled on the ground, but that wasn't the end to it; it looked like someone had painted the walls on either side with the stuff. Even a cursory look showed Alex where spatter and cast-off lines rose up the walls. Several wooden crates had been smashed, their wooden bits spread out from the epicenter of the event. This wasn't a simple murder scene, someone had been butchered here.

Alex whistled as he looked around.

"Who was the victim?" he asked.

"No idea," Danny said. "The body was too badly mangled for an identification."

"What can you tell me?"

Danny flipped open his notebook.

"The body was that of a female, badly disfigured. She had red hair with no sign of greying, so we assume she wasn't elderly. Dr. Wagner thinks someone went after her with an axe."

Alex shivered. He hadn't seen the body, but his mind's eye pictured it in all its vivid, gory detail. It made him sick.

"Is there anything you can tell me?" Danny asked.

Alex stepped closer, being careful not to step in the coagulating blood.

"I hate to admit it," he began, "but I'm pretty sure Wagner's right about the weapon." He indicated the lines of cast-off blood on the right-hand wall. "This is from the killer swinging the axe up and over his head. See how high up they go? That means the weapon was long. There are some medieval weapons like that, but an axe makes the most sense."

"Anything else?" Danny said, taking notes in his book.

Pound of Flesh

"Whoever did this was either insane or they really hated the victim.," Alex said. "This amount of blood explains why Adam was covered in the stuff."

"You think he's our killer?" Danny asked. "I thought you said he was sitting down when he got the blood on his trousers."

"I might have been wrong," he admitted. "I think if Adam had been the killer, he'd have more blood on him."

"But you can't be sure."

Alex shrugged.

"No. There's just too much blood here to sort out what happened. All I can really tell you is that it was incredibly violent."

"Thanks," Danny said, clearly not meaning it.

Alex opened his bag and pulled out his multi-lamp.

"Silverlight won't be any help," he said, "but maybe the killer used some kind of magic."

Lighting his ghostlight burner, Alex swept the scene. It didn't take long for him to determine that nothing magical happened in the alley.

"Well, it was worth a try," Danny said. "Sorry to bring you out for nothing."

"Not exactly nothing," Alex said, pulling out his rune book. Fortunately, Iggy had been thorough in replacing his more complex runes, so Alex found what he was looking for quickly.

"I can help you identify your Jane Doe," he said, turning the book so Danny could see the complex and colorful rune.

Danny chuckled and shook his head.

"And what's that?" he asked.

"Temporal restoration rune," Alex said. "Remember Jerry Pemberton?"

"Pemberton?" Danny said, his eyebrows furrowing. "The burned body in the recliner?"

"This is the rune I used to restore his body."

Danny shivered at the memory but then nodded.

Alex tore the rune out and offered it to Danny.

"I've got to go, but you can use this just as easy as I can. You just have to remember that once you use it, you've only got five minutes before the body turns to dust."

"Thanks," Danny said, carefully folding the paper and slipping it under the cover of his notebook.

"I'll send you my bill," Alex said, picking up his bag.

"What's your hurry? I figured you'd want to see the body."

"Based on your description, I think it's better if I don't," Alex said. "When you use that rune, be sure to send anyone who's eaten recently out of the room."

"Never figured you for a weak stomach," Danny said, giving him a probing look.

"I have a date with Sorsha," Alex explained, "and I've got a lot of lost time to make up for."

"It's good to have you back," Danny said, slapping him on the shoulder as he turned.

"It's good to be back."

5

DINNER CONVERSATION

Alex walked until he found another dark alley and ducked inside to use a vault rune. Checking his watch as he closed the heavy door behind him, he found that he only had fifteen minutes before he needed to meet Sorsha.

"And you smell like blood and garbage," he said.

Moving quickly, he crossed to the brownstone door, then exited out into the upstairs hallway just outside his room. He was disoriented for a moment but realized Iggy must have moved the door during his long convalescence. Turning to his room, Alex went inside, then showered and put on his tuxedo. As he threaded his cufflinks through the holes in the shirt, he smiled at the memory of the time he'd asked Iggy if he had a tux Alex could borrow. In the end he'd used a disguise rune to simulate the high-end garment. After that incident, Alex wanted a Tuxedo of his own, and, a year after he'd started working with Andrew Barton, he'd done it.

"Barton," Alex mumbled as he pulled on the glossy black tuxedo coat. "I should have called him. He's going to be angry that I didn't come to him first." Alex chuckled as he headed back out into the hall, toward his vault door. "He's probably got a dozen new ideas he wants help with."

Pushing thoughts of the eccentric sorcerer from his mind, Alex crossed his vault to the back wall where the cover door to Sorsha's castle stood. As he reached it, he pulled out his pocket watch and checked the time.

"Six on the dot," he congratulated himself.

The door to Sorsha's castle had binding runes and protection runes on it just like all the other cover doors in Alex's vault. Iggy had insisted, saying that the security of the brownstone required it. Alex would have been just as happy with a simple bolt on both sides, but his mentor was insistent.

Concentrating on his pocket watch, Alex tried to disengage the runes that kept the door closed, but the little symbols in the watch didn't glow or react to his touch. A bolt of panic went through him, then his grip on the watch loosened.

"You have no magic," he whispered, a sinking feeling in his gut. He'd known it, of course, from the moment he saw the damnation rune, but this was the first time he'd faced it. The first time he'd tried to do magic and felt nothing.

He thought about yelling to Sorsha, to have her use the rune key he'd created for her to open the door, but even though the door was only made out of wood, the runes prevented sound from passing through.

Alex's breathing came quicker, and he had to lean against the door as his knees went weak.

How did you get through the brownstone door? he thought suddenly. He remembered just reaching out and opening it, like it wasn't locked at all.

Iggy must have disabled that lock so Sorsha could come in and out while he was unconscious.

I don't have another key, he thought. *I'll have to have Iggy make one.*

Iggy had obviously made one for himself; he wouldn't have been able to get through Alex's vault to check on him if he hadn't.

"Looks like I'm going to be late," he said, forcing his arms to stop shaking.

As he pushed away from the wall, there was a clicking sound from the door, and it swung outward. Sorsha stood framed in the opening, a sardonic grin on her perfect features and a silver key blank in her hand.

"Ignatius said you might need a little help with the door," she said.

Alex straightened up, tugging on the front of his jacket to smooth it out.

"You look dashing," she said, keeping the half-smile on her lips.

"And you look beautiful," Alex replied.

The great thing about dating Sorsha, from Alex's perspective, was that she always looked good. Tonight was a bit strange, however. Sorsha wore a teal-green flapper dress that looked like it had been painted on her. The dress was at least a decade out of style and had a row of fringe around her waist. A headband of some embroidered material encircled her brow, and both her shoes and her cigarette holder matched the dress.

"Since we're staying in tonight, I thought I'd dust off one of my old favorites," she said, reading his expression. She gave a quick shake of her hips, sending the fringe flying, and beamed at him.

"What do you think?"

"It suits you," Alex admitted. Of course that really wasn't much of an admission. Sorsha could wear a sandwich board and make it look good.

He stepped through the door, shutting it behind him, and took Sorsha's arm. Together they walked across her cavernous foyer, but when Alex turned to head toward her formal dining room, she resisted.

"This way," she said, with an enigmatic smile.

Alex allowed himself to be led through the door under the stairs and back toward the kitchens. When they arrived, he found a small table laid out for dining with a chair on either side. The smell of cooking food permeated the room, but Alex saw no sign of Sorsha's talented cook.

"I've given the staff the night off," she said, gesturing for Alex to sit.

"The whole night?" Alex asked, standing by the chair Sorsha indicated and lighting a cigarette. "Don't some of them live here?"

She favored him with a sly smile.

"I have arrangements with the Seville," she said, referring to the hotel. "Whenever any of my staff have a day off, they always have a room waiting for them in the city, in case they stay out too late to return here."

"Fancy," Alex said.

Sorsha lifted the lid from a pan on the nearby stove, then used a wooden spoon to taste it, adding spice from a jar when she found it wanting.

"You cooked?" Alex asked, genuinely curious. "You didn't just snap your fingers and make the food appear?"

Sorsha raised an eyebrow at that.

"Is that all you think I can do?" she asked, a hint of danger in her voice.

"Not at all, but I've never heard you even talk about cooking food."

Sorsha's dangerous expression turned to a smile.

"Well, I guess you don't know everything about me, now do you?"

"That is very true," Alex said, leaning against the little table. "You know almost everything about me, but, come to think of it, I actually know very little about you."

"A girl needs her secrets, Alex," Sorsha said, using a ladle to move the contents of the simmering pan to a china bowl.

When she finished, Sorsha put a lid on the bowl and put it on the table. She quickly followed it with a loaf of brown bread, a cake of butter, and a bowl of rice that looked like it had been shaped into a perfectly round mound.

"What's all this?" Alex said, moving behind Sorsha's chair, ready to pull it out once she finished.

"Butter chicken," she said, sitting down and allowing Alex to help push in her chair. "I went to India once and fell in love with it."

"Sounds delicious," Alex said. Growing up poor, he'd learned to eat almost anything, so it really didn't matter so much to him.

Not that I'm going to tell Sorsha that, he thought.

"Give me your plate," she instructed once Alex was seated.

He did as he was told, and she laid down a bed of rice, then ladled a lumpy orange stew over it. Handing the plate back, she sat waiting until Alex took a bite.

Pound of Flesh

"I see why you like this," he said, dabbing at his mouth with his napkin. "You really cooked this?"

She smirked at him as she raised her spoon.

"Don't act so surprised," she said.

Alex enjoyed the meal, and Sorsha couldn't have been better company. They talked about everything from her business, to politics, to the cases Alex had picked up on his first day back. Alex could feel the stress of losing six weeks of his life melting away, and it felt good.

"That was amazing," he said once dinner was done. "Since you cooked, I guess I'll do the washing up."

He stood, but Sorsha held up her hand.

"I know you and Ignatius have that arrangement, but I am a sorceress." She waved her hand, and the dishes, the leftover food, the tablecloth, and even the table itself, vanished. When she stood, the chairs disappeared as well.

"I need you around when Iggy cooks," Alex said.

"You can't afford me," she replied, slinking forward and closing the gap between them. "There's an old saying," she said, putting her arms around his neck, "that the way to a man's heart is through his stomach."

"Well, you can't be faulted on that front," Alex admitted.

"Good," she said, releasing him and heading away toward the parlor. "Come with me and we'll put that little axiom to the test."

Alex had no idea what she meant, but he was excited to find out.

"We need to talk about us," Sorsha said when they reached the parlor.

Alex's excitement level dropped immediately to zero.

"Us?" he said, his voice suddenly hoarse.

Sorsha snapped her fingers, and a roaring fire sprang up in the stone hearth.

"Yes," she said, moving to the liquor cabinet. "You were raised by a priest, correct?"

"Uh, yes," Alex said, still not sure where the sorceress was going with her line of inquiry.

Sorsha turned with two drinks in her hand, one mostly clear, the other golden brown over ice.

"Why did God make Eve?" she asked, moving to Alex and handing him the glass with the dark liquid.

Taking the glass, Alex had to shift mental gears quickly. Father Harry had drummed the Bible into his head for most of his teenage years, not just requiring Alex to read it, but quizzing him on its contents.

"Because it was bad for man to be alone," he managed, finally.

"From what I've seen of men," Sorsha said, her face a mask of imperious disapproval, "it *is* bad for men to be alone. Especially if that man is you."

"Now hold on a minute," Alex protested. "Sure, I've got myself in my share of scrapes, but those things were always started by someone else."

"These 'scrapes' you mention," Sorsha said, sipping from her glass, "would that be a mad runewright who wanted to make himself a god? Or perhaps using Limelight to cure your girlfriend?"

"To save her life, I think you mean."

"What about going into business with a gangster, or trying to take down a blood mage by yourself, or jumping in front of a machine gun?"

"That last one was to save Danny, and I'd do it again," Alex growled. "What's with this assault on my character? You know damn well I did the best I could in those situations and came out better than most."

"Don't be vulgar," Sorsha admonished him for his curse. "And you know very well that you'd have fared much better if you hadn't taken on those things by yourself."

Alex sipped what turned out to be a Scotch on the rocks to give himself time.

"So you want to what? Appoint yourself my guardian?"

He waited for an answer, but Sorsha just glared at him.

"You want to put a muzzle on me," Alex went on, "maybe a leash?"

Sorsha took one step toward him and slapped him. She must have used some magic because even with her tiny frame, she made him stagger back.

"What was that for?" he demanded.

"I'm in love with you," she said.

"I thought that was a foregone conclusion," he said, "otherwise what have we been doing for the last two years?"

"You misunderstand me," Sorsha said, her voice cold and even. "I've dated before. I've had lovers before."

"If you're thinking I'm going to be shocked, forget it," he said. "I'm not pure as the wind-driven snow, and I never expected you to be."

"I've had lovers," she reiterated, "but I've never been *in* love."

Alex pressed the cold glass against his cheek.

"You've got a funny way of showing it."

Sorsha whirled on him, raising her hand again, but he didn't flinch.

"I refuse to love a man who's going to destroy himself," she spat. "If you're just going to run off and get yourself killed then I..."

She clamped her jaw shut and breathed through her nose. Alex could tell she was biting back a sob, an emotion she was too proud to let slip.

"Then I'm through with you," she finished at last.

"Can I talk now?" Alex asked after a short silence.

"That depends," Sorsha said, firmly back in control of her emotions. "Do you have anything useful to say?"

"I'm sorry," he said.

"For what?"

"For doing what I had to," he said. "I'm sorry I risked my life to save yours, but in my book that was a fair trade."

"That's the problem," Sorsha said. "You're only going by *your* book."

Alex wanted to slap himself in the face. He'd been so busy listening to what Sorsha was saying that he completely missed what she wanted.

"I suppose I could be more careful in the future," he said, scratching his chin as if in thought. "That might be hard, though. You know how impulsive I can be when people are in trouble."

Sorsha didn't answer him, just crossed her arms and raised an eyebrow.

"I've got it," Alex said, snapping his fingers. "What if I worked more closely with someone a bit more level-headed?"

"Someone who can curb some of your more insane ideas," Sorsha said, the ghost of a smile tugging at her lips. "Someone who can help you instead of letting you do everything on your own."

Alex nodded sagely.

"All right," he said. "It's decided. First thing in the morning, I'll ask Iggy to be my business partner."

The smile evaporated from Sorsha's face, replaced by a sudden snarl as her eyes went wide, glowing from within.

"Why you..." she started, then stopped when she saw Alex's sly grin. "It's like you want to get slapped," she growled.

"Was that the wrong answer?" Alex asked, his voice positively dripping with insincerity.

Sorsha's eyebrows dropped down over her glowing eyes.

"Look," he said, putting a hand on her shoulder. "There's a lot of sense in what you're saying, and I'm sorry I've scared you so often. That said, don't you have a company of your own to run, not to mention working with the FBI?"

"My people handle most of the day-to-day at Kincaid Refrigeration," she said, then she sighed. "And the FBI disbanded their magical crimes unit."

Alex didn't know about that, and he suddenly felt like a heel.

Some detective you are, he admonished himself. *Your girl loses a job that's important to her, and you don't even know about it.*

"Well, how about you come work with me," he said. "It doesn't have to be every day, but whenever you can spare the time."

She smirked, then leaned in and kissed the cheek she'd slapped.

"Thank you, Alex," she said. "I know what it cost you to offer that, but I'm not looking for a job. I don't want to be at your office every day; after all, a little of you goes a long way. I just want you to call me whenever you need help. Not Ignatius. Not Danny. When you run into trouble, you call me first."

"I promise," Alex said, putting his arms around her and pulling her into a kiss. Strangely, he meant it too.

Pound of Flesh

A phone was ringing somewhere.

The clattering, insistent jangling seemed to echo, as if it were down in a stone basement. Alex knew he must be dreaming. His phone was right beside his bed and would have awoken him instantly. This phone was clearly meant for someone else.

He took a deep breath and tried to go back to sleep, but for some reason he couldn't roll over. His drifting mind returned to wakefulness, and he looked down at the curtain of platinum hair that hid Sorsha's face as she nestled in the crook of his shoulder. He grinned like an imbecile, then ran his hand up her bare shoulder, causing her to shiver.

"Get the phone," she murmured. "I don't want to."

He was about to ask what phone, still convinced that the sound he'd heard was in his dreams. At that moment, however, the phone rang again. From the sound, it was located in the hall outside Sorsha's bedroom.

"Right," he said, disentangling himself and rolling off the massive bed. Striding naked out into the hall, Alex found a small table with a phone on it and the label 'Ignatius' on a printed card next to it.

Iggy must have run a wire from my vault so he could contact Sorsha while I was sick, Alex reasoned.

"Hello?" he said, picking up the receiver.

"Alex," Iggy's voice greeted him. The old man sounded a bit flustered. "I'm sorry to wake you but something's come up."

"What's going on?"

"Well, I just got a call from a young man named Rick Hannover," Iggy said.

Alex felt his blood run cold.

"Did something happen?" he demanded.

"According to the young man, someone broke into his house tonight and assaulted his mother. She's in the hospital and the police are at the house. I figured you'd better head right over before they trample all the clues."

"Right," Alex said. "I'll grab my kit and go to my office."

"I'll call a cab and have it waiting for you outside Empire Tower," Iggy said, then hung up.

"What is it?" Sorsha asked, coming up beside him.

"Apparently a ghost just put one of my clients in the hospital," Alex said.

6

THE MISSING

It was after two in the morning when Alex stepped out of a cab in front of Melissa Hannover's stately Victorian house. The ambiance was reduced a bit by the two police cars parked along the curb, but Alex had expected there to be more.

The police must be finished with the scene, he thought.

There wasn't an officer outside the door, but all the lights in the house were still on, so maybe there were a few cops still going over the place. When he knocked, it took almost a full minute for a uniformed policeman to open the door.

"Who are you?" the officer growled.

"Alex Lockerby," Alex said, holding out one of his cards. "I'm a private detective in the employ of Mrs. Hannover, the owner of this property. Her son called me and asked me to look into tonight's events."

"She ain't here," the cops said. "They took her to the hospital, so I suggest you go there."

He started to close the door, but Alex blocked it with his foot.

"As I mentioned," he said, keeping his voice pleasant, "she had her son call me to look over the house."

"Lockerby?" a familiar voice called from inside the house.

Alex could hear the sound of someone coming down the stairs, then the door was pulled open and he was face to face with Detective Robert Arnold of Detweiler's division. He looked very much as Alex remembered him, short with a mop of red hair and a rumpled overcoat. A crooked smile lit up his face and he put out a hand.

"Alex Lockerby," he said as Alex took his hand. "I heard you were laid up for a while."

Alex nodded.

"Had a bad reaction to a potion," he supplied. As excuses went it wasn't the most solid of explanations, but he doubted anyone would probe too deeply into it. He made a mental note to talk to Iggy and work out a more plausible explanation for his convalescence.

"Oh, that's terrible," Arnold said. "My wife is always worrying about getting a bad potion. Her mother got a cold cure from a street vendor when she was little and it turned her purple for a week."

Alex smiled at that, but had the good manners not to laugh.

"Her mother took a picture, but it was only black and white back then, so she looks like she's got an impressive tan. What I wouldn't give for that in Technicolor."

Alex smiled again, glad the detective hadn't pressed too hard about his excuse.

"So what happened here?" he asked.

Alex had glanced around a bit while they'd been speaking, and he noticed the mirror that had been on the wall earlier was gone and three of the balusters were missing from the staircase handrail.

"Well, it's a pretty clear case of assault," Arnold began. "According to the boy, Rick, his mother heard something downstairs and went to investigate. As near as we can figure, she was assaulted right as she reached the foyer."

"Did she see anything?"

"There's no way to know," Arnold said. "When we got here, she was unconscious so I had a few of my officers take her to the hospital."

"I assume Rick called you?" Alex said.

"Not right away," the detective said, consulting his notebook. "According to his statement, when he heard the assault, he grabbed a

Pound of Flesh

bat and came down to help. He said he hit the man in the back and he ran off."

"Ran where?" Alex asked. "Did he go out the front door?"

Detective Arnold grinned at him.

"See," he said, "that's what I like about you, you're always looking for the details. Rick said the front door was locked with the key and that the man ran that way."

Arnold pointed into the opening that led to the parlor.

Alex knew from his visit yesterday that just outside the windows of the parlor was the wrap-around porch. That would make it easy for a burglar to get in and out, so of course Detective Arnold was far too smart to have missed that.

"I take it all the parlor windows are locked," he said.

"Got it in one."

"What about the kitchen door in the back?" Alex asked. "Maybe our burglar ran that way because Rick was blocking the hall."

The kitchen was straight back from the foyer along the hall that ran next to the stairs. There was, however, an opening in the parlor wall that led into the formal dining room and then to the kitchen so the man could have gotten out that way.

"The back door was locked with the key as well," Arnold said, "and we found the key ring upstairs in Mrs. Hannover's room."

"No chance he could have been upstairs before he was discovered?"

Arnold shrugged.

"It's possible, I suppose, but not really likely, I mean if Mrs. Hannover heard him down here, she certainly would have heard him upstairs."

Alex couldn't disagree with that statement, so he didn't try.

"Do you know what he was doing in the parlor?"

"Looking through photo books," Arnold said, motioning for Alex to follow as he moved to the parlor.

The room looked mostly as Alex remembered it, except the front cabinets of a narrow credenza along the wall had been opened and their contents pulled out. Most of what Alex could see was the kind of junk people accumulated, mementos, tchotchkes, and sentimental brick-a-brac gathered over a lifetime. These had been pushed to the side in a heap. Clearly the burglar had no interest in them. What had occupied his attention were two bound photo albums. Both were open and there were pictures littering the ground all around them.

"Any idea what he was looking for?" Alex asked.

"Beyond a specific picture?" Arnold said. "Not a clue."

Alex stared at the pile, as if that act alone could make it reveal its secrets.

"Would you mind if I looked around a bit with my lantern?" he asked at last.

"We're pretty much done with the place," Arnold said. "I only stayed because Rick called you and I wanted to see if you could find anything we missed."

It was quite the admission coming from the police department, but Alex's experience with Detective Arnold told him the man had no ego. He wanted to solve cases and he didn't care how that happened.

"Well, it'll be a bit before I can tell you anything," Alex warned. "Assuming there's something to find."

Arnold pointed at the couch along the back wall of the parlor.

"You think there's any evidence on that?"

"I doubt it," Alex chuckled.

"In that case," the detective said, sitting down on the couch, "I'll wait for you here."

Without another word, the little man turned and laid down, putting his hat over his eyes.

Leaving Arnold to his nap, Alex opened his bag and began assembling his tools. The first thing to do was to determine how the burglar had gotten in and out of the house.

Lighting his silverlight burner, he reached for the silk wallet that held his pince-nez speckles but hesitated. He'd been over this house less than a day ago and found nothing, but maybe he missed something. Leaving the wallet, Alex unclipped his oculus from its place under the lid of his kit bag and slipped it over his head. The spectacles did the job of showing what his lamp revealed, but the oculus was more powerful, more versatile, and more accurate. Normally he used the spectacles and only switched to the oculus if he needed it. This seemed like one of those occasions.

Dialing the oculus' magnification back a bit, Alex began to move through the room. There were no new fingerprints on the credenza, which suggested that the intruder wore gloves. There were new prints on the photos but Alex suspected that was from the police handling them.

Moving slowly and meticulously, Alex swept the room. Knowing that the burglar wore gloves, he wasn't expecting to find fingerprints, but that didn't mean the man didn't leave behind anything else.

"Like that," Alex said, kneeling down. There was a round rug with a decorative fringe around the edge that almost filled the room. As Alex leaned down, he moved some of the fringe to reveal a small drop of glowing blood. It wasn't enough for a finding rune, but it meant that Rick had hurt the man with his Louisville Slugger.

It was also the first real evidence that someone other than Rick and Mrs. Hannover was actually in the house.

"You still with me, Detective Arnold," Alex said, keeping his voice low in case the man was asleep.

"I'm awake," Arnold said from under his hat. "You find something?"

"That depends," Alex said. "Did that kid, Rick, have any wounds when you got here? Was there any blood on him?"

Arnold picked up his hat and tilted his head so he could see Alex.

"Why?"

"Because there's a small drop of fresh blood here," Alex said, indicating the floor, "and if it didn't come from Rick, then it means someone else was here."

"You thought there wasn't?" Arnold said, raising an eyebrow.

"Never assume," Alex said, absently, tearing a blank page from his notebook and placing it next to the blood drop. "Do you know what happened to Rick's bat?"

"My boys put it on the table in the kitchen," Arnold said. "You going to look for blood on it?"

"That's the idea," Alex said. "But I've still got a lot of ground to cover between here and there."

Arnold dropped his hat back on his face and got comfortable.

"Let me know if you find anything else."

Hours later, Alex sat at the kitchen table and stared at the baseball bat. He knew he should blow out the multi-lamp but he was just too tired. The pale light of morning was beginning to bleed through the windows behind him and it felt like he'd been up for three days straight.

Worse than all that, he was no closer to understanding what happened in Mrs. Hannover's Victorian mansion than he was three hours ago.

"You look like I feel," Detective Arnold's voice assaulted him out of the semi-darkness. "Since you didn't run in to wake me, I'm going to assume your search wasn't a rousing success."

"That's about the size of it," Alex said, leaning forward to blow out the lamp. "I did find the edge of a footprint in the parlor. It's too big to be either Rick or his mother. It was by the first window in the room, so I assume that's how he got in and out."

"Assume?" Detective Arnold said, skepticism in his voice.

Alex sighed and leaned back again.

"There's no evidence that anyone opened that window in the last six months."

"Maybe he went into the dining room."

"No," Alex said, rubbing his eyes, "the wall juts out there. The passage door to the dining room is a good four feet back from the window. The only reason for that footprint to be there is if our burglar was headed for the window."

"The window that hasn't been opened."

Alex sighed and nodded.

"The window that hasn't been opened," he agreed.

"Magic?" Arnold asked.

"No," Alex said. "I checked. There's almost no magical residue anywhere in the house at all, just a few barrier runes in Melissa's handbag and a fever remedy potion in the medicine cabinet."

"Is that unusual?"

"Not really," Alex said. "Most people only seek out magic when they need it, so there isn't much residue in their homes. Dr. Bell and I are lousy with the stuff, but we're an aberration."

"My wife has a stack of mending runes at least an inch high," Arnold said. "She can be a little clumsy at times."

"If it's okay with you, Detective, I'm going to go home and go to bed," Alex said, picking up his multi-lamp and replacing it in his kit bag.

"I think that's an excellent idea," Arnold said. "I've got to call my lieutenant and give him a report, then I'm going to do the same."

By the time Alex stumbled downstairs to the brownstone's main floor, it was after noon. Iggy was waiting patiently for him in his greenhouse reading a Margaret LaSalle novel.

"You look done in," he observed as Alex filled the percolator with water.

"Coffee," Alex mumbled.

Ten minutes later Alex sat at the table with Iggy, sipping his third cup of coffee.

"So you know someone was in the house, but not how they got in or out," Iggy summed up Alex's tale of the night before. "You know what that means?"

"If you quote yourself about removing everything impossible and looking for what remains, Iggy I swear..."

The doctor chuckled and sipped his coffee.

"All right," he said. "I shall restrain myself, but you and I both know that ghosts don't leave footprints and men don't walk through walls."

"Don't be ridiculous," Alex countered. "I walk through walls all the time."

"Using a rune that would leave behind enough residue to light up the street by ghostlight." Iggy shook his head. "No, you're missing something. Maybe the entire window comes out of its frame, or there's a loose panel in the wall."

Alex could only shrug at that as he hadn't even considered such a possibility.

"There's no way something like that could exist without leaving scuff marks or collecting fingerprints."

"You said the intruder wore gloves," Iggy pointed out.

"Let's assume for a minute that there is something tricky about the house," Alex said, not really believing it. "How would the intruder know about it and not Mrs. Hannover?"

"Well, he'd have prior knowledge of the place," Iggy declared. "How much do *you* know about it before it belonged to Mrs. Hannover?"

"I had Sherry do a basic records search, but that's it."

"I think perhaps you'd better do a more thorough investigation."

Alex drained his coffee and took his cup and saucer to the sink.

"Then I'd better get her started," he said.

"After that I suggest you call Detective Arnold and have him meet you at the Hannover house."

Alex gave him a quizzical look.

"Why? I've already been over every inch of that house, twice actually, and I didn't find anything. What would be the use of going again before I learn anything new?"

Iggy gave Alex a penetrating look while he sipped his coffee.

"Out with it," Alex insisted.

"You said that the intruder pulled old photographs out of an album," Iggy said. "That makes me wonder what photos were in that album, and what do the ones the burglar removed have in common."

"I assumed he was looking for something specific in the photos," Alex said. "When he found a picture that looked close to what he wanted, he took it out, then dropped it if it wasn't right."

"That sounds like a sensible reason for a burglar to bother with a photo album," Iggy said.

"What if he found the picture he wanted and took it?" Alex said.

"Go through the album and count the spaces where pictures are missing," Iggy said. "If it matches the number of loose pictures, then he didn't find what he was looking for."

"And if I'm short, it will tell me how many pictures the burglar took away with him."

"Now your brain is working again," Iggy declared as Alex picked up his suit coat from the back of his chair and put it on. "All you have to do now is figure out why a thief, who may or may not have a connection with the house, would go through photo albums belonging to the new owner."

Alex paused for a long moment. Iggy had brought up a very good question.

"I'll ask Mrs. Hannover about it when I see her," he said, heading for the front door. "I need to stop by the hospital first and check up on her anyway."

"Good luck," Iggy called after him. "If you need me, I'll be amongst my orchids."

7

RESIGNATIONS

The closest hospital to Melissa Hannover's house was Bellevue, so Alex caught the crosstown crawler headed east and south. A short ride later, he inquired after his client's room and was directed to a doctor on the fifth floor.

"Mr. Lockerby," Rick's voice greeted him when Alex got off the elevator. He jumped up from where he'd been sitting on a wooden chair in the hallway.

"Hey, Rick," Alex said, "how's your mom?"

Rick suddenly looked down. He looked exhausted and Alex wondered if he'd eaten today.

"She's asleep," he said, "but no one will tell me anything."

Alex put his hand on Rick's shoulder.

"Don't worry, kid," he said. "I'll go talk to the doctor. Cool your heels here till I get back."

Alex left Rick in the hall and made his way down the hall to where a bored-looking nurse sat behind a heavy desk.

"I'm here to see Melissa Hannover," he said. "What room is she in?"

Pound of Flesh

The nurse checked a clipboard, then shook her head.

"I'm sorry, but Mrs. Hannover is in a seclusion room, she isn't allowed visitors."

"On whose orders?" Alex said, lighting a cigarette.

"Dr. Lazlo," she said. "He's her physician."

"Can you page him for me?" Alex asked, giving her his most charming smile.

"I'm sorry," the nurse said again, "but the doctor is very busy."

Alex passed her one of his cards.

"Mrs. Hannover is my client," he said. "She was assaulted in her house last night, so I need to talk to her."

The nurse looked at his business card, then back at Alex. She seemed to hesitate for a minute, then she picked up the phone on her desk and paged Dr. Lazlo. Alex thanked her, then headed down the hall to where Rick was waiting.

"The doctor who's looking after your mother will be here soon and we'll find out how she's doing," Alex said.

Rick didn't answer, he just nodded wearily.

Poor kid's been here all night, Alex thought. *That's a long time to be worried about his mom.*

It was also a long time to sit on a chair.

"Do you have some relatives here in town?" he asked.

Rick thought about that, then nodded.

"I've got an uncle in Brooklyn," he said.

Alex fished a nickel out of his pocket and pressed it into Rick's hands.

"Go give him a call," he said. "Tell him you need to stay with him until I catch whoever keeps trying to break into your house."

Rick looked at the nickel for a long minute as his tired mind assimilated Alex's instructions.

"Okay," he said at last, then headed down the hall to where a public phone hung on the wall.

"Are you the reason I'm here?" an officious voice came from behind Alex.

Turning, Alex found a thin, balding, bespectacled man in a white coat standing behind him. The man had a long, snipe nose, like a beak, and dark, beady eyes under furrowed brows.

"Dr. Lazlo?" Alex asked, putting on a friendly smile. "I need to ask you about Melissa Hannover."

"Are you her husband?"

"Uh, no," Alex said, fishing out one of his cards. "Mrs. Hannover is my client."

Lazlo scoffed and threw the card over his shoulder.

"Mrs. Hannover needs rest," he said. "She is not to be disturbed so she can recover, and I am not to be disturbed by sightseers. There are people in this hospital who depend on me and I don't have time for the likes of you."

He started to turn away, but Alex grabbed him by the arm.

"Unhand me," Lazlo growled.

"I don't think you understand me, Doc," Alex said, pushing the man back against the wall of the hallway. "You see that kid over my shoulder? He's been sitting here, in this hallway, all night not knowing if his mother is alive. Now you're going to let him see his mother or you're going to need to see a doctor of your own."

"You let go of me or I'll summon the police," Lazlo hissed.

"I've got friends over at the Central Office," Alex said, "including the captain of detectives. If I give him a call, he's going to wonder why a doctor at this prestigious hospital is keeping a young man worrying about the fate of his mother."

To reinforce his point, Alex squeezed the doctor's arm hard, glowering down at him from his six-foot-one frame.

The doctor's angry look melted away and he cleared his throat.

"I, uh, I suppose I could take a few minutes to explain Mrs. Hannover's condition to the boy."

"That's the spirit, Doc," Alex said, releasing his arm and slapping him on the shoulder.

"My uncle will be here to get me as soon as he can," Rick said as he made his way back to where Alex and the doctor stood.

"That's great," Alex said, noting that the boy's face seemed more tranquil. "This is Doctor Lazlo, he's the doctor taking care of your mother."

Pound of Flesh

"Is my mom okay?" Rick asked, worry replacing the relief on his face.

"Well," Lazlo said, clearing his throat, "her injuries are healing, but she isn't out of the woods yet."

"What does that mean?" Rick asked.

"When they brought your mother in, she was unconscious," Lazlo explained. "After I treated her wounds, she still hadn't regained consciousness."

"Is that bad?" Alex asked, regretting the question immediately when Rick's face paled.

"It could mean she suffered a brain injury," Lazlo said. "In such cases, it's best to allow the body time to heal itself. Right now, Mrs. Hannover is receiving dream syrup to keep her asleep along with a regenerative draught to speed up her healing."

"But when she wakes up, she'll be okay, right?" Rick demanded.

"That's the hope," Lazlo said.

"When will you take her off the dream syrup?" Alex asked.

"On Friday."

"What happens if she doesn't wake up then?" Rick asked, his voice hoarse.

"The blow to her head doesn't seem too serious," Dr. Lazlo said. "I have every confidence that this treatment will work."

"But what if it doesn't?"

"If your mother still doesn't regain consciousness, there are further treatments we can use," Lazlo said.

"Don't worry, Rick," Alex said, "the doc knows what he's doing. Let's go wait for your uncle downstairs. We'll grab something to eat in the cafeteria."

Rick's face brightened at that and he nodded. Alex put his arm around the young man's shoulder and led him down the hallway toward the elevator. He did look back to give Dr. Lazlo a last glare, but the man had already turned away and headed for the nurse's station.

Nice bedside manner, he thought.

Half an hour later, Alex walked through the front door of his office. He was still tired from his late night, but Sherry's smile when she greeted him gave him a bit of a boost.

"Hey, Boss," she said. "I was worried when you didn't come in."

"Late night," Alex replied.

"Well, no one else is sympathetic about your schedule," she said, tearing a page from one of her notebooks. "Andrew wants to see you as soon as you come in." She handed him the paper then tore another one off the pad. "That alchemist, Linda Kellin called. She wants to see you at her shop."

Alex looked at Linda's name on the paper.

"Linda..." he said, trying and failing not to think about Jessica. He couldn't remember the last time he put flowers on her grave.

She deserves better than that, he chided himself.

"Well, she seemed pretty out of sorts when she called," Sherry said.

Alex sighed and nodded.

"I'd better go see Andrew first," he said. "If I don't, he's liable to follow me to Linda's."

Alex got off Andrew Barton's private elevator directly into the Lightning Lord's office. The sorcerer was literally a force of nature and Alex tended to think of him like the Rock of Gibraltar: eternal and unchanging. What greeted him when he got off the elevator put the lie to that idea.

Andrew's office was almost completely changed from what Alex remembered. The huge windows that ran up thirty feet along the back wall were still there, of course, as was the left-hand trophy wall that held the sorcerer's awards, photos, and mementos. It was the center of the space that had changed.

The last time Alex had been in Andrew's office, the center of the floor had been occupied by an enormous desk. It was easily fifteen feet long with a thick marble slab for a top and polished steel undercarriage that looked more like an impressionist sculpture than simple legs. It was an imposing edifice that reflected its larger-than-life owner very well.

To Alex's great surprise, the desk was nowhere to be seen in the giant room. A smaller desk of polished wood now stood off to the right side of the room, illuminated by a light fixture that hung down from the ceiling. Alex knew this was Andrew's new desk because of all the papers and blueprints piled on top of it.

In the center of the room, where the original desk had been, sat something that looked like a giant birdbath. In simple terms it was a shallow dish that had to have a diameter of at least ten feet. Below the dish was a heavy marble post that had to be as big around as a manhole cover. The post held the dish about waist high and, as Alex approached the strange device, he could see that the inside of the dish contained a silky black substance. It reminded him of coal dust.

"Well, it's about time," Andrew's voice boomed at him.

Alex expected the sorcerer to be angry, but when he turned to where the sound emanated, he found Andrew smiling broadly.

"I heard you were pretty sick," he said, crossing the floor and throwing his arms around Alex in a brief hug. "I'm glad you're back, young man."

He pushed Alex to arm's length, holding him by the shoulders.

"You look healthy," he declared before letting go.

"I am," Alex declared, "thanks to Iggy."

Andrew's face clouded over briefly.

"Yes, Dr. Bell was very tight-lipped about your condition," he said, his voice dipping into a slight growl. "Still, that's water under the bridge now. I've got two new projection towers being built and there's a dozen new ideas on my desk waiting for you to tell me how we can enhance them with rune magic."

"Why don't you start with this," Alex said, nodding in the direction of the birdbath.

"You like it?" Andrew said, smiling like a child with a new toy. "I came up with this to help your police friend and that FBI stiff," he went on. "The black stuff is magnetic sand. All I have to do is put some current through it," he reached down and touched the side of the dish.

A shudder ran through the sand, emanating out from the point where Andrew touched it and spreading like a ripple on water.

"Then think about what I want and..."

The sand shifted into a map of Manhattan, complete with buildings that raised up above the surface.

Alex was impressed and he admitted it.

"Here are the locations of my new towers," he said, and the surface shifted again. This time it was a map of the U.S. As Alex watched, the two New York towers rose up along with the one being built in Jersey City. Then came the two in Washington D.C., and finally one by the tip of Lake Michigan, and one on the California coast.

"Chicago and Hollywood," Andrew said.

Alex understood Chicago, it was the second biggest city in America.

"Why Hollywood?" he asked.

Andrew chuckled at that.

"Movies are the best way to spread a message," he said, "so I want those writers and directors to love my power projection."

"And mention it in their movies," Alex guessed.

Andrew winked and tapped the side of his nose.

"As soon as the tower goes up, I want you to get the vault passage up and working," he continued.

Alex's smile froze. With the damnation rune on his body, he wasn't sure he'd be able to modify his vault. As far as he knew, he was the only one who could change the shape of his vault, but without access to his magic, how would he do that?

Maybe Iggy will have some ideas, he thought.

"Something wrong?" Andrew asked.

Alex sighed.

"There's something you should know," he began.

"That sounds ominous," Andrew said, sitting on the edge of his desk.

"Part of my recovery involves a special rune that Dr. Bell tattooed on my chest," he said. "I was exposed to too much magic, it...well it's like it poisoned me. The rune keeps me from using magic until my body heals."

Andrew's eyebrow shot up in a look of confusion and surprise.

"You can't do any magic?" he asked. "At all?"

Alex shook his head.

"If you want to find someone else to do your rune work, I'll understand."

Andrew thought about that for a long moment, then he stood up and began to pace.

"You remember Bradly Elder?"

"Your former runewright with the god complex?" Alex scoffed. "Yes, I remember him."

"Well, he was very jealous of you," Andrew said.

Alex remembered that too; he'd used the man's jealousy to keep him talking while the construct he'd written overloaded and killed the man.

"Well it wasn't your penmanship he was jealous of," Andrew went on. "He was jealous of your mind, the way you can conceptualize complex magical interactions with the most basic of magics."

"I still can't write whatever I might think up," Alex pointed out.

"That's what Ignatius is for," Andrew said with a smile. "I'll even compensate him if I need to. The point is that I don't need you to write runes, I can get someone else to do that, I need your mind to help me optimize my projects. So no, I won't be firing you."

"Just checking," Alex said. "Now about your passage to the Hollywood tower, I'm going to assume you want the passage so you can pop out there to take actresses to dinner without having to teleport."

Andrew laughed at that and waggled his eyebrows.

"Not all of us are dating dangerous women," he said. "Now, let me show you some of the things I've been working on."

Alex wanted to put the sorcerer off, but Andrew was on a roll now and there was no stopping him. He checked his watch and there were still three hours before Linda would shut up her office, so he took a deep breath and followed the energetic sorcerer over to his desk.

"Alex," Linda exclaimed as he walked through the alchemy shop door. "Thank you for coming."

Alex took off his hat and gave her a smile. Linda wore a typical shop apron over a simple dress with her blonde hair up in a mass of curls. In some ways she was very different from her mother, but Alex could see the shadow of Jessica in her face.

"Sorry it took me so long," he said, slipping out of his overcoat and hanging it on the rack by the door. "I had to meet with Andrew Barton and he can be a bit long winded."

Linda crossed the shop floor and gave him a quick hug.

"I'm just glad you're here," she said.

"Me too," he said, returning the hug. "So why am I here? Sherry said you sounded worried on the phone."

Linda went back behind her counter and bent down to pick up a round bottomed bottle with a cork stopper. As she put it on the counter, it reminded Alex of the kind of potion bottles the wicked witch in a fairytale might use. Inside the bottle was what looked like a cup's worth of shimmering blue potion.

"What's that?" he asked.

"It's called Behring's Antiserum," she said. "It's a potent cure for people who've been poisoned."

Alex held up his hand.

"I appreciate the thought," he said, "but I was sick, not poisoned."

That wasn't true, of course; Alex had, in fact, poisoned himself. The problem was that adding more magic to his body wasn't going to help. Now that he thought about it, Linda's potion wouldn't even be able to affect him with the damnation rune in place.

Linda gave him an amused look.

"It's not for you," she said. "I know Dr. Bell knows his stuff, I'm sure he knows about this." She held up the little bottle again. "The reason I asked you here is because I had five of these last week and now this is the only one left. Understand, these have been here so long that they were brewed by my mother."

Alex was starting to see where she was going with this train of thought.

Pound of Flesh

"So four people have come in looking for a cure to poisoning in the last week?" he asked.

"No," she said. "I had four people come in complaining of the same symptoms. It took me a while to figure out the first one, but the antiserum cured the others as well."

"Do these people have anything in common?" Alex asked. "Other than buying their alchemical cures here, I mean."

Linda gave him a sly smile and picked up a notepad.

"I should be insulted by the tenor of that question," she said with a smirk, "but I knew you'd ask it, so I wrote everything down here."

She handed Alex the paper and he scanned the list of four names. Below each name was an address. Most of them lived in the same general area, south and west of the core.

"Any idea what could have poisoned them?" Alex asked. "I mean poison cures are all different, right? You can't cure someone from arsenic with the same stuff you use for a rattlesnake bite."

"True," Linda said, "but Behring's Antiserum is good against a lot of things. Its effectiveness also changes depending on the body chemistry of the person injecting it."

"So you got lucky when you gave it to your customers," Alex said.

Linda blushed a bit at that.

"People like to think of alchemy as an exact science," she said, "but it's magic, just like runes or sorcery. Sometimes it does what it wants to."

Alex looked at the list of names and back up to Linda. She wasn't trying to hire him, she thought people were in danger and she wanted his help. He wasn't above working a few pro-bono cases, and Linda was an important person in his life.

"I take it you don't know what kind of poison it was or how it was administered."

"No idea what it might have been," Linda said, "but unless they were bitten by something, the usual way to administer poison is to put it in food or drink."

"All right," he said, tucking the list into his shirt pocket. "I'll talk to your sick clients and find out how they might have been poisoned."

"Thank you, Alex," Linda said, hugging him again.

"Anytime, Linda," he said, turning and heading for the coat rack. "Two things," he said as he put on his coat and hat. "If anyone else comes in with whatever the other four had, let me know immediately."

"What's the second thing?"

"How long does it take to brew that antiserum?"

"About a week."

"I think you'd better get started on some more, I've got a feeling you might need them."

8

THE MYSTERIOUS CLIENT

Linda Kellin still lived and worked in the house her mother had established as her shop and laboratory, so Alex left the house and walked south until he hit One-Hundred Tenth street. From there he caught a crawler to Central Park West, then changed to a southbound skycrawler and in less than thirty minutes he was getting coffee at Marnie's coffee bar.

"I haven't seen you in forever," she said, wrapping her thin arms around Alex and hugging surprisingly tightly for her small frame. "Sherry said you were sick but she wouldn't tell me what was wrong."

"It wasn't her fault," Alex said, happy to get a hug from her. For a long time now he'd thought of her as family and it was nice that she felt the same way. "And I was here yesterday, but you weren't"

"I have to get my beauty sleep," she said, squeezing him again. "I'm just glad you're here. Are you back in the pink?"

Alex nodded as she let him go.

"Fit as a fiddle," he lied.

"Well don't scare me like that anymore," she instructed, swapping him a full thermos for an empty one.

"I'll do my best," Alex said as he headed for the elevator.

Ten floors up from Empire Station Alex got off the elevator on the twelfth floor and turned left, moving down the hall to a polished door of dark wood at the end. It always made him smile to see the brass plate beside the door that read, *Lockerby Investigations*. This time he was torn. In some ways it was like he'd been here every day, week in and week out, but he knew it had been more than a month since he was a regular in his own office.

"Hey, Boss," Sherry greeted him when he walked in. "What did Ms. Kellin want?"

"She thinks someone is trying to poison some of her clients," Alex answered, hanging up his hat and coat. "Gave me a list. I'll talk to them and look for any possible commonalities."

"I could do that for you," Sherry offered.

"Nope," Alex said, stopping in front of her desk to light a cigarette with the touch tip lighter. "Someone broke into Mrs. Hannover's house last night, she's in the hospital."

Sherry gasped.

"Is she okay?"

Alex shook his head.

"The doc I spoke to is keeping her unconscious and hoping her body heals itself," he said.

"How did they get in?"

"Well that's the rub," Alex said, puffing on his cigarette, "I don't know. As far as I can tell, all the doors and windows were locked."

"So it is a ghost?" Sherry asked.

"Ghosts don't leave size ten footprints or drops of blood on the floor," he said. "Whoever he is, he got inside that house in a way I couldn't find."

"Boss?" Sherry said, her voice tentative. "Are you sure you're able to use your lantern as well as you used to?"

Alex raised an eyebrow at her, holding her gaze for a long moment.

"Iggy told you?" he guessed.

She nodded.

"He wanted to make sure I didn't take cases that required you to write runes in the field," she said, suddenly looking down.

"Well, he wasn't wrong, but I don't need my magic to use

silverlight. Whoever got into the Hannover house used some kind of trick to do it."

Sherry looked like she was about to speak but Alex cut her off.

"And he did it without magic. Ghostlight works too."

"So what are you going to do?"

Before Alex could answer, the door to the back hallway opened and Mike Fitzgerald emerged. He was as unchanged during Alex's missing month, still short and thin with dirty blond hair and bushy mustache.

"Alex," he said, his expression brightening. "Sherry told me you were back, but I didn't believe it."

"Good to see you, Mike," Alex said, shaking the smaller man's hand. "Sherry tells me you've been handling some challenging cases while I was out."

"That I have," he said, beaming. "I did have to consult with Dr. Bell on a few of them, but he steered me right."

"I'd like to go over your work in a minute," Alex said, "if now's a good time?"

"Now's fine."

Alex turned to Sherry.

"I've got a job for you while I catch up with Mike," he said. "Go over to the hall of records and find out everything you can about the Hannover house. I want to know who built it, who paid for it, and who's lived in it since it was built. Names and addresses if you can get them."

Sherry didn't bother to take notes, she was familiar with a full records workup.

"Can I get lunch on the way back?" she asked.

"Take some cash. I'll cover the phone while you're out."

Sherry opened the cashbox on the third try, took a few dollars and left.

After she'd gone, Alex had Mike walk him through the cases he'd taken in Alex's absence. Most of it was standard detective work, but Alex was impressed by how good an investigator Mike had become.

"This is excellent work," he admitted at last. "How's your rune writing?"

Mike pulled out the blue-backed rune book he carried and handed it to Alex.

"Did you write all of these?" Alex asked, paging through the book.

"All but the major restoration runes and the temporal restoration rune," he said. "I'm afraid those are still beyond me."

"Do you think you could do one of my climate runes?" Alex asked.

Mike blushed at that.

"I've been trying," he admitted. "It'd be nice to not be cold all the time. So far I haven't been able to manage it."

"Keep trying," Alex said. "I don't like being cold either."

After that, Mike excused himself to go write some runes and Alex turned to the list of names Linda had given him. He didn't really want to deal with this, but if Linda was wrong, and the four clients that had come needing Behring's Antiserum hadn't been poisoned, then that was one heck of a coincidence.

"And I do love a good coincidence," he remarked, voice dripping with sarcasm.

Resolved to take the matter seriously, Alex picked up the phone and called the first of Linda Kellin's clients.

Alex hung up the phone and sat back in Sherry's chair. He'd spent the last hour and a half on the phone, calling Linda's clients. Most confirmed what she'd told him, although one of them was a certifiable nutcase.

Picking up his notepad, Alex reviewed his findings. As far as he could tell, the four people who had required a dose of Behring's Antiserum were complete strangers to one another. None of them lived or worked in the same parts of the city, they had no discernible friends or organizations in common, and they didn't frequent the same diners. As far as Alex could tell, the only thing connecting them was their alchemist, and they only sought her out after they felt sick.

With a frustrated sigh, Alex threw the notepad back on the desk and took out a cigarette. He didn't doubt Linda; if she said customers needing Behring's Antiserum were rare, then they were rare. In Alex's

Pound of Flesh

experience, an outlier like that meant something sinister was afoot. That said, coincidences did happen.

That didn't mean Alex had to like them.

He picked up the phone and reported his findings to Linda.

"You really think it's just a coincidence?" she asked when he finished.

"I don't want to," Alex said. "I hate coincidences, but without any more data I don't think there's anything more I can do."

"So, all you can tell me is to brew more batches of antiserum?" she demanded, frustration leaking into her voice.

"No," Alex replied. "Keep your ear to the ground. If any more of your clients show the same symptoms or if you hear of anyone else like that, call me. Maybe with more information I can figure out if anything is really going on."

"All right," Linda groused.

It was clear to Alex that she was just as unsatisfied with the idea of coincidence as he was. He bid her good day and hung up.

The phone on Sherry's desk had rung a few times between Alex's outgoing calls, but it had always been minor stuff, the kind of jobs that routinely went to Mike. Alex had dutifully taken notes and stacked them neatly on the corner of Sherry's desk. He knew his secretary wouldn't be back for several hours yet; searching city and state records was a time-consuming task.

For himself, Alex quickly got bored.

He had just resolved to go back to his desk and get those case files Sherry had put together for him, when the phone rang.

"Lockerby Investigations," Alex said, scooping up the receiver.

"Alex?" Danny's voice greeted him. "Have you been demoted?"

"Temporarily," Alex chuckled. "Sherry's off doing a records search so I'm holding down the fort."

"Well, I was calling for you anyway."

"Need more help with that murder in the alley?" Alex guessed.

"No," Danny said, "We've got that well in hand. Thanks to your disgusting rune, we got pictures of the victim. From that we made up some sketches and showed them around in the neighborhood where the body was found."

"So, who is she?"

"She's a waitress named Amanda Keeler," Danny explained. "Her boss at the diner didn't know where, exactly, she lived, so I've got men canvassing the nearby apartments. Shouldn't be too long before we get lucky."

Alex was impressed. He liked it when investigations progressed as they should.

"Sounds like you've got it all but wrapped up," he said. "How do I merit a call?"

"We showed around a drawing of Adam," Danny said, referring to the bloody amnesiac. "Nobody in the neighborhood knew him, but Amanda's boss at the diner said Adam was there last night and that he got up and left right after Amanda got off shift."

"He followed her out?" Alex said. "That's not good."

"It gets worse," Danny said. "A couple of uniforms found blood on a trash bin a few blocks from the scene. When they opened it up, they found an ax covered in blood. Adam's fingerprints were on it."

Alex considered that for a long moment.

"We arrested him about an hour ago," Danny said.

"You think his amnesia is a put-up job?" he asked at last. "Maybe he's setting up for an insanity plea?"

"I don't know about that," Danny said. "Bellevue is sending over someone to evaluate his mental state, but he isn't here yet."

"That brings us back to what you called me for."

"Adam wants to hire you," Danny said.

"Hire me?"

"Yep," Danny went on. "He swears he didn't kill Amanda, though how would he even know? Anyway, what he does know is exactly one private detective, so he asked me to call you for him."

"And he wants me to prove he's innocent," Alex stated.

It certainly was an interesting case. The first thing Alex would have to do is figure out who Adam really was, and then if he had any actual motive to kill Amanda Keeler.

"All right," Alex said after thinking it over. "Tell Adam I'll be by to see him in a few minutes. Also, I'll need to look at that file you've been building on him."

"Yeah, I know the drill," Danny said, a bit of an edge in his voice. "Just remember not to make the department look like a bunch of jackasses if Adam is innocent, and by department I mean me."

"Don't worry," Alex reassured his friend. "Based on what you told me, you didn't have any choice but to arrest Adam. It would have been derelict of you not to."

"Listen," Danny said, his voice getting serious. "A couple of reporters have already picked up on this story. I'm putting them off, but you can bet your rune book they'll print the most sensationalized version of that bloody alley if they manage to figure out what happened."

"That won't go over well with the public."

"It'll cause a panic," Danny agreed. "So I'd take it as a personal favor if you can nail Adam down sooner rather than later."

"What happens if he's innocent?" Alex asked.

"That would be extraordinarily bad news," Danny said. "If Adam's innocent, it means there's someone loose in the city who has no qualms about chopping pretty women into little chunks."

Alex shivered at the thought.

"Tell Adam I'll be right over," Alex said, then he hung up and punched the intercom button, calling for Mike.

This time, when the elevator deposited Alex on the fourth floor of the Central Office of Police, the desk sergeant escorted him down to one of the smaller interrogation rooms. Adam was inside, wearing prisoner clothes and looking morose.

"Take as long as you need," the sergeant said. "There'll be a man outside the door to let you out when you're ready."

Alex nodded, then stepped inside the little room and took the seat on the opposite side of the table from Adam. He worried for a moment that he might be locking himself in a box with a man who chopped up a person with an axe, but his instincts were telling him Adam was innocent of that crime.

That and Alex was relatively certain he could take Adam as long as he didn't have an axe.

"Thank you for coming," Adam said, his voice full of relief. "I...I don't know what to do."

"Well, we'll figure that out," Alex said. "Have you remembered anything?"

Adam shook his head.

"No," he admitted. "I don't know who I am, or where I work. I don't even know if I can pay you."

"I'm pretty sure you can," Alex said. "When I first met you, your clothes were good quality and in good repair, so it's highly likely you have a job. Based on the callouses on your hands, and how your jackknife was so sharp, I'd say you're some kind of tradesman. A skilled one if I had to guess."

Adam looked up, hope suddenly on his face.

"Will that help you find out who I am?" he asked.

"Probably not," Alex said, as gently as he could. "It is a piece of the puzzle, but there are thousands of skilled tradesmen in Manhattan."

Adam's hopeful look bled away, draining his face of life.

"Don't worry," Alex went on quickly, "If you are a skilled tradesman, someone will miss you pretty soon and they'll eventually call the police to report you missing. It might take a while, but we'll know sooner or later."

"What if I live alone?" Adam said. "What if I work alone?"

Alex shrugged.

"It might take longer, but sooner or later, someone will wonder where you went," he assured Adam. "But we're not going to wait around for that to happen. First I'll check the missing persons list; if you do have a wife, she should have called in by now. If that's a bust, I'm going to take another look at your clothes and the things you were brought in with and see if I can find anything there."

Adam let out a pent-up breath and nodded.

"Okay," he said, then he reached over and grabbed Alex's wrist. "I may not know my name," he said, his voice a hoarse whisper, "but I know who I am, and I'm not a murderer." He let go of Alex and rubbed his palm with the thumb of his other hand. "There's no way I could have chopped up someone with an axe."

Alex wasn't sure he believed that. For all Adam knew he was a mass-murdering psychopath, but deep down Alex doubted that. Something about the man seemed vulnerable and genuine, and it didn't feel like the memory loss talking.

"You sit tight," Alex said. "I've got some ideas and I'll get started right away." Alex started to stand up, but hesitated, dropping back into his seat. "My friend, Lieutenant Pak, mentioned that the police want this case closed quickly, so they'll probably offer you some kind of deal to plead guilty for a lesser sentence or better treatment. Do me a favor and give me at least a day to work, don't admit to anything."

"I couldn't admit anything if I wanted to," Adam said. "I don't remember."

Alex chuckled and gave Adam his most reassuring smile.

"That won't stop an ambitious prosecutor," he said, "so just sit tight and keep your mouth shut."

9

PRINTS

Alex rode the elevator up one floor to the detective's bullpen, then made his way around the perimeter to Danny's office.

"So, what do you think?" his friend asked as Alex entered.

"I don't think he's your killer," Alex reiterated. "I can't be sure, though. Amnesia makes it hard to get a read on him."

"I agree," Danny said. "Do you think you can figure out who he is?"

Alex shrugged, offering Danny a cigarette from his pack.

"You know that sooner or later someone is going to miss him," he said. "Is the D.A. really likely to offer him a deal?"

Now it was Danny's turn to shrug.

"I don't know, but everyone wants this matter settled before news of Miss Keeler's murder gets out. That way we can say we've caught the killer and there's no more danger."

"Still seems fast," Alex said.

Danny leaned down and opened a drawer in his desk.

"You haven't seen this," he said, holding out a photograph.

Accepting the photo, Alex turned it over to reveal a beautiful young woman. She had strong cheekbones with a button nose and a

Pound of Flesh

high forehead. Her hair was a mass of natural curls and even though the photo was in black and white, he could tell she was a redhead.

"This Amanda Keeler?"

Danny nodded.

"If the public finds out that she was chopped into chum, every tabloid from here to Washington will be screaming that we've got a new Ripper on our hands."

"So we need to find out who Adam is and where he came from fast," Alex said, handing the picture back. "In case he's not the killer."

"What are you going to do about that?"

"I figure I'll check the missing person's sheets first," he said. "With any luck his worried young wife has already called in looking for him."

"And if no one's looking for Adam?"

"Well, then it gets tricky," Alex said, tapping the ash off the end off his cigarette. "The only evidence we've got are his clothes and the things from his pockets. I'll have to go through those again."

Danny reached under his desk and pulled out a cardboard box.

"This is it," he said, putting the box down on his desk.

"Mind if I take these to my vault?" Alex asked. "I may want to run a few tests on the clothing."

Danny hesitated for a long moment.

"This is a very important case, Alex," he said. "If anyone found out I gave you the evidence, I could lose my badge."

"I'll be careful," he said, picking up the box. "And I'll have it back to you by five, don't worry."

Danny gave him a long look.

"Just find out who Adam is," he said. "I want this case in the 'closed' column as soon as possible."

Alex gave his friend a wink, then headed down the hall toward the janitor's closet. It was, quite conveniently, large enough for Alex to open a vault door inside.

Alex spent the next hour going over Adam's clothing and pocket items again. He'd subjected them to ghostlight and silverlight but saw nothing he hadn't seen before. In a fit of despondency, he called Iggy to come and take a look.

"I don't see anything you don't already know," the old fox said, opening Adam's jackknife. "The keys are the kind you could find in the pocket of any man in the city, the change purse is unremarkable, the watch is expertly cared for and set correctly, and the clothes have no identifying marks in them."

Alex sighed and rubbed his temples.

"Here," Iggy said, holding the knife out, "smell this."

Alex leaned forward and inhaled just above the open blade.

"Tobacco," he said, recognizing the faint odor. "Some American blend."

"Indeed," Iggy said. "I believe that explains why the knife is so sharp, your man Adam trims cigars with it, good ones by the smell."

"So he's not just a simple tradesman," Alex said. "He's got enough money to buy good cigars."

"He might have recently come into money," Iggy suggested. "That would explain the callouses on his hands."

"Maybe he changed jobs," Alex suggested.

"Also a good possibility," Iggy admitted. "Though I have no idea how to determine his identity based on just that."

"Well, thanks for taking a look," Alex said.

"Any ideas on what you'll do next?" Iggy said, using his own pocketknife to trim a cigar from his pocket humidor.

"Yeah," Alex said, giving his mentor an enigmatic smile. "A couple of uniforms found that bloody axe in a trash bin. I wonder how thoroughly they searched the bin once they found the axe?"

"What an excellent idea," Iggy said, heading for the brownstone door. "Do take care to wear your coveralls while you're rooting through the trash."

"Right."

By the time Alex changed clothes, dropped of Adam's belongings to Danny, and made his way to the alley where the bloody axe had been found, it was almost four. The sun was heading for the horizon and the alley where the trash bins were stored was pretty dark. Alex decided to use his multi-lamp as a lamp, something he hadn't done in years, and found a protruding nail on a nearby building to hang it up.

A lot of detective work consisted of tedious, boring tasks that most right-thinking people wouldn't want to do. These days Alex had a lot of help with things like research and stake-outs, but unsurprisingly, no one ever volunteered to help him root through a garbage pile.

Pulling on a pair of heavy gloves, Alex tipped over the nearest bin and began pulling the trash out of it, spreading it around the ground. He'd learned from previous experiences that one should always wear thick gloves when sorting trash because people had a tendency to throw out sharp bits of metal and broken glass.

As he began to sift through the trash, there was quite a bit of it that had blood on it, no doubt from the axe. He switched his lamp to the silverlight burner, then separated all the bloodstained trash into a pile. Once he had his regular oil burner back in the lamp, Alex started his examination of the bloodstained trash. Most of it was scrap leather, obviously from the cobbler shop that abutted the alley. The remnants of someone's half eaten lunch complete with a brown paper bag yielded no usable information, other than perhaps the fact that the cobbler disliked liverwurst.

On and on it went, with Alex peeling apart scraps of paper, torn envelopes, bent nails, a few broken tools, and piles of scrap leather. After an hour or so of searching, Alex gave up. He'd searched both the bins behind the cobbler's shop thoroughly and come up with exactly nothing. With a frustrated growl, he scooped the refuse back into the bins and returned them to their spot behind the shop.

He'd just blown out the oil burner in his lamp when he had an idea. Something he probably should have thought of before he spent all that time digging through the trash.

Setting his oil burner aside to cool, he took out the silverlight burner again and lit it. This time, instead of focusing on the bins, he shone the light around the alley. After all, whoever put the axe in the bin had to have walked along the alley at some point.

Alex moved up the alley toward the far end but didn't find any evidence of blood. Turning around, he went back to the end closest to the cobbler's shop. This time there was a definite trail of drops. They came from the mouth of the alley and ended just before the trash bins.

Moving out to the street, Alex lost the trail. Too many people had walked the sidewalk during the day, obliterating the trail. Again, Alex had found something that turned out to be utterly useless when it came to learning Adam's real identity.

As he turned back to where he left his crime scene kit, Alex froze. Something at the far end of the sidewalk was fluorescing in the light from his lamp. He moved to it and found a crumpled bit of paper stained red. Turning it over in his hands, Alex could see small lines printed on the paper as well as what looked like writing.

"It's a piece from a spiral notebook," he guessed, having seen that exact paper every time he made notes in his own flip book.

Taking his gloves off, Alex carefully tried to unfold the paper. Unfortunately, the dried blood had stuck it together as efficiently as any glue.

"Not to worry," he told himself. "A little water will loosen you right up." It would be nice if he could use a cleaning rune on it, but that might strip away the writing, so he was forced to use more primitive methods.

He had no idea if the paper held anything useful, but this felt like something important. For the first time since he took this case, he felt encouraged, like finding Adam's identity was something he might actually be able to do.

Humming cheerily to himself, Alex moved to his kit and took out a small jar with a screw on lid. Once he had it open, he deposited the bit of bloody paper inside and replaced the lid. Blowing out the burner in his multi-lamp, Alex set it aside to cool, then stood and tucked his heavy gloves under his left arm. From a hidden pocket inside his overalls, Alex produced his rune book, paging through it until he found a cleaning rune. The alley was deserted, so he could use his vault to get back to the office, but doubted Sherry would appreciate his coming in smelling like garbage and old blood.

Sticking the rune to his coveralls, Alex donned his gloves again, then lit the rune and held his arms out as the magic stripped the dirt, sweat, and grime from his clothing.

Alex wanted to work on the bloodstained paper the moment he returned to his vault, but a quick check of his pocket watch told him it was half past five. There was still a chance that Sherry would be in the front office, and Alex wanted to know what, if anything, she'd found out from her afternoon of research.

Setting his kit bag on one of the workbenches near his armory, Alex crossed the great room, turning right, then down the hall to his office. When he reached the front room, he found Sherry sitting on one of the two couches, reading a fashion magazine.

"Hey, Boss," she said when he entered. "I figured you'd be by before too long."

For Sherry, it really wasn't much of a guess. Her abilities gave her a keen sense of other people's schedules.

"I take it you found something?" Alex said. He knew she had information to give him, because if she'd found nothing, she would have just left him a note saying so.

"Mrs. Hannover's house has a very interesting history," she said, reaching into the back of the fashion magazine and pulling out a blue file folder. She tossed the magazine on the end table next to the couch, then opened the folder.

"The house was built in twenty-five," she read, "for a woman by the name of Thelma Rubison. There wasn't anything about inspections or permits in the records office, but I did find a mention of the house in the *Times* from the month the house was finished. According to the reporter, who apparently talked to the builder, Mrs. Rubison spent somewhere in the neighborhood of fifty thousand dollars to have it built."

Alex whistled.

"It must have been quite the place back in its day," he said. "It's not that grand now."

"Well, it was just a guess," Sherry said. "I kept looking but I couldn't find any more references to the house or to Mrs. Rubison."

Alex deflated a bit at that. He'd hoped that there'd be more.

"You might be interested to know that Mrs. Rubison sold the house in thirty-three to a banker named Floyd Watts. Apparently he used the house as a rendezvous for his various mistresses."

"Charming," Alex said. "Why did he sell to Mrs. Hannover?"

"According to the court filing, his wife found out about his extracurricular activities and filed for divorce. Selling the house was part of the settlement."

"That explains how Mrs. Hannover came to own it," Alex said, folding his arms in thought. "So, what's so important that someone has to break into the house?"

"You said he was looking through the family pictures," Sherry suggested. "Maybe he's looking for something left by one of the previous owners."

"Must be the banker," Alex said. "Anything left behind by the original owner would have been long gone by the time Mrs. Hannover moved in. Maybe one of our banker's ladies was someone important."

"Someone married who's in the public eye?" Sherry said.

Alex nodded. He was liking this line of thought.

"Get me an address on Mr. Watts," Alex said. "I'll go see him tomorrow and find out which of his mistresses has a husband or boyfriend who's willing to brain an innocent woman to keep her secret."

"I'll track him down first thing in the morning," Sherry said, standing up and picking up her handbag. "Right now, I have a date."

"Say 'hi' to Danny for me," Alex said as she headed for the door.

Sherry whirled on him.

"How do you know about us?" she demanded.

Alex gave her a half smile and a wink.

"You seem to forget that I'm a detective," he said. "I was in Danny's office this morning and when I hung up my coat, his coat smelled of your perfume."

"That's cheating," Sherry said with a wry grin.

Alex winked at her, then turned and headed out into the hall.

Alex returned to his vault. The paper with the blood just needed a little moisture to unstick it, so Alex removed it from the jar where he'd kept it and dropped it into a petri dish on his workbench. That done, he picked up a bottle with a rubber dropper in the lid. Adding a few drops to the paper, he massaged it in with a cotton swab.

Gradually the paper began to release as Alex added more water and worked it in to the parts of the paper that were stuck. Eventually, he managed to get the paper straightened out in the bottom of the dish.

Tipping it up, he dumped the little bit of accumulated water out onto the workbench, then took out a magnifying glass. The paper was clearly torn from a flip notebook like the kind he and Danny carried. There was only writing on one side, so Alex used a pair of long-nosed tweezers to turn the paper over.

"Mandy Keeler," he read. "Red's Corner Diner, noon to seven shift."

Alex sat back and just thought for a moment. 'Mandy' was clearly short for Amanda, so that fit. He couldn't be certain the bit of paper belonged to Adam; it might just as well belong to the killer, assuming that wasn't Adam. One thing was certain however; whoever it belonged to was looking for Amanda. They knew when and where she was going to be, and it was quite likely that knowledge got her killed.

A shiver ran up Alex's spine as he sat thinking. If someone went to Red's looking for Amanda, that would mean her death wasn't a crime of passion, but rather a premeditated one. Had someone planned to murder her and then make it look like it had been done by a madman or a jealous lover?

Alex glanced back at the scrap of paper, wishing it had more to reveal. After a minute of fruitless staring, he suddenly sat up.

Picking up his tweezers again, Alex moved the paper from the dish to the workbench, then pulled out his rune book. Paging to the middle, just after the high-use section and before the expensive rune section, Alex tore a page from his infrequently used rune section. It was simple, just a few heavy lines made in pencil, but it was very useful in the right circumstances.

Reaching into his kit, Alex withdrew a small, round tube with a threaded tin lid. Unscrewing the tube, he shook some of the black soot inside onto the top of the scrap of paper. That done, he replaced the tube of graphite filings, then folded the rune and dropped it on top of the scrap and the filings. Lighting the rune paper produced a symbol that resembled a squinting eye inside a circle. As it burned, the filings on the scrap of paper jumped up in a puff, then settled back down. Most settled around the edges of the paper, but a small amount adhered directly to the face of the page.

As Alex scrutinized the shape left in the wake of the revelation rune, he realized it was a name, just written backwards. It must have been written on the page above the back side of the bloody scrap.

Taking care, Alex transcribed the word, writing each letter in turn until he could read a name.

"Gallagher," he read.

It was a name, the only real question was whose? Was it Adam's real name?

"No," Alex answered his own question. "Why would Adam write his own name on a notepad?"

Could it be the killer? Alex thought.

"Only if Adam was following the killer," he reasoned, "but then why would he have Amanda's name in his book?"

Alex had to face the fact that the name Gallagher might not relate to Amanda's death at all. It could just as easily be the name of Adam's grocer since it had been written on a previous page in the notebook.

"And you're assuming the paper belongs to Adam in the first place," he told himself.

That, at least, was an easy problem to fix. Removing his silverlight burner, Alex clipped it into his multi-lamp and lit it. Slipping on the blue spectacles, Alex held the magnifying glass over the scrap of paper until he found what he was looking for. Right on the top left corner was a beautiful thumbprint.

Alex grinned and stood up to retrieve his fingerprint lifting kit.

"Gotcha," he said.

10

THE PERSONALS

By the time Alex got downstairs, he wanted nothing more than to turn around and go back up to bed. Iggy warned him that his body would need time to adjust from being sick, but it hadn't really bothered him as he was going through the day, it just seemed to save everything up to hit him at home.

"None of that," Iggy said as Alex leaned on the wall of the little hallway between the library and the kitchen. "Dinner will be ready in a quarter of an hour or so, not enough time for you to take a nap, unfortunately."

"Very funny," Alex said, pushing off the wall. "I just overdid it a bit today."

"I warned you," Iggy said. "Too bad you're basically immune to magic at this point, because I hear Linda is making a scaled down version of her mother's rejuvenator. That would fix you right up."

Alex moved into the kitchen, circling the massive table the long way to stay out of Iggy's space as he moved around the stove.

"I'll just take the old-fashioned route," he said, picking up the percolator and pouring himself a cup of coffee. If it had been cooler, he would have drained the cup in one go, but as it was, he sat down at his usual place at the table and nursed the cup until Iggy joined him.

"Say grace," Iggy said, putting his napkin in his lap. "Then you can tell me all about your new cases."

Alex did as Iggy asked, then began a narrative on his time back at the office. When he finally finished, his food was cold and his coffee was gone.

Iggy took out a cigar as they sat in silence, trimming it with his cigar cutter. When he finished, he clamped it between his teeth and lit it, puffing out fragrant clouds of smoke before he sat back in his chair.

"What are your thoughts about Adam?" he asked at last. "How do you find someone who can't remember who he is?"

Alex got up and poured himself another cup of coffee.

"I'm pretty sure all I have to do is wait," he said. "Sooner or later someone will come looking for him. The worry is the D.A. I'm pretty sure he's getting political pressure to put this case to bed."

Iggy chuckled at that.

"Oh, you may be sure of that," he said. "With the special election to fill Senator Copeland's seat coming up, everyone's posturing like it was a Presidential election."

Alex had forgotten about the special election. Senator Copeland had died back in June and it had taken the state officials in Albany this long to actually hold an election to fill his seat. Iggy was right, any aspiring politician would use the story of Amanda Keeler's grisly death as fuel for their political aspirations.

"So," Iggy continued when Alex didn't speak, "how can you find out who Adam is before the D.A. pressures him into taking a deal? I mean, as far as he knows, he might be guilty. With the evidence the police have, Adam might start to believe it whether he's guilty or not."

Alex reached in his pocket and pulled out the scrap of bloody paper with Amanda's name on it. Placing it on the table, he went back into his suit-coat pocket and withdrew a white card with a fingerprint on it.

"I found this in the alley where the axe was found," Alex said. "It wasn't near the trash bin, but the silverlight picked it up."

Iggy leaned forward and took the scrap of paper, holding it up to the light.

"I see it has the name of the dead woman on it, along with where and when she worked," he said. "Also, the word 'Gallagher.' Since's it's backwards, I assume you used a revelation rune for that."

Alex nodded and Iggy continued to scrutinize the paper.

"Do you have any idea what 'Gallagher' means?"

"None," Alex said. "As far as I know the name is wholly unconnected to Adam's identity."

"They appear to have been written in the same hand," Iggy said. "Though that's not surprising since it's unusual for more than one person to write in a flip notebook."

"I missed the handwriting," Alex sighed, rubbing his eyes.

"Think nothing of it," Iggy said, dismissing the error with a puff of smoke from his cigar. "That's why it helps to have multiple eyes on a piece of evidence."

"Did I miss anything else?"

Iggy ignored the question and tapped the paper with his index finger.

"What do you make of the victim's name and particulars?" he asked.

"I'm pretty sure it means Adam didn't know Amanda," Alex said.

"Indeed," Iggy agreed. "If you wanted to find Daniel somewhere, you might put down his first name, but certainly not his full name."

"That likely leaves us with some hired thug," Alex admitted, a wave of weariness pressing down on him like a physical weight. "Kidnapper? Maybe a hit man?"

"Oh, I don't think so," Iggy disagreed. "If Miss Keeler had any money, she wouldn't be working in a middling greasy spoon. If her family had money, her picture would have been in the evening paper."

"That rules out kidnapper," Alex nodded. "What about hit man?"

"The whole point of a hit man is to kill your intended target in a public and flamboyant manner," Iggy said. "It's designed to send a message in such a way that the information is clear but there isn't a trail back to the instigator. No, Miss Keeler's death was violent, visceral, and unless I'm very much mistaken, personal."

"So the killer knew her," Alex summed up, "and since Adam had to write her name in a notebook, it's almost certain he didn't know her."

"That's how I see it," Iggy said, "assuming this paper actually belongs to Adam."

"You think it doesn't?"

Iggy shrugged.

"It's certainly possible, though since you found it in the same alley where the police found the axe—"

"With Adam's fingerprints on it," Alex cut in. "The police checked as soon as they picked Adam up."

"Indeed," Iggy agreed. "Bearing all that in mind, I suspect that this paper most likely belongs to Adam, and you should proceed on that assumption until it's proven otherwise."

"Danny can get Adam to write something and then we can compare the handwriting," Alex offered. "Assuming his amnesia hasn't affected his handwriting."

"It shouldn't," Iggy said. "Handwriting is something we do habitually and amnesia doesn't affect that, so that might be a good way to verify the note."

Iggy sat back in his chair and puffed on his cigar with a self-satisfied smile. Alex didn't have the heart to tell him that was exactly the same conclusion he'd reached earlier. It was nice to have it confirmed, though, and Iggy had managed to rule out kidnapping and murder for hire.

"So what was Adam doing spying on Amanda?" Alex wondered aloud.

Iggy chuckled at that.

"You need to get some sleep," he admonished.

Alex could tell from his tone, that the old fox had figured it out.

"Just tell me," he said.

Iggy gave Alex an amused look and waggled his bushy eyebrows.

"A man has the name and particulars of a person in a flip notebook, much like those used by the police," he began.

"If Adam was a cop, someone would have recognized him." Alex interrupted.

"So who else uses flip notebooks and is in the habit of following complete strangers?"

Alex groaned and slapped his open hand over his face.

"He's a private detective."

"Something you should have thought of, I dare say."

Alex considered that. There were hundreds of private detectives in New York and every one of them had to get a license from the city. Of course the records office would have a list of everyone who applied for a license, but they had no way to know who was actually working as a private detective, meaning he'd probably have to sort through a thousand applications looking for Adam.

"It's a place to start," he said.

"If you mean the city's hall of record," Iggy said, "I think there might be a quicker way to find your man."

"Enlighten me," Alex said, a shot of excitement rousing him.

"Since Miss Keeler was unmarried and, according to what Daniel found out, not in a relationship, it's safe to say that whoever hired Adam wasn't after a cheating spouse."

"Unless they thought Amanda was the other woman," Alex countered.

"Unlikely," Iggy pushed back. "If she was seeing an older man, it's likely he would have met her at the diner once or twice, assuming he didn't meet her there in the first place."

"Okay," Alex said. It was a stretch, but he wanted to see where Iggy was going.

"So," Iggy went on, "if Adam wasn't following Miss Keeler to see where she spent her nights, what was he doing?"

"Missing person," Alex guessed. "Amanda Keeler might have been in hiding, or maybe she got separated from her family in the big war. Someone is looking for her."

"Exactly," Iggy said. "She was the right age to have been a war orphan."

"Let's assume you're right," Alex said, "and that's a big assumption at this point."

"Agreed."

"How does that help me find Adam?"

"When people are looking for someone, they don't usually employ a private detective right off," Iggy gave Alex a penetrating look. "Do they?"

Alex sat up straight, his coffee forgotten.

"No, they don't," he agreed. "They check with police and city records."

That could be a viable line of inquiry, though there were thousands of missing persons alerts in the police's cold case files.

"I rather think you should start with the papers," Iggy said. "Running an ad in the personals is much cheaper than hiring a private detective."

That made sense. There were always notes in the personals section of the paper, people seeking to reconnect with old friends, to find lost loves, and even looking for missing family members. Whoever hired Adam would probably have run ads looking for Amanda first. If he could find one of those, he'd find Adam's client, and that would lead him back to Adam.

Alex grinned at Iggy and the old man nodded back to him, hiding a self-satisfied smile behind his cigar.

"Now," he said, tapping the ashes of his cigar on his plate before standing. "I believe I shall do the washing up tonight. You need to retire immediately and get some sleep."

Alex opened his mouth to protest, but Iggy shot him a stern look.

"Doctor's orders," he said.

"All right," Alex said, ironically not having the energy to argue. He picked up the bloody scrap of paper and the fingerprint card, putting them back in his pocket, then headed for the stairs.

"Be careful," Iggy called out, causing Alex to turn back. "Whoever hired Adam to find Miss Keeler may very well be the person who killed her."

That made an unfortunate amount of sense. Whoever hired Adam to find Amanda was willing to pay private detective rates to locate her. Alex didn't know why someone would do that just to kill her, but stranger things had happened.

"I'll be sure to meet him somewhere public," he said.

By the time he reached his room, he had just enough energy left to take off his clothes and fall into bed. He was asleep before he could pull his covers up.

Alex knew something was wrong. His mind was barely awake but he could tell that his room wasn't as it should be.

"Wha-," he mumbled as he forced his eyes open.

Despite the odd feeling, his room seemed just as he left it. That's when he realized his clothes were missing. Not the undergarments he was wearing, but the shirt, coat, pants, and shoes he had shed so carelessly on his way to his bed last night. He distinctly remembered tossing his coat on the foot of the bed and his shirt made it onto his reading chair.

Which was now occupied, but not by his shirt.

"It's about time you woke up," Sorsha said, setting the book she'd been reading aside.

"Wha-," he tried again. "What time is it?"

Sorsha raised an imperious eyebrow, then reached for the clock on his bedside table.

"It's eight fifteen," she reported, then put the clock back where Alex could easily see it. "Your landlord insisted that you needed your sleep."

She clenched her teeth as she said it and Alex had never heard her refer to Iggy as his 'landlord.'

"I would have thought," Sorsha went on, "that you'd had quite enough sleep over the last month."

"I don't think that's how it works," Alex said, choosing his words carefully. He started to pull the covers back, but hesitated when he realized he was only dressed in his underwear.

"Oh, please," Sorsha scoffed. "Two nights ago you were in my bed and you were naked."

"Sorry," Alex said, getting up. "Father Harry taught me to never put a lady in an awkward position."

The ghost of a smile crossed Sorsha's lips but then her eyes hardened.

"That is exactly the problem I came here to discuss with you," she said, watching him as he went toward the bathroom to wash his face and run a comb through his hair.

"Problem?" Alex said.

"Yes," Sorsha said. "I thought we discussed it yesterday, but apparently you didn't fully understand me."

Alex wasn't sure what she meant, so he finished buttoning up his shirt, then went looking for some trousers.

"You said we needed to work together more," he said. "So far all I've done is some research and looked at a crime scene. One with a dozen cops watching it, so I was perfectly safe."

"I *am* concerned about your safety," Sorsha said, suddenly behind him as he buttoned up his trousers. She slipped an arm over his shoulder and another around his waist, hugging him from behind. "Maybe I let my worry for you talk too loudly," she said, her cheek against his back.

"You aren't wrong to be worried," Alex said. "I am usually the one to rush in where angels fear to tread."

"Yes," Sorsha agreed, "but I didn't just mean that we should work together when things get dangerous. I meant that we should be together when we aren't working."

Alex took her hand and turned to face her.

"You want us to be more of a couple."

She looked up at him with her pale blue eyes sparkling in the morning light.

"You don't mind," she said, "do you?"

Alex thought about that for a moment. Ever since he first met Sorsha he'd considered her the most beautiful woman he'd ever met. They hadn't gotten off on the right foot back then, but he'd worn her down. When he thought about it, she was really the only woman who he could talk to about his life and magic. Even Sherry didn't know what Sorsha knew, despite working with him every day.

"I don't mind," he said. "I do need you to explain it to me though. Sometimes I'm not the sharpest knife in the drawer."

"I've already talked with Ignatius," she said, looking up at him. "When you eat here, I'll be joining you, assuming I'm available. And twice a week, you and Ignatius will dine with me at the castle."

"Is that all?" Alex asked, knowing full well it wouldn't be.

"No," she said. "We need to go out and we need to stay in."

"You mean without Iggy."

"Most definitely," she said. "Though I know you'll need time for your little talks."

Alex laughed. She said she'd talked to Iggy and Alex knew he would have insisted on maintaining at least some of their evening chats.

"This sounds kind of complicated," Alex said. "Why don't we just get married? Then we can adopt Iggy and he can live with us."

"You are not funny," Sorsha said, then her face fell. "You know we can't get married. You'd never be able to go anywhere again. Everyone who wants something from me would try to get it through you."

Alex hadn't really had anyone try to ply him to get access to Sorsha and he said so.

"That's because everyone thinks you're just a passing fling. Someone that caught the Ice Queen's eye. They expect that I'll move on at some point."

"But if we were married, people would know that you listened to me," Alex guessed.

"You'd also be a target for rival sorcerers, or anyone who wanted to exert power over me."

"Won't those people figure it out when we're still going out together next year?"

"Eventually they will," she said, snuggling up against his chest again. "We can get married then."

"Promise?" he said.

"Yes."

"You're a very practical woman," he accused her with a smile.

"You mean I'm not romantic?" she said, arching an eyebrow.

"No," he said, putting his arms around her. "I mean that you do things deliberately. You're romantic when the opportunity arises, and serious when you need to be."

"Would you prefer a softer woman?" she asked in a soft voice.

"What use would I have for a woman who couldn't challenge me?" Alex asked.

Sorsha sighed, then pushed him back, looking up with a mischievous grin.

"I'm going to remind you that you said that," she said. "Probably when you'll least appreciate it."

"I'd expect nothing less," Alex chuckled. He wasn't entirely sure what had just happened. It seemed that he had married Sorsha in everything but name. He really didn't mind, he was half-way through his thirties, a time when most men had not just a wife, but a family as well. If he was honest with himself, it was a situation he had never really considered.

"Are you happy?" she asked, her face and tone earnest.

Alex leaned down and pressed his lips to hers in a brief but passionate kiss.

"I believe I am."

11

LADIES' NIGHT

Alex had a smile on his face when he crossed his vault to his office. His conversation with Sorsha had been unexpected, but now that he thought about it, he'd felt it coming for some time.

"You look like the cat who ate the canary," Sherry said as he entered the front room. "Did you figure something out about the mystery man?"

"In fact I did," he said, brushing off her interest in his grin. He went on to explain about Adam's possibly being a private detective and how finding Amanda Keeler's name in the personals might lead to learning his identity.

"That makes sense," Sherry said, "I take it you want me to dig into the classifieds?"

"That depends," he replied, "did you get an address for Floyd Watts?"

Sherry tore the top sheet off a notepad, handing it to Alex.

"He lives in California now," she said. "A place called Palo Alto."

Alex looked at the address and sighed. He made enough money for the long-distance call, but it wouldn't be a quick conversation.

"What about the wife?" he asked. "You said she divorced him for using the Hannover house to keep his mistresses, right?"

Sherry nodded, leaning back in her chair and crossing her legs.

"So it's likely she knew about the women that Floyd kept in that house. She'd have needed their names and maybe even their testimony to win her case."

"She would need at least one of them, yes."

"What is ex-Mrs. Watts' name?"

Sherry picked up one of her notebooks and flipped through it, stopping after a few pages.

"Lydia," Sherry read. "Lydia Watts, now Lydia Bergen since she's gone back to her maiden name."

"Any idea where Mrs., uh... Miss Bergen is living now?"

"She got their apartment in the divorce," Sherry said, copying down an address from her notes onto a fresh pad. Tearing the page off, she handed it to Alex.

"All right," he said. The address on the paper was for an apartment building in the core. "You take the personals, go back a few months and see if you can find any mention of Amanda Keeler or the name 'Gallagher.' I'll go see the former Mrs. Watts and find out what she knows about her ex's paramours."

"I'll get Mike to cover the office," Sherry said, standing up with her handbag. "He's writing runes this morning, so he can just move in here."

Alex nodded, then turned and headed back out the door.

The apartment building where Lydia Bergen lived was a block from Empire Tower, so Alex didn't bother with a cab and just walked. The building itself was a perfect example of the excess of the roaring twenties, even though it hadn't been built until the early thirties. It was built of gray stone, rising up twenty-five stories, and housed some of New York's wealthiest citizens.

"Who are you here for?" the doorman out front asked.

"Miss Lydia Bergen," Alex said.

Pound of Flesh

The doorman was broad shouldered and athletic, with the kind of bigness Alex associated with men who did manual labor. Since he was a doorman for the ridiculously wealthy, his size meant he exercised to keep his physique. He was not the sort of man to be trifled-with.

"Our residents value their privacy," he said, leaning into Alex's personal space. "What's your business here?"

Thinking fast, Alex pulled his rune book from his shirt pocket, then flipped to the back pocket where he kept business cards and important papers. Pulling out a linen card with gold leaf embossing, he handed it over to the burly man.

The card was one Andrew Barton had given him when they'd started working together. The card was one of the fanciest Alex had ever seen, with his name embossed in gold with the important sounding title of 'Chief of Runic Development.' Alex had never shown it to anyone, not even Iggy, but he'd kept it in the back of his rune book in case he ever needed it to sound important.

"I'm Alex Lockerby," he said. "As you can see, I'm a representative of Barton Electric. Miss Bergen may have received some Barton Electric stock from her ex-husband in their divorce and Mr. Barton wanted me to discuss it with her."

The doorman hesitated. While he appeared to be a more than competent guard dog, his face bore the blank expression of the unimaginative. He was exactly the sort of man who would be intimidated by the name, 'Andrew Barton.'

"I'll...I'll announce you," he said at last.

Two minutes later the elevator operator, a perky young blonde with a crooked smile, let Alex off at the penthouse level. There were only two apartments on this level, which meant they were huge, and expensive. Alex was getting a pretty good idea how Floyd was able to afford the Henderson house as a place to keep his mistresses.

"Who is it?" a feminine voice came from behind the heavy door once Alex knocked.

"My name is Alex Lockerby, ma'am," he said. "I'm a private detective. I need to ask you a few questions about a house you sold recently."

There was a long pause, then the lock in the door clicked.

When it opened, Alex was greeted by an attractive woman who looked to be in her early forties. Her skin had an olive complexion, Greek or Italian descent if Alex had to guess. She had raven hair with a streak of silver that grew from the left side of her forehead. On some other woman it might have made her look old, but Lydia wore it like an accent or a beauty mark. The entire effect was stunning.

Floyd must be nuts, Alex thought.

"What about that house?" she said.

"Someone broke into it the night before last and tried to murder the new owner," Alex said. "They were looking for something."

"Is the owner all right?" Lydia asked, still not opening the door all the way.

"Mrs. Hannover," Alex explained, "and she's still in the hospital. The doctors don't know if she's going to be all right."

"Who hired you?"

"She did," Alex said. "She thought there was a ghost in her house making noises after dark. She was attacked the following night."

"So why are you here?"

"Since Mrs. Hannover just moved in, I assume that whoever attacked her was looking for something belonging to, well, one of the previous occupants."

"That wasn't me," Lydia said, starting to close the door.

"No," Alex agreed, "but you had a detective of your own, didn't you? You needed to know who your husband was keeping there."

The door hesitated, then opened a bit.

"My husband was an ass," she said. "I don't want to be reminded of him."

"You don't have to tell me anything," Alex said. "Just call your man and have him tell me who he found."

"You really think this is about one of my husband's floozies?"

Alex just shrugged.

"Maybe one of them had a husband," he offered. "Maybe a jealous lover, or an overprotective father. Someone who wants to make sure there's no evidence left behind by whoever they care about."

She opened the door fully and leaned on the jamb, raising a

Pound of Flesh

cigarette to her lips. She wasn't the beauty Sorsha was, but she was an extremely handsome woman.

"The kind of woman my husband fancied weren't important people," she said. "Waitresses, secretaries, musicians, dancers," she paused to take a drag on her cigarette, "those were the women that my husband courted. The kind that were impressed by his wealth. He'd wine and dine them, then put them up in that house until he got bored with them, then send them back to whatever was left of their lives."

Bitterness dripped from her voice and Alex felt sorry for her.

"I'm sorry to ask this of you," he said, meaning it. "But whoever broke in was definitely searching for something."

"Doesn't it make more sense for your intruder to be looking for something belonging to the Hannover woman?"

"No," Alex said. "If he wanted something from Mrs. Hannover or her son, he wouldn't have attacked her, he would have questioned her."

Lydia Bergen stood there smoking for a long minute before she shrugged.

"All right, Mr. Lockerby," she said. "Come in. I'll get the investigation files for you."

She stepped back and Alex entered her massive apartment. His vault was big, but this apartment was enormous.

"Have a seat there," Lydia said, closing the door. "You can look at the files all you want, but you have to do it here. I can't risk losing them in case my husband tries to contest the divorce decree."

"Fair enough," Alex said, sitting on a white couch with a coffee table in front of it.

Lydia disappeared into a back room for a few minutes, then reemerged with a cardboard file box. Setting it down on the coffee table, she took off the lid, revealing dozens of folders in neat rows.

"I'm Lydia," she said as she sat next to Alex. "But you knew that already. It's okay to call me Lydia, though. Most people call me Miss Bergen, which makes me sound too young or too old."

"And you can call me Alex," Alex said.

"These are the files you want," Lydia said, indicating a group of folders separated by a paper divider. "Every tramp, hussy, floozie, and whore my husband ever put up in that place."

Alex picked up the folders and set them on the table, then moved the box to the floor. Taking out his notebook, he opened the folder on top of the file and began making notes. After an hour he was more than halfway through the files. Whoever Lydia had hired had been especially thorough. There were notes on all the girls, where Floyd had found them, their families, how long they'd spent with Floyd, and what had ultimately happened to them. There were a few files that were little more than a name, but most were thick with detail.

"Would you like a drink?" Lydia asked. She'd sat on the other side of the couch from Alex, reading a book of poetry and answering the occasional question while Alex searched the files.

"Whiskey," Alex said without thinking. "If you have it, that is?"

"I do," she said, setting her book aside and rising. "I'll be right back."

Alex kept making notes until Lydia waved a glass of amber liquid under his nose.

"Sorry," he said, sitting back and accepting the glass. He sipped it while Lydia resumed her seat.

"I don't see a ring," Lydia said, crossing her legs. "Are you spoken for?"

Alex almost laughed, but realized Lydia might take that the wrong way.

"Actually," he said. "I'm engaged."

That wasn't strictly true, but it was the best way to describe his unusual arrangement with Sorsha.

"Figures," she said. "All the prime cuts are taken and it's only the grindings left at the butchers."

"Sorry," Alex said with a shrug.

"Do you mind if I ask you a personal question, Alex?" Lydia said.

"No."

"If you were available, would I have had a shot?"

Lydia had to be five years older than Alex, not an insurmountable difference by any means. She was beautiful and shapely, and filthy rich. What wasn't to like?

"You would," he said.

She gave him a shy smile, then picked up her book.

"Thank you, Alex," she said and went back to reading.

Alex wondered how much her innocent-sounding question had cost her.

The files he'd been reading told the stories of pretty young women, young being the operative word. It must have torn Lydia apart when she found out about her husband's predilections.

Alex refocused his efforts on the files and half-an-hour later, he was done. Of the many women Lloyd Watts was involved with only seven had been residents of his mansion in the core.

"Thank you, Lydia," he said as he returned the folders to the file box and replaced the lid. "I appreciate your help."

Lydia scoffed.

"I can't have brutish men assaulting innocent women," she said. "Not after my divorce anyway."

She led Alex back to the front door and waited for him to step back into the hallway.

"Alex," she said just as he started to turn away. "If that engagement of yours doesn't go through, be sure to remember me."

Alex put his hat over his heart in a gesture of earnestness.

"I will," he said, "A woman like you is impossible to forget."

Then he put his hat on and headed for the elevator, leaving Lydia smiling after him.

When Alex got back to his office, Sherry was still out. That wasn't surprising as she had a lot of newspapers to go through. It was Mike who greeted him when he walked through the front door.

"How's it going?" Alex asked him as he hung up his overcoat and hat.

"We've had a few calls," Mike said, his blond mustache turning up as he smiled. "A couple of records searches and a missing necklace. I'm meeting with all of them this afternoon to get their particulars."

Alex was impressed and he said so. Mike was not only becoming a serviceable detective in his own right, but his business skills were coming along nicely too. Excusing himself, Alex made his way down the short hallway to his office. Now that he had the names of Floyd Watts' paramours, he'd need to call them. He couldn't just come right out and demand information from them, so he'd have to tread carefully.

An hour later, Alex had crossed four of the seven women off his list. Once he'd tracked them down, talking with them removed them as suspects. They had only basic educations and didn't have strong family ties. The ideal person to be swayed by Floyd Watts' promises of luxury and decadence.

He asked if any of them had permitted Floyd to take dirty pictures of them, but they all denied it. So far the search for someone with motive wasn't going very well.

Before Alex could pick up the phone to locate woman number five, a dark-haired southern belle named Victoria Blackburn, the intercom on his desk buzzed and Mike's voice emerged.

"Begging your pardon, Boss," he said, "but I've got an alchemist on the line named Linda Kellin. She says she really needs to talk to you."

Alex was puzzled for a brief moment, but then remembered the calling he did yesterday. He probably should have called Linda right away after that. He made a mental note to apologize to her.

"Put her through," Alex said, after depressing the talk button on the intercom box.

A moment later, his desk phone rang and Alex picked up the handset.

"This is Alex."

"I've got five new cases of poisoning for you," she said by way of greeting.

"I thought you only had one dose of that antiserum stuff left."

"I cannibalized some potions with the same basic structure and used them to make more," Linda said. "It only took two days."

"I looked into the previous four and didn't find any area of intersection," Alex said.

"Well, this should give you more information to work with."

"Linda," he began, "you said that this antiserum stuff works differently on different people. Are you sure they needed it, or rather that it actually cured them?"

Pound of Flesh

"Alex Lockerby," Linda fumed, "I may not be as good an alchemist as my mother was, but I know when someone has been poisoned. And," she hastened to add, "I'm not the only one this time."

"What do you mean by that?"

"I mean that a doctor from Presbyterian Hospital came in looking for Behring's Antiserum. He's seen a rash of cases there too."

Alex was only paying partial attention, but now his brain snapped into focus.

"What's this doctor's name?"

"James Kitteridge," Linda said. "He told me he has three cases and I've had another two."

Alex took a deep breath and let it out slowly. Linda thought that having more people meant it was a sure thing someone was poisoning them. Unfortunately, the more people, the less likely someone was poisoning them. This was more like some kind of bad food or chemical spill, only in cases like that it was easy to track everyone back to a single point of exposure. Based on what he already knew about these incidents, there wasn't any way to track the sickness back to a common point because the original five people he called didn't intersect.

"All right," he said. "I didn't find any commonality among your first four victims, but maybe with more data, we'll be able to see a pattern."

"I hope so," Linda said. "So far we've been lucky, but sooner or later people are going to start dying."

Alex took out his pen and notebook, cradling the phone receiver on his shoulder.

"Give me the numbers of your new clients and that doctor, and I'll make some calls."

"Is there anything I can do?" Linda asked.

"Yes," Alex replied, "make up as much of that antiserum stuff as you can."

12

STATISTICAL SIGNIFICANCE

Alex called Dr. Kitteridge as soon as he got off the phone with Linda. The man was very different from Phillip Lazlo, the doctor watching over Michelle Hannover. Kitteridge sounded earnest and kind, and like Linda, he was very concerned about the three patients he'd given Behring's Antiserum. According to him, he'd heard from several other doctors at other hospitals who were seeing similar patients.

Copying down the patients Dr. Kitteridge had seen, Alex asked the man to get patient names from any doctor who reported prescribing Behring's Antiserum. Kitteridge promised he would and Alex hung up.

Setting aside the contact information for the three patients, Alex turned back to the list of Floyd Watts' paramours. Despite the call from Linda and his conversation with Dr. Kitteridge, Alex wanted to keep the momentum he had working on the mystery of Hannover House. There were still three women he needed to call in the hope of discovering a motive for Mrs. Hannover's attacker.

Picking up the folder on his next vixen, Victoria Blackburn, Alex hesitated, then put it back down. Pulling out his address book, he looked up the number for The Philosopher's Stone, then picked up his phone.

Pound of Flesh

"Philosopher's Stone," Charles Grier's voice came over the line. "Proprietor speaking."

"It's Alex Lockerby, I've got a question for you."

"Alex," Charles said, with obvious delight. "I'd heard you were laid up for quite a while! It's good to hear your voice. What's your question?"

Alex took out his flip notebook and opened to a blank page.

"What can you tell me about an alchemical potion called Behring's Antiserum?" he asked.

"I can tell you I had ten bottles of the stuff in stock last week and now I've only got one," Charles said. "But I'm going to assume that's not what you wanted."

"No," Alex agreed.

"It's an older formula," Charles explained. "Most of what it does is covered by modern anti-toxin and anti-venom potions."

"Most," Alex repeated, latching on to the word, "but not all."

"There are a few physiological phenomena and even a few toxins that only respond to Behring's Antiserum. That's why we keep it around."

"How do you know when to try it?"

"That's easy," Charles said with a chuckle, "when other antidote potions don't work."

"Is it exclusively used as an antidote for poison?"

"Primarily," Charles said. "It is also useful for cleaning out parasites like tapeworms, flukes, trichinosis, that sort of thing."

"I heard that it doesn't always work on every person," Alex said.

"That's true," Charles admitted. "The working theory is that it's sensitive to the person's diet, though nobody really knows for sure. Is there a reason you're asking the particulars of a potion that's suddenly flying off my shelves?"

"Linda thinks that people are being poisoned," Alex explained. "She's sold out of Behring's Antiserum in the last week, and a Dr. Kitteridge over at Presbyterian Hospital has had to treat three different patients with the stuff."

Charles was silent for a long moment.

"I suppose that's possible," he said. "But I would think that if someone was poisoning people it would be easy to trace. The easiest way to poison someone is through the food they eat. Liquids are a close second, but many poisons have a strong odor or taste, so you'd need something strong to hide that."

Alex had read Iggy's monograph on poisons, so he already knew what Charles was saying, but the man was on a roll, so he didn't interrupt.

"If someone had poisoned the soup at a restaurant, all the people who got sick would lead right back there. Have you checked the victims?"

"I did, no connections so far," Alex said. "A couple of them work near each other, but everyone else is all over the map."

"I suppose that leaves individual poisoning," Charles said. "Your man, if he even exists, must be administering doses one on one. I don't see how that's even possible."

"I do," Alex said, sitting up a little straighter as his mind latched on to an idea. "What about a cabbie," he suggested. "That would explain why the victims don't overlap in any meaningful way."

"And just how is this cabbie administering this poison?" Charles asked. "No passenger in a cab is going to let the driver inject them."

"What about smoke?" Alex said. "Could our man soak a cigar in the poison, then just smoke it when people are in his car?"

"How does he keep from getting poisoned?"

"Maybe he has a stash of Behring's Antiserum," Alex guessed. "Or he's immune."

"Typhoid Larry?" Charles said with a laugh. "I suppose that could happen, but it doesn't sound likely, does it?"

Alex was forced to admit that it didn't; still, the idea of a killer cabbie wasn't far-fetched, there had been one a few years ago. Killing, or attempting to kill, with a poison that was only cured by an unusual antidote was also strange. If someone wanted to poison a large group of people, they usually did it where people congregated.

A sudden chill made Alex tremble as images of the Brotherhood of Hope mission flooded his mind. Last of all was the sight of Father Harrison Clementine lying on the floor of a meeting the hall. He'd stopped an outbreak of magical plague, but it had cost him his life.

You need to go see his grave and pay your respects, he thought, mortified that it had been almost a year since he'd been.

Alex shook his head to clear it.

"I suspect you're right," he admitted to Charles. "If someone wanted to poison a lot of people, he wouldn't do it one person at a time."

"I'm rethinking that," the alchemist replied. "So far you've only got a handful of cases, correct?"

"Yes, but based on how many potions you've sold, there's at least nine more I don't know about."

"That's still a relatively small number of people," Charles pointed out. "Maybe the idea of a one-off poisoner isn't so far-fetched."

Alex liked the cabbie idea and he wasn't ready to give it up just yet.

"Can you get me the names of the people you sold Behring's Antiserum to?" he asked.

"None of them were regular customers," Charles said, "but if anyone else comes in, I'll let you know."

"Thanks," Alex said, then Charles wished him good luck and hung up.

Alex pushed aside the file on Victoria Blackburn and opened the file he'd started on Linda's clients. When he'd interviewed them, he'd asked about their routines, where they lived, worked, ate, and shopped. What he hadn't asked, was how they traveled.

Not wanting to call them all back right away, Alex focused his attention on the three new names that Dr. Kitteridge had given him. Selecting a name at random, he picked up the phone and dialed the number.

When Alex hung up the phone it was already three o'clock in the afternoon. He'd called the three new potential poisoning victims, then gone back through the four Linda had given him. All but one had taken a cab in the last week. He would have felt better if it had been all of them, but it was a strong lead. That last person could have been infected in some other way, but Alex couldn't even say that because he still didn't know how the poisoner was plying his trade.

He'd had thinner leads.

"You need to discuss it with Iggy," he said out loud.

If there were holes in his theory, ones he was missing, Iggy would find them.

It was still two hours till closing, so he tapped the intercom key and got Mike's voice in response.

"Sherry still isn't back?" he asked.

"No," Mike reported, "she called in about half an hour ago and said she's still working her way through the agony columns. I do need to know if you want to shut up the office, though. I've got to go meet with those leads we talked about earlier."

"I'll come up and cover," Alex said, rising from his desk and picking up the files on Floyd Watts' lovers. With two hours left until five, he had plenty of time to call the remaining three and get their stories.

When Alex left his vault for the upstairs hallway of the brownstone, he felt like he'd run a marathon. It wasn't a natural feeling for him; Alex only ran when someone chased him. Still, he'd been on the phone, following leads all day and had very little to show for it. That always drained him.

Instead of heading downstairs, he turned and entered his room. The least he could do was have a belt and splash some water on his face. Since Sorsha was joining them for dinner, he ought to at least look presentable.

As he poured himself two fingers of single malt from the bottle in his liquor cabinet, there was a knock on his door.

"Come," he said.

"I thought I heard you come in," Iggy said, standing in the now open door in his tan tweed suit with a cigar in his hand. "I understand that Sorsha will be joining us for dinner."

Alex lowered his glass.

"I thought she worked that out with you."

Pound of Flesh

"She did," Iggy admitted, puffing on his cigar. "That was my attempt at small talk."

Alex hesitated, then picked up his Scotch bottle again and poured another glass.

"Since when do you need an excuse to talk to me?" he said, holding out the glass to his mentor.

Iggy crossed the room and took the glass, then turned and sat in Alex's reading chair.

"I'll admit that after the last few weeks, I'm feeling the need to keep a closer eye on you," he said, sipping the Scotch. He gave Alex a mischievous smile and puffed on his cigar. "You look just as exhausted tonight as you did at dinner last night. You're overdoing it."

"No, I'm not," Alex argued. "I visited with a source this morning and spent the rest of the day making phone calls."

"I take it you didn't have much success," Iggy observed, tapping the tip of his cigar into the ashtray on Alex's bedside table.

"As a matter of fact, I didn't. Why is that significant?"

Iggy leveled his gaze at Alex.

"You're avoiding what happened to you by throwing yourself into your work," he said. "It's a way of coping with uncomfortable realities, but getting so wrapped up in your work that you're exhausted all the time is bad for your physical health."

"So I'm supposed to not work?"

"No," Iggy said, sipping the Scotch again, "I think not working would be worse for you."

"Then what *are* you suggesting?"

"I think that for the time being, you need to use Sorsha and myself as sounding boards, especially when you run into difficulties."

Alex masked his hesitation by sipping his own glass. One of the symptoms of Limelight exposure was a loss of cognitive function.

"You think I've lost a step?" he asked. "Because of the Limelight?"

Iggy shrugged at that.

"It's possible, though I've not seen any evidence of that," he said with a dismissive wave of his hand. "What I *am* saying is that having a competent investigator at your disposal will help share the load, so to speak. And we can tell you when you need to take a break."

"I do not need a nursemaid," Alex said, draining his glass.

"I'm your doctor, boy," Iggy growled, "and I say you do."

Alex's grip tightened on his glass. He'd never resented Iggy's interference in his life, but he was feeling belligerent. Of course he could tell off the old man, Iggy probably wouldn't even resent it, but all he had to do was tell Sorsha about his concerns and she'd make sure Alex would follow his doctor's orders.

That's what you get for dating a sorceress, he thought.

"All right," he said, "I do want to get better, after all."

He was surprised how much that admission irritated him, but the more logical part of his brain knew that Iggy was just looking out for him.

And you do feel like ten miles of bad road, he told himself.

"Well," Iggy said, draining his glass and setting it aside. "Let's not keep Sorsha waiting." He stood, tapping his cigar in the ashtray, then headed for the door. "I look forward to hearing all about your current cases over dinner."

The last time Alex ate with Sorsha, she'd given her staff the night off and cooked for him herself. They had a romantic dinner at the little servants table in her kitchen. This time they ate in her formal dining room and her personal chef prepared the dinner. For Alex's money, the chef was much better, not that he'd ever tell Sorsha that. He wasn't surprised, however; the man was a professional, after all.

As they ate something French that Alex couldn't pronounce, he told them about his research problems. He thought having two people to talk to instead of one would make his dinnertime conversation last twice as long, but Iggy and Sorsha let him go until he'd gotten the whole story of Adam the possible detective out.

"So what did Sherry find out?" Sorsha asked when he finished.

"I don't know," he confessed. "When I left the office, she hadn't returned or called in. I expect she wanted to stay late so I'll talk to her in the morning."

"That's not a good sign," Iggy said. "If she'd found the name Amanda Keeler, she would have come back or called in right away."

Alex had come to the same conclusion and he nodded.

"I suspect she had to go back and look for the name Gallagher."

"It's not much of a lead," Sorsha said, chewing on her fingernail in thought, "but it's the best one you've got at the moment."

"Maybe the police canvass will turn up something," Iggy mused.

"I think they stopped their canvass yesterday," Alex said. "They found the diner where she worked, but nothing about where she lived."

"I thought you said that Daniel was rather keen to get this case solved," Iggy said. "Tell him to reinstate the canvass, only this time have them focus on all the banks in that part of the city. Miss Keeler must have kept her money somewhere."

That made sense. Alex would call Danny right after dinner and get him going on that. There was still the possibility that Amanda wasn't the dead woman's real name, but Alex would bet money that if she was hiding, her bank account would be in her assumed name.

"So," he said after a long moment of silence, "did I miss anything else?"

"Not that I can see," Sorsha said. "If nothing else, you're right about the missing persons reports. Sooner or later someone is going to wonder what happened to Adam and Amanda. Once that happens, you'll wrap things up quickly."

"What about your other case?" Iggy asked.

"Which one?" Alex said. "The case of the not so haunted house or the case of the strange illnesses going around the city?"

Sorsha expressed a desire for the former while Iggy indicated the latter. Alex went with Sorsha's request and told them about his phone calls to Floyd Watts' mistresses. Of the girls he called, only one, the southern bell, Victoria Blackburn, cared about Floyd. In her case, he'd gotten her pregnant and disappeared. She was very grateful and talkative once Alex revealed that Floyd was now living in Palo Alto, California.

"Sounds like the kind of woman who might send some muscle into the old house to look for Floyd's whereabouts," Iggy mused.

"She swears she didn't," Alex said.

"And you believe her?" Sorsha asked.

Alex nodded.

"She already knew that the house had been sold per the terms of Floyd's divorce," he explained. "She had no reason to break in, because she knew he wasn't there."

"Maybe," Iggy said, stroking his mustache. "That's certainly likely, but I wouldn't rule her out completely. A single woman with a child on the way could bring out the knight in shining armor in a man. Such a man might take it upon himself to locate the object of her misfortune."

Alex hadn't thought of that. It didn't seem likely, but he couldn't rule it out.

Maybe Sherry will have something for me in the morning, he thought.

"Now," Iggy said, moving on, "about this sickness that you say is going around."

Alex explained Linda Kellin's worries and the information he got from Dr. Kitteridge and Charles Grier. Everyone agreed that it might be something, but that if people were being deliberately poisoned, the only way to track it down would be to wait for a pattern to appear. In the end Sorsha and Iggy came to the conclusion that the only thing Alex could do was wait for more data.

Back in his brownstone bedroom, Alex took off his suit and put on a pair of thick pajamas to help fight off the late November chill. He hung up his clothes to keep them neat, then moved to his reading chair and sat down. Picking up the candlestick phone on his bedside table, Alex dialed Danny's number.

"Crawley, is that you?" Danny's voice demanded when the line connected.

"It's Alex."

Danny swore then apologized.

"I didn't know you cared," Alex ribbed his old friend. "What's the trouble?"

"Remember how I said that if one of the people running to fill

Senator Copeland's seat found out about the murder of Amanda Keeler it would get bad?"

"Is that a rhetorical question?" Alex asked, knowing that it wasn't.

"Well one of them did," Danny growled. "This lowlife Alderman named Malcom Snow found out somehow and he's all over the evening papers calling for justice for Amanda."

"How long will you be able to keep the heat off Adam?" Alex asked.

"Not long," Danny said. "I think I can keep the D.A. at bay until lunchtime tomorrow. Please tell me you have a lead."

"Iggy and I were thinking you should take a look at the banks around the diner, Amanda probably had an account at one of them."

"That's it?" Danny asked, clearly still irritated.

"It's the best we could come up with ," Alex admitted, "but with any luck I'll have something for you tomorrow."

Danny growled something under his breath and hung up.

Alex didn't blame him as he set the phone aside. Getting up, he took the glass in which he'd had Scotch earlier as well as Iggy's glass and washed them in his bathroom sink, returning them to his liquor cabinet. He intended to stay up and read a little, but thought better of it and went to bed.

He was going to need to be up bright and early.

13

THE COST OF DOING BUSINESS

True to his intentions, Alex was up early the next morning so he could be at his office before the morning paper arrived. When it did, Alex easily found the comments of Senatorial hopeful Malcom Snow. There was no picture attached to the article, but the alderman's name was writ large across the top of the page, just below the masthead.

The text was a free-flowing interview with an obviously sympathetic Times reporter. Alex skimmed the article looking for any hint where Snow got his facts. Wherever it was, his source was good, for he seemed to know even more about the murder of Amanda Keeler than Alex did. Clearly he had access to the police file.

"Or he's the killer," Alex added. It wasn't an impossible idea, but it didn't seem likely. If he were the killer, he'd have pushed this story to the papers the day after it happened. After all, the election was Tuesday of next week and it takes time to whip up a movement.

Focusing back on the article, Alex reread it for content. Snow used his position as an alderman to weave a story of rampant crime in the city, ending in the brutal murder of an attractive young woman as she walked home from work. He stopped short of calling her death the work of an American Jack the Ripper, but that was the obvious conclusion to make for anyone who read the interview report.

"He's going to start a panic," Alex muttered as he started to read the rest of the paper. After a minute of scanning the police blotter, he shook his head to break out of the routine, then folded the paper and put it on his desk.

The clock on the back wall read seven fifty-two, so Sherry shouldn't be in for a few more minutes, but the moment Alex put the paper down there was a knock at his door.

"Come in," he said, moving the paper aside.

The door opened and Sherry came in, right when he needed her.

As usual, the sarcastic part of his brain added.

"Good morning," she said, taking one of the seats in front of Alex's massive desk. "I figured you'd want a report first thing."

"Please tell me you found something," Alex said, opening the file folder on Adam.

Sherry took a breath and then shook her head.

"I found lots of people looking for women named Amanda, but not Amanda Keeler," she said. "I couldn't find a mention of any Gallagher either. I went through everything twice just to be sure."

Alex refused the urge to curse, taking a deep breath instead.

"Thanks anyway," he said. "I know you did your best."

"What now?" she asked. "Are you just going to wait until someone comes looking for Adam?"

"No," he said, handing her the newspaper. "The papers know about Amanda Keeler's murder now. Politicians are involved, and that means the police and the D.A. will be under tremendous pressure to wrap this case up."

"So what are you going to do?" Sherry pressed.

"I'm not sure," he admitted. "It's unlikely Adam would actually go to prison even if he is charged. As soon as the papers print his picture, someone will recognize him and he'll be off the hook."

"Unless he's from out of town," Sherry pointed out.

"Is there anything you can tell me about him?" Alex asked. Maybe if she did a reading for him, she could give him something solid.

"I haven't been able to read anyone but you, me, and Danny for six months," she said.

Alex gave her an earnest look and she finally rolled her eyes.

"All right," she said. "I'll try once I'm back at my desk."

"Thanks, doll," Alex said as Sherry stood. "You're the best."

Sherry stopped and put a finger to her chin in an exaggerated pose of deep thought.

"You're right," she said, "I am the best."

Smirking over her shoulder, she headed for the door, but stopped again once she had it open.

"There is one other thing, but it's about the Hannover house," she said.

Alex didn't have time to think about that right now, but since the case of the amnesiac P.I. wasn't going anywhere, he decided to listen anyway.

"What is it?"

"When I looked into the house, I found a record of the house being built, but the building permit itself was missing."

Alex sat up a little at that. Lots of paperwork went mysteriously missing in the labyrinthian halls of government bureaucracy, but it usually took decades. The Hanover house was built in nineteen-twenty-five, just thirteen years ago. Paperwork shouldn't be vanishing from folders that recent.

"That could mean something," he admitted.

"That's what I thought, so I had a friend in the records office try to track it down. She called me yesterday evening and said she'd found it."

"Anything suspicious about that?" Alex asked, his curiosity pulling him along.

"No," Sherry admitted, "she found it on the floor near the shelf where it was supposed to be filed. It probably fell out of the folder when I requested it."

"But something's off or you wouldn't have brought it up, right?"

Sherry hesitated and Alex felt his energy draining.

"I don't know," Sherry said. "According to my friend, everything was in order on the permit, it's just the estimated cost that the builder listed."

"Too much?" he guessed.

Alex actually didn't find that surprising. A lot of disreputable builders would pad their bill, estimating a job for twenty or even fifty percent more than they thought it would cost. He'd seen that more than once in his tenure as a P.I.

"According to the building permit, the original owner, Thelma Rubison, paid fifty thousand dollars to have that house built, and that doesn't include the land, because she owned that already."

Alex shook his head. Their earlier research had suggested such an outrageous price, but Alex hadn't actually believed it . Fifty thousand dollars would build a mansion with a dozen bedrooms and a tennis court. Some of the houses in the core cost that much, but they actually were mansions with tennis courts, and there was no reason for the modest three-story Victorian to cost more than ten thousand. It was possible, if the original owner got a frugal builder, to have the house for significantly less.

So why did the original owner pay so much? he mused to himself.

"From the look on your face, I'm guessing that's important?" Sherry asked.

"It might be," he said. "It definitely means I need to take another look at that house. Good work chasing that down."

Sherry gave him a wide smile, then headed down the hall to the front office. For his part, Alex opened the file on the Hannover case and made a few quick notes. The cost of the building suggested there was more to that house than met the eye, the question was what?

Gold pipes? he wondered. *Hidden underground pool in the back yard?*

Whatever it was, it might be the reason someone would break into the house to look for it. That could mean that the break-in had nothing to do with Melissa Hannover or her son. It probably didn't have anything to do with Floyd Watts or his mistresses either.

"So what is it about?" he asked himself.

The only way to know was to go back to that house and go over it again, inch by inch.

Maybe amberlight will reveal something, he thought, since he hadn't used it in his previous sweep.

Before he could muse further, the phone on his desk rang.

"It's Danny," his friend greeted him.

"Wow," Alex said, checking the clock. "It's barely eight o'clock. It must be bad over there."

"You have no idea," Danny said. "The captain is on the warpath about the leak and I don't know who leaked it."

"You want me to come over and interview the detectives?" Alex joked.

"Why not? I've been meaning to retire to Florida and now is as good a time as any."

Since Danny was only in his mid-thirties, Alex took that statement as humor.

"You keep your folder locked in your office?"

"In a locked file cabinet in my locked office."

"Is it still there?"

"I've got it right here on my desk," Danny said. "I took it out of the locked cabinet after unlocking my office."

Alex thought about that for a moment.

"I've only seen the *Times*," he said. "Is that alderman blathering his story in any other paper?"

Danny considered that and Alex could hear him shuffling paper on his desk.

"It's in most of the morning papers," he said, "and even a few of the tabloids."

"Is it all the same story or are they different?"

"Different," Danny said after more paper rustling. "But," he went on after a long pause, "it looks like the *Times* article is the original and all the others are using it as their source. Is that important?"

"I think so," Alex said. "It means that your alderman—"

"Malcom Snow," Danny supplied.

"It means that Mr. Snow has a confidant at the *Times*—whoever wrote that article."

"The interview did seem a bit complimentary," Danny agreed. "So Snow handed the story about Amanda Keeler's murder off to his pet reporter, not exactly a shocking revelation. How does that help me find my leaker?"

"It means that whoever leaked the file, leaked it to Snow and not the *Times*," Alex said. "Snow's an alderman, he's bound to have needed police protection in the past."

"You're thinking he might have requested specific officers a time or two?"

"Makes sense," Alex pointed out. "If he's got a favorite cop, that's going to be your leaker."

"That still doesn't explain how the leaker got into my office and my filing cabinet," Danny said.

"He probably didn't. That file, or pieces of it, have been all over your office going from hand to hand. All your man would need is a few minutes alone with the file and a camera."

"Okay," Danny said, "that's enough help to fix my problem, provided I have a little bit of luck. Do you have anything new on our pal, Adam?"

Alex sighed.

"Nothing useful," he said. "Sherry went over the classified and the agony columns and came up empty. Nobody's been looking for Amanda Keeler or anyone named Gallagher."

"Well, it was worth a shot."

Alex could hear the weariness in his friend's voice; this case was getting to him. It was saturated with politics and public scandal, two things that could end a good cop's career faster than sleeping with the mayor's wife. Too bad no one was looking for Amanda other than Adam.

That thought made Alex pause.

"You know," he said into the silence that had taken over their call, "maybe whoever is looking for Amanda tried to find her previously."

"You said the papers were a bust."

"Not the papers," Alex said, "the real old-fashioned way. What if they came to the police?"

"I already had one of my boys go through the missing persons book," Danny said. "She's not there."

"The way I figure it, she'd have to have been gone a long time for someone to hire a P.I. What if that's not a forward-thinking view of detective work, what if it's the last gasp of a desperate person?"

"So Amanda would be in one of the cold case books," Danny said. "I'll turn Crawley loose on them, though it might take a while."

"At least it's something," Alex pointed out.

Danny sighed.

"All right, I've got a stool pigeon to find. Where are you going to be if I need you?"

Alex described the Hannover case and referred his friend to Detective Arnold if he needed to call the house.

"Sounds fun," Danny said once Alex explained his intent to meticulously go over every square inch of the house.

"You're a riot," Alex sneered, then bid his friend good luck and hung up.

He wanted to stay in his office and do more work, but he didn't have any excuse to do that, so he stood up and headed into his vault to refill his kit.

Alex used the keys he'd gotten from Rick to enter the tall Victorian house on the little hill. Before he started his sweep, Alex walked through the house to make sure he was alone. As he went, he found everything the way he'd left it after his last investigation. He'd given Detective Arnold a quick call before he came, so Alex knew that the police hadn't been back in his absence.

After his tour of the house, Alex broke out his oculus and the multi-lamp. Despite his theory earlier that using amberlight might reveal something, the odds of that weren't good, so Alex started with his old standby, silverlight.

Hour after hour, Alex progressed through the house, investigating every fluorescing fingerprint or stain. When he got to the kitchen, it looked like there might be a hidden trap door down to a cellar, but once Alex traced all the grout in the floor tiles, he had to admit there was no opening in the floor, hidden or otherwise.

Frustrated but undefeated, Alex blew out his silverlight burner and switched in the ghostlight. Unlike the silverlight, ghostlight would react brightly to any hint that magic had been used in the house. This

Pound of Flesh

time Alex decided to start in the parlor where the mysterious intruder had disappeared. Magic would definitely explain how the man had simply vanished without a trace.

When Alex finished with the parlor, he was ready to throw his multi-lamp across the room. His hands, elbows, knees, and back were throbbing from his crawling around looking under everything and up to now he'd found absolutely nothing.

"Is it possible Rick came downstairs with his bat and hit his mom in the dark?" Alex mused. He didn't believe anything like that happened, especially since there was a footprint that couldn't have been Rick's in the parlor.

"Come on, Alex," he told himself out loud. "You found that footprint, there's got to be more evidence."

Slightly encouraged, Alex slipped his oculus back over his eye and picked up his lamp, heading for the hallway between the foyer and the kitchen.

Alex stood in Mrs. Hannover's bathroom with his hands on his hips and swore at the top of his lungs. Iggy and Sorsha didn't hold with swearing, so Alex had lots of select turns of phrase saved up and it took him more than a minute to get them all out.

"Well, that felt good," he said once the echoes of his profanity-laden tirade faded.

It felt good, but he'd been over the entire three stories of the Hannover house and found exactly nothing.

Nada.

Bupkis.

From where he stood, the man who put Mrs. Hannover in the hospital could only be some kind of vengeful ghost.

Of course that couldn't be true because ghosts didn't exist.

"Get ahold of yourself," he growled, picking up his multi-lamp.

He blew out the burner and slipped the oculus off his head. Since he'd left his kit bag sitting on the kitchen table, Alex headed for the stairs and returned to the first floor. He wasn't surprised to find his kit sitting right where he left it. The only signs anyone had been in this house in the last two days were his own foot impressions in the carpet runners and in the dust of the unused rooms.

Since the multi-lamp had been lit for the last few hours, Alex set it aside to cool. Using a thick rag to extract the ghostlight burner from the lamp frame, he set it aside as well. His brain urged him to call Danny and see if anything had turned up in the old missing persons file.

His mind wanted him to make that call, but his pride was arguing against it. Alex had spent the better part of the morning doing his best to find something, anything, and now here he was with nothing to show for it. That was not a conversation he wanted to have with anyone, let alone Danny.

Or Iggy, or Sorsha, or Sherry, or Mike, or anyone else he could think to call.

He looked down into his bag, wondering how long it would be before he could store his lamp and the ghostlight burner. The inside of the leather strip where the other burners were held with wire clips showed signs of being singed from the times Alex didn't wait for the burner to cool before returning it to its place.

Right next to the gap where the ghostlight burner would fit was the least used of his burners, the one with amberlight in it. Amberlight was both the most and least useful of his burners. When you wanted to reconstruct a crime scene, it was invaluable, because it showed Alex where discarded items had been kept before being moved. He'd even used it once to track a stolen delivery truck back to the place where it had been stored.

The downside of amberlight was that if nothing had moved, or if a discarded object had moved too much over a long enough period of time, there was no way to find its point of origin.

"Why not," he muttered to himself, making the decision to remove the burner from his bag and clip it into the lamp. "You can't find any more nothing than you already have."

Carrying the lamp into the parlor, Alex lit it and strapped on the oculus. He didn't bother looking at the credenza and the disturbed photos since he knew they'd been moved and he knew where they'd been stored. Instead he moved along the windows, drawing the curtains to keep out the bright light of day.

Amberlight worked best in the dark.

Turning to the corner where he'd found the footprint, Alex swept the ruddy brown light from the lamp over the floor. There was nothing to be seen, but he really didn't expect there to be. Whoever had moved through here hadn't lingered long enough to leave a trace that amberlight would reveal.

He was about to turn away, when his vision was interrupted by a faint line. It was so subtle that he wouldn't have seen it if he hadn't walked right through it while under the amberlight.

Stepping back, Alex held the light out. What he'd seen was a curved motion line that originated from the bit of wall that filled the space between the window to the outside and the doorway to the dining room. It was about three feet long and maybe a bit more, and held a framed photograph of Empire Tower that was flanked by two magelights in decorative sconces.

As Alex examined the line, he began to get the idea that the entire bit of wall had swung inward until it was pressed up against the window. Turning his attention to the wall, Alex found a faint smear of a motion line around the base of the left-hand sconce.

Setting the lamp aside, Alex ran his finger along the bottom of the sconce and felt a groove running parallel to the wall. Slipping his fingernail into the groove, Alex pulled. There was a clacking noise and the left edge of the wall popped free from the dining room door's frame.

Alex reached into his coat and produced his Colt 1911, gripping it tightly in his right hand. With one fluid motion, he pulled on the newly discovered secret door, swinging it open. Stepping back, Alex let the door pass him, then stepped forward again, leading with his weapon.

He didn't know what to expect, but he wasn't at all surprised when he was greeted with the sight of a dusty stairway descending down into the darkness below.

14

THE SPEAKEASY

Alex just stood there, at the top of the dark stairs, trying his best not to breathe. There was enough light to see large footprints in the dust of the stairs, meaning this was how the assailant had entered and left the upper part of Mrs. Hannover's house. It didn't seem likely that the man was still down there, not with all the lights off, but Alex was taking no chances.

After a long couple of minutes just holding his gun angled down into the depths of the secret space, Alex stepped closer and glanced around just beyond the frame of the hidden door. As he expected, there was a light switch on the wall just inside.

Switching his 1911 to his left hand, he pressed the switch and was rewarded with another electrical clack and light bloomed below. With the aid of the lights, Alex could see that the stairs were made of some rich-looking amber wood that had been polished to a shine that was obvious even under years of dust. The wall board had been papered, showing a pattern of purple and white vertical stripes, and there were pictures hung every few feet.

This was not some secret basement for storing valuables or some mad scientist's hidden laboratory; whoever decorated this meant for it to be elegant.

Alex put his foot on the first step and began going down as slowly and silently as he could. The stairs creaked a little under his weight, but they felt well-made and sturdy. When he reached the bottom, Alex found himself facing a heavy door. It was closed but not locked, so Alex carefully turned the handle until he felt the door come free from the latch.

He held his breath again, listening for any sign that someone was waiting for him on the other side. When he'd finally gotten his fill of nothing, Alex pushed the door open and quickly stepped inside.

What greeted him was beyond description.

The space was open, like the chapel at Father Harry's old mission, but instead of having tables and benches, this place had couches, overstuffed chairs, chaise longue, and well-built wooden chairs. These were scattered around in an eclectic pattern, as if the purpose was so that people could group in small clutches or large parties and still be seated near one another. In between all this furniture were low coffee tables, and tall end tables, each holding crystal ashtrays while some few held Tiffany lamps.

As Alex's gaze swept the space, he saw that there were many blank spaces on the walls, as if pictures had recently been taken down, leaving evidence of their former positions in the dust.

On the right side of the open area was a long, polished bar made of cherry wood. A brass rail ran along the floor in front of it, and there were tall stools covered in padded leather standing in front of it. Behind the bar were sturdy shelves built over a mirrored back. Dozens of bottles, some labeled and some not, stood on the shelves caked in dust. A barman's rag was shriveled up on the bar and several glasses with thick handles and bottoms were standing nearby, a few of them on their sides.

If it wasn't for the thick rime of dust covering everything, Alex would have assumed it was a bar just after closing time.

"It's a speakeasy," he gasped.

Younger Alex never had much money, so speakeasies weren't part of his formative experience. He'd been to one that was nothing more than an empty warehouse with a bar made from scrap wood laid across some beer kegs in one corner. He'd often heard that speakeasies had good beer but, because of his aforementioned lack of funds, he'd never developed a taste for beer. He remembered the place smelling of wastewater and the beer tasting about the same.

The experience wasn't exactly a highlight of his youth.

As he looked around at the opulent barroom, however, Alex reconsidered his memory of the Roaring Twenties. If the speakeasy he'd visited had been like this, he might have gone out more.

"Nah. Not with Iggy's private stash available to me," Alex muttered.

During the dark days of prohibition, Iggy had introduced Alex to the joys of bourbon, whiskey, cognac, port, and various kinds of wine. Given Iggy's tastes, Alex had only the best, leaving him no desire to chase after back-alley beer. That had changed once Alex opened his detective agency and he had to purchase his own spirits. By then, of course, he'd learned the names of a few smugglers who could bring him bourbon. It was rot-gut compared to Iggy's stuff, but Alex had been okay with that. By the time he'd moved to his mid-ring office, Prohibition was on its last legs anyway.

Alex just stood there, taking everything in, sparing a moment of reverence for a bygone era. As his eyes swept the room, however, he remembered why he was there. Leaning over the bar, he saw that part of the floor had been pulled up, revealing the bare dirt below. The work was new, and Alex could see the dust still clinging to the tops of the broken boards. Along with the dust, there were large handprints where the vandal had removed the flooring.

"This was the construction noise Mrs. Hannover heard," Alex mused.

Gripping his pistol tightly, Alex kept it at the ready as he stepped behind the bar. There were old, dusty bottles lined up underneath the bar along with several old kegs that appeared to be slowly leaking rancid beer, judging by the smell.

A short hall ran away from the main room, perpendicular to the bar. Predictably there were two bathrooms marked 'Ladies' and 'Gents,' along with a heavy door that led to a ransacked office. The remains of a desk had been overturned, smashed to kindling, and thrown into an empty corner. A sturdy chair sat, upside down, atop the pile with dozens of empty folders and the remnants of office supplies.

Behind a comfortable chair that would have been behind the desk before it had been destroyed, was a wall safe with its door open. Stepping around the chair, Alex surveyed the safe. The interior was lined with dark velvet, a technique usually used by jewelers to prevent overlooking tiny stones. It was also good for keeping track of loose coins, which seemed much more likely in an underground bar. Alex leaned in, looking at the hinges of the heavy door. Based on the dust, he could tell the door had been left open when whoever owned this place left.

"That has to be Thelma Rubison," Alex mumbled. "This certainly explains why this house cost fifty large."

What it didn't explain was why someone would tear the office apart and tear up the floor behind the bar. Whoever had done that was looking for something, and they wanted it very badly.

Not bothering to dig through the debris in the office, Alex moved back out into the bar area. If there was anything to be found in the pile, the person who made it would have already found it.

Now that Alex was paying attention, he began to see signs that the vandal had been busy out in the main room as well. Everywhere he looked, pictures had been taken off the walls and thrown on nearby furniture or on the floor. A quick survey of the nearest unhung photographs showed smiling, drinking people taken in this speakeasy and a different one that looked remarkably similar.

A sister bar? Alex wondered.

It was possible, of course, but one thing Alex did know about speakeasies was that if they ever got raided by the Feds, they would move locations. Still, as he looked around at the opulence of this place, he knew it had never been raided. This speakeasy obviously catered to the wealthy and the powerful; those people had connections and having connections meant they could keep the authorities at bay.

"So what was the intruder looking for?" Alex wondered aloud. Based on the condition of the office, he'd figured the man wanted something valuable, but then why take down so many pictures?

Setting aside the photograph he'd picked up from the floor, Alex moved to the wall and leaned in to one of the pictures that hadn't been taken down. Unlike the ones on the floor, this one showed a picture of Central Park. The one next to it showed Empire Tower under construction over a brass nameplate that read, Empire State Building, the original name of the structure.

The difference, in every case Alex checked, was that the pictures taken down were of people in one of the two speakeasies, but the ones that were still up had been taken elsewhere. The conclusion seemed obvious.

"The intruder is looking for someone in one of these pictures," Alex said, stroking his chin. There were hundreds of pictures covering the walls and the intruder seemed to have been through all of them. "That means that whatever he's looking for, it's hard to find, or it isn't here." Alex looked back at the torn-up floor behind the bar. Whoever was doing the looking, they weren't going to give up until they were absolutely sure they found what they were looking for.

"Whoever that is," Alex said. With this many pictures there were hundreds of different people in them. There was no way Alex could figure out what or who the intruder wanted, even if he went through all of them.

With a sigh, Alex tucked his gun back into the holster, then mounted the hidden stair back up to the house to retrieve his kit.

"I guess I'll have to figure it out the old-fashioned way."

He wasn't looking forward to the hours of work it was going to take to examine such a large space, but he was relatively certain that if he found any fingerprints they'd belong to the intruder. Any prints left over from when the speakeasy was open for business would have degraded years ago.

As he tromped back down the stairs, the sound of his footfalls echoed through the room, bouncing off the walls and reverberating. The echoes continued after Alex reached the floor, and they even went on as he crossed to the bar.

It was a testament to how much being laid up affected his skills that Alex only realized what he was hearing when a door behind him opened. Instinct drove him and he dived over the bar as a shot rang out. The bullet tore a chunk out of the bar as Alex dropped onto the pile of boards and rolled down to the exposed dirt floor. Another shot rang out and one of the leaking beer barrels began pouring out foul liquid.

Coming up into a crouch, Alex pulled his 1911, then raised it up over the bar and fired blind. As soon as he shot, the man on the far side of the room shot back, but Alex had already moved. Scrambling down to the end of the bar, Alex ducked out and brought his gun up.

On the far side of the room stood a large man in a heavy overcoat. He wore a fedora pulled low, which prevented Alex from seeing his face. He carried a large bore revolver, .44 or .45 if Alex had to guess, pointed at the bar where Alex had been.

Alex fired twice but between his shots, the man pivoted, shooting at Alex's new location. The incoming bullet punched through the bar but it still had enough movement to bite into Alex's foot. Alex's second shot made the man cry out and he spun around, running back through the open door. All Alex could hear after that was the sound of receding footsteps going up a flight of stairs, followed by the bang of a closing door.

Wanting to pursue his query, Alex pushed up to his feet. The second he put any weight on his injured foot, however, he came crashing right back down to the floor. Muttering a word that Sorsha would have slapped him for saying, Alex pushed up to his hands and knees. He gave a momentary thought to going after the man, but he was in no condition for a foot pursuit.

Besides, he thought, *he doesn't know I'm injured. He's probably got to a car by now and is long gone.*

Looking down at his shoe, Alex could see a hole in the top and a copious amount of blood running out of it.

"That's not good," he said aloud.

Reaching out, he tried to slip the shoe off his foot, but it exploded in pain when he tried.

Swearing again, Alex pulled himself up to one foot and hopped to the end of the bar. Grabbing his kit, he kept hopping until he hit the wall just beyond the bar. Moving as quickly as he could, Alex took out his chalk and leaned down while keeping his injured foot up and chalked a door on the wall. It wasn't his best work, but with the use of only one foot, it would do.

Tearing a vault rune from his book, Alex licked the back and stuck it to the wall, between the chalk lines. One flick of his lighter and the paper vanished while the steel door appeared, melting out of the wall like a phantom.

Fumbling with his key, Alex finally managed to get the door open and he hopped through. He reached out to close the door, but thought better of it, choosing instead to swing the metal cage door closed instead. This would allow him to return to the hidden speakeasy quickly, but would keep the intruder, or anyone else out.

Satisfied that the door was secured in place, Alex hopped over to his drafting table and picked up the telephone on the nearby rollaway table.

"Iggy?" Alex said when the line connected. "I've been shot."

"Where?"

"Through the foot," Alex said, trying to sit in his work chair and keep his leg straight at the same time.

"Not where have you been shot," Iggy growled, "where are you?"

"In my vault."

"Oh," Iggy replied, his voice calmer. "I'll be up in a tick."

Alex hung up and focused on trying not to bleed on his carpet. Looking back along the path to his caged vault door, he saw a mostly uninterrupted trail of red that had ruined three of his rugs. With the cold, inter-dimensional stone that made up vaults, rugs were an absolute necessity.

"Well, that looks messy," Iggy said, coming out of the brownstone hallway with a medical bag Alex hadn't seen before. "Can you get to your medical room or do I need to help you?"

"I can manage," Alex said, lurching up to his one good foot.

He heard Iggy stifle a laugh as Alex hopped to his first aid room but he was in too much pain to care.

"Get up on the table, but don't lie down," Iggy said, setting his bag on the counter next to the sink. He dug around in the bag for a moment, then withdrew a glass bottle with a cork stopper. Next came a tumbler like the kind Alex used for his whisky. Into the tumbler, Iggy poured about one finger of cloudy liquid from the bottle.

"Drink this," he said, pushing it into Alex's hand.

Alex did as he was told and almost immediately he felt numb.

"What is that stuff?" he demanded, having trouble focusing his eyes.

"Laudanum," his mentor replied.

Laudanum was a powerful pain killer made from opium, and Alex knew Iggy disliked it because it had addictive properties.

"You're immune to most potions because of the damnation rune," Iggy explained, drawing another liquid into a long syringe. "Now hold still, this is going to hurt."

Alex gripped the side of the medical table and nodded at Iggy.

He only thought he was ready because once Iggy pulled off his ruined shoe, the doctor stuck the needle most of the way through his foot and Alex felt like he'd been stabbed instead of shot. As someone who'd been both stabbed and shot, Alex knew that the latter was preferable to the former. Bullets did their bit and the pain of their impact faded almost immediately. Knives, on the other hand, hurt going in and they hurt coming out.

Alex did his best not to swear as Iggy stabbed him three more times with the syringe. By the third jab, whatever Iggy was injecting started to take effect and Alex barely felt it.

"Well, that's a nasty bit of work," Iggy declared once he cleaned up the wound. "The bullet went right through. I'm going to have to use some alchemical flesh filler to close it. Fortunately, that stuff reacts with itself, not you, so it should work fine."

Alex wanted to comment but his brain was getting foggy.

"Dare I ask what you were doing to end up shot through the foot?" Iggy continued.

"Oh, you'll like thish one," Alex said, slurring his words. "I found a schecret schpeakeasy, left over from Prohibishon. It looked like the people jusht walked away and...and left it."

"That sounds fascinating," Iggy said from what sounded like a great distance away. "You'll have to show it to me."

Alex liked that idea, but before he could agree, he lapsed into a drug induced sleep.

15

BACK DOORS

Alex felt like he was floating in a dimly lit space. It was hardly a new experience for him, since he'd woken up from a six-week nap in just the same way only three days ago.

"-ye mums," a British voice was saying.

Alex assumed it was Iggy, but the timbre didn't sound right.

"Yime rot pappy," a female voice replied. "Could've respected fist."

Based on his previous efforts to speak when coming out of a drug induced nap, Alex decided to just wait for his vision to clear. When it did, he wished it hadn't. Sorsha was arguing with Iggy and her usual porcelain skin was bright pink.

"I'm sorry, Sorsha," Iggy was saying in the kind of placating voice Alex heard mothers use with children. "It was more complex than Alex's original notes, so I had to do a number of trials before the gap was covered."

"He didn't need it to be perfect," Sorsha fumed.

"My shield design?" Alex managed. "You got it working?"

"Yes, I did," Iggy said, stepping around Sorsha. He grabbed Alex's arm and took his pulse from the wrist.

"You," Sorsha said, her eyes narrowing into slits. "I thought I told you to stay out of dangerous situations."

Alex was still a bit groggy, so it took him a moment to process what she'd said. Reaching out to take her hand, he pulled her close enough that Iggy had to step back.

"I was in an abandoned speakeasy underneath an inner-ring house in the middle of the day," he said. "That's about as safe a place as I can imagine."

"And yet you still have a hole in your foot," she said, some of the edge gone from her voice.

"Yeah," he said, glancing down to where he could see his bandaged left foot. "When will I be able to walk?"

"You'll need crutches," Iggy said. "The flesh putty in the wound will regenerate your foot much faster than natural healing, but your immunity to magic will mean that your foot will only bond to the transformed putty at the body's normal healing rate."

"What does that mean?"

"It means you'll be on those crutches for a while," Iggy said. "Don't put any weight on that foot or you'll risk dislodging the transformed flesh before it can fully bond with your foot."

"Swell," Alex muttered.

"I am not at fault for your bad decisions," Iggy replied, drawing himself up to his full height. "If you'd destroyed that Limelight like you should have, I could have had you up and walking normally half an hour ago."

"I know," Alex said, keeping his voice conciliatory. "I appreciate you not letting me bleed to death."

Iggy's mustache bristled but he made no further comment. Sorsha took the opportunity to lean down and give him a kiss on the cheek, then wiped her lipstick off with her thumb.

"Thank you for not getting yourself killed," she said. "But from now on, when you're investigating old houses or abandoned warehouses, you call me first."

Alex took her hand and squeezed it.

"I promise," he assured her. Based on the day he'd been having, he even meant it.

"All right," she said. "I have to get back to work, but I'll come by your office and make sure you get home for dinner."

With that, she squeezed his hand back and headed out into the main part of Alex's vault, turning in the direction of the cover door that led to her office bathroom.

As soon as she was gone, Alex gingerly lifted his foot and then swung his legs off the table.

"Take it slowly," Iggy said, gathering a set of crutches from Alex's equipment closet. "So, tell me," he went on as Alex gingerly put his good foot on the floor, "you found a secret, preserved speakeasy?"

"How did you know it was a secret speakeasy?"

"I may have looked through your cage door while you were recovering," he said with a sly wink. "It looks like it was quite the high class place."

Alex pulled out his pocket watch and found it was almost three-thirty.

"I need to get moving," he said, picking up a crutch and tucking it under his left arm. "Can you help me fix my pants?"

Iggy hadn't needed to cut his pants off to work on his foot, he'd just rolled up the cuff, but there was blood all over it. Alex had cleaning runes in the repair box on his workbench, but he'd need help to use them.

Iggy nodded and headed out into the vault's great room. For his part, Alex let the crutch take his weight, then slung the second one under his right arm. Alex had the crutches because he'd needed them before, and it surprised him how easily he fell back into the rhythm of using them. The only problem was his 1911 that kept pinching his side when the crutches caught it wrong. When he reached the workbench where Iggy was waiting, he pulled out his gun and slipped it into the outside pocket of his suit coat.

"Expecting more trouble?" Iggy asked.

"These days? Always."

Iggy chuckled at that and motioned for Alex to lean up against the table. Reaching down, he gently grabbed Alex's ankle and raised his leg up a bit. Sticking a cleaning rune to the rolled cuff, he flicked his lighter to life and activated the rune. For a moment Alex's trouser roiled as if the surface were liquid, then thousands of motes of dirt and grime puffed away from the fabric. They swirled around like angry insects until Iggy touched the wooden bucket where Alex had carved a linking rune that connected to his stock of cleaning runes. As soon as it activated, the cloud of swirling filth streamed over Alex's leg and down into the bucket.

"Now that that's done," Iggy said, setting the bucket aside, "show me this fascinating speakeasy."

Alex nodded, but turned back toward his desk.

"I have to call Detective Arnold first, since we now have a suspect in Mrs. Hannover's assault."

An hour later, Alex sat at one of the tables in the abandoned speakeasy with his injured foot up on a chair and an open bottle of Scotch from behind the bar next to him. Iggy had assured him the Scotch was still good and, after cleaning out one of the speakeasy's tumblers, Alex had to agree.

He heard a light footstep on the stairs that led up to the main house and Alex looked up to find Detective Arnold and a uniformed policeman standing on the landing. Arnold looked around, taking in the place, then whistled.

"Now this is impressive," he said. "I haven't seen a speakeasy since my days as a patrolman."

"Detective Arnold," Alex said, pointing at his bandaged foot, "I'd stand, but..."

"I hope that's not evidence you're drinking," Arnold said, making his way through the maze of tables to Alex. He turned one of the chairs around, sitting in it backwards with his arms crossed on the chair back.

"Payment for my injured foot," Alex said, raising his glass before finishing it.

Alex wiped out a glass at a nearby table, then pushed it toward Detective Arnold.

"So are you going to tell me," Arnold said, tipping the dusty Scotch bottle up over the glass, "or am I going to have to ask?"

Alex took the bottle from him and refilled his empty tumbler.

"I found this place this morning," Alex said. "Obviously, it's how Mrs. Hannover's attacker got in and out without leaving a trace." Alex set the bottle down, then pointed around the room at the places where pictures had been taken down. "I'm convinced he was looking for a picture of someone or something."

"Explains why he went through Mrs. Hannover's pictures," Arnold said. "Any idea what he's looking for?"

Alex took a sip of the exceptionally smooth Scotch, then put his glass down.

"I was trying to figure that out when the man himself came through that door," he pointed at the door in the back of the bar. "Fortunately I had my gun handy and I managed to drive him off, but not before my foot caught a stray bullet."

"I thought you lived with a doctor?" Arnold said, using his glass to point to Alex's crutches.

"He does," Iggy said, stepping through the back door where Alex's assailant had entered earlier. "Unfortunately by the time he got back to me, we had to treat it the old fashioned way."

"Doctor Bell," Detective Arnold said, standing. "Nice to see you again."

"I hate to interrupt, but these stairs lead up to a tool shed on the back of the property," Iggy said, making his way to the table. "There's a hedge all the way around the property, but the tool shed has an exit out to the back street behind the house. Perfect for getting people in and out discreetly back when it was a speakeasy."

"Not to disagree with you, doctor," Arnold said, "but the nearest crawler station is blocks from here. I don't see anyone who'd come to a swanky place like this walking to get here."

"No doubt they had some sort of taxi service," Iggy suggested.

"Probably a few of them," Alex said. "After all, a bunch of parked cars in one place might look suspicious."

"Well, that really doesn't matter," Arnold said. "What matters is why someone is breaking into an old speakeasy." He looked around, then leaned over to another table to wipe his finger in the dust. "I'd say this place hasn't been used since Prohibition was ousted. So why is someone here now?"

Pound of Flesh

"It took me two days of investigation, going over this house multiple times to find this place," Alex said. "Maybe whoever our intruder is had the same problem."

"I doubt it," Iggy said. "I mean perhaps it was a contributing factor, but your man came in through the tool shed. I doubt he found that by accident."

"You're thinking he knew this place existed, just not exactly where it was," Arnold said.

"Makes sense," Alex agreed. "This place had to have been built when the house was built, which explains why the owner sank fifty large into the construction."

"Do you know who paid for it?" Arnold asked, fishing his notebook out of his coat pocket.

Alex mimicked the move, taking his notebook from the pocket of his shirt.

"Thelma Rubison," he read. "She already owned the land when she built and the only address for her was an inner-ring hotel, The Grand. She put it on the building permit."

"Probably stayed there while this place was being built," Detective Arnold agreed. "Anything else?"

Alex shook his head and closed his notebook.

"I didn't look her up because I never thought she had anything to do with the case."

"Well, if nothing else, the hotel might have a record of her stay," Iggy said.

"I'm sure we can find her in the city records," Arnold said, closing his book as well. "The real question is whether she'll know why someone is breaking into her hidden bar that hasn't been used for at least five years," he looked around at the state of the place then shrugged, "probably more."

"It's a long shot," Alex said, "but she might remember what's in some of those missing pictures."

"It's a place to start," Arnold agreed, then he reached out his hand. "Thank you, Alex, you've been a big help."

Alex took the man's hand and shook it.

"I'm going to leave a few of my boys here," the detective said. "I'll head over to the records office and see what I can find out about Miss Rubison. With any luck she'll know what this is all about."

With that Detective Arnold turned and headed for the steps up to the Hannover house.

Alex waited until he was gone before pulling out his rune book. He was just opening it when Iggy cleared his throat.

"I'm parked out back," he said, giving an almost imperceptible nod in the direction of the uniformed officer who was standing by the door to the back stairs.

"Right," Alex said, slipping his book back into his inside coat pocket. Using the table, he pushed himself up, then accepted his crutches from Iggy. He wasn't looking forward to hopping up the stairs to the tool shed, but he couldn't use his vault to leave where someone could see him.

"Where are we going now?" Iggy asked as Alex made for the stairs.

"I'm going back to my office," Alex said. "I have to make some calls and follow up with Danny, so I won't need a nursemaid."

Iggy gave him a skeptical look, then shrugged.

"If you say so," he said. "Just stay off your foot while the alchemical flesh filler hardens up and starts bonding with your natural skin."

"Yes, mother," Alex droned.

One trip through his vault later, Alex flopped down in his desk chair. He hadn't even put his wounded foot on the floor and it was throbbing. The idea that he'd have to wait for weeks for it to heal up properly made him feel like he was living in the dark ages.

"You have no one to blame but yourself," he said, doing a fair impersonation of Iggy.

He wanted to blame his predicament on Iggy and Moriarty, but he couldn't quite believe that lie. The damnation rune was his only chance and it had been necessary because of his own actions. Knowing that didn't make it better, though. He'd done what he'd done because he had to, didn't he? If he hadn't, Sorsha would be dead.

"Hell," he growled, "I'd be dead."

Pound of Flesh

The words sounded ridiculous as he said them. Using the Limelight should have killed him already.

He tried to push the thoughts of the Limelight from his mind, but the presence of the damnation rune forced him to linger on it. Images of a jar of green powder infiltrated his mind and refused to leave, fanning the fire of a deep-seated need.

"Get back to work," he admonished himself.

With a great effort of will, Alex cleared his mind and picked up his telephone.

"Bad news," Danny said when Alex got him on the line. "Adam is being arraigned right now. The D.A. is going to pursue a trial as soon as he can, probably within the next few weeks."

"Well, we knew that was coming," Alex said, feeling a bit guilty despite having done all he could to find Adam's identity.

"Do you have anything to go on?"

Alex suppressed a sigh.

"Nothing," he said. "Sherry didn't find anything in the library archives. I guess I could go over myself and go through it again, but Sherry's top shelf when it comes to research, so if she didn't find anything, there isn't anything to be found."

"All right," Danny said, resignation in his voice. "I'll get Adam's picture out to the press. If they print it in the paper, maybe someone will recognize him."

"Be sure to tell them he's an amnesiac," Alex said.

"I can't," Danny said. "I've been given explicit instructions not to let the press know that."

Alex whistled.

"Somebody wants this case to go away," he said.

"The mayor if I had to guess," Danny said. "That alderman, Snow, was in the morning paper using Amanda's murder as a cudgel to beat the current administration."

"He's not going to be alone for long," Alex guessed. "His political rivals will have to pick it up to stay competitive."

"Which means the mayor and the D.A. are going to do everything in their power to button this case up as quickly as they can. Hence why I'm not allowed to mention Adam's amnesia."

"I'll leak it," Alex said.

Danny hesitated.

"If this leaks, they're going to blame me," he said. "I'm their best fall guy."

Alex didn't like that, but he couldn't refute it.

"I'll go through Sherry's notes again," he said. "If I find anything, I'll call you."

Alex hung up and spent a full minute just going over the Keeler murder in his head. Finally, in frustration, he reached out and depressed the front office key on the intercom.

"Sherry?" he said.

"It's me," Mike's voice came back. "What is it you need?"

"Where's Sherry?"

"She said she wanted another crack at that research at the library archives," he said.

"Does she think she missed something?" Alex asked.

"No," Mike said in a very matter-of-fact tone. "She's just frustrated. I figure it can't hurt to go over it again, though, so I told her I'd mind the store."

"Good work," Alex said. "I've got some calls to make, so I'll be here if you need me."

With that, Alex released the key and the little intercom went silent. He'd wanted to go over what little Sherry found during her last trip to the library's newspaper graveyard, but it seemed like she beat him to the punch there.

His fists tightened in anger, but he forced himself to relax. He wasn't mad at Sherry, but at the situation. He couldn't be certain Adam hadn't murdered Amanda Keeler, even though he doubted it. What he needed was more time to find out who Adam really was.

Two possibilities to make that happen sprung into his mind simultaneously and rather than choose one, he decided to do both. Picking up his phone again, he dialed the number for the police operator at the Central Office.

"Callahan," the captain's voice rang out once the operator connected them.

"This is Alex Lockerby, can you talk?"

Pound of Flesh

The line went quiet for a moment, then the captain came back on.

"I heard you were back among the living," he said. "And if you mean, 'can I talk freely,' I can."

"Good," Alex said. "I'm going to leak the information about the amnesiac suspect, Adam, to the press."

Alex could swear he heard Callahan's teeth grinding.

"You do that," he said in a gravelly voice, "and you'll be putting my butt in a sling, not to mention your pal, Danny."

"Even if Adam's guilty, they're railroading him. Somebody's got to stop them. You used to accuse me of leaking to the press all the time, so this time it'll be true."

"You don't get it," Callahan said, his voice calm and even, "this case is poison. If anything gets in the D.A.'s way, heads are going to roll."

"Starting with Danny's?"

"Starting with mine," Callahan said.

"Well, that's why I called," Alex said. "Did you have Adam examined by a doctor when he came in?"

"Of course," Callahan said, starting to sound a bit insulted. "We've got a specialist all the way from Bellevue, Fredrick Dyle. What of it?"

"What if, strictly hypothetically you understand, a reporter found his way over to Bellevue and was seen walking the halls and flirting with nurses and receptionists for a while," Alex said. "And then, hypothetically of course, security had to throw him out."

"And then the evening edition had the story about Adam's amnesia," Callahan guessed. "Hypothetically."

"Hypothetically," Alex agreed.

"Well, if the security guard called us and had a uniform go down to take a statement, then that would make it pretty obvious how the story got into the press," Callahan agreed. "You know any reporters who like you enough to play their part in a scheme like this?"

"Hypothetically?" Alex asked. "I do."

"Well, I don't know anything about it," Callahan said, "hypothetically or otherwise, and we never had this call."

"What call?" Alex said, then hung up.

With a smile on his face, Alex lifted the receiver again and dialed the offices of the infamous tabloid, *The Midnight Sun*. After a few minutes, he was connected with Billy Tasker, one of their top reporters.

"Alex, it's good to hear your voice," Billy said. "Last I heard, you were laid up with some mysterious disease."

"I got better," Alex deflected. "Look, I've got something hot and I need a way to get it in the press without anyone knowing where it came from."

"Something hot, eh?" Billy said.

Alex could practically hear the man drooling through the phone.

"You know me, Alex," Billy went on, "I'm the soul of discretion."

"Not this time," Alex said. "This time I need you to plant a false trail."

"It's three o'clock, Alex," Billy said. "I need time to get whatever this is into the evening edition soon."

Alex thought about that for a moment.

"Do you have a young, handsome reporter in your office?" he asked. "One who isn't an idiot and can follow instructions?"

"In the tabloid game, we have to be good looking and charming," Billy said. "It's part of the game, I mean nobody really wants to talk to a tabloid."

"Do you or don't you?" Alex pressed.

"I've got five of those," Bill scoffed.

"Well pick the smartest of the bunch, call him to your office, and sharpen your pencil," Alex said. "Because I've got a story for you."

16

WHAT'S IN A NAME

Alex sat at his desk, foot throbbing, and stared at the folder Sherry had prepared on Adam. It was frustratingly thin, and he'd been through it a dozen times or more without learning anything new. Now he was irritable and in desperate need of a sandwich and a drink. He toyed with the idea of sending Mike down to the cafe in Empire Station, but every time he thought about toggling the intercom something stopped him. Something in the back of his mind was nibbling at his consciousness, but it wasn't making itself known.

One thing he was reminded of was the Lunch Box. He hadn't been to his favorite greasy spoon in at least six months. In the old days, he ate there because it was close to the brownstone and he couldn't afford to eat anywhere else. Now he could eat at the Ritz's dining room every day, though he doubted he'd like it. The food would be exquisite of course, but the conversation was sure to be...

"Conversation," he said out loud as his mind latched on to the word. "Adam went to the diner where Amanda worked," he went on, his mind racing along lines of connection. "If he was looking for her on someone's behalf, he wouldn't have confronted her cold. He would have gone when she was off. He'd have talked to the staff, the waitresses and the cooks, asked them about her."

He stood up as this thought took firm hold of his mind, then sat down again quickly as his foot exploded with pain. Cursing, he got to his good foot more carefully, then slung his crutches under his arms. Limping down to the front office, he struggled his way through the door.

"Alex?" Mike asked as he came through the door. "What happened to your foot?"

"I nearly caught the man who assaulted Mrs. Hannover," Alex said. "He didn't want to be caught and shot me in the foot. I'll be all right in a week or so."

"Did you tell Dr. Bell?"

"He's seen to it," Alex said in a voice that warned off any further discussion. "I'm going out to follow up on something Danny's boys were working on. It's on the other side of the core, so I'll be out for a couple of hours."

"I'll hold the fort then," Mike said. "Do you mind if I write runes here on Sherry's desk? I'm trying to get your preservation rune down. Dr. Bell is very insistent about that one."

Alex hadn't thought about the preservation runes since he'd gotten out of his sick bed, but he should have. Lucky Tony wouldn't be happy that Iggy had made the last delivery of the preservation runes. He was a man who liked things to run a certain way.

Better give him a call today, he thought.

"Go ahead," Alex told Mike, "just don't get ink on Sherry's desk. That won't make her happy."

Mike nodded.

"I'll be careful."

Alex turned to go but stopped, looking back over his shoulder.

"Hey Mike," he said, then waited for the little man to look up from his work. "Thanks for filling in for me with the runes and, well, everything. I appreciate it."

"You bet, Boss," he said, then went back to his work.

It took Alex almost five minutes to extricate himself from the cab he'd taken across town to the dirty street in front of Red's Corner Diner. Despite Alex's current financial situation, he'd seen more than his fair share of dog wagons, so nothing about the run-down little building with dirty windows bothered him.

When he shouldered the door open, he was greeted with the smell of hamburgers, bacon, and burned toast, all undercut with the faint aroma of industrial cleaner. In a strange way it made him feel like he'd come home.

I've got to go by the Lunch Box and see everyone, he thought as he made his way to the counter. The thought made him feel a bit like a heel.

"What can I get you?" a smiling young girl in a gingham apron asked from behind the counter. She was fresh faced and pretty in a plain kind of way, with brown hair and freckles.

He'd wanted a sandwich, but now that he was here, he wanted his old standby.

"Poached eggs on buttered toast," he said.

"Coffee?" she offered, holding up the pot.

"Just water," he replied. He might be reliving his memories of diners, but he lived in a world where Marnie's coffee existed, and there was no coming back from that.

Alex waited until his food arrived, then began plying the waitress for gossip.

"I don't know much," she said in response to Alex's probing questions. "I just started working here and I was lucky to get it." She leaned in closer as Alex ate his eggs. "I did hear that the last girl died, though."

Alex let the conversation pause for a moment. It wouldn't do to seem too eager.

"That's terrible," he said after chewing for a moment, "what happened?"

The waitress looked left and right as if she feared being overheard, then she leaned in. "They say she was murdered," she whispered, covering her mouth with her hand. "The police came in and everything."

"Why did the police come?" Alex paused with a bite of egg halfway to his mouth. "She wasn't killed here, was she?"

The young waitress gasped and shook her head.

"I heard the owner talking to the cops," she said, keeping her voice low, "they were asking if someone came in here looking for her, you know, before she died."

Alex looked around to see if anyone was listening. He knew there wasn't, no one had come in the diner since he had, and the only other patron was at a booth on the far side. The look was to make the waitress feel comfortable enough to talk.

"Did someone come in?"

"Well, I wasn't here," she said in a conspiratorial voice, "but one of the other waitresses remember someone asking about a waitress named Ann."

"I take it no one named Ann works here," Alex said, taking another bite of egg.

"No," she confirmed.

"What was Ann's last name?" Alex asked as nonchalantly as he could. "Maybe she was the sister of someone who worked here."

"I don't know," the waitress said, "that's all Lisa remembered."

"Oh, well," Alex said with a shrug. "That's life in the city."

The waitress agreed with a smile and a flirtatious nod but was pulled away when the bell over the door jingled.

Alex would have liked to have a definite last name to go with Ann; that would make any research efforts surer. Still, if it was Adam who had come in asking about Ann, then her last name was likely to be Gallagher.

It was a start and it was more than he had this morning, so Alex finished his eggs, and then hobbled over to the phone to call a cab. The phone was an older model, without a rotary dial, so he gave the operator the exchange of a cab company and gave them the address of the diner. Once that was done, he dropped a nickel into the slot and waited for the operator.

"Empire one, seven-five-three," he said when the operator returned.

"Lockerby Investigations," Mike's voice said a moment later.

"It's me," Alex said. "Sherry still out?"

"Yeah. I heard from her just a bit ago, she's still over at the library going through newspapers."

Since the library was closer than his office, that worked out well for Alex.

"I'll head over there," he said. "I found something that can help her investigation."

"Before you go, Boss," Mike cut in before Alex could hang up, "Linda Kellin has called for you twice, Billy Tasker wants you to call him, and Captain Callahan would like a word. That last one sounded very urgent."

Alex sighed. He knew that even with Callahan's blessing, leaking Adam's condition would draw official scrutiny, he just didn't expect it this quickly. As worrying as that was, he reasoned he'd better call Billy first, in case something had gone horribly wrong.

"Thanks, Mike. I'll call in again once I'm done with Sherry."

With a sigh, Alex hung up and dropped another nickel in the phone. This time it was Billy who picked up.

"Brother, you really came through for me this time," he said once Alex identified himself. "The afternoon edition sold out. We haven't done that since your buddy Danny caught the Dolly Anderson killer. We're having to print more to get them out to the newsstands by five. I owe you."

"I'm glad to hear that," Alex said, meaning it. "How did the authorities react?"

"Like a hornet's nest that got kicked over. I've had calls from the mayor's office, the administrator from Bellevue, even your friend Captain Callahan called. I told them the story you gave me and I'm pretty sure they bought it. My reporter made a real nuisance of himself, so they've all got the paper trail."

"Can you take the heat?"

Billy scoffed.

"This isn't the worst reaction to a story I've had this year," he said. "I suspect that everyone but the mayor's office thinks Adam is getting a bum steer, so they didn't push too hard."

"Well, let me know if they get too persistent," Alex said, "or if they poke any holes in our story."

Billy promised that he would and hung up. He didn't want to admit it, but Billy's casual attitude about the objections from city hall didn't jibe with Callahan's urgent call. As he fished another nickel out of his trouser pocket, however, he heard his cab honk from the street.

The New York Public Library was a massive edifice that resembled nothing more than a Greek temple, complete with a long stair leading up to it. Alex had been here many times during his career, but the sheer gravitas of the place always impressed him.

Mounting the stairs, Alex limped painfully up using his crutches. After a brief rest at the top, he turned left and approached the bank of public phones along the wall. These were modern phones, so Alex dialed the number for the Central Office switchboard and told the operator to ring the captain.

"Something is very wrong," Callahan said when he picked up the phone.

"Wrong how?" Alex asked. "My guy Tasker at *The Midnight Sun* said that our story was solid."

"It is," Callahan growled. "But that's not going to calm down the important people that have been in and out of here all morning. The lieutenant governor was in here with the chief and the mayor, and they were not happy."

"That's nothing you couldn't handle, Captain," Alex said.

"Normally yes," Callahan said, "but it was the way they were unhappy that's bothering me."

That took Alex by surprise and he hesitated.

"Once I told them about a reporter mucking around at Bellevue," Callahan said, "they immediately started talking about that alderman, Malcom Snow. I still don't know how he found out, but everybody in my little meet and greet was afraid of him."

"Afraid how?" Alex asked. "Like afraid he would sneak in their homes at night and kill them?"

"No, afraid that he's going to use this poor girl's murder as a stick to beat them with," Callahan said. "Like this could destroy their political careers."

"Isn't Snow running for the U.S. Senate?" Alex wondered. "Even if he uses Amanda's murder to give the mayor a black eye, the election is in less than a week. After that, Snow will either be an uninterested private citizen or off to Washington not to be heard from till the next election."

"That's what's bothering me," Callahan said. "I get that the mayor doesn't want to look bad, but people get killed in this city every day and he's not up for reelection for two years. By the time this could hurt him politically, no one will remember it."

Alex didn't like the idea that a beautiful young woman like Amanda could be so brutally murdered and then be utterly forgotten. Since no one had come forward looking for her, Alex assumed she had no family, at least not any in the city. It might be a very long time before anyone missed her, if ever.

"Any guesses?" Alex said.

"I was going to ask you that," Callahan shot back. "There has to be some connection, something personal for someone involved."

"You like the mayor better than the lieutenant governor or the chief?"

"Chief's not in this, he was uncomfortable the whole time, but Lieutenant Governor Phelps was hot under the collar."

"And we don't know why," Alex summed up the conversation.

"Do you think you can look into this?" Callahan asked. "Discreetly."

"I suppose that if I'm working the case with Danny that would give me an excuse to keep investigating."

"Done," Callahan said, "I'll call him and square it. You just find out who our dead girl really is and why that amnesiac detective was following her."

"There is a problem with that," Alex said. "Adam asked me to do P.I. work for him and find out who he really is."

"Did he pay you a retainer?" Callahan asked.

"No."

"Then that never happened," the Captain replied. "I'll have Danny talk to Adam and let him know what we're doing. You just focus on finding out who Adam really is."

"I don't have anything new on Adam," Alex said, "but I might have a lead on Amanda."

"Whatever's going on here could blow up in our faces, scribbler," Callahan said, "so keep me in the loop."

"Cross my heart," Alex said, then hung up.

He stood there in the phone booth for a long moment, before pushing the door open. The conversation with Callahan bothered him more than it should. Amanda's murder had been brutal, and if she'd been someone from the core, Alex would have understood all the political hysteria, but Amanda was a nobody working in a low-rent diner.

Or was she? he thought.

If he was right, Adam had been looking for her under another name. Could Ann Gallagher have been someone important? The runaway daughter of a connected family?

"Callahan was right," he said as he left the booth, "this could blow up in our faces."

He had no doubt who would be chosen to be the scapegoat if that happened. Callahan liked him, sure, but he wasn't going to put his own neck or Danny's on the block if it came to that. Alex resolved to stay alert and look over his shoulder often.

Shaking off the oppressive weight of the call, Alex headed downstairs, going slowly with his crutches, to the sub-basement where the newspaper archive was housed. It wasn't hard to find Sherry as there were only about ten people in the entire archive. She sat at a table near a reading lamp with a dozen or so newspapers spread out on the long table.

After spending two days crawling through old newspapers looking for a single name, Alex assumed she would have looked exhausted. Instead, Sherry was rapidly moving between multiple papers and taking copious notes on a pad that had several pages already rolled over the top.

"Tell me you've found something," Alex said as he walked up on her.

Sherry gasped as she looked up.

"Alex," she said in an out of breath voice. "You scared me."

"Sorry, doll. I was in the neighborhood, so I thought I'd stop by and see how you were doing."

"What happened to your foot?" she asked.

"I had a disagreement with a man in a speakeasy," he said.

Sherry's eyebrows went up and she smiled.

"That sounds like an interesting story," she said. "Care to share?"

"Later," he said. "Right now I'm desperate for a lead on Adam or Amanda Keeler."

Her smile widened into a grin, showing a lot of teeth.

"I think I'm on to something," she said. "I came back today, because I could swear I saw the name Gallagher, but not in the classifieds. It took me a while, but I finally found the story."

"Was it about a pretty redhead?"

A brief cloud crossed Sherry's face and she shook her head.

"The story didn't have a description, just a name."

"Ann Gallagher?" Alex asked.

Sherry just gaped at him.

"How did you know that?"

"Adam was in the diner where Amanda worked a few days before she died. He was asking about a woman named Ann."

"Well, aren't you clever," Sherry said, sitting back in her chair.

Alex pulled up a chair and sat next to her.

"So, why don't you tell me who Ann Gallagher was?"

Sherry picked up a paper, turning it over and dropping it onto the table in front of Alex. Across the top, the banner headline read; *Police Break Up Prostitution Ring*. Before Alex could read more, Sherry dropped another paper with a less prominent headline that was still above the fold. This one read; *Gallagher Evidence Brings Down Connolly mob*.

"Well that explains a little," he said, taking the paper and scanning the article. It wasn't as detailed as Alex would have liked; clearly the police and the D.A. were keeping a lid on as much of this case as they could. What it did say was that a girl named Ann Gallagher had produced evidence of some kind that had taken out one of the Irish mob families.

"Looks like this might be a simple case of revenge," Sherry said.

Alex checked the date of the paper; September sixth of twenty-seven.

"After eleven years?" Alex said. "Mob guys are usually more pro-active than that."

"She was living under a fake name," Sherry pointed out.

Alex mused that over for a moment, but it didn't feel right.

"Adam found her, and I doubt he was at it for eleven years."

"Maybe his client just got out of prison," Sherry offered.

Alex consulted the paper again. It didn't give details of any individual mobsters who were caught up by the police, but it did mention that the head of the family, Aidan Connolly, had died in a shootout with police, along with several of his lieutenants. The opinion of the reporter was that Connolly and his men simply refused to be taken alive.

"I don't know," he said. "The kind of hardcore mobster who would beat a young woman into a literal bloody pulp is the kind of guy who'd get life. Anyone who only got ten years was an accountant, or maybe the guy who drove their bootlegging truck."

"Still might have been devoted to their Boss," Sherry countered. "Most mobs are built around families."

"Fair point," Alex said. "I guess we've got some digging to do."

17

CORRELATION

Alex pushed away the stack of newspapers and lifted up his injured foot, resting it on a nearby chair. He and Sherry had combed through eleven-year-old newspapers looking for any mention of Ann Gallagher or the Connolly mob. Despite the salacious nature of the case, the news reporting was surprisingly thin.

"I think we're done, Boss," Sherry broke through his wandering thoughts. "There just isn't anything more. Even the tabloids don't have the details, though the stuff they made up was interesting."

Alex chuckled and nodded. One of the tabloid stories about the case said that Ann was a Cailleach, bringing down the Irish Mob with magical abilities. From context Alex inferred that a Cailleach was some kind of witch. As amusing as that was, it wasn't the most ridiculous take on the story. Some of the more salacious rags had stories that even the Brothers Grimm couldn't have imagined.

He heard Sherry stand up on the other side of the table and start gathering the stacks of papers.

"I'll get these put away," she said. "You go call Mike and tell him we'll be back soon."

Alex sighed and nodded, then took his foot back down from the chair. It had ached a bit while he'd been going through the papers, but now it was only a dull throb that bothered him when he moved it the wrong way.

Pushing up with his good foot, Alex stood and grabbed his crutches. Hobbling toward the stairs, he wondered if he'd reach the top before Sherry finished returning the papers.

It felt like ten minutes later when he finally hopped up the last step onto the landing and made his way across the polished floor to the phone booths. During his slog up the stairs, he remembered that Linda Kellin wanted him to call, so, before he called Mike, he dialed the number for Linda's shop.

"Alex?" Linda answered, a note of desperation in her voice.

"Good afternoon to you too," Alex said, trying not to grin. "I hear you're looking for me."

"Alex, you have to help," she said, her voice shifting from relief to anger. "Two dozen people are dead and over a hundred have been poisoned. Every alchemist in the city is making Behring's Antiserum as fast as we can."

Alex pinched the bridge of his nose. His gut still told him there wasn't some mad poisoner running around the city making people sick, but if Linda was right, people were dying. It was something he couldn't afford to ignore.

"All right," he said. "Do you and your doctor friend have data on the victims?"

"We have addresses," Linda admitted, "but we don't know where they might have been exposed."

Last time Alex had been the one to get medical histories on all the people that Linda and Dr. Kitteridge identified. This time around, the job was too big for just him, and Sherry had already done two days of research without a break.

"Okay," Alex said. "I'll help you find out where this is coming from, but I need you and all your doctor friends to do something first. Call everyone who got sick, and the families of everyone who died. I need to know where they work, and, more importantly, where they eat any meals that they don't eat at home."

"That's a lot of phone calls, Alex," Linda said. "Are you sure it's necessary?"

Pound of Flesh

"Ever hear of a doctor called John Snow?" he asked. When she said she hadn't, he went on. "How about William Farr?"

"Why are they important?"

"Because," Alex explained, "back in the eighteen-fifties, England was having a problem with cholera. Basically, if you drink water that's been polluted by sewage, you can get violently sick and die."

"I know what cholera is," Linda growled at him, "I know four different potions that treat it, but what does that have to do with this poison?"

"William Farr was a mathematician; he used records of the cholera spread, and the deaths, to prove that cholera was coming from the River Thames. He thought it was because of the stink coming off the water, but that's not important. Farr's data allowed a doctor called John Snow to isolate an outbreak in a neighborhood called Soho, well above the river. Turns out if you know where the dead people were getting their drinking water, you can pinpoint the source of the infection, and that's just what Dr. Snow did. It's known as finding the focus of an infection."

"How do you know all this stuff?"

"Iggy wrote a whole monograph about it," Alex explained. "I'm sure he'd be happy to get you a copy, but let's get back to your sick people. If there was an obvious connection, like them all having been to a Dodgers game at the same time, your doctor friends would have found it already. I'm guessing that whatever is making the people sick is one step removed from where they were infected, maybe two."

"So you think that someone's, what? Poisoning foodstuffs before they go out to diners?" Linda asked.

"That makes more sense," Alex said. "Most of the food eaten in the city is shipped in from all over the state. That means the focus of infection might be something tainted that came in on a boat or train that's been sent to random restaurants and lunch counters."

"Then how will knowing where the sick people ate help? Won't there be dozens of these focuses?"

"If we can identify even one focus of infection, like a diner or bar, we can find out who their suppliers are. With any luck that will lead us to one common source."

"Is this what you do all day?" Linda asked.

"Some days," Alex admitted.

"It makes me tired just thinking about it," Linda fired back. "I'll call Dr. Kitteridge and get everyone going on that information."

"I'm going back to my office," Alex said. "When you get information on thirty or so of the sick people, bring it there and we'll lay everything out on my big map."

Linda promised that she would and Alex hung up. He thought about calling Danny and telling him about the mob angle in Amanda Keeler's killing, or rather Ann Gallagher's killing, but his foot was hurting again and he wanted to make that call from the comfort of his desk chair. The good news there was he didn't have to call Mike, he'd see him in less than a quarter an hour. Resolved to catch the skybug from Library Station, he hitched up his crutches and headed outside.

By the time he'd reached the bottom of the stairs, Sherry had caught up with him and they both took the skycrawler back to Empire Station. Mike was relieved to see them and quickly gathered up his rune writing gear as Sherry glared at the mess on her desk.

"I've got to call Danny about what we learned," he told Sherry as she waited to reassume her position as head of the office, then he shuffled down the hall to his comfortable chair.

"Danny," he said, once the police operator connected his call. "How's it going with Adam?"

Danny grumbled something Alex couldn't make out.

"What's that?"

"Chief Montgomery and the D.A. are on the warpath over here," Danny said in a low voice, as if he feared being overheard. "With the news about Adam in the papers, and that alderman talking to every reporter he can find, it's given the whole department a black eye. Half the papers say we're incompetent, the other half say we're railroading Adam. The only thing they have in common is that everyone wants answers."

"Well, I may have a few for you, but you're not going to like them," Alex said. He pulled out his notebook and began walking Danny through what he and Sherry had learned. When he finished, his friend groaned.

"The Irish mob?" he said. "If that gets out, the papers will have a field day. A third of the department is Irish, they'll say we're complicit."

"It might not be so bad," Alex said, "maybe they'll just settle for incompetent."

"Very funny," Danny growled, his voice dropping to a whisper. "The papers are already slanting their stories to imply that Amanda's murder was to protect someone in the police or in the mayor's office. If they get ahold of this angle, they'll take it as confirmation."

That's about the way Alex figured it. Distrust in the management of the city would skyrocket and Alderman Snow would look like a crusading warrior of the people.

"What are they going to do when they find out that Adam's pretty much off the table as a suspect?" he asked.

"Blame rolls down hill," Danny said. "I'm sure they'd love to point the finger at me, but they're going to have a tough time convincing anyone that I'm Irish."

Alex chuckled in spite of himself, then the reality of that statement hit him.

"Callahan," he said.

"The only way he could be more Irish would be if he was a redhead," Danny agreed. "We need to figure out if Amanda's death was retaliation for the Connolly mob."

"The file on that case is going to be an inch thick," Alex said.

"And likely restricted," Danny pushed back.

"Can you get access?"

"Are you kidding?" Danny said, with a self-satisfied chuckle. "As soon as I tell Callahan about this, he's going to give me anything I want."

"Don't abuse your newfound power," Alex said, stifling a laugh. "Or, if you do, get a bigger office."

"I'll do my best," Danny said. "Once I get the file, I'll bring it by the brownstone after work, so we can go over it."

"Stop fishing. I'll get you an invite to dinner."

"You really *are* a good detective," Danny said with a smile Alex could hear. "See you tonight."

With that, Alex hung up.

There wasn't much to do without the police files on the Connolly case, so Alex pulled out his notes on the illnesses Linda Kellin and Dr. Kitteridge had reported to him previously. He'd done two city maps from that data, one showing where everyone lived, and one showing where everyone worked. The work map was centered around the west side, just north of the industrial district, but it covered an enormous area, at least half a mile in diameter.

Out in the country, that would be as good as a glowing light pointing the way to the source of whatever was making people sick, but half a mile on Manhattan covered a dozen ethnicities, fifty places to eat, and a few thousand residents. It was quite possible that Linda was right and something, or someone, in that radius was poisoning people, but it was like looking for a needle in a haystack.

Not that he'd ever done that, but the idiom was fairly self-explanatory.

Before his thoughts could wander to the origins of some of Iggy's favorite folksy sayings, the intercom on his desk buzzed.

"Sorry to bother you, Boss," Sherry said, her voice scratchy and tinny over the intercom's tiny speaker, "but Detective Arnold is on the line, he'd like a word."

Alex pushed the notes on the illnesses away, then sat up and reached for the phone.

"Detective," he said, putting the receiver to his ear. "Did you figure out who's stalking Mrs. Hannover's secret speakeasy?"

"Well, that's kind of the problem, Alex," Arnold said. "The woman who had the house built…"

"Thelma Rubison," Alex said without bothering to consult his notes. How could he forget such an interesting name? It was like peanut brittle for the brain.

"Yeah, that's the name on the building permits and the original title," Arnold went on, "but as far as I can tell, there's no such person."

Well, that explains why her name is so interesting, Alex thought. *The first rule of an alias was to make it memorable.*

"Weeellll," Alex said, dragging out the word to give himself time to think. "I guess I'm not surprised that the woman having a luxury

Pound of Flesh

speakeasy built for New York's rich and powerful did it using a fake name."

"In hindsight it does make sense," Arnold said. "The question now is how do we find out who she really was?"

"Smart guy like you, you've already checked the bank records and contacted the builder," Alex said.

"The payments to the builder were drafted from Manhattan Metropolitan Bank," Arnold said, obviously reading from his notes. "The bank manager didn't remember Thelma Rubison, but that was the name on the account. It was opened a year before the construction began and closed a week after the builder handed over the keys."

"What did the builder have to say about building an underground speakeasy? He must have talked with Rubison about the details, surely he could…I don't know, describe her."

"I'm sure he had lots of conversations with her," Arnold said, "unfortunately he's been dead for three years. I spoke with his son, Phillip Buxton, but he wasn't part of the business back in twenty-five, he was at school upstate."

"What about the job foreman?" Alex said. "The supplier for tools and the building materials?"

"You know, I asked about that, and it was the darnedest thing," Arnold said, "the son went through the records for the whole year and there wasn't anything about the building of Thelma Rubison's property."

"What about the other properties built that year? I doubt the builder hired a new foreman for each job, he'd need a foreman he could trust for a top secret build and trust like that takes time."

"Yeah, I thought of that," Arnold said, an amused tone creeping into his voice. "You might want to sit down for this one. According to Buxton, the usual foreman was a guy named Sam Wainwright. He retired from building last year. I called him and he remembered that job very well. He said it was the only job Phillip's dad ever took on that he didn't use Sam as the site foreman. Sam figured he did the foreman job himself."

"Sounds like something Sam would have been curious about," Alex offered, "or mad about."

"Nah," Arnold scoffed, "Phillip's pop had Sam run a job in Brooklyn by himself while the speakeasy was being built. He's still so proud that his boss trusted him to run his own build that I think he popped a shirt button while I was on the phone with him."

Alex chewed on that for a moment, letting the conversation lapse.

"Did Sam or Phillip know about any other secret jobs the company took on?"

"No," Arnold said. "I asked about that because having Sam do his own jobs would make it easy for Phillip's dad to do other things on the side, but Phillip started working at the company two years later and nothing like that came up."

"So the builder is a bust," Alex declared.

"That's the way I see it," Detective Arnold said. "I'm kind of stuck about where to go from here."

"What about the speakeasy?" Alex asked. "Any idea what it was called?"

All speakeasies had names, that's how their patrons would identify them, and a ritzy place like Thelma Rubison's would definitely have a name.

"I'm sure it did," Arnold said. "As far as my boys have been able to find, however, there's no mention of the name on anything left behind in that place. And, before you ask about the clientele, there's no chance anyone rich or powerful enough to have been a patron is going to talk about it."

Alex wasn't sure he agreed with that, but he wasn't ready to argue the point. He'd pursue that angle later if he needed to.

"That only leaves the elusive Miss Rubison," he said.

"You have an idea on how we can find her?"

"Maybe," Alex hedged. "For as opulent as that speakeasy was, it wasn't built until nineteen twenty-five."

"That's right in the middle of Prohibition, but no one could know it would end in thirty-three," Arnold said. "She probably built it for the long haul."

"I agree," Alex said, "but do you think you could do it?'

"Do what?"

"Have a full-blown speakeasy built in a few short months. I mean, how did Thelma, whoever she is, know what a high-end speakeasy would need? How many tables? Where to get hard liquor as well as beer?"

"You think this wasn't her first time running a speakeasy," Arnold said. "Do you know how many speakeasies there were? Prohibition lasted thirteen years and there was practically one on every corner."

"It's a daunting task," Alex agreed, "but I wonder how many of those speakeasies were run by women? That's not likely to be a big number."

There was a pause and Alex imagined he could see the rumpled little detective nodding his head and stroking his chin.

"I see where you're going with this," he said at last. "I'll have my boys start pulling Prohibition arrest records; it shouldn't take too long to go through them looking for women."

"That's the spirit," Alex said. "Let me know how you make out."

He was about to hang up, when Detective Arnold spoke again.

"I was wondering if you'd be willing to check the newspaper archive for me," he said. "You're really good at that, and I'm going to need everyone I've got on this end just to go through the police reports."

"Is that helping in an official capacity?" Alex asked.

"I'll square it with my lieutenant, but yes," Arnold said.

Alex looked at the clock, which told him it was after four.

"I can't get started tonight, is tomorrow soon enough for you?"

"It'll be tomorrow afternoon before I can even get the files out of storage," Arnold said. "Assuming they're all in one place."

"I'll call you the moment I learn anything," Alex said, then he bade the detective good evening and hung up.

He was about to stand up and limp his way to the front office to see Sherry. Since he didn't really have anything to do right now but wait for data from Linda, he figured he'd go home early. Before he checked with Sherry to make sure his calendar was clear, however, he picked up the phone and dialed the brownstone. Iggy wouldn't mind having Danny over for dinner, but he'd have Alex's hide if he wasn't properly informed.

18

THE SALON

Iggy puttered in the kitchen, humming to himself while Alex read the evening paper. Danny had been right, every article about the Keeler murder had an undertone of scandal and conspiracy. Some figured the police were deliberately mishandling the case to cover up for one of their own, while others implied subtly that Amanda was the mistress of someone high up in government, possibly even the mayor himself.

As Alex skimmed the stories, he did take solace in one thing...no one thought Adam was the killer anymore. When he picked up the last paper, a salacious tabloid called *The Lamplighter*, he found that not everyone had abandoned Adam as a suspect. Like *The Midnight Sun*, they too claimed to have an inside source at Bellevue, and their source claimed that Adam was only faking his amnesia.

Alex chuckled, interrupting Iggy's humming.

"Find something amusing?" he said as he continued to putter over the stove.

"Did you read the Lamplighter?"

"No," he admitted, "It only just came in as I was starting dinner. I usually save that particular rag for my after-coffee chuckle in the greenhouse. Did you know that they have twice published stories that I'm alive, or rather that Conan Doyle is alive, and working on a new Sherlock Holmes story?"

"I hadn't seen that," Alex chuckled, "but I'd pay a tidy sum to have been there when you read that."

Iggy harrumphed at that, but said nothing.

"You know," Alex continued, using the tabloid to hide the smile on his face, "you ought to write some new Holmes stories. Have your publisher say they were found in a drawer or something."

A long frosty silence greeted him, and Alex did his best not to snicker.

"Funny," Iggy said at last, his voice flat and even. "You know very well that I spent years trying to get out of Sherlock's shadow. Now that I'm out, I'm never going back, so I'll thank you to keep your humorous observations to yourself."

"Do you ever think about writing again?" Alex asked, his tone turning serious.

"Sometimes," Iggy said, "but then I come to my senses."

"Why not write something different," Alex suggested, his impish tone returning. "I hear romantic stories are all the rage with young women."

"Perhaps someday," Iggy chuckled. "If I run out of money."

"How come you didn't get wiped out in the crash?" Alex said, asking a question he'd been sitting on for years.

"My money was in a British bank at the time of the crash," he said. "I didn't convert it to dollars until I came here. Even then, the money I brought with me was just what I had in a rainy day fund. I...I left the rest for my family."

Iggy hadn't come to America of his own volition, of course. He'd been fleeing a secret society called the Whalers, kind of a precursor to the Legion. They wanted the Archimedean Monograph and suspected, rather than knew, that Iggy had it. For the safety of his family and friends, he had to fake his own death and run.

Alex really hadn't thought about Iggy's money, other than to acknowledge that he had more than enough. It made sense that he'd left the bulk of it with his family, but that gave rise to other questions.

"How are you so rich if you only brought your rainy day fund?" he asked.

"I put it in the market," Iggy said, as if that were the most obvious answer possible.

"But the market took a beating, why'd you risk that?"

"Because, dear boy, by the time I got here the market had already suffered the worst. It was, and still is, steadily building back, and my money is building with it."

"What if it crashes again?" Alex wondered.

Iggy just shrugged at that.

"I own this brownstone outright," he said, "along with a few other properties that I picked up for a song, thanks to the market crash. I also have some gold and precious stones in case I need to sell something for cash. If the market has trouble again, I'll be fine."

Alex raised an eyebrow at that. He understood the concept of fungible goods, things that could be bought and sold easily; a lot of mob families and crooks kept their money in those kinds of things in case they needed to make a quick getaway. It was also a good way to hide ready cash from the IRS.

Maybe it's time to start doing some of that yourself, he thought. His bank account was starting to get large.

He was about to ask Iggy where a good place to start would be when the doorbell rang.

"That'll be Danny," he said, setting the tabloid aside and standing gingerly.

True to Alex's prediction, he found his friend standing on the stoop with his hat in his hand and a heavy-looking briefcase at his side.

"Sorry I'm late," he said, raising the briefcase up to chest level. "You won't believe the trouble I had getting this." He looked like he wanted to go on, but hesitated when he saw Alex on crutches. "What happened to you?"

"I had a disagreement with a burglar," he said with an awkward shrug. "It took too long to get it treated for a quick heal."

"Ouch," Danny said, stepping inside as Alex moved back. "I'd love to hear your burglar story, but some other time."

"Not to worry," Alex chuckled, "It isn't an interesting story."

Danny set down his heavy case, then hung his hat and overcoat on the pegs in the short hallway just inside the vestibule, while Alex limped toward the kitchen.

"Hello, Daniel," Iggy said as they entered the kitchen. "You look like a man in need of a good meal."

Danny chuckled at that but there was no humor in it.

"I had to tell the captain that I was coming here to talk to the two of you before he let me leave the Central Office with this," he said, setting the heavy briefcase on the table.

"That bad?" Iggy asked as Danny slumped down in one of the heavy chairs that stood around the table.

"Not quite," he said, "and we want to keep it that way. The sooner we find out who Adam is or why Amanda Keeler, or rather Ann Gallagher, was murdered, the quicker we can get the newspapers off our backs."

Danny opened the briefcase, fishing inside, then pulled out two thick folders full of loose papers. Dropping them on the table wasn't enough to shake the massive piece of furniture, but the sound of it resounded off the ceiling with a bang.

"What are you doing in there?" Sorsha's voice came from the library.

Alex turned in his chair to find her rounding the corner by the stairs and crossing into the library. She was dressed in her usual work clothes, a pair of high-waisted slacks with a white shirt, a burgundy vest and matching lipstick. Clearly she'd come though his vault from her office. Her platinum hair shimmered in the light of the fire in the library grate and one of her makeup-darkened eyebrows was raised.

"Danny," she said, with a smile blooming on her face. "Are you joining us tonight?"

"The police are having a spot of bother over the killing of that young lady," Iggy said. "Alex thought we could put together a bit of a salon to review the facts. You know, see if we can't help out."

"I thought you had a suspect," Sorsha said as Alex stood awkwardly in order to pull out a chair out for her.

"That's Adam," Alex supplied. "He's the one with amnesia."

Sorsha thought about that for a moment.

"I would think that would make him an excellent suspect," she said. "He can't, credibly, defend himself."

"Except the tabloids are running with the story that he's being railroaded," Danny explained.

"Yes, that would make trying him difficult," Sorsha admitted. "It definitely means that the D.A. can't use him to have a speedy trial and make the case go away."

"You have expressed the problem with both alacrity and accuracy," Iggy said, motioning for Danny and Alex to sit as well. "As I understand it, though, another thorny problem has reared its head. Alex…"

"Uh," Alex said, realizing that Iggy was looking to him for an explanation, "I think Danny is better informed on this subject."

"I'm not sure I'd say that," Danny growled, but he gathered the folders together next to the place-setting in front of him. "Alex found out that our murder victim, Amanda Keeler, was actually Ann Gallagher. According to this," he patted the stack of files, "Ann was instrumental in bringing down the Connolly mob back in twenty-seven."

Iggy whistled at that.

"I thought Miss Keeler, or rather Miss Gallagher, was in her early twenties," Iggy observed as he brought a plate of baked potatoes to the table.

"That's what the coroner figures," Danny said.

"That would mean that she was somewhere between eleven and thirteen when she helped bring down the Connollys," Sorsha said. "What could a child do to topple an established crime family?"

"She could give the police copies of their books," Alex said.

"How could a mere child obtain copies of a mob family's accounts?" Iggy asked.

"I suspect that's what's in here," Danny said, patting the stack of folders again. "Why don't we eat and then we can go through everything?"

"An excellent idea," Iggy said, bringing over a plate of roast. "The food is hot and that's the best time to eat it. We can talk while Alex is doing the dishes."

"How am I going to do dishes with one foot?"

Iggy gave him an amused look.

"Lean on the sink."

Alex rolled his eyes at that, but reached for a bowl of blanched green beans without comment.

An hour later the plates had all been cleared away and the enormous oak table was now covered in files. When Danny had first opened the folders after dinner, he'd discovered that many people had been through the documents since nineteen twenty-seven, and none of them had been particularly vigilant about putting them back properly.

"I've got a page of the report on the Connolly's west side bootlegging operation," Iggy said, handing Danny a loose page.

Iggy, Alex, and Sorsha stood on one side of the table sifting through the stack of loose documents and attempting to identify their subject matter. Once they did, they passed them to Danny, who would stack them into organized piles. Alex had his left knee on a chair to avoid using the crutches, which worked well enough to keep his foot off the floor.

"Here's one about a brothel on twenty-third street," Alex said, passing it over. "That's the third brothel we've found."

"Is that a lot?" Sorsha asked.

"Depends on how big their territory was," Danny said, sorting the paper into a stack by the end of the table.

"According to this, they had almost twenty bookmakers spread all over the lower west side," Iggy said, handing another page to Danny. "It's a slightly different color than most of the rest of this," he went on, "It's rather light on details, so it might be part of a summary of some sort."

"Here's another," Sorsha said, picking a page out of the stack that was slightly more yellow.

"I've got two here," Alex said, picking two sheets out of the pile.

It only took Danny a few minutes to put the pages in order as Iggy and Sorsha found three more.

"This is a summary of the case file," Danny said at last. "There are at least seven different files in this mess, representing more than a decade of police work."

"The newspapers said that Ann Gallagher was instrumental in bringing about the Connolly's downfall, so at her age, what we're looking for has to be in the most recent file," Alex said.

"That's helpful," Iggy said, "but we'll still need as much of this information as we can get for reference. We'll need to finish sorting all this."

Sorsha and Alex sighed simultaneously, then looked down at the table when Iggy glowered at them.

"Both of you should know better," he growled. "There are no shortcuts in an investigation."

"Yes, sir," Alex said, managing to sound sincere. At this point he'd welcome a police raid if it got him out of sorting paper, but Iggy was right. Whatever Ann Gallagher had done, it was just the tipping point, and the information in the other files was the evidence the police would have used to put the Connollys away.

Alex was certain that the leaders of the Connolly mob had been swept up immediately and, if they allowed themselves to be taken alive, they were undoubtedly still in prison. That meant that the killer was likely someone low on the mob's totem pole. Someone who only did a few years of jail time, or even someone the police missed entirely.

He wanted to sigh again.

He'd hoped that crawling through these files would yield a viable suspect, but the more he thought about it, the less likely that seemed. There were likely to be dozens of low-level associates and even uninvolved family members that would fit the bill, and even with the might of the New York Police Department, it would take weeks to track them all down.

Half an hour later, Danny put the last of the loose pages onto one of the stacks, then handed each person at the table a file to organize and read. It didn't take Alex long to organize his, so he started reading.

"This is the Gallagher file," he said as the others finished their own sorting.

"What's it say?" Sorsha asked, putting a hand on his forearm and leaning in to read over his shoulder.

"According to the summary, she came to America with her mother Katherine as some kind of indentured servant," Alex began.

"Indenturement's illegal," Sorsha said, anger creeping into her voice. "It's been illegal since the Thirteenth Amendment, that's..." she did some quick math in her head, "that's over seventy years ago."

"Some practices die hard," Danny said. "A lot of people want to come here, especially from Ireland during the famine. Things like indentured servitude still exist if someone wants to emigrate but can't afford the boat ride."

"Even today?" Alex asked.

Danny nodded.

"It's not institutionalized like it used to be," he explained, "there aren't any friendly societies raising money or investors offering contracts publicly, but private deals happen."

"How can those deals be enforced?" Sorsha asked. "All anyone in that situation would have to do is tap a policeman on the shoulder and tell their story."

"That's why the mob was doing it," Alex said, tapping the report he'd been reading. "As soon as Katherine and Ann got off the boat they were separated. Ann went to one of the family homes to be a maid and Katherine was sent to one of the Connolly brothels to work off her debt. According to this, the Connollys had a habit of doing that with any pretty girls they brought over."

"That's monstrous," Iggy declared, his mustache ruffling with outrage.

"That's what Katherine thought," Alex went on. "Some of her clients were members of the mob and she started listening to what they were saying."

"She was gathering evidence?" Danny said.

"Looks like it," Alex said, turning the pages of the report. "According to this, she learned the names and locations of the family businesses, even the name of their mob doctor and their accountant."

"Then why is Ann in all the tabloid stories?" Sorsha asked.

"The straw that broke the camel's back seems to be when Ann turned twelve," Alex said. "Katherine learned that the godfather, one Angus Connolly, was going to marry her off to one of his lieutenants. It doesn't say here, but I'm going to assume he was a real piece of work, because Katherine took the book she'd been keeping her notes in and got it to her daughter. Ann ran away from the home where she was being kept and got the book to the cops."

"Brave girls," Iggy said, "both of them."

"The cops grabbed the accountant," Alex said, still reading. "He cut a deal and the police rolled up the whole organization."

"What about Katherine?" Sorsha asked.

"Her body was found, beaten to death, when the police raided the brothel," Alex said. "I guess that lieutenant didn't like being deprived of his child bride."

"That's horrible," Danny said in a quiet voice.

"Well, it has a happy ending," Alex said, "if you can call it that. That lieutenant was linked to a dozen murders, and he got the chair in twenty-seven."

"Good riddance to bad rubbish," Iggy declared.

"And Ann changed her name and disappeared," Sorsha said. "Only to be found, thirteen years later, and murdered."

"Assuming Adam was the detective who found her," Danny asked, "how did he do it?"

"That doesn't matter," Iggy declared. "Without knowing who Adam really is, we can't check his office or his files to find out who hired him or how he ultimately located Ann."

"Even if we did, his employer likely used an alias," Sorsha pointed out.

"So we need to figure out who's left of the Connolly mob, and who of that group might want revenge bad enough to beat Ann Gallagher into a bloody pulp," Alex gave voice to the conclusion he'd reached earlier.

Danny held up the file he'd been reassembling.

"According to this, the Connolly mob was primarily made up of three families, the Connollys, the Faheys and the Cohans. There are a few other minor families, but they're all low-level muscle."

"That's pronounced Co-han in Ireland," Iggy said, correcting Danny's New York reading of the name Cohan.

"I wondered about that," Danny said. "It sounded Jewish, not Irish."

"What happened to the ringleaders?" Alex probed, trying to bring the discussion back to the principals.

Danny checked his paper, then flipped the page and read more.

"According to this, Angus, his underbosses, and most of his lieutenants were tried and convicted. Some got the chair, but others are still in prison with no chance of parole."

"Most?" Iggy asked.

"There are three names of Connolly lieutenants here with no notes beside them," Danny said. "That could mean they're dead, or that they escaped, or maybe whoever made this report forgot to list their conviction."

"That sounds like a promising place to start," Sorsha said, giving Alex a sly smile. "I mean what are finding runes for, after all?"

"How would I establish a connection with a mobster who's been gone for thirteen years?" Alex asked.

"Quite right," Iggy said. "Any physical evidence in police storage will have lost its connection years ago. We'll have to locate them the old-fashioned way. Now, just whom are we looking for, Daniel?"

"James Fahey, Michael Cohan, and Liam Cohan," Danny said.

"That's a bit of good luck," Alex declared. "Two Cohans. They've got to be at least cousins, if not brothers."

"You think they've stayed in touch?" Sorsha asked.

"If they're still alive, I'd bet they live in the same neighborhood," Alex said.

"Family is a big deal to mobsters," Danny agreed.

"Well then," Alex said. "Let's start with them."

19

THREATS AND DEALS

Having a direction in the murder of Amanda Keeler, or rather Ann Gallagher, gave Alex that feeling that always inspired him to action. It felt like the case was moving again, like there were things to be discovered, just waiting for him to find.

The reality that greeted him as he entered his office the following morning was that of having the names of three long disappeared gangsters and no obvious way to find them. The best he could come up with was more records crawling. The missing gangsters had families, wives, kids, maybe a few nieces or nephews. If he could locate any of them, there was a chance he'd find the missing men.

A very slim chance, he reminded himself with a sigh.

He'd almost rather be shot again than spend another day in the library.

Almost.

Leaning his crutches up against the bookshelf behind his desk, he eased himself into his chair. He'd have to get over to the city records office eventually to look up marriage and birth records while Sherry would take the library to look for any hint of the missing men or their legacy. As much as Alex didn't want to spend the day at the records office, he didn't envy Sherry the task of crawling through newspapers looking for any hint of the missing mobsters. It wasn't like looking for a needle in a haystack, it was like looking for a specific haystack in Kansas.

The only saving grace was that Alex needed to wait for Danny to call before he could get started. They'd spent several hours going through the Connolly mob's file looking for everything they could find on James Fahey, and Michael and Liam Cohan. There wasn't much, but since they were known criminals, Danny pointed out that they would each have individual files in the police records. Those would naturally have more specific information on the three. Maybe enough information to track them down, so before Alex and Sherry wasted a day, he wanted to make sure it was absolutely necessary.

With another sigh, Alex opened his right-hand drawer and pulled out a tumbler and his good bottle of single malt Scotch. Pouring two fingers into the tumbler, he sipped it, then lit a cigarette and took a long drag. It was barely eight o'clock and he felt tired.

Since he had time to kill while Danny and the police tracked down their files, Alex picked up the top folder on his pile of work. Opening it, he found the information he'd gathered on Linda Kellin's supposed poisoner. He wanted to just shut it and move on, but he was sure she would call again today whether she managed to track down enough of the potential victims or not.

Before he started in on the file, he took another sip of the Scotch then tapped the 'talk' key on his intercom once, the signal to Sherry that he was in. Before he could settle into the mysterious poisoning folder, however, the intercom clicked twice then once more. That was the signal that someone was waiting for Alex in the front office, someone who wasn't a friend.

Alex wanted to swear. His usual procedure for this was to go back into his vault, then through the door to his Empire Tower apartment. From there, Alex would travel down the restricted elevator to Empire Station, then back up to the twelfth floor and into his office.

The circuitous path only took a few minutes, and would make sure to keep his vault entrance a secret. Of course that depended on his being able to walk normally. Looking up at his crutches, Alex was not excited to make the trek. He considered just going down to the front office and pretending he'd come in before Sherry, but if the unfriendly visitor had been waiting outside the office early, he'd know that was a lie.

"Terrific," he growled, downing the rest of his Scotch before levering himself out of his chair and gathering up his crutches.

It took nearly fifteen minutes for Alex to limp his way through his emergency client route. As he approached the door to his offices, he heard a man's voice raised in anger. It had the timbre and energy of someone used to raising his voice and Alex decided that whoever it was, he was going to throw the fellow out.

"Alex," Sherry called out in relief as he came in, "This is Alderman Snow, he's been waiting for you."

"I heard," Alex said, pushing a hard edge into his voice as he closed the door behind him.

The man waiting in his office was almost as tall as Alex, but paunchy, a former athlete gone to seed. He had a bald head and a square jaw with hard, dark eyes and the stub of a cigar clamped between his teeth. Iggy had often told Alex that politics wasn't a gentleman's game, it was a knife fight in a dark closet. If Iggy was right, Alderman Snow looked like the kind of man who could make that work for him.

Alex remembered the name, Alderman Malcolm Snow, the man who was using Ann Gallagher's death to stir up trouble before the special election. He wondered what Snow was doing in his office first thing in the morning?

"It's about time you got here," Snow growled, turning from Sherry to Alex.

"Shut up," Alex growled right back, "this isn't your district, Alderman, you don't have any weight to throw around here. You shout at Miss Knox again and I'll throw you out on your ear."

It was clear Snow wasn't used to being addressed like that and his face clouded over in rage. Before he could explode, however, he mastered himself; whatever he wanted in Alex's office was more important to him than venting his rage.

Okay, Alex thought, *why are you here, Mr. Alderman?*

Pound of Flesh

"Cute," he said, using his cigar to indicate Alex's crutches. "I see you have trouble keeping your mouth shut as well."

When Alex didn't respond, he went on.

"I'm running to fill Senator Copeland's Senate seat, God rest his soul," Snow said. "I think the country is headed in the wrong direction and New York City is leading the way."

"And what?" Alex asked. "You want to put a campaign sign on my door?"

Snow chuckled but it was a mirthless sound.

"I want to get federal money into this city," Snow said. "We've pared the mobs back, crushed the street gangs, but still people can't walk home at night."

"You're referring to the murder of Amanda Keeler," Alex said, being careful not to call her Ann Gallagher.

"Yeah," Snow said, leaning in close, "that was a real mess. That poor girl was cut up by some psycho and the cops...well, they covered it up."

Alex wanted to ask how the alderman thought the cops covered it up? It wasn't common for the police to invite the news boys to a crime scene, especially one so gruesome.

"What's your point, Mr. Snow?" he asked instead.

"The city ain't safe, and the cops are incompetent," Snow said with no trace of sarcasm. "At least that's what I thought yesterday morning. But then I came across an interesting bit of news. You see, I've got friends everywhere, even down at that rag, *The Midnight Sun*. One of my friends, he called me and said that right before the Sun printed that story about the guy with amnesia, one of their head guys sent a reporter over to Bellevue, told him to schmooze with the nurses."

"So?" Alex said. "I'm sure tabloids do all kinds of sleazy things to get their stories."

"Yeah, but that reporter, the one their top brass sent over to Bellevue? He didn't have any instructions on what to look for, just who he needed to talk to."

"You said you have friends everywhere, Mr. Snow," Alex retorted, "I'm sure the tabloid does too."

Snow laughed at that, this time with genuine humor.

"You're very smooth, Mr. Lockerby," he said.

"I'm in the people business," Alex fired right back, leaving his voice gruff and uninviting simply for the irony of it.

"You know, I had the same thought," Snow said, thumping Alex with the hand that held his cigar and sending a cascade of ashes falling down onto the rug. "I found out that you've got lots of friends, like one of the bigwig reporters at *The Midnight Sun*, Bill Tasker. You're also friends with that Chinaman lieutenant, Danny Pak."

"Pak is a Korean name," Alex growled, forgetting for a moment that the origin of Danny's name wasn't common knowledge.

"Whatever," Snow said, waving his cigar dismissively. "The point is, lots of people over at the Central Office know that you and he are friends, that you helped him crack the Addison Smith case, the one that made him a detective in the first place."

"It isn't a secret that Danny and I are friends," Alex said. Snow seemed to be trying to imply something but he hadn't managed to make himself understood yet.

"And when I found that out," Snow continued, "I had one of my friends look into your pal's expense reports." Snow leaned in again. "You'll never guess what I found."

"Danny drinks too much coffee?" Alex hazarded a guess.

"I already knew he was at the Amanda Keeler crime scene," Snow said, "but imagine my surprise when I found out that he added a consultant to his expense report."

Alex had to force his face to remain impassive.

"So what?" he said. "I consult for the police all the time, and not just for Lieutenant Pak."

"I just think it's awfully coincidental that you were at the Keeler crime scene and then you went and leaked the story to your pal Tasker over at *The Midnight Sun*. Oh, you spiked the DA's case, but good. The cops wanted this to go away and you threw them to the wolves."

"Are you going to get to the point sometime soon or do we still have to change trains somewhere?" Alex demanded, letting anger flow into his voice.

"The point is this," Snow declared, mirroring Alex's anger, "what do

Pound of Flesh

you think would happen if I took this story to your friend Lieutenant Pak's boss? What would he say about your activities?"

Alex wanted to laugh out loud, but he bit the inside of his lip hard. Callahan wouldn't have much to say, he'd been in on Alex's leaking Adam's story to the press.

"He'd say that your little story lacks evidence," Alex said.

That clearly wasn't the response Snow had anticipated, and his face soured.

"Well then what would happen if I told my story to the *Times*?" he demanded.

"I suspect," Alex said, choosing his words carefully, "that if you try to sully my reputation with slanderous lies, I'd be forced to find out who your little friend at the *Times* is and expose them. Maybe look into every story they ever wrote, especially any that said nice things about you. It wouldn't take me long, Mr. Snow," Alex continued, raising his voice, "this is what I do, after all. How do you think your Senate campaign would weather that exposé?"

Snow didn't get to be an alderman, and now a Senate candidate, by being foolish. He knew when to pick his battles and he knew he was beat here. The look in his eyes as he stormed out of Alex's office, however, said that this wasn't a defeat, but rather a strategic retreat.

"He's going to be back," Sherry said once the heavy tromp of his footsteps faded away, "isn't he?"

"He is," Alex said, keeping his eyes on the door as if he expected Snow to be back.

"What was he after?" Sherry went on. "It was like he was trying to get you to back off a case, but he never mentioned anything."

"He wants to stir the pot," Alex said. "The story about Amanda's death, or rather the brutality of her death, has got the city talking. It's good press for Snow, since he's talking about reform."

"That still doesn't explain why he showed up here."

"The story had shock value, but it's running out of steam," Alex explained. "People can only be shocked for so long before they move on. He needs to turn the story in a more sensational direction by implying that the police are either incompetent, or better yet that they're corrupt."

"How could he make it look like the police are corrupt?" Sherry asked.

"If he had evidence that the police were trying to hide the murder, make it go away, that would look bad."

"You mean like if they tried to railroad a man with no memory of the crime?"

"Exactly."

"That still doesn't explain why he came to you," Sherry pointed out.

"He thinks I leaked the story about Adam to the press because I thought the police were involved in a cover up," Alex said. "He came here hoping to find a friend. When he didn't, he tried to bully me into staying out of his way."

"So what happens now?"

"Now, he's trying to figure out what happened. He knows I'm on the side of the police, so now he's wondering why the police would release the story about Adam."

"Do you think he'll figure it out?"

Alex wasn't sure. Snow was a brash bully, that much was clear, but there had been a cruel intelligence behind the man's bluster. He pivoted from fishing for an ally to his extortion tactics without a pause.

"I think that whatever story Mr. Snow tells himself about this meeting, he'll try to use me as a pawn in his election game."

"Should we worry?" Sherry asked, an edge of fear creeping into her voice.

Alex let out a pent-up breath through his nose.

"No," he said at last. "If he becomes too much of a bother, I'll have Andrew turn him into a toad."

Sherry snickered at that.

"Why not Sorsha?" she asked.

"Are you kidding?" Alex shot back. "Sorsha would kill him."

That broke the tension in the room and they both laughed.

"One good thing about Mr. Snow's interruption," Alex said. "I remember that I was supposed to do some research today for Detective Arnold."

"When Danny called me last night, he said we'd be doing research for him," Sherry said.

Pound of Flesh

She had a slight smile on her red-painted lips, but then, she always did when she mentioned Danny.

"Once he calls, we probably will be," Alex admitted. "Until then, I think I know how to save us some time on Detective Arnold's case."

With that, he limped back to his office and eased down in his chair again. The cigarette he'd left burning in the ash tray had gone out, so he lit a new one and picked up the phone. Dialing the number of *The Midnight Sun* from memory, he waited until their front office secretary connected him with Billy.

"Alex," his friend greeted him. "Thanks for that last story, it did gangbusters."

"Hey, Billy," Alex said, "do me a favor and go close your door."

Billy complied, then came back.

"You want to tell me why I did that?" he asked once he'd picked up the phone.

"You know that alderman, the one who's running to fill Senator Copeland's seat?"

"Malcom Snow," Billy said. "He's making a lot of noise in the press these days, especially about that murder in the alley."

"Well, he came by my office this morning, said he had an inside source at your paper and they implied to him that I gave you the story about Adam."

There was a short silence on the line, then Billy came back.

"Did he say who?"

"No such luck," Alex said. "I'm not going to let that worry me, I just thought you ought to know."

"I'm guessing that's not the only reason you called," Billy said. "You could have told me that with the door open."

"I always knew you were smart," Alex said. "Listen, I've got this other case I need a bit of help with, might be right up your alley."

Billy hesitated.

"I guess I do owe you," he said. "What do you need?"

"*The Midnight Sun* was around during Prohibition, right?"

"Oh, yeah," Billy laughed. "Those were prime days for the tabloids. Why do you ask?"

"I need to find out the names of any women who might have run high class speakeasies. Do you think your records would have something like that?"

"I'd have to ask some of the old timers," Billy said, "but it sounds like the kind of background information we'd keep around to help flesh out a story."

"Good. Have someone dig through that and give me a call if you find anything."

"This woman speakeasy boss," Billy said in an all too casual tone of voice, "would that lead to an interesting story?"

Alex hadn't given it much thought, but the discovery of a secret speakeasy in a nice, quiet inner-ring neighborhood might make an excellent story.

"It's got potential, but I have to okay it with my client before I let you in," he said.

"Promise me you'll do your best."

"Always," Alex said before hanging up.

20

ACTIONABLE

Alex reached for the folder full of Linda Kellin's sick people but hesitated. Reaching past the folder, he poured himself another two fingers of Scotch, then sat back in his chair and sipped it. Even if Linda managed to scrape together enough data to populate his big map, it was likely he'd be down at the hall of records with Danny.

"Boss?" Sherry's voice came from the door, causing him to look up. She was leaning against the frame with her legs crossed one over the other and one hand behind her back. "Are you still talking with Miss Kellin about people getting sick?"

"Is that a rhetorical question?" Alex said, sipping his Scotch, "I hope."

Sherry pulled her hand from behind her back and held up a copy of the *New York Observer*, one of the minor papers in town. Across the top in large block letters was one word; *Outbreak?*

"Damn," Alex said, finishing his Scotch in one go. "Give me the highlights."

Sherry turned the paper over and looked at the article.

"They say that their reporters have seen a lot of people coming into the local hospitals, they also say calls to independent doctors are up as well."

"Any specifics?" Alex asked.

"Nothing concrete," Sherry went on. "Mostly it's a lot of scary language and innuendo suggesting that there might be some new disease stalking Manhattan."

"What about an alchemical elixir called Behring's Antiserum?"

Sherry scanned the article again, then shook her head.

"Nothing about alchemy at all."

"Well thank God for small favors," Alex groused. "The city's alchemists will have time to make as much of the antidote as they can before there's a full-on panic."

"Won't this cause a panic?" Sherry echoed Alex's thoughts.

"Not till the *Times* picks it up," Alex said. "Some people will believe the *Observer* story, but most will wait for confirmation. I hope," he added.

"Glad I could brighten your day," Sherry said, then she dropped the paper on his desk. "What are you going to do?"

"I've got to call Linda," Alex said. "She and her doctor friends need to keep their traps shut. If one of these muckrakers hears the word 'poison,' there'll be blood in the streets."

"Good luck," Sherry said, then she turned back into the hall and headed back to her desk.

Alex picked up his phone and dialed Linda's number, waiting as the phone rang on the other end.

"Kellin Alchemy," Linda's voice greeted him.

"It's Alex."

"Did you talk to the press?" she demanded before Alex could get a word in edgewise. "There was a story in the *Observer* this morning, Dr. Kitteridge is in a panic."

"No," Alex said, forcefully enough to stop the flow of words. "Whoever wrote that story either noticed a lot of sick people at the hospitals or someone you treated talked."

"What are we going to do?" Linda cried. "Alex, you have to help, we have to find out where this is coming from. If there's a panic, a lot of people will get killed."

"I know," Alex said, trying to keep his voice calm and even. "What did you and your doctor friends find out?"

"We managed to track down forty-two of the poisoning victims."

"Don't say 'poison' again," Alex insisted. "Just call them 'sick.' We don't want to run the risk of anyone overhearing."

"Okay, we've got the information you wanted on forty-two of the sick people," she said.

"Good. Do you have it with you?"

"I've got a few, but Dr. Kitteridge has the rest."

"Close your shop and get over here right away," Alex said. "Call Kitteridge and have him meet you here with his list. The sooner we find out where this is coming from, the better."

"I'll catch the skycrawler right away," she said.

"I might not be here when you arrive," Alex said. He could hear her take in a breath to protest but he rushed on before she could. "I've got to help the police track down a killer, but my apprentice Mike Fitzgerald will be here. He can plot your data on the big map just as easy as I can and once you can see it laid out, you'll know where whatever this is came from."

There was a short pause on the line, then Linda agreed and hung up.

Alex replaced the handset in the phone's cradle and sat back, letting out a slow breath. It wasn't even nine o'clock and his day was stacking up with enough work to keep him busy for a week.

"And all of it a five-alarm emergency," he sighed. He was tempted to take another drink, but the way things were going, he'd need his wits about him. Speaking of wits, maybe he should call Iggy and have him help Mike.

Alex discarded the idea as soon as it crossed his mind. Plotting locations on the big map was something Mike did every day when he used finding runes, so he didn't need a nursemaid.

There was one thing he needed to do and he pressed the 'talk' key on his intercom.

"Sherry, would you ask Mike to come in here for a minute?"

"Will do, Boss," she replied and a few moments later, Mike was in Alex's doorway. He was a small man but with the kind of energy one usually associated with a cocker spaniel. When Alex first met him, Mike was hocking simple runes on Runewright Row, but he had excellent foundational knowledge. With a little training and encouragement, Alex reckoned he'd make an excellent runewright, and Alex had been right. Now Mike handled most of the basic cases Lockerby Investigations took on, freeing Alex up for more complex problems.

If Alex was honest with himself, Mike would be ready for some of those big cases sooner rather than later.

"You wanted to see me, Alex?" he said.

"You know Linda Kellin?"

"The alchemist? I've heard her name, but I've never met her."

"Well, you're about to," Alex said. "She's on her way over here with a doctor named Kitteridge. They're tracking this bout of sickness, and I want you to help them plot the locations where the sick people live, work, and eat on the big map, then point them at the source."

"Should I go with them after that?"

Alex considered that. If it was a case of someone actually poisoning people, there might be an element of danger.

"Use your own judgement," Alex said, "but before you go, call Captain Callahan over at the Central Office and ask for a patrolman to go with you."

"Will do," Mike said, then he headed back to his office.

Before Alex could pick up the extinguished cigarette in his ash tray, his intercom buzzed.

"I have Danny on the line for you," Sherry said.

Alex pressed the 'talk' key and asked her to send the call to his phone.

"Ready for a scintillating day of government efficiency?" Alex asked as he picked up the phone, not bothering to keep the ennui out of his voice.

"That'll have to wait," Danny said, with an indecent amount of energy in his voice. "I got ahold of the files on our missing gangsters and lo and behold, one of them, Liam Cohan married a girl from a wealthy family named Camilla Stone."

Alex's morning had already been long enough that it took him a moment to process what his friend said.

"Does the Stone family have a big house somewhere where the family gathers?"

"Jersey City," Danny said.

"You think maybe he and the missus have a little place close by?"

"I made a quick call to the Jersey City land office this morning," Danny said, "and the Stones own a mansion in the Heights and a beach house on Long Island."

"Nothing suspicious about that," Alex said.

"Strangely, they also own a house in Hoboken."

"Well, that's not as tony as the Heights," Alex noted.

"It's also not a very big house," Danny said.

"You mean it's the ideal kind of place for a wanted man to lay low and blend in," Alex said.

"You up for a trip to New Jersey?" Danny asked.

"I'll be waiting on the sidewalk," Alex said.

Danny promised to be there in fifteen minutes and hung up. Alex was not content to wait in his office for the chance to actually do something, so he grabbed his crutches and his coat and headed for the street.

As much as Alex was craving some action, he spent the next three hours just waiting. The trip from Manhattan to Hoboken in Danny's car was both uncomfortable on Alex's injured foot and boring. The only exciting bit was the trip through the Holland Tunnel where all Alex could do was imagine the millions of tons of water pressing down on the man-made structure.

Magic was something Alex could trust, but he was never quite sure about engineering. Engineers were way too enamored of their slide rules.

Once Danny reached New Jersey, they had to wait for a lieutenant from the Jersey City police to meet them, then wait some more for their captain to organize a sufficient number of officers to surround the house in Hoboken.

"Wake up," Danny said as he climbed back into the driver's seat of his green Ford. For as old as it was, the car was still in excellent shape, if a little out of style. Alex would have liked the ability to put his seat back, but with only one row of seats, that wasn't an option either.

"I'm up," Alex said, moving his stiff leg and throbbing foot off the dashboard. "Have the Keystone Cops finally figured out what we're doing?"

"Don't start," Danny cautioned, pushing the button that brought the engine to life.

"We should have just showed up on Liam's doorstep and grabbed him," Alex grumbled.

Danny laughed at that.

"Yes, I can just see you giving chase if he decided to run."

"You've got your gun, right?"

"That'd be even better," Danny said. "Kill our only witness before we could question him? Callahan would have my badge."

Alex crossed his arms and slumped in his seat as Danny pulled out behind a Jersey City police car.

"Don't sweat it," Danny continued. "The Jersey City cops are going to turn Liam Cohan over to us, we just have to follow protocol."

Alex didn't like that and he said so. Danny just laughed again and concentrated on following their escort car. They headed north into a residential area with neat little homes on small plots of ground. Eventually, the houses and the lots got a bit bigger and perfectly painted and level picket fences were in evidence.

"Looks like this is it," Danny said as the squad car ahead of them pulled over to the curb. "Stay in the car," he said as he shut off the car and jumped out.

Alex waited while Danny and four officers from the front vehicle ran up to the house, then opened his door and dragged himself out. Two patrol cars pulled to the curb behind Danny and more uniformed men swarmed along the curb and up to the house.

From what Alex could see as he limped behind them, Danny and the Jersey City lieutenant were pounding on the front door while the uniforms swarmed around the house to cover other exits. After half a minute, Danny and the lieutenant stepped aside so an officer with broad shoulders and no perceivable neck could hit the front door with his shoulder, smashing it in.

For all the waiting he had to do for Danny to set all this up, he had to admit the Jersey boys were efficient.

A tide of uniforms entered the house and Alex took his time limping up the sidewalk on his crutches. As he approached, he could hear the officers clearing the house room by room and floor by floor. By the time Alex reached the front door, they'd finished, but there was no indication that they'd found their man.

"All clear," the Jersey lieutenant called, then he swore.

"No Liam?" Alex said as Danny and the Jersey lieutenant reached the landing on the main floor.

"I thought I told you to stay in the car," Danny said, a bit of attitude in his voice. Clearly he was irritated.

"I got lonely," Alex said, offering the two men a cigarette as an ice breaker. "Has our little bird flown?"

"Who is this guy?" Jersey said. He was a wiry man about five foot ten with rough features, a five o'clock shadow, and a no-nonsense attitude that seemed to roll off him in waves.

"Alex Lockerby, meet Lieutenant Tom Miller," Danny said. "Lieutenant, this is Alex Lockerby, one of my best consultants."

"Consultants?" Miller scoffed. "Don't you guys handle your own police work across the river?"

"Alex is a special case," Danny said with no trace of embarrassment.

"I'm house trained," Alex added.

"Uh-huh," Miller mumbled noncommittally, then he turned back to Danny. "What do you want to do now?"

"This is where Alex comes in," Danny said. "When we checked the master bedroom, there were open drawers, clothes on the floor, and no sign of a jewelry box. There was some makeup in the bathroom, but not much."

"Signs Mr. and Mrs. Cohan left in a hurry," Alex concluded, turning to Miller. "Someone tipped them off."

To his credit the lieutenant didn't snap back at either Alex or Danny, he just clenched his fists and nodded.

"That's the way I figured it," he said, "And I didn't need a consultant."

"That's not what we need Alex for," Danny said. "We need him to find Liam now that he's on the run."

Alex looked at Danny, then at the stairs leading up to the second floor.

"All right," he sighed, then handed his crutches to Danny and hopped up the stairs. It wasn't exactly dignified, but Alex had nothing to prove to Miller or his boys.

"What are we doing?" Miller asked as he and Danny followed Alex up.

"Looking for what the Cohans left behind," Alex said, taking his crutches back from Danny.

He didn't have to be told which was the master bedroom, as it was much larger than the other two on this floor. The bed was neatly made, but loose clothing and personal items were strewn chaotically across it. Both dressers had drawers pulled open, many with articles of clothing hanging out of them.

"Whenever the Cohans got the call, they moved fast," Alex observed.

"Old habit," Miller guessed.

The dressers in the Cohans' bedroom were two different styles. One was tall with a drawer on the top, then a double cabinet door in the middle with two drawers beneath. This was typically a man's dresser with drawers inside the cabinet to hold ties, socks, cufflinks, and other such things. The shorter dresser was the kind women used with three drawers on either side. Between the two sets of drawers was a middle portion with a lowered top and a large mirror so the lady of the house could sit and do her makeup.

Alex made his way to the ladies' dresser first and began pulling the drawers open one by one.

"What are you looking for?" Miller asked, when neither Alex nor Danny explained.

"Something of importance to Mrs. Cohan," Alex said. "She left in a hurry, so it's very likely that she left something here that's important to her by accident. If I can find it, I can use a finding rune to locate her."

Pound of Flesh

"A finding rune!" Miller exclaimed. "They've got a range of a hundred yards tops. Do you think they're hiding in the cellar?"

Danny put a restraining hand on Miller's shoulder.

"Alex's finding runes are a bit more powerful than that," he said.

"What if they split up?" Miller said. "Even if you find Camilla, it might not lead us to Liam. Why aren't you searching his stuff?"

"If they split up, we'll use Camilla's wedding ring to track Liam," Alex said. "And I'm not searching Liam's things because he was a lieutenant in the Connolly mob. A man like that knows how to travel light and how to go on the lam. He probably doesn't have keepsakes."

"His wife, on the other hand," said Danny, "doesn't have years of running from the cops to fall back on."

"Exactly," Alex said, turning over the contents of a drawer that appeared to contain nothing but lacy undergarments and gauzy robes. At the bottom, tucked into a back corner was a small bundle of letters tied with a red ribbon. "Bingo," Alex said, holding his prize aloft.

As the others gathered around, Alex pulled the top envelope from the bundle and extracted the letter. It was a brief note from Liam telling Camilla that he was safe and that he'd be coming for her soon. Beneath the letter, Liam had written the phrase, 'with all my love.'

"He must have written this when he went on the lam thirteen years ago," Danny guessed.

"Okay," Miller said, "so this is special to Camilla, what happens now?"

Alex set the letters on the dresser top, then opened his rune book. He wasn't about to open a door to his massive vault in front of the Jersey City cops, letting them see his best tricks, so he paged through until he found a safe rune. This would open a small door into his vault that ended in a wooden box that Alex had mounted to the wall. From the outside, it would look like a sealed space in the shape of a box, just like it had when all Alex could use were safe runes.

Tearing it out of his book, he licked it and stuck it to a bare patch of wall. Once he was done, he chalked a square around it, then used his gold lighter to ignite the rune. It flared to life and a moment later a square steel door melted out of the wall.

"Well I'm impressed," Miller said in a neutral voice.

"This is just the warm-up," Danny said. "The real show is about to start."

Alex tried not to roll his eyes as his friend buttered him up. He opened the safe door with an ornate key from his trouser pocket, then took out his kit bag. Actually it was a duplicate of his kit bag that he kept in the safe box for just this kind of occasion. He'd have to be sure to restock it next time he was in his vault, but that was a task for later.

Removing the bag, Alex shut the safe and the door melted back into the wall, leaving nothing but the chalk outline.

Easing down to his knees, Alex set aside the crutches, then pulled out his rolled-up map. Since the map was of Manhattan, Alex set it aside and pulled out a large piece of folded paper that usually never left the bottom of his bag. Unfolding it revealed a map of most of New York state, along with New Jersey, New Hampshire, Vermont and a lot of Pennsylvania.

Setting this down, Alex took out his finding box and removed a new tin compass. Setting the compass on the map, Alex placed the bundle of love letters atop it, then flipped through his red-backed rune book for a finding rune. Once he'd extracted one, he added it to the pile, then took out his lighter.

"Focus on Liam and touch the map," he instructed.

"We didn't know him," Danny said.

"No," Alex admitted, "but you know a lot about him. Trust me, it will help."

Danny and the lieutenant exchanged glances, then both of them put their hands on the map. Alex touched the map with his left hand, then lit the rune with his right. It erupted into a shower of orange sparks that eventually solidified into a spinning rune. Alex held his breath as the rune spun. He'd never really been sure if his runes worked so well because of how they were written, or because of how he used them. It was probably some combination of the two, but he hoped his lack of magic wouldn't hamper the rune's ability to work.

Much to Alex's relief, the rune began to slow its rotations until it finally stopped and then burst into a shower of sparks. Reaching out to take the letters off the compass, Alex observed that the needle was pointing northeast rather than straight north.

"Found her," he said with a grin.

"What?" Miller said, obviously confused.

"Follow the needle," Alex said, sliding the compass slowly across the map until the needle began to spin. He picked it up then, revealing the part of the map it had covered.

"Long Island City," Miller read from the map. "They can catch a train there to anywhere."

"Not anywhere," Alex corrected him. "If they wanted to go west, they'd just catch the train here in Hoboken. If they went east to Long Island City, they have to either be going north to Connecticut or further east to Long Island itself. Liam is a city boy, but lots of mob families bought property on the north shore back in the day."

"How much do you want to bet that's where they're going?" Danny asked with a grin.

"No bet," Lieutenant Miller said, shaking his head. "That's some trick, scribbler," he said with no trace of mockery. "It looks like you boys can handle the mobster from here, but I might have some work for your skills, Lockerby. If you don't mind crossing the river, that is."

Alex fished into his pocket for one of his business cards and handed it over. He wasn't thrilled about being on the Jersey City policeman's radar, since he had more than enough work as it stood. That said, it would be nice to have another regular client.

"Call me anytime," he said.

21

RUBY

Alex grumbled as the Jersey City police crawled through Liam Cohan's house looking for anything that might mark him as Ann Gallagher's killer. He'd come along with Danny in the hope of catching Liam, not to do five minutes of investigation and then be sent to sit on the couch in the parlor.

Unfortunately, in the time it had taken to gather up his kit, Liam had moved too far away even for Alex's finding rune. The compass had lost its connection and now doggedly pointed north. Without that pointing the way to the missing gangster, no one was in a hurry to leave.

In the old days, the rune wouldn't have been able to find Camilla even as far as Manhattan with the Hudson in the way, but Alex had come a long way since then.

"Having fun?" Danny asked, a sarcastic grin on his face.

"Heaps and heaps," Alex said in a complete deadpan. "Are you planning on leaving any time soon?"

"That's the good news," he said. "I've given the authorities in Long Island City Liam's description and Captain Callahan is having it sent to all the stations along the line. So, there's nothing holding us here."

"What if these Jersey boys find something?" Alex asked, not looking forward to coming back out here in that case.

"Lieutenant Miller knows what he's doing," Danny said, "if they find anything here, they'll let us know."

Alex had to admit that Miller seemed competent, but Iggy always told him not to trust police when it came to searches and investigations. Most patrol officers were good men, but they weren't trained investigators; their work might be thorough but it wasn't necessarily complete. So far, all his trip to the Garden State had gotten him was a sore foot and a chronic case of boredom. He'd almost rather be at the hall of records.

Almost.

"So we can go?" Alex said.

"Unless you've gotten comfortable," Danny said, his smirk widening.

"Just for that I should use my vault to get back to my office and leave you to drive the tunnel alone."

"You know it's not smart for you to use your vault to travel," Danny said, lowering his voice and looking around, "or to talk about it when some Jersey flatfoot might overhear."

"Relax," Alex said, pushing himself onto his good foot. "There are eleven officers in the house and eight of them are searching upstairs. Two are out back, going through the tool shed, and one is on the front door to keep away the curious public."

"How do you do that?" Danny asked, handing Alex his crutches.

"Count?" Alex said. "I learned that trick in school."

Danny gave him a flat look.

"I mean keeping track of eleven men."

"It's not all that tough," Alex said. "There were four men with Lieutenant Miller when we were upstairs. When we came down, I counted three men on the second floor, and there were three men in the kitchen when I came in here. Two of the men in the kitchen said they should check the tool shed, then they went out to the back yard. The last guy went upstairs about ten minutes ago. See, easy."

"Uh-huh," Danny said, clearly unconvinced. "You really are bored."

"Very," Alex affirmed as he headed for the front door.

An hour and a tunnel ride later, Danny pulled up in front of Empire Tower to drop Alex off. Despite his sour mood and his throbbing foot, Alex thanked his friend and headed inside to the elevator. Twelve floors later he was outside his office with a sigh of relief.

He walked in to find Sherry on the phone, and he stopped long enough to hang up his coat. As he did, however, he caught Sherry's conversation.

"No, he just walked in, Detective. Stand by for a minute."

Alex sighed and turned to face his pretty secretary.

"Detective Arnold?" he guessed.

Sherry nodded.

"He says he'd like your opinion on some evidence he dug up in the secret speakeasy case."

Alex thought about putting him off, but the little man could be doggedly determined when he wanted to be.

"Tell him I'll be with him in a minute, then send the call to my office," Alex said, limping heavily on his crutches. "Make that two minutes."

Almost exactly two minutes later, Alex's desk phone rang and he picked it up.

"Detective Arnold," he said, "I would have thought you'd have a suspect in custody by now."

"Have you ever been to a fancy dinner party?" Arnold asked.

Alex paused at the non-sequitur.

"I have," he admitted. Much to his chagrin, Sorsha had been dragging him to fancy parties and upper crust social events for the better part of a year now. "Why do you ask?"

"You know when they bring you that tray with all the little finger food on it?"

"Hors d'oeuvres," Alex supplied.

"Yeah, those," Arnold said. "Well whenever I get passed one of those trays I always take too long to pick something, because, well, there's just too many options."

"I take it your search for female speakeasy bosses was successful."

Pound of Flesh

"Excessively so," Detective Arnold said. "There were seventeen speakeasies that were run by women during Prohibition. Now, I eliminated the ones that couldn't be our girl, mostly they were either dead, in prison, or they were operating in bad parts of town when Prohibition ended."

"What about women who were working in speakeasies after the Hannover house was finished?" Alex said.

"We looked at that," Arnold admitted, "and that brought the number down to six."

"And all of them have gone to ground?"

"That seems to be the case, yes."

Alex thought about that for a moment, tapping his pencil on his notebook.

"What about the timing of building the new speakeasy?" Alex asked. "That probably means Thelma lost her old one."

"You think it got raided?" Arnold said. "The original one, I mean?"

"It's possible," Alex said. "Give Thelma a month or two to get her finances in order and buy the land, then the time to actually build the new speakeasy. Was there a high-class speakeasy that was shut down around that time?"

Alex waited while Detective Arnold checked his notes.

"There is one," he said, finally. "It was called the Silken Cushion, and it was raided in February of twenty-five."

"The house was built in the summer of twenty-five, so that tracks," Alex said. "Who's the lucky proprietor who operated the Silken Cushion?"

"That's one of our six," Arnold confirmed, "a Miss Ruby Tomlinson, but she went by Ruby T."

"That sounds an awful lot like Thelma Rubison," Alex observed, "just with the letters reversed."

"Seems a little obvious," Arnold said.

"Nobody knew who she really was," Alex countered. "As long as she didn't just use the same name, she could have called herself anything."

"Fair point," the detective admitted. "But that probably means Ruby Tomlinson was an alias too, so how do we find out who she really was?"

"Just look up the raid on the Silken Cushion," Alex suggested. "There has to be a record of her arrest, maybe even a mug shot."

"Well, that's a bit of a problem," Detective Arnold said. "I've got files on most of the speakeasies in question, but not on the Silken Cushion. There's two others without files as well."

That didn't make sense, since most speakeasies were known to police, even if the police didn't know exactly where they were. It wasn't likely they didn't have a file on the Silken Cushion.

Unless they did, Alex thought.

"The speakeasy under the Hannover's house was a high-class kind of place," Alex said. "The kind that would cater to the rich and famous."

"I can't argue with that," Arnold said.

"What if the file on the Silken Cushion is missing because it catered to the same clientele?" Alex suggested.

"You mean someone with influence got the file pulled?" Arnold said.

"Or destroyed," Alex added.

"Let's not jump to conclusions," Detective Arnold said. "If it was purposely misfiled or tagged as classified, it might just be somewhere else in the records room."

"Happy hunting," Alex said. "I'm going to check on Mrs. Hannover later today, so call me if you find something."

Detective Arnold promised that he would and Alex hung up. He hadn't intended to go visit Mrs. Hannover, but it had been a couple days since he'd been to the hospital, so he needed to check up on his client. In the meantime, however, he wanted to find out more about the Silken Cushion.

Reaching for the phone, intent on calling Billy Tasker, Alex was stopped by a knock on his door.

"Come," he said and Mike Fitzgerald stuck his head in.

"Sorry to bother you," he said, "but could you come take a look at the map?"

Alex had completely forgotten about Linda Kellin's poisoning map, but he covered that with a curt nod.

"Of course," he said, managing to suppress a sigh.

Pausing long enough to light a cigarette, Alex pushed himself back to his feet as Mike handed him his crutches. A few moments later, Alex followed Mike into the map room where Linda Kellin and an older man stood looking at the enormous map that occupied the top of a massive conference table. The man was older, probably in his mid-forties, with a Roman nose, dark, focused eyes and a square, clean shaven jaw. Based on the man's dress, a good suit coat and trousers over a silk vest, Alex guessed that this was Dr. Kitteridge.

"Alex," Linda said, a note of relief in her voice. "We did what you said, but this doesn't make sense."

"Nice to see you too," Alex said, but with a genuine smile. Linda wasn't exactly the spitting image of her mother, but every time he saw her he saw the ghost of Jessica in her face. The fact that he hadn't been to visit her grave in at least six months pained him once more, and he shifted his gaze to the man.

"Dr. Kitteridge, I presume," he said, limping to the table. "I'd shake your hand, but..." he shrugged with the crutches.

"And you must be Mr. Lockerby," Kitteridge said, in a low, calming sort of voice. "Linda's told me a great deal about you. I must confess, though, this quest to find out where our strange toxin is coming from isn't going according to plan."

Alex leaned over the map, where Mike had put flat-bottomed glass beads on every location Linda and the doctor had given him. Some of the beads were black while the rest were red.

"Which ones are homes and which are workplaces and diners?" he asked Mike.

"Black are the homes," Mike supplied. "The rest where the people work and eat."

As Alex had anticipated, the black beads were spread out in a line on the lower west side, from Hell's Kitchen down through the West Village and part of Greenwich. Most of the beads were in the outer ring, but a few made their way inward to the mid ring. That told Alex that, if the sick people were, in fact, being poisoned, it wasn't happening where they lived. With all the space the black beads covered, there should be more sick people in those areas if the poison was something in the city water.

Shifting his attention to the red beads, Alex found them much more concentrated. One was located just south of the Garment District where a halo of red beads encircled a spot on Twenty-Second Street. In truth, Alex had expected the red dots to be a lot more congested, piled up in one place where everyone who got sick ate, but there was no obvious location.

Worse still was the second halo.

Four blocks south and to the west was another grouping around a spot just north of an industrial area that bordered the Meatpacking District. If whatever was making people sick was, in fact, food-borne, it was entirely possible that it came from the meat packing plants. Unfortunately, just like the upper halo of red, there was no definitive location here. All around the area was a swirl of red, but there just weren't any clusters.

"What does it mean, Alex?" Mike asked after giving his mentor a few minutes to study the map. "Did I do it right?"

"You did, Mike," Alex said, straightening up.

"But what does it mean?" Linda repeated Mike's question.

"It means that it's time to get the police involved," Alex said. "This pattern means that people aren't getting sick from a single source." He looked up at Linda. "You were right. Someone is poisoning people."

Since Danny and Detective Arnold were busy, and Captain Callahan had his hands full with an impending P.R. nightmare, Alex asked for Lieutenant Detweiler when the Central Office operator picked up.

"Lieutenant," Alex said, putting on his most chipper voice. Since Danny got promoted to Lieutenant, Alex hadn't had much to do with the irascible Lieutenant of Division Three. Technically, Detective Arnold was in Detweiler's division, but Alex got the impression that Arnold and his boss didn't talk much.

"Who is this?" Detweiler demanded.

"It's your old pal, Alex Lockerby."

Detweiler mumbled something that Alex assumed was a curse.

"What do you want, scribbler," he said. "I'm busy."

"Did you see that bit in the *Observer*? About an outbreak of people getting sick?"

There was a short pause, then a much more hesitant Detweiler came back on the line.

"What about it?" he asked. His tone made it clear that he wasn't going to like the answer no matter what it was.

"By tomorrow, the papers are going to be all over this story," Alex said. "So far over one hundred people have gotten sick."

"How do you know any of that?"

"Because one of the alchemists who makes the treatment for this mysterious illness figured it out a few days ago," Alex explained. "We've been working on it with a doctor from Bellevue ever since."

"That wouldn't be the same doctor who let the cat out of the bag about our amnesiac killer, would it?"

"No," Alex said, resisting the urge to chuckle. "This is serious, Lieutenant. The doctor had been in contact with other hospitals and they're seeing the same illness crop up."

"What's that got to do with me?" Detweiler asked.

"I used the doctor's data to plot an infection map, only there's no single point where everyone got sick."

"That's not possible," Detweiler said. "Unless you're saying the city water is tainted."

"Nothing like that," Alex assured him. "If the city water was the problem, we'd have a lot more sick people, but you're on the right track. It looks like someone, or a group of someones, is infecting random people on purpose."

"You can prove this?" Detweiler asked, interest blossoming in his voice.

"No," Alex admitted, "I don't have the manpower, but a motivated police lieutenant might."

"That sounds like the kind of thing that would land a motivated lieutenant on the front page," Detweiler said. "Why aren't you tossing this softball to your pal, Danny?"

"Danny's busy," Alex said, not wanting to go into it. "Are you in or out? If you're in, I'll send you the doctor, the alchemist who first discovered it, and all my research. You get all the credit."

DAN WILLIS

"What if this craps out?"

"If it turns up nothing, then who's the wiser?" Alex said. "Right now the captain is up to his neck in a political nightmare, he probably won't even notice."

The line went silent for almost a minute, then Detweiler came back on.

"All right, scribbler, send over the doctor and everything and I'll look into it."

Alex thanked him and hung up before the irascible little man could change his mind. After that, he had Mike mark the placement of the red and black beads on a spare copy of the map Alex carried in his kit, and sent him, along with Linda and Dr. Kitteridge, over to the Central Office.

Detweiler might be a hard-bitten pain in the neck, but he wasn't stupid. Once Mike explained what the data meant, he'd have a small army of patrolmen canvass both areas. If something suspicious was going on, they'd find it.

As Alex leaned back in his comfortable office chair, he allowed himself a satisfied smile. So far today, he'd managed to locate a gangster who'd been missing for over a decade, figure out who used to own Mrs. Hannover's house, and put the police on the trail of a potential poisoner. The gangster and Thelma Rubison were still in the wind, but that was a problem for the police.

All in all, it had been a good day.

Alex had barely put his foot up on an open desk drawer, however, when the intercom buzzed.

"I've got Billy Tasker on the phone for you," Sherry said.

"Put him through," Alex said.

Alex scooped up the receiver a moment later when the phone rang.

"Billy," he said. "Did you find out anything?"

"Alex," Billy said, false acrimony in his voice. "I'm offended. You didn't tell me you were looking for Ruby."

"Ruby T?" Alex asked, remembering the name Danny had found.

"I don't know if she used a one letter last name," Billy said, "but Ruby was one of the most infamous speakeasy operators during Prohibition."

Pound of Flesh

"How come no one seems to have heard of her?" Alex said.

"Because she was a myth," Billy said, "or more accurately, a legend. No one knew who she was or if she even really existed."

That tracked with what Detective Arnold had learned. Even the police didn't seem to know Ruby's real name, or, if they did know it, they were still covering for her.

"What do the stories say?" Alex asked.

"Supposedly, she ran some high-class joint," Billy said. "It was the kind of place the rich and famous frequented, only the biggest of the big-wigs."

"Meaning it was protected," Alex said, giving his thoughts a voice.

"Yep. There was a story in our archives about the place being raided once but the police didn't arrest anyone and Ruby was nowhere to be found."

"Were the police looking for her?"

"I wouldn't think so," Billy said. "She was probably told about the raid ahead of time so she could clear out."

"Well if they weren't after her, and no one was arrested, why did the police raid the place?"

Billy hesitated.

"The guy that wrote this story speculated that the police were looking for someone called the Central Park Butcher."

"Who?" Alex said, trying to remember anything like that.

"I don't know," Billy said. "I was hoping you knew. I'm having my guy look for anything on this Butcher, but with a name like "the Butcher," it's bound to be something big."

Alex couldn't disagree.

"Do me a favor," he said. "Don't run anything on this until I get back to you."

"This is big stuff, Alex," Billy said, hesitation in his voice.

"True," Alex admitted, "but if there's anything to this Butcher business and Ruby knows something about it, it will be a much bigger story after I've had a chance to run it down."

"You guarantee me the first bite at the apple?"

"Always," Alex said. "Always."

205

22

THE BUTCHER

Alex looked up at the clock in his office and found the little hand pointing to three. He still had time to go see Mrs. Hannover before heading home for dinner. After his conversation with Billy, he wanted to go straight home and pick Iggy's brain. The raid on Ruby's speakeasy happened thirteen years ago, long before Alex had opened his detective agency in the little basement office in Harlem. Iggy, however, had been in the habit of reading the papers for interesting cases since before he fled to America.

If anyone knew about the Central Park Butcher, it would be Iggy.

That would have to wait, however. Detective Arnold had reminded him that he had a client, one that was currently in the hospital. Alex had pursued the case for the sake of her son Ricky, but he hadn't been back to check on his client and that was a serious lapse in his professional behavior.

Butcher or no Butcher, Alex needed to check up on Mrs. Hannover.

"Sherry," he said, after pushing the 'talk' key on the intercom. "Is there anything that needs my attention?"

"I've got a few things for you to look at," Sherry said, "but nothing that's time critical."

"I'm going out and I probably won't be back. I'll call in before closing."

"Okay," Sherry said, "I'll hold down the fort."

Alex looked at his crutches and sighed, then picked them up and limped down to the elevator.

Since there was a skycrawler station right in front of Bellevue Hospital, Alex got off the elevator at Empire Terminal and limped across the marble floor to the platform. At this time of day there weren't too many people in the station, so Alex slumped down onto one of the long wooden benches to await the next train.

With nothing better to do, he looked around at the other people waiting. Iggy had trained him early on to always be aware of his surroundings. That had graduated to what the old man called the deduction game. For that, Alex had to observe people and make educated guesses about them based only on what he could see. It was a skill that hadn't gotten as much of a workout since he started working in Empire Tower, and the connection to the brownstone through his vault didn't help either.

He still used those skills when he met clients and when investigating crime scenes, but he wasn't even doing that as much as he used to. As he thought about it, he decided he missed the game and resolved to shake the dust off his skills.

He started at Marnie's coffee bar. She wasn't there at the moment, but that would have been too easy; Alex had known Marnie for the better part of five years. Even at this time of day there was a young man behind the counter in a white shirt with a deeply red apron and a pair of spectacles. He was pouring out coffee into a paper cup for a man in workman's clothes.

"The kid goes to school and works here to pay his bills," Alex said. It was rather obvious after all. He wore spectacles because of excessive reading and there was an ink stain on the index finger of his left hand. Based on the way he held the heavy coffee with his left hand to pour, that would make him left-handed, so the ink stain was from writing.

"The workman is a bricklayer," Alex said, moving on to the other man. He was older, in his mid-thirties if Alex had to guess. His thickly calloused hands and muscled shoulders told Alex he worked with hard, heavy objects, and the traces of brownish dust clinging to his denim trousers meant stone of some kind. Since there was a crew repairing some of the cobblestones on the south side of Empire Tower, Alex surmised he came from there.

"Too easy," he said, shifting his vision.

There were the two security guards that protected the special elevator that went up to Barton Electric, but Alex knew both of them. The older man was Bert Cummings, and the younger one was Bob Benjamin. Bert was a pleasant enough fellow, but he kept to himself, while Bob was a chatterbox who talked to Alex every chance he got.

Moving on, Alex looked across the platform. Five people were there; a businessman attempting to rub a stain off his tie, a young woman with a little girl in tow, a portly gentleman who kept checking his watch, and a man in a dark suit who sat opposite Alex reading a newspaper.

The man with the stain had clearly just eaten in the terminal cafe and spilled something on his tie. The woman held onto the little girl's hand and the girl made no effort to pull away. Clearly mother and daughter, though why they were out in the city at this hour was still a mystery. The portly man was clearly a stockbroker. He was checking his watch to ensure he could get back to his office before the market closed.

Alex felt a subtle shift in the air, followed by the smell of ozone. He'd ridden the elevated crawlers enough to know the signs of an approaching skybug. The southbound car would be pulling into the station in less than half a minute.

Grabbing his crutches, he stood, then put on his hat. By the time he limped over to the platform, the others had heard the approaching crawler. The only one who hesitated was the man with the newspaper.

Now that Alex thought about it, the man had been sitting casually, with his legs crossed, but hadn't turned a single page in the newspaper the entire time he'd been sitting there.

"He was also turned away from the platform," Alex said. "Like he didn't want anyone to see his face."

Alex turned back to the platform as the skycrawler rumbled to a stop on its dozens of churning purple legs. With a hiss and a crackle, the car settled down onto the support blocks provided for it and the rear door hissed open. Several people got off, then the others began to board. Looking over his shoulder, Alex noted that the man with the newspaper now had it tucked under his arm, but walked with his head down so his hat brim concealed his face.

When it was Alex's turn to board, the man with the stained tie held his crutches while Alex hopped up into the car. He continued to hop to the first row of backward facing seats before sitting down. From that vantage point, he could get a good look at the newspaper man once he got on board.

When the man boarded, however, he took off his hat and made his way up the circular staircase to the upper deck of the crawler. He made the act of taking off the hat seem casual, but he kept it high as he went, concealing his face until he was up the stairs.

Everyone else had stayed on the main level, but the woman with the child and the man with the stained tie wouldn't have been able to see his face as he boarded. The only person who could have seen him, if not for the hat, was Alex.

So he's following me, Alex thought. *He feels safe in the upper deck, since it will take me time to get off with my crutches.*

Alex considered moving to sit next to the door so he could hop off quickly at his stop and put some distance between himself and the other man. It wasn't a bad idea, since his 1911 was safely secured in his vault. Still, it was unlikely the man would try to grab him on the platform outside Bellevue; there would be too many people there, even at this hour.

Ultimately, Alex rejected the idea. He didn't know who this man was or what he wanted, and that information would no doubt prove extremely interesting. All Alex needed to do was lure the man into the hospital, then use a vault rune to grab his gun. Once the man made his move, Alex would be ready for him and then he'd get some answers.

When the train stopped at Bellevue Station, Alex got off as if nothing out of the ordinary was happening. The reading man got off after him, but never actually got close. He moved at a leisurely pace as if he had nowhere to be anytime soon.

As Alex slowly descended the skycrawler platform, he wondered what the man wanted? Since the missing Irish mobster was the only case anyone might know he was working, he wondered if this was a calling card from Liam Cohan. That didn't seem likely as Liam was currently fleeing the law, but telephones existed and trains stopped to refuel.

It didn't seem likely his shadow was related to any of his other cases; no one knew that he was helping Detective Arnold with the speakeasy break-in or that he had helped identify the location of a potential poisoner.

Could it be someone from my past? he wondered.

Whatever the man wanted, Alex felt certain it wasn't to congratulate him on a former closed case. He shouldered his way through the front door of the hospital lobby and headed for the elevators.

"Hold the elevator," he said as one opened up a few yards away.

Ducking inside, Alex let go of his right crutch and punched the button for the top floor. As he pulled the cage closed behind him, he saw the dark suited man running. He wasn't going to arrive before the outer doors rumbled closed, but he could watch the floor indicator to see where Alex got off.

The elevator would take at least thirty seconds to climb the seven floors to the top, so Alex didn't have much time. Fortunately, the middle aged nurse riding in the car with him got off on the third floor. Once the door was closed again, Alex put his injured foot on the floor to hold his weight while he chalked a square on the wall of the elevator. Opening his left hand, he took out the folded vault rune he'd palmed on the crawler and stuck it to the wall. Lighting it quickly, he dug out his key and slotted it into the steel safe door that melted out of the elevator wall.

Pulling the safe door open, Alex ignored the spare crime scene kit, instead reaching all the way back to the rear wall and running his fingers down the right side until he felt a small groove. Pushing his fingernails into it, Alex pulled, causing the panel to slide out past a seam in the door, sticking out into the elevator. In the cavity behind the panel was Alex's .38 Special and several boxes of bullets.

The elevator began to slow, so Alex grabbed the pistol and dropped it into his coat pocket. He wanted to grab more bullets, but the outer

Pound of Flesh

door began to open. Sliding the hidden panel back into the safe, Alex closed the door and picked up his crutch, stepping in front of the disappearing door as someone outside pulled the door cage open.

"Oh," a pretty woman in a nurse's uniform said when she stepped inside. "Let me get the door for you."

Stepping back, she held the automatic outer door while Alex limped off. He thanked her and turned down the hallway toward the far end of the building. Alex figured he'd have about thirty seconds for his shadow to arrive, maybe less if he managed to catch the second elevator quickly.

Moving as quickly as he could without appearing to be in a hurry, Alex made his way to the desk where the ward nurse was on duty. The woman behind the desk was older, with bits of gray in her hair and a look of world weariness on her face. As Alex walked up, she was speaking with someone on the phone and she held up a finger for him to wait. Alex glanced at the patient roster hanging on a clipboard behind the desk.

"How can I help you?" the nurse asked as she hung up the phone.

"I'm here to see Harold Weis," Alex said, with his most charming smile. "What room is he in?"

"Are you a family member?" she asked, consulting the clipboard.

"No, ma'am, I'm his attorney, just here to go over a few points regarding his will."

Alex had used that one before. Many people who ended up in the hospital began feeling their mortality and made or altered their wills.

"Room seven-oh-five," she said, nodding further down the hall. "Just down there."

Alex thanked her and limped in the direction she indicated. The odd-numbered rooms were on the opposite side of the hall from the nurses' desk, so Alex ducked into an even-numbered room when he heard the elevator bell announce the car's arrival.

Inside the room was an older woman sleeping in the bed, so Alex quietly closed the door, leaving just a crack. As he listened, he heard the regular rap of dress shoe heels on the tiled floor. A moment later the footsteps stopped and he heard the voice of the bored nurse.

"Can I help you?" she asked.

211

"I'm with the Federal Bureau of Investigation," a smooth tenor voice said. "Did you see a man on crutches come by here?"

Alex clenched his hand into a fist. Of all the things he expected, the idea that the FBI was following wasn't one of them.

"Yes," the nurse said, "he went to see Mr. Weis in seven-oh-five. It's down that way."

The clack of the FBI man's shoes picked up again and Alex pushed the door he was hiding behind all the way closed. He wanted to get a look at the mysterious Fed, but unless the man was an idiot, he'd be looking for open doors so no one could slip behind him.

Alex held his breath as the footsteps passed the room where he was hiding, then waited until they became muffled, no doubt from the man entering room seven-oh-five. He was tempted to wait for the man to return, but there was a decent chance the man would search all the rooms on this floor, rather than believing Alex had fled on his crutches.

Pulling out his chalk again, he drew a door on the back of the hospital room door, then fumbled with his rune book, searching for a vault rune. Tearing one out, he licked it and stuck it to the chalk door before lighting it and stepping back.

Just as the steel surface melted out of the back of the room door, Alex heard the FBI man step back out into the hall. Trying to be as quiet as he could, Alex slotted his vault key into the plate in the center of the door and turned it with a click that sounded far louder than he remembered.

Years ago, Alex had rigged his vault door to swing inward rather than outward. He'd done it to prevent anyone from blocking his door open. To prevent the opposite problem, Alex had installed a pressurized gas cylinder attached to a piston that would, when activated, force the door closed with the force of a moving car. So far, Alex had never triggered the mechanism, but it was primed and ready to go.

The footsteps in the hall stopped as the FBI man was doubtless listening to see if he could detect Alex. Having no desire to answer FBI questions, or to be caught with a gun in his pocket, Alex leaned on his door, pushing it open. His crutches squeaked on the tile floor as he limped inside, and suddenly the hospital room behind him spun around.

Alex held his breath. The Fed had opened the room door, but hadn't seen the vault opening on its back. He could just shoulder the door closed and it would disappear without a trace, but it would take a second or two for the minor cleaning rune woven into the pattern to remove all traces of his chalk line. The only thing he could do was stay silent and wait.

The Fed's footsteps continued as he entered the room, though he didn't go far, just a couple of steps. With the room door open all the way against the wall, there wasn't any reason for the man to look behind it and, a moment later, he went back out into the hall, pulling the door closed behind him.

Alex waited until he heard the man move down toward the end of the hallway before he gently pushed his vault door closed and turned the inside handle. A moment later it disappeared entirely, melting into the gray stone that made up the vault itself.

23

SUSPICION

Alex limped through his office but paused as he crossed the great room, looking at the phone on the rollaway cabinet by his drafting table. He wanted to stop and make a few calls, but the idea of sitting on the tall chair that served the drafting table made him limp on toward the door to his office.

As he settled behind his desk, he thought about tapping the 'talk' key on the intercom box to let Sherry know he was there, but thought better of it. He didn't want to be interrupted.

His first call was to Bellevue, to the nurse's station by Melissa Hannover's room. He was informed that Mrs. Hannover had regained consciousness for a brief time yesterday, but that the doctor was keeping her asleep for another day.

Satisfied that his attempt to visit her would have been fruitless anyway, Alex thanked the nurse and hung up.

He thought for a few minutes about who he should call next. There were several options, but ultimately he realized there was only one person that fit the bill.

"Redhorn," the gruff voice on the other end of the line said.

"This is Alex Lockerby."

"Well, long time," Agent Redhorn said. "I assumed if you needed something from the Bureau, you'd talk to your girlfriend. What can I do for you?"

"I was followed by a man in a black suit today," Alex said. "He tailed me all the way from my office over to Bellevue Hospital. I gave him the slip, but before I did, I heard him tell one of the nurses that he was FBI."

"Interesting," Redhorn said after a pause. "Are you asking if it was me?"

Alex chuckled at that.

"Of course not," he said. "I would have recognized you right off. No, this guy was a little too obvious."

"You thinking he was just pretending to be an agent?" Redhorn asked. "Our guys tend to work in pairs when surveilling a subject."

"I didn't see anyone else," Alex said, "but that's not proof of anything. I guess what I really want to know is if the FBI has any reason to be curious about my whereabouts?"

"I haven't heard anyone mention your name in months," Redhorn admitted, "but if you were suddenly a person of interest, I'd be the last person to know about it. I mean, my old boss is dating you."

"You think you could ask Director Stevens about it? If he wants to know what I'm up to, I'll be glad to brief him."

"I'll ask," Redhorn said, "but first, I need you to tell me if you're working anything shady? Anything that might make Uncle Sam curious about you?"

Alex stopped to think, but he only had the few cases he was working since he'd been back, and he doubted Mike had anything of national significance on his plate.

"The only things I'm working are that girl who was hacked to death in Alphabet City, a woman whose house has a forgotten speakeasy in the basement, and some people who might have been poisoned down by the Meatpacking District."

There was a pause on the line and Alex heard Agent Redhorn sigh.

"You don't happen to need a partner, do you?" he asked.

"Why?" Alex asked.

"Because I've been doing paperwork all week," Redhorn said, "and it sounds like you get all the interesting cases. All three of those have been in the paper."

"You think that's why some agent is following me around?" Alex asked. "They know something about one of these cases that I don't?"

"I doubt it," Redhorn said. "Nothing in the newspapers mentioned your name. How would the Bureau know you were involved?"

"I suppose they could have called the Central Office," Alex guessed. "Although if they did that, the police would have told them everything I know."

"That's exactly what would have happened," Redhorn said. "It's still possible the Bureau is looking into something about you, but it's just as possible your shadow is a fake."

"Which would make him very dangerous," Alex concluded.

"I'll talk to Director Stevens about this," Redhorn said. "Until then, try not to go anywhere by yourself. Take Danny or Sorsha with you. Call me," he chuckled, "I'd love the distraction."

Alex didn't like the idea that he needed a babysitter, but Redhorn made a good point. In his condition, he couldn't outrun an arthritic grandmother.

"Will do," he said.

"Stevens is out," Redhorn went on. "I'll talk to him in the morning. Give me a call around ten, I'll have an answer for you by then."

Alex agreed, then hung up.

He hadn't really expected Agent Redhorn to know anything about his federal stalker; if Redhorn had known, he'd have told Sorsha before now. Still, Director Stevens might know something, so it was worth the phone call, although Alex was sure he'd owe the FBI man a favor after this.

It was still before five, according to the clock on his office wall, but Alex wanted to talk to Iggy about the mysterious Butcher. Reaching for his intercom, he tapped the 'talk' key, explained his premature return to Sherry, and asked if there was any pressing business.

"Nothing that can't wait," she said once he'd explained his desire to leave. "Do you want me to wait to hear from Lieutenant Detweiler before I go?"

"No, he probably hasn't had time to organize his men yet," Alex said. "I don't expect to hear anything on that front until at least noon tomorrow."

"All right, then," Sherry said. "I'll close up at five."

Alex thanked her for her diligence, then released the intercom key.

Despite his desire to get home, he stopped to light a cigarette. Mostly he was putting off using his crutches. Between going all over town and dodging a purported FBI tail, he'd been on his feet too much and his foot throbbed.

"How did people put up with this before healing potions were discovered?" he grumbled. "Probably why people in the Middle Ages died at thirty."

Realizing he couldn't put it off anymore, Alex got to his feet and took his crutches under his arm.

At least I'm almost done, he thought as he headed out of his office and into his vault. Once he got home, he could stay off his feet for the rest of the day. Pausing at the cover door to the vault, Alex opened it with the gold key on his key ring, then proceeded though his vault to the brownstone door.

Once he'd managed his way down to the ground floor, he found Iggy in the kitchen, reading the paper while something that smelled wonderful baked in the oven.

"You're not going to believe this," Alex said as he limped into the kitchen. "I was followed today by someone who claimed to be from the FBI."

Iggy lowered his paper and raised an eyebrow.

"Well, that might explain those two fellows across the street," he said.

Alex turned and limped back through the library to the large front window. Since the bombing incident with Paschal Randolph, Iggy had installed gauzy curtains between the window and the heavy curtains that provided privacy and blocked outside light. The inner curtains were semi-transparent, allowing light in, but blocking the view of anyone outside.

Leaning toward the window, Alex looked out through the gap between the upper curtain rod and the top of the frame. Across the street, he saw a dark sedan parked. It was already dark, so he couldn't see inside, but as he watched, a cigarette suddenly glowed from the darkness of the passenger side of the vehicle.

Private detectives and hit men worked alone, so if there were two, that could only mean law enforcement. Alex hadn't been sure if his shadow from earlier had been an actual FBI man, but with the watchdogs outside, he was beginning to believe it.

"Do you think your friend, William Donovan, is behind them?" Iggy called from the kitchen.

"I doubt it," Alex said, limping back. "Donovan is a hands-on kind of guy, and he's not bashful about showing up in person."

"In that case, Uncle Sam seems to have taken an interest in your movements," Iggy said.

"You mean they're suspicious about my vault?"

"I did warn you that someone would begin to notice if you seemed to just magically appear back at your office and here," Iggy said in a matter-of-fact tone.

Alex ground his teeth as his sore foot seemed to throb in time with his heartbeat.

"Well, that's just great," he growled.

"I am sorry, lad," Iggy said, seeming to understand Alex's foul mood. "You should probably go back to your office and catch a cab back here."

Alex suppressed a swear word, then hitched up his crutches and headed for the stairs.

Forty-five minutes later, Alex hopped up the stone stairs in front of the brownstone. He bit his lip as he fumbled with his key ring, looking for the one that would open the front door. Finally finding it, he tapped it against the knob and lurched inside.

Ever since the cab dropped him off, he'd listened for the sound of a car door. That would herald the men in the car getting out, no doubt, to intercept him. So far, however, all they were doing was watching. Still, as Alex closed the door behind him, he heaved a sigh of relief.

"What took so long?" Iggy asked when Alex came limping back into the kitchen.

"My foot hurts," Alex said, as if it were the most self-evident thing in the world. "I had to sit on my front office couch for a quarter hour before it stopped throbbing."

"I thought maybe the Feds had picked you up," Iggy admitted. "I was just about to call Sorsha and have her go looking for you."

"Thanks for the concern," Alex said, easing down onto one of the heavy chairs that encircled the enormous dining table. "I was worried the guys across the street would try to stop me when I got back, but they stayed put."

"They have to know you saw them," Iggy said, stirring something on the stove.

"Maybe," Alex said. "Danny and Callahan know better, but most Feds don't think too highly of private detectives."

"Or they're gathering information about your habits," Iggy said.

"I already called Agent Redhorn," Alex said. "He didn't know anything about this, but he said he'd ask Director Stevens in the morning."

"In that case," Iggy said. "I suggest we table this discussion until we know more."

"Suits me," Alex said. "I've got something else I wanted to ask you."

Alex explained what Billy Tasker had told him about the raid on the Silken Cushion, the speakeasy run by Ruby Tomlinson, and the possible connection to someone called the Central Park Butcher.

"This Butcher character would have been in the news prior to the raid in twenty-four," Alex said. "Do you remember anything about that?"

"I'm afraid you're forgetting your history," Iggy said. "I didn't arrive here in the colonies until twenty-seven. Before that, I kept up with the news in the London Times, not the *New York Times*. That said, with such a dramatic name, I imagine it won't be hard to track down the story."

"More library time," Alex sighed.

"You've been at this long enough to know that investigation isn't all car chases and shootouts," Iggy said. "Speaking of which, I think it's time I re-bandaged your foot."

"What about dinner?" Alex asked, loath to get back on his crutches.

"Sorsha called," he said, "she's running about half an hour late, so we have time."

Alex sighed and followed Iggy through the vault door in the kitchen and through to his vault.

"Take your shoe off and get on the table," Iggy said when they entered his surgery.

Alex complied and Iggy began to unwrap the bandage. As he got further inside, Alex could see traces of dried blood on the bandage. When at last Iggy set the bandage to the side, the old man just stood there, staring at Alex's foot.

"Something wrong?" Alex asked.

"Yes," Iggy muttered, rubbing a calloused finger around the hole where the bullet penetrated. "A good portion of the packing cloth has almost completely transformed, but the rest is still cloth. No wonder your foot is sore."

"What does that mean?"

Iggy thought about that for a moment before responding.

"I'm not sure," he admitted, "but if I had to guess, the damnation rune is causing the alchemical putty to transform the cloth."

"I thought it stopped my ability to use magic," Alex said. "And you said the putty would work because its magic wasn't being applied directly to me."

"If I said it, it's true, of course," Iggy said, voice filled with mocking self-aggrandizement. "But the rune on your chest is doing more than just blocking access to your magical abilities." He turned from the table and crossed his surgery room to a tall cabinet and pulled out a rubber block. Using this to prop up Alex's foot, he pulled up a chair to put himself at eye level with the wound.

"What else is it doing?" Alex prodded his mentor.

"Well," Iggy said, opening a nearby drawer of instruments. "The Limelight you took subjected your body to large amounts of magic that left magical residue behind. The damnation rune on your chest is designed to leech that residue from your body."

That didn't sound pleasant, and Alex said so.

"That's why," Iggy said, picking up a pair of long-nosed tweezers, "it's doing the job very gradually. If it did it all at once, it might send you into shock, or just kill you outright."

He prodded Alex's wound with the tweezer, causing Alex to flinch and suck air through his teeth.

"Steady on, lad," Iggy said, prodding with the tweezers again. This time he tugged and Alex's foot erupted in pain. "Well, that's no good," he said.

"You're sure about that?" Alex asked, his voice dripping in sarcasm. It had felt like Iggy was trying to extract a tooth, but from his foot.

"Oh, definitely," Iggy said, ignoring Alex's tone. "I'm afraid the damnation rune is drawing magical energy from the cloth, up through your body to the rune. That's why the cloth touching your skin has completely transformed into new skin, while the stuff in the center is still cloth."

Alex's stomach turned when he realized the implications of what Iggy was saying.

"You mean the rune pulled the magic out of the cloth, making it merge with my foot from the outside in, but it didn't finish?"

"In a word, yes," Iggy declared.

"How are you going to get the stuff that didn't transform out?" Alex asked, picturing his mentor having to literally cut it out of his foot.

"I suspect Sorsha will be able to help with that," he said. "It should be easy for her to simply teleport the remaining cloth out of your foot."

"Isn't that just going to leave another hole in my foot?"

"Yes," Iggy admitted, "but a much smaller one than you had before. I'm afraid it will take a while to heal fully, but the good news is that, once we get the cloth out and fill the hole with wound putty, you should be able to walk with just a cane."

That didn't really thrill Alex, but a cane was better than the crutches.

"I guess I can live with that," he said.

"Perhaps," Iggy replied.

"What's that supposed to mean?"

"It means that the damnation rune wants to absorb any magic close to you," Iggy said. "It's supposed to pull the residual magic out of you so your body can heal from all the damage the Limelight and life transference has done to you."

Alex recalled their discussion about transfer toxicity. Normally it didn't affect runewrights, but Alex had used both quite liberally and it had weakened his body.

"The problem," Iggy went on, "is that it's pulling new magic into your body from any source near you, then dragging it up to your chest where the rune is."

"You mean that instead of purifying me so I can get better, the rune is adding new magic to my system."

Iggy sighed and nodded before reaching out to take Alex by the shoulder.

"In your weakened state, more magic could kill you outright," he said. "You're going to need to divest yourself of your tools: your flash ring, your pocket watch, and especially the shield talisman I made for you. That one's tied into a vast pool of magic thanks to the linking runes."

Alex quickly took off his ring and pulled the silver arrowhead necklace Iggy had given him over his head.

"What about my rune book?" he asked as he added his pocket watch to the pile.

"That one is probably safe," Iggy said. "Runes don't produce magic until you activate them, after all. Still, you might want to carry your book in your kit bag for now, at least until I figure out if they're safe for you to carry."

Alex took out his rune book and handed it to Iggy, but held on when his mentor tried to pull it away.

"If the damnation rune has been draining the magic from the runes in the book, shouldn't they be weaker than normal?"

"Good point," Iggy said. "Some of the basic barrier runes might have been drained entirely." He put Alex's book into the pocket of his suit coat. "I'll test a few of them after dinner and let you know."

"Ignatius?" Sorsha's voice came from the general direction of the kitchen. "Alex?"

Alex opened his mouth to call her, but Iggy held up a hand.

"I'll tell her that the alchemist cloth was faulty," he said. "Don't tell her about the problems with the damnation rune."

"Why not?"

"Do you want to have her accompany you on every case from now until you can use magic again?"

Alex hadn't thought of that. Iggy was absolutely right, if Sorsha knew that Alex couldn't wear the shield talisman, she'd worry about him constantly. He couldn't put her through that.

"Right," he said. "Let's just have her remove the cloth from my foot and have dinner then."

"An excellent plan," Iggy said.

24

REVELATIONS

Just like Iggy said, Sorsha was able to remove the cloth from Alex's foot in just a few seconds. Instead of teleporting it out, however, she simply dissolved the woven material, leaving Alex's foot still injured but feeling much better.

"Thanks, doll," Alex said, breathing much easier. He wouldn't admit it, not even under torture, but he'd been worried about her pulling out a chunk of his foot. Normally that would be an easy fix for alchemical medicine, but in his current condition, he'd be stuck on the crutches for months while that healed. So far, he'd only had them a day and he was already sick of them.

"Don't you 'doll' me," Sorsha snapped, pulling his wandering thoughts back to the present. She looked from Iggy to Alex and back again. "So, both of you think I'm an idiot, do you?"

She put the back of her hand against her forehead and mimicked a fit of weakness.

"I'm just a poor stupid girl," she gasped, her voice high pitched and breathy. "I'd never be able to tell that Alex's new rune leached the magic out of the regrowth cloth and now his shiny new shield pendant won't work. Why, if I knew that, I'd be so worried about him, I'd never have a moment's peace."

"All right," Alex said, giving her an unamused look. "We just didn't want you to worry."

"With the amount of scrapes you get in, I'm within my rights to worry," she declared.

"Fair point," Alex admitted. "I assumed you'd demand to never leave my side until I was better. I guess I sold you short."

Sorsha gave him a knowing look with an accompanying half smile.

"Oh, I will be spending more time at your side," she said. "I am your fiancée, after all."

Alex reached out and took her hand. He was always surprised how warm she was, given her proclivity for cold-based magic.

"As long as you don't come with me on stakeouts," he said.

"Why not?" she said.

"A beautiful dame like you in the car? You'd be too distracting."

Sorsha blushed slightly, and Alex pulled her in for a quick peck on the lips.

"Now, now," Iggy said at last, shooing Sorsha away from the table. "I've got to pack Alex's wound with some anti-biotic paste and re-wrap it before we can go out to dinner."

"I suppose that's my cue to go get the food on the table," Sorsha said. "Hurry out."

With that, Sorsha turned and headed out of Iggy's surgery, back toward the brownstone.

The following morning, Alex woke early intending to make it into his office by eight. He hadn't heard back last night from Billy about the mysterious Central Park Butcher, so he expected a call first thing.

True to Iggy's prediction, Alex hadn't needed his crutches to walk this morning, but only just. His foot felt much better, but he still needed to keep off it as much as possible. Iggy had suggested he use a cane, but Alex didn't own a cane, so he planned to send Mike out to get one after his apprentice had a chance to finish up any work left over from yesterday.

Alex limped out of his room and into the hall where his vault door

DAN WILLIS

now stood against the wall. Tapping it with the gold key on his ring, he passed inside and headed for the great room. The hallway to his office was just on the opposite wall and he was grateful for that with his sore foot.

His vault had magelight installed all along the halls and in the ceiling of the great room. Since the cover doors that kept the vault secure didn't block Barton Electric's power projection, Alex's vault was always well lit. This time, however, as he passed out of the brownstone hallway and into the great room, he noticed something off. The lamp on his reading table was on.

The reading table stood next to a comfortable, wing-back chair that faced the fake fireplace on the wall. This was Alex's library, and the fireplace was flanked by two rows of bookshelves on either side with a rollaway liquor cabinet standing by. When Alex read in here, he used a pair of boiler stones to simulate the warmth of a fire, then poured himself a Scotch and switched on the lamp. All in all, it was a very comfortable situation.

As he noticed the illuminated lamp, his eye traveled past it to where a small tumbler sat, along with a bottle of white wine.

"Sorsha," he greeted her where she sat in his reading chair with a book in her hand.

"You need a better wine selection," she said, snapping the book closed. She swapped the book for the tumbler and downed the remaining liquid in it as she stood. "A mediocre vintage at best."

Alex chuckled as he limped his way over to her.

"I guess my tastes aren't as refined as yours," he said, "and it's my liquor cabinet."

Sorsha smirked and slunk up to him, sending her hips side to side. She wore a simple white dress with a half-jacket over her shoulders, and her walk made the dress bunch and slide as she moved.

"Are you saying I'm not welcome here?" she said, pressing her hip against him.

"No," he admitted. "Just that I hadn't considered your palate when choosing my liquor."

"Well, you do have excellent bourbon and Scotch," Sorsha admitted, "but it's a bit early in the day for those."

"Speaking of early," Alex said, slipping his arm around her tiny waist. "To what do I owe the honor of seeing you at this hour?"

Her smirking face broadened out into a delighted smile. It was ravishing.

"I have a present for you."

Turning, she slipped his grip and moved back to the reading chair. Reaching behind it, she withdrew a long silver cane with a polished ivory handle and a solid tip on the bottom made of white rubber.

As she turned back to Alex, she held the cane in both hands, like a medieval lady about to present a sword to her knight.

"For you," she said, doing a little curtsy before holding it out to him.

Alex whistled as he took it. As canes went it was magnificent. The body seemed to be made of a single piece of metal that had been polished to a high shine. It looked like silver, but Alex knew better; silver was much too soft a metal to make a good cane. The handle had a flat spot on one end, almost like it was designed after a war hammer, with the rest of the handle pointing backward from that point. As Alex held it up, it felt light in his hand, more like it had been made of wood instead of metal.

"You just happened to have this laying around?" he marveled, turning the cane over several times in his hand.

"Don't be absurd," Sorsha said with a laugh. "I made it for you last night, just look at the inscription on the front."

Alex held the cane up and found what looked like a polished shield just below the hammer head.

Alex Lockerby, The Runewright Detective, it read in flowing script that Alex recognized as Sorsha's handwriting.

"You made this?" he said, wonder in his voice.

"I am a sorceress," Sorsha said in an irritable voice. "You seem to forget that a lot. I might have to dream up ways to remind you on a regular basis."

Alex wanted to give her a playful retort, but he was too focused on Sorsha's gift.

"Thank you," he said, lowering it down to his side.

Sorsha slipped her arms around his neck and looked up at him.

"Well, I can't have my fiancé running around with some old stick in his hour of need, now, can I?"

"I guess not," Alex said before leaning down to kiss her.

It was well past eight when Alex finally limped into his office. He knew Sherry would be down the hall at her desk, managing the ins and outs of his business like an admiral directing a fleet. If Billy had called before he got in, Sherry would know about it.

"I'm here," Alex said after sitting down at his desk and tapping the 'talk' key on the intercom. "Any calls for me?"

"Not yet, Boss," Sherry said. "You expecting something?"

"Billy Tasker," Alex said. "If he calls, I don't care what I'm doing, put him through."

"Will do," Sherry said, and the speaker went silent.

Alex sat back, then realized he was still holding on to his new cane. Chuckling, he hung the cane on the edge of his desk where it would be out of the way, then admired it for a moment. Alex had never really had many possessions of his own, not that he really needed things. He had his tools, of course, but until he started buying more expensive suits, he'd never really had nice things. It still didn't seem like he needed a fancy watch or lighter, but he had to admit, he smiled every time he pulled out the gold lighter Sorsha had given him.

"I suspect that's because of the giver," he said. "I should probably get her something nice."

Before he had a chance to pursue that train of thought any further, his phone rang.

"Lockerby," he said, even before the receiver reached his ear.

"I've got Danny on the line for you," Sherry said.

Alex was happy to hear from Danny, but it felt like a bit of a letdown in lieu of Billy.

"Put him on," he said.

"Alex?" Danny said, then went on before Alex could speak. "I really need your help."

"You didn't catch up with Liam Cohan?" he said. "I thought you had him pretty well boxed in."

"Well, yes and no," Danny said. "He did manage to give us the slip, but then Liam walked into a police station in Northport and turned himself in."

That didn't make sense and Alex said so.

"Well, you're not going to believe this," Danny continued. "I'm not sure I believe it and I was here for all of it." He hesitated a moment, then went on. "So, when Liam took off, he went straight to his cousin's place in Northport."

"His cousin, Michael Cohan?" Alex asked, remembering the list of missing mobsters.

"That's the one," Danny said. "When he got there, he found that Michael had been murdered, beaten to death with a bat two days ago."

Alex whistled at that.

"You think it's the same person who killed Ann Gallagher?"

"Liam does," Danny said. "When he walked into that police station, he said that he'd tell us everything we want to know if we offered him protection."

Alex thought about that for a moment.

"What kind of guy sends a mobster running?" he asked.

"The same kind that would hack a young woman to death," Danny said.

It was a good point; whoever this killer was, he wasn't afraid of the public or the law.

"Sounds like you're in the catbird seat," Alex said. "What do you need me for?"

"Liam says that the only person who could have known about his cousin and would have a grudge against Ann is our other missing mobster, James Fahey."

"He's sure?"

"Says Fahey is the only one who could know. Everyone else is either dead or in prison."

"So why me?"

"Back in the day, Liam stole a watch from James," Danny said. "According to him, James Fahey held a grudge over it for years."

"So it's the ideal thing to use in a finding rune," Alex said.

"That's what Liam suggested."

"Okay," Alex said, glancing at the clock. "Give me a minute to grab my kit and I can be over there in twenty minutes."

"See you then."

Twenty-two minutes later, Alex limped off the elevator onto the fifth floor of the Central Office of Police. With his cane in his left hand and his kit in his right, he made his way down the hall to the back of the building, then turned left, moving along the row of glassed-in offices.

When he finally reached Danny's, he found his friend sitting behind his desk, leaning back in his chair with his feet up on an open drawer. He had his hands behind his head and a cigarette between his lips.

"You don't look nervous at all," Alex said. "I mean if you don't find Fahey, the press could still make trouble for the department."

Danny lifted his feet off the drawer and sat up, taking the cigarette out of his mouth. He reached down to his desk and tossed a folded newspaper across it to Alex.

"You obviously haven't seen the morning edition."

Alex picked up the paper and scanned the headline above the fold.

Retired Mobster Gives Cops the Slip

Alex read the first few lines, which suggested that Liam was the man who killed Ann Gallagher. It didn't name him, but the implication was that the cops let him escape on purpose.

"They're going to be disappointed when they find out Liam turned himself in," Alex said, dropping the paper back on the desk.

"Only if we catch James Fahey," Danny fired back. "If we don't get him the papers will just imply that they meant Fahey all along."

"There's always an angle," Alex observed. "Where is this pocket watch that Fahey wants so badly?"

Danny reached into his coat pocket and removed a shiny brass watch. The case was covered with intricate engravings, culminating in a large, calligraphic letter 'F' in the center of the cover.

"Doesn't look like much," Alex said, as he opened his kit bag.

"Apparently it belonged to Fahey's grandfather," Danny said as Alex rolled out his map of Manhattan on the desktop. He waited until Alex weighed the map down with his jade figurines, then set the watch in the center.

Alex set his battered brass compass on the map, then put the watch on top of it. Reaching back into his bag for his red-backed rune book, he flipped through the pages until he located a finding rune. Tearing it out, he folded it and placed it on top of the watch.

"Okay, I need you to think about finding James Fahey and touch the map," Alex said, pulling out his lighter.

"I meant to ask you about this last time," Danny said, "is this because of your ... illness?"

"Yes," Alex said, "having someone else focus helps." Without being able to connect to the rune as the magic worked, he needed someone else thinking about the goal. Since Danny already knew abut the Limelight and the damnation rune, he didn't have to conceal the truth..

Flicking the lighter to life, Alex touched the flame to the flash paper and it burst into orange fire, finally coalescing into the finding rune. Alex held his breath while the rune spun above the compass. As he watched, the rune began to slow down, but then stuttered and sped up again.

"Well, damn," Alex said as the rune burst into a shower of orange sparks. "Did Liam have any idea where Fahey is living now?"

Danny shook his head.

"He said that James is a native New Yorker, but that's it."

Alex rubbed his chin as he thought. He'd watched the rune closely, and it had definitely slowed for a second, like it wanted to connect but just couldn't.

"Let me try something," he said at last.

Reaching back into his bag, Alex pulled out a leather bag with a drawstring top. Tugging open the top, he dumped three small metal squares out onto the map.

"What are those?" Danny asked as Alex picked up the cube nearest to him.

Alex checked the cube, turning it until a large letter 'J' was revealed.

"This is a piece of Barton Electric's power projection tower in Jersey City," Alex said, dropping it back in the bag. "This one is for the Bronx." Alex turned the cube so Danny could see the letter 'X' written on it in black paint. "That leaves this one for Brooklyn," Alex said, setting it on top of the compass.

"What's it do?" Danny wondered as Alex dropped the bag back into his kit.

"Well, I've never tried this before," he admitted, "but if I'm right, it will use the Brooklyn power tower as the center of my finding rune."

"You mean it'll be like you're casting the rune in Brooklyn?"

Alex nodded, picking up the watch and the other stacked elements and handing them to Danny. Removing the map of Manhattan, Alex replaced it with one of Brooklyn and the bottom of Long Island.

"Let's hope this works," he said, setting the watch, compass, and steel cube down on the new map.

Alex tore out another rune and this time when he ignited it, the spinning slowed almost immediately. Below the hovering rune, he could see the compass needle begin to spin with the rune, gradually slowing down until it pointed off to the east and south.

"Does that mean what I think it means?" Danny asked in a whisper.

Alex grinned back at him.

"It means two things," he explained. "First, my power tower idea works, and second, James Fahey is living in Brooklyn." Alex slid the compass across the map until it started spinning in a little neighborhood just south of the Brooklyn Bridge.

"Right there."

25

ANCIENT HISTORY

Alex dozed on the couch in Danny's office while his friend coordinated with Callahan and Captain Morrison of the Brooklyn Office of Police. It was more of a loveseat than a couch, so it was too small for Alex's six-foot one-inch frame, but at least it allowed him to keep his injured foot elevated.

"You awake?" Danny said as he came hustling in.

Alex made a noncommittal noise from under his hat.

"The Brooklyn Police are moving on Fahey's place right now," he said, opening his center desk drawer and retrieving his police .38 Special. He tucked it into his shoulder holster, then picked up his hat. "Callahan and I are going to meet them, but by the time we get there it will be all over."

"The Brooklyn P.D. going to give you Fahey without a fight?"

"Callahan says their captain owes him a favor."

"Well, what are we waiting for?" Alex said, swinging his legs over the side of the couch and sitting up.

"Callahan told me to have you wait here," he said, "but don't worry, we should be back in an hour. You can finish your nap."

"Mind if I use your phone?"

"Help yourself," Danny said, grabbing his coat off the rack by the door and heading out.

Alex waited a minute before opening one eye and listening. The commotion in the bullpen had died down and he heard the ding of the elevator door at the far end, meaning Danny and Callahan were gone.

He stood up from the couch and moved around to sit behind Danny's desk. Other than his friend's chair being too tall, it felt like his old desk in the mid ring. Picking up the phone, Alex dialed the number for Billy Tasker.

"What have you got for me?" he asked when Billy picked up the phone.

"Alex?" he said when he recognized the voice. "Sorry I haven't called, but this rabbit hole about the Butcher is twisted and deep."

"What can you tell me?"

"The story starts back in twenty-two," Billy began. "A city gardener named Anton Wells was tending a flower bed in Central Park when a woman started screaming. Anton, being a good citizen, went to investigate and found that the woman's children had been playing with a stray dog. The dog had been digging and found a bone."

"Let me guess," Alex said. "A human bone?"

Billy snorted on the other end of the line, clearly unimpressed.

"I'm telling you a story about a guy named the Butcher of Central Park, of course it was a human bone."

"Everybody's a critic," Alex groused.

"Anyway," Billy said. "Anton follows the dog and finds a patch of dirt that had been dug up in one of the flower beds. He digs it up and finds more bones. Lots of bones."

"How many?"

"Bones?" Billy asked. "No idea, but when the police got their coroner on scene, he said there were at least three bodies buried in that flower bed. Children's bodies."

"Dear God," Alex hissed, appalled.

"Oh, it gets worse," Billy said. "The police swept the park and found two more flower beds and seven more bodies. All of the victims were between ten and fifteen."

"Ten kids," Alex said, pulling out his notebook and starting to scribble. "How is this not still front-page news?"

"They were just bodies," Billy said. "There were no clothes, no personal effects."

"No way to identify them," Alex finished.

"And it was in the early days of the Depression," Billy added. "They might just have been starvation victims that some destitute family couldn't afford to bury."

Alex could see that. What better place for a penniless family to bury a beloved child than a flowerbed in the park?

"So that means they found more at some point," he guessed.

"Got it in one," Billy said. "A year later, in the fall of twenty-three, a man fishing in the reservoir hooked a denim coat. At first the police didn't think much of it, but a woman named Delia Brown had a daughter that went missing the previous winter."

"She came in when the papers reported it?" Alex asked.

"The coat had the name Sarah sewed into the lining. Sarah was Delia's daughter's name; she was fourteen."

"What did the police do?" Alex asked.

"At first?" Billy said. "They did nothing. Then Delia started talking to the press."

"I bet the cops liked that."

"Whether they liked it or not, it got them out from behind their desks," Billy said. "They dragged the reservoir and found over a dozen sets of clothing along with more bones."

Alex felt his stomach churn at the thought.

"According to the official report, the police recovered a total of twenty-four bodies," Billy said. "Six of them were positively identified, all coming from a three-block area on the west side."

"Six kids went missing from that part of town and the cops weren't looking for them?"

"That's what I thought," Billy said, "but I've got an old guy here who remembers those times. Lots of kids joined the army or took off for greener pastures. If there was any decent excuse about where they might have gone, the cops didn't take it too seriously."

Alex swore. He knew there were bad cops, lazy cops, and even jaded cops, but Danny wasn't like them, so he'd been largely insulated from that sort. Still, how did an investigator hear the pleas of a parent with a missing child and then do nothing?

"So what happened when the cops finally figured out the missing kids were dead?"

"They moved pretty quick once that was established," Billy said. "There was a neighborhood handyman, named Herman Franks, that the kids were always hanging around. He was their prime suspect."

"Sounds like he was their only suspect," Alex said.

"Anyway, by the time the cops had a name, Herman was in the wind. One of his neighbors claimed to know where Herman worked, but the police weren't able to find him. Weeks went by with no news, then months, then a year."

"No wonder there's nothing in the papers these days about this," Alex said.

"Well, the police did get a break fifteen months later," Billy went on. "Someone walking his dog at night spotted someone dumping a body in the reservoir. He sicced his dog on the man and it tore up his leg before the guy was able to get away. Cops followed the blood trail to the home of a man calling himself Adam Canfield. It didn't take them long to figure out that he'd raped and murdered a sixteen-year-old girl from his building."

"So, was he the Butcher?" Alex asked.

"The cops thought so," Billy said. "They announced that the Butcher was Adam Canfield and that he was dead."

"Wait," Alex interrupted, "when did Canfield die?"

There was some paper rustling then Billy came back on.

"When the police arrived at Canfield's building, he saw them coming," Billy said. "He tried to go out a fire escape and when police cornered him, he started shooting. According to the coroner's report, Canfield had eleven bullets in him and that was before he fell over the railing and took a five-story swan dive."

"So he fit the profile and he was dead," Alex said. "The perfect patsy to close the Butcher case."

"What makes you think he was a patsy?" Billy said.

Pound of Flesh

"Because you're telling me details I don't need to know if Canfield was the Butcher."

Billy laughed at that.

"Well, you're right," he said. "The reporter who put this file together had connections in the department, and he got ahold of the original report. The description the police had from Herman Franks' neighbors didn't match Adam Canfield."

Alex swore.

"So the Butcher is still out there," he said, "and nobody is looking for him."

Something was bothering Alex about this whole story, something beyond the level of civic incompetence on display.

"What does any of this have to do with Ruby T or the Silken Cushion?"

Billy hesitated, then sighed.

"As far as I can tell, nothing," he admitted. "The only possible link is a note in our file. The man who put it together linked the police raid on the Silken Cushion to Herman Franks. It was just a guess, but he thought that the only way the cops would raid a place like the Silken Cushion was if there was someone there they desperately wanted."

"Why did he think that?"

"Honestly," Billy said, "I don't know. The guy who put this file together passed last year, so unless ouija boards really work, you and I know everything there is to know."

Alex thought about that, turning the whole twisted story of the Butcher over in his mind. No matter how he looked at it, there wouldn't be a connection with the speakeasy.

"It doesn't make sense," he said at last.

"What doesn't?"

"The Silken Cushion was a high-class joint," Alex explained. "Herman Franks, a handyman from an outer ring neighborhood, would never get past the doorman."

"Maybe he worked there," Billy said. "I mean there was that one neighbor who said he knew where Franks worked, so maybe someone figured it out."

Alex thought about that for a long moment.

"A high-end speakeasy wouldn't have waiters, they'd have waitresses," he said. "But there's still a few male positions, bouncer, doorman, something like that."

"So, what if the file is right?" Billy said. "What if Franks worked at the Silken Cushion?"

"That would explain why it was shut down and rebuilt in secret," Alex reasoned. "As soon as Ruby T learned about Franks, she'd want to make sure he couldn't find the new one, to say nothing of the cops that raided the original speakeasy."

"Why would Franks care if Ruby reopened the Silken Cushion?" Billy wondered.

Alex thought about that, but couldn't come up with a good reason. After all, if the police were hot on his trail, he'd be busy moving to Montana, not worrying about his old job.

"Anything?" Billy prompted.

"No," Alex said. "Let me think about it."

"You will tell me when you figure it out," Billy said, "right?"

Alex laughed at that.

"Not only will you be the first to know if the police are about to make an arrest, but I have it on good authority that the police will soon be arresting the man who hacked that girl to death in Alphabet City."

"Reeealy," Billy said, stretching the word out. "I'm going to owe you big for this, aren't I?"

Alex just smiled.

"With any luck," he said, then he hung up.

Alex stood and went down the hall to get a drink from the water cooler. His foot was still sore, but his mind was busy turning the Butcher and the Silken Cushion over and over. By the time he got back to Danny's door, he had a headache. Deciding to give his mind a break, he continued past Danny's office, down to the office of Police Lieutenant James Detweiler.

Knocking on the doorframe he waited in the hall till the pudgy man looked up from his desk.

"You've got a lot of nerve coming here after sending me on that buggy ride," he growled. "If it wasn't for that Bellevue doctor, I'd have sworn out warrants for the lot of you."

"What are you talking about?" Alex asked, genuinely confused.

"I've had men searching every street and diner since last night and they've turned up exactly nothing."

Alex almost laughed, but Detweiler wasn't the type of man who would take a little friendly ribbing.

"You aren't going to find anything until eleven at the earliest," he said. "If Linda and Dr. Kitteridge are right, these people are being poisoned when they eat lunch. Get your men out in the street and have them watch where people eat."

Detweiler gave Alex a dark look.

"That fancy doctor said someone was poisoning people," he said. "What was I supposed to do? Can't have a lunatic running around with a syringe and some chloroform, right?"

"Right," Alex said. "Just have your men pay attention to where people eat."

"Are you Alex Lockerby?" a voice came from behind him.

Alex turned to find a young patrolman he didn't know standing behind him in the hall.

"That's me," he said.

"Captain Callahan is on the phone for you."

Alex turned back to Detweiler and shrugged.

"Gotta go," he said. "Let me know what you find."

Following the patrolman down the hall, he led Alex into Danny's office where the phone cradle rested on the desk.

"Callahan?" Alex said when he picked it up. "Fahey give you the slip?"

"You could say that," the Captain's gruff voice broke over Alex. "When the Brooklyn boys got here they found him in his living room with his head bashed in. Looks like someone went at him with a baseball bat."

"Like Michael Cohan?" Alex asked, more than a little surprised.

"Just like Michael Cohan," Callahan said. "Get your bag of magic tricks and Officer Penrose will bring you here."

"It'll be faster to take the crawler," Alex said. "Have someone meet me at the station by Barton's power tower. I'll be there in twenty minutes."

Alex handed the receiver back to Officer Penrose, then picked up his cane and his overcoat before heading down the hall. Since his kit bag was in his vault, Alex turned away from the elevators and entered the janitorial closet. Closing the door behind him, Alex chalked a door on the wall, exactly like he'd done at least a dozen times. If he could figure out how to make a cover door work in here, he'd have done it a long time ago.

Since he didn't have his bag with him, Alex kept his rune book in the outside pocket of his overcoat. Slipping the coat on, he removed the book and tore out a vault rune.

A moment later, Alex crossed his vault's great room, picking up his kit as he went. He stopped in front of an ordinary-seeming shelf filled with various powders and inks used in the rune writing process. Reaching up to the top shelf, Alex ran his hand along the top until his fingers found a short metal rod. He pressed it down, eliciting a soft click, and the right side of the shelf came away from the wall.

Alex pulled the shelf open like the door it was, revealing a metal cover door hidden behind it. This was the single place where Alex's main vault connected to the Barton Electric Transport Hub. Technically, it was all Alex's vault, but the hub existed so Andrew, and occasionally Alex, could move between the various power towers quickly and without having to teleport.

The door led into a round room with cover doors over six different hallways. Each door had a label indicating where they went; five led to the existing power towers and one led to Barton's office on top of Empire Tower.

Alex entered the hub, then turned and closed the shelf and then the steel cover door. Turning, he selected the door for the Brooklyn tower; opening it with his gold key he limped inside and shut it behind him. Beyond the cover door was a short hall that led to another cover door that connected to the control room on top of the Brooklyn tower.

Alex headed for the elevator that went down to the main floor, passing the bullet holes in the concrete that still hadn't been patched from the time Alex fought Nazi saboteurs in this very room.

Two minutes later, Alex exited the elevator on the main floor, then moved out to the street. The skycrawler station was across the street and Alex limped to it, taking a seat on one of the benches by the stairs to await the police.

"How long have you been waiting?" Danny asked when he pulled up to the curb by the station.

"Twenty minutes," Alex admitted, standing up and limping to the car.

"Cheater," Danny said with a grin.

By the time Alex got in the passenger seat, however, his expression changed.

"Tell me," Alex said.

"Fahey's not our man," Danny said. "Someone caved his head in, at least two days ago from the smell."

"I assume that the Brooklyn boys have been all over the scene," Alex said. "What do you think I'll be able to find?"

Danny rolled his eyes.

"Do what you can," he said. "Callahan wants this guy found today. The longer he's free, the more Alderman Snow is going to vilify us in the papers. There's already some of the trashier tabloids calling for Chief Montgomery and Captain Callahan to resign. It won't be long before it's me they'll be coming after."

"I won't let that happen," Alex said, his voice full of fervor. "If there's something to find at Fahey's house, I'll find it."

"I never doubted you," Danny chuckled. "You don't know how to fail."

"Stop laughing and drive."

26

THE DOG WAGON

For a retired mobster, James Fahey lived in a very modest house. Alex had been through it twice in less than an hour. Sitting room, kitchen, bedroom, office, bathroom — nothing. There was also nothing in the unfinished attic or in the tool shed in the back yard.

As Alex knelt to repack his kit, Danny and the Brooklyn captain gathered around him.

"Did Fahey let the killer in?" Captain Morrison asked.

The captain of the Brooklyn office was a thin man of medium height with a bottle brush mustache and a receding hairline. Alex wasn't sure if his men feared him or respected him, but he ran the crime scene with practiced efficiency.

"No," Alex said, leading the way to the back door. "See this?" He pointed to the lock in the back door. "See the scratches? They're shiny and new."

"Someone picked the lock," Danny agreed, "someone who wasn't a pro."

"And Fahey didn't hear that?" Morrison asked.

Alex could only shrug at that.

"It wouldn't make much noise and the killer could see through the window in the door. He'd know if Fahey came out of the back rooms, so all he had to do was wait for his opportunity."

"That's how he was able to sneak in and attack him unawares," Danny added.

"Is there anything else your consultant wants to look at?" Morrison said to Danny.

Danny looked to Alex.

"That's all for me," he said, and returned to repacking his kit. There had been plenty of evidence in the little house, just none that pointed to Fahey being Ann or Michael Cohan's killer. If he was the killer, Alex would have expected to find calluses, or failing that, bruises, on the palms of the mobster's hand. Unfortunately, Fahey's hands looked like the heaviest thing he picked up during his time on the lam was a shot glass.

The house was simple and basic, the ideal place for someone in hiding. Alex found a gun stashed under a loose floorboard along with some cash, but based on the amount of dust inside, that secret compartment hadn't been opened in years. Beyond that, there was nothing to suggest that Fahey was anything other than a regular person.

"What do you think?" Danny asked, coming to stand beside Alex as he stripped the burner from his multi-lamp.

"I think James Fahey isn't your guy."

"Funny," Danny growled at him. "You realize this puts us right back at square one. The press is going to have a field day when they find out."

"There's already reporters outside," Alex said.

Danny sighed and looked out the front window.

"I guess you can't have a murder in a nice, quiet neighborhood like this without people taking notice."

"The fake ID in Fahey's wallet said he was calling himself Phillip West," Alex said. "Give the reporters that name and it should buy you a day or two."

"Until someone figures out that Phillip didn't exist before he bought this house."

Alex closed his kit and stood up.

"With Fahey dead, where does that leave you?"

"With Liam," Danny said. "And he's been on the run since yesterday. It's possible he did this before we caught up to him..."

Danny just let the sentence run out.

"If he's the killer, why did he turn himself in?" Alex observed. "My gut tells me we've missed someone."

"I checked," Danny said. "Everybody from the Connolly mob is either dead or in jail."

"How is that possible?"

"Between the evidence Kate Gallagher provided and the informant the police had, they rolled up the whole gang in a weekend."

"Well, they missed James and the Cohan boys," Alex said. "They must have missed someone else."

"Someone who's killing their own people?" Danny asked. "After all these years?"

Alex thought about that for a moment, then shook his head.

"That doesn't make much sense, does it?"

Danny didn't answer, just ground his teeth.

"If you're done," Alex said, picking up his cane, "can you drop me back at the crawler station?"

"Unless you're in a hurry, you can ride with me back to Manhattan."

Alex thought about that and decided he wasn't.

"Sounds good to me," he said.

An hour later, Alex limped off a crawler in the Meatpacking District. With skycrawler lines running all over the city, Andrew Barton had the bright idea to use the rails themselves as power projectors. It didn't cover all of the outer ring, but it did make it possible for crawler service to cover most of Manhattan, something Alex was grateful for as he limped toward the end of the block.

He was tempted to stop at a bored-looking woman with a food cart at the corner and see if she had coffee, but he was certain it would be undrinkable.

Turning the corner, he made his way west, toward the docks. There were several large industrial buildings lining the far side of the street, with a nondescript office building on Alex's side. Beyond the office building were smaller industrial businesses, everything from leather goods to a cobbler's shop. As Alex expected, there was a five and dime squeezed between the big buildings across the street and two diners on his side.

"About time you got here," Lieutenant Detweiler growled as he looked up over the newspaper in his hands. He was leaning against the front fender of a police car and Alex could see a bored-looking uniformed officer sitting behind the wheel.

"What made you think I was coming at all?" Alex asked, genuinely puzzled.

"I called Lieutenant Pak fifteen minutes ago," he replied. "Told me he'd dropped you at the crawler station so you could come here. I decided to wait."

"Does that mean you've found out where the tainted food is coming from?"

Alex wasn't one hundred percent certain that it was food making people sick, but it was the best bet by a long shot.

Detweiler chuckled at that, folding up his paper before tucking it under his arm.

"We checked the diners and the lunch counter over there," he jerked his thumb over his shoulder at the five and dime, "but there was no sign of anything out of the ordinary."

"How did you test their food?" Alex pushed back.

"Your little friend, the alchemist—"

"Linda," Alex supplied.

"Right," Detweiler said, "Linda said that the stuff that cures the sick people—"

"Behring's Antiserum."

Detweiler gave Alex a hard look.

"Whatever," he said. "The point is that it's almost exclusively used to cure things that are magically induced. That's why there isn't much call for it. Once we knew that, we called for a sorcerer to come take a look at our eateries."

That made sense. A sorcerer would be able to detect magical

residue, even if it had been a few days since something tainted had been served. Alex could have used ghostlight to do the same thing, if he'd been available, but with his sore foot, he was glad he didn't have to.

"Anyway," Detweiler went on, "your girlfriend was on call today, so she came out and took a look, didn't find anything."

"I thought you said you did find something?" Alex said.

"Well other than liking you, Miss Kincaid seems pretty smart," Detweiler said with a chuckle. "You see, an hour ago there were half a dozen dog wagons here."

Street vendors. Alex's mind snapped into focus. He remembered the woman with the cart on the sidewalk before he'd turned the corner. It was such a common sight, the fact that she sold food didn't even register with him.

"Any of the vendors stick out to Sorsha?" he asked.

"None of them had any magical aura, if that's what you mean. But when we questioned them, they all said that this is a hot spot for the lunch trade."

"How many?" Alex asked.

"As many as three dozen," Detweiler said. "All up and down this block and the next one on both sides of the street, selling everything from hot dogs, to ready-made sandwiches, sweets, there's even one that sells cold beer, if you can believe that."

"So they congregate here for the lunch rush," Alex said, looking around at the empty street. It was already one-thirty, so he wasn't surprised the dog wagons had moved on to greener pastures. With the shift workers back on the job, and almost no foot traffic, it simply wasn't worth staying. He suspected the only reason the woman around the corner was still there was due to the proximity of the crawler station.

Which gave him an idea.

"Get in your car, Lieutenant," he said, hobbling over to the rear door behind the driver. "We need to get over to the other hotspot, the one near the garment district."

"It's after the lunch hour there too," Detweiler said, although he hurried around the car to the passenger side and got in.

"Is it?" Alex asked. "A lot of places in the garment district take late lunches so they can be in their shops when everyone else is on their lunch break."

He wasn't surprised that Detweiler didn't know that, since detectives and lieutenants usually took lunch when they could get it, and some days went without.

The ride to the garment district only took five minutes since traffic in this part of town was light. When the driver turned the last corner, however, traffic nearly came to a standstill.

There had to be at least a hundred people on the sidewalks, moving up and down in spite of the chill November air. Most huddled together with steaming cups of coffee or soup bought from the vendors as they spoke in quiet voices. The diner across the street had no open seats at their counter and a short line of people waiting to take away their order. A few heartier folk had round lunchboxes and sat on the curb in the cold, watching the activity around them as they ate.

Detweiler whistled.

"It's a madhouse out there," the uniform in the driver's seat said as he eased the car over to the curb.

"That's a lot of people eating outside in the cold," Detweiler observed.

"I guess they need a change from work," Alex said.

"You want me to call for backup?" the driver asked.

Detweiler turned to Alex.

"You think you can investigate all of those with your lamp and fancy monocle?"

"If I have enough time," he said. "Problem is those vendors aren't going to stay put. We know at least one of them wheeled their cart all the way here from the Meatpacking District. As soon as the lunch rush dies down, they're going to move on."

"So we need backup," Detweiler declared. "Though by the time they get here it'll probably be too late."

Alex didn't argue; the little man was right. There was maybe fifteen minutes left before the throngs on the street would be gone.

"What we need," Alex said with a grin, "is faster backup. Can you get a Central Office switchboard operator on your radio?"

"Miss Kincaid?" the southern drawl of Carolyn Burnside burst from the intercom on Sorsha's desk. She'd been reviewing sales and inventory figures for Kincaid Refrigeration and now she was going to have to start again.

"What is it, Miss Burnside?" she asked, managing not to sigh or sound irritable. She'd given specific instruction that she was not to be disturbed and Carolyn was an extremely competent woman. If she'd interrupted her employer, it was because the matter at hand was serious.

"I have Mr. Lockerby on the line," Carolyn said, "he claimed to have an urgent matter he'd like to discuss with you."

Sorsha smirked at that. Alex could be excessively charming when he wanted something, and while Carolyn wasn't completely resistant to his charms, she'd been burned by him before, so she never took anything he said at face value.

Where Alex is concerned, Sorsha thought, *that's probably a wise position.*

"Thank you, Carolyn," Sorsha said, putting down the pencil she'd been holding and stretching her arms above her head. "Put him through."

The intercom clicked off and Sorsha reached for the phone. It was an ornate model that had been a gift from Bell Telephone when one of their salesmen had negotiated a bulk order of cooling disks. Sorsha had to admit, that salesman knew his business, the phone was boxy, with the new dial mechanism on a slanted panel that made up the top of the phone. A silver-plated arm rose up behind the dial, ending in a spring-loaded fork that supported the cradle. The handset was silver with white leather wrapped around the middle and blue accents.

It was the perfect phone for her office, and, despite its being just a bit ostentatious, Sorsha liked it.

Taking hold of the handset as the phone began to ring, Sorsha lifted it to her ear.

"It's about time you called me," she said in her most imperious tone. "Even before your accident, you were terribly negligent in your communications."

"I was under the impression you didn't like to be disturbed at work," Alex's voice greeted her.

He was right, of course. Sorsha hated being interrupted when she was working, and, as a powerful and dangerous sorceress, she usually got her way.

"That is for people I'm not engaged to," she said, not giving him an inch. "I believe the proper amount of work interruptions for a fiancé is at least six a week, twelve if the wedding date is actually set."

"Uh," Alex stammered.

Sorsha almost laughed, but that would have given the game away. Like most men, the idea of matrimony was both desirable and uncomfortable for Alex. That knowledge gave Sorsha a distinct edge when it came to their verbal sparring, one she intended to wield liberally and with impunity.

"Sorry, doll," Alex managed after a full second, "I'm still recovering from being unconscious all those weeks, so I'm not back to full strength."

As rejoinders went, this one wasn't bad and Sorsha smiled to herself. He had called her 'doll,' a term of endearment she disliked, but Alex knew she disliked it and used it on purpose. That was him trying to get her off balance.

She'd had offers of marriage before, some from men that actually interested her, but no one could spar with her like Alex. She reveled in the idea of a man who was just as smart as she was, smarter in some areas.

"Well," she said, not lessening her imperious tone a whit, "that's certainly a good excuse, so I shall forgive you...this time."

"I've always said you were a merciful woman," he replied, affecting the most pitiful cockney accent imaginable.

This time Sorsha couldn't resist and she laughed.

"Why are you calling?" she said. "I spent my lunch hour sniffing around an industrial street for that other lieutenant you sometimes work with."

"I'm afraid Lieutenant Detweiler and I both need your sniffer again," he said.

That made her smile vanish. She'd already teleported twice today and she wasn't looking forward to doing it again.

"I'm sorry," Alex said when she explained her hesitations. "Whatever it is that's making people sick, the alchemists aren't able to keep up with demand for the antidote. If we don't find where this is coming from, and fast, a lot of people are going to die."

Sorsha wanted to complain. She wanted to tell Alex that she wasn't wearing the right shoes to go walking all over creation. After all, most men liked it when their significant other played helpless once in a while; it made them feel appropriately manly.

Unfortunately for her, Alex was a different breed. He liked her strength. What's more, he was right about people dying, and according to Linda Kellin, several people were already dead.

"All right," she said, rubbing her eyes. "Do you know any poetry?"

"Poetry?" Alex replied in a voice that conveyed the absurdity of the notion. "I know a limerick about a sailor and a fishwife."

"Don't you even think about it," Sorsha said, sending her senses down the phone wire. "Just keep talking, recite something."

There was a pause on the phone and Sorsha lost contact with the thread of power that filled the phone line.

"The Lord is my shepherd," Alex said, "I shall not want."

Sorsha had forgotten that Alex had been raised by a devout priest and she smiled as her magic took hold of his voice and began to follow it back along the wire.

"He maketh me to lie down in green pastures," Alex continued, "He leadeth me beside the still waters."

Sorsha's magic tether hit a sudden obstacle, as if Alex's voice left the wire. She quickly realized the operator in the Central Office must have linked the phone to the radio in Lieutenant Detweiler's car.

"He restoreth my soul: He leadeth me in the paths of righteousness for His name's sake."

Sorsha felt the distance jump as her magic reached out to the radio car, and found it.

"Yea, though I walk through the valley of the shadow of death, I will fear no evil: for Thou art with me."

Sorsha closed her eyes and the world lurched to the side, pitching and rolling like someone going over a waterfall in a barrel. Her skin stretched tight, like she was about to be pulled apart, but just before she lost all cohesion, she was dumped unceremoniously onto a dirty sidewalk just outside the garment district.

Strong hands gripped her as she swayed on her feet, encircling her and holding her steady. She took a deep breath through her nose, letting it out slowly as her stomach continued to churn as if it had not fully materialized yet.

"You can let go now," she said, opening her eyes as the sensation passed.

"You're a bum sport," Alex said, letting her slip from his arms.

She shot him a dirty look, then turned to his companions.

"Lieutenant," Sorsha greeted the balding little man. "I assume you need me to look at some more diners."

"Just those," Detweiler said, pointing up the street.

Sorsha turned, taking in the mass of humanity.

"You think it's one of the dog wagons?" she asked as she looked at them all.

"It has to be," Alex said. "It's the only thing that explains how people got sick around two completely different locations. The street vendors wheel their carts wherever the business is."

Sorsha understood. She was a little embarrassed that she hadn't thought of it herself. It only made sense that vendors with mobile carts wouldn't just stay in one place all day.

Closing her eyes, Sorsha summoned her power, then opened them again and looked up the street, then down.

"I'm guessing," Alex said, "that if you get close enough, you'll be able to tell if one of those carts is leaking magical energy.

She didn't have to get close. One of the carts, run by a shaggy man with brown hair and a crooked smile, was actively glowing.

"That one," she said.

27

THE LUSH

Alex followed Sorsha's pointing finger to a rickety cart with a sign proclaiming that it sold hot dogs. The man pushing it looked just like all the other vendors, though a bit scruffier and more unkempt. His clothes were decent and sturdy, but they'd seen better times, and Alex could see that his shirt collar and cuffs were threadbare.

The man himself looked to be in his thirties, with the rough hands of someone who pushed a cart all day and the brown skin that indicated work in the outdoors. His hair was long and brown, like the color of old leather, and it hung about his face like a curtain. Alex could see his dark eyes peering out from beneath that curtain and the brim of the tan flat cap he wore.

As Alex looked at the man, his eyes suddenly jumped up to look back. Alex realized too late that he was actually looking at Sorsha, and her accusatory finger. With a strangled cry, the man turned and ran.

"Stovall," Detweiler yelled at the patrolman, "go get him."

Officer Stovall didn't have to be told twice and took off like a shot, shouting for people to get out of his way.

"Take charge of that cart," Detweiler said to Alex as he ran for the patrol car.

When he reached it, he jumped in and eased the vehicle away from the curb. Alex watched as he pulled out into the crowded street and maneuvered off in the direction that the unknown man and Officer Stovall had gone.

"Well," Alex said, offering Sorsha his arm, "shall we?"

She gave him an amused look, then took the offered arm and walked toward the abandoned cart.

The cart itself, much like its vanished owner, was sturdy, but showing signs of age and disrepair. A small puddle had formed underneath it where what looked like a teacup's worth of water had dripped from the bottom of the cart. The push handle had been made of an old length of lead pipe and there were slight indentations in the soft metal where the owner had put his hands when moving it.

The top of the cart had two trap doors in it, each with a porcelain-covered knob sticking up from it. A cursory examination of both revealed a steamer compartment for the bread and a compartment of hot water for the hot dogs. A few waterlogged sausages bobbed in the water and, even though he knew they were tainted, Alex had to admit, they smelled delicious.

"You always take me to the nicest places," Sorsha said with a smirk.

"Oh, this is just the fare for us common folk," he said, smirking right back at her. "I wouldn't expect a high-class dame such as yourself to know about the joys of hot dogs."

He expected her to spar right back at him, but instead, her expression turned wistful, almost sad.

"I used to eat them all the time," she said, "but that was before... well, just before."

Alex assumed she was referring to the days before she came into her power. If he remembered what he'd heard about her, she was well into her fifties. No one would ever know, since she didn't look a day over twenty-five, and she'd keep looking like that for another century or so. Alex had never heard the story of what Sorsha had been, or where she'd come from prior to receiving her magic.

She'll tell you when she's ready, he admonished himself. Not that it really mattered; Alex was in a relationship with the woman she was, not the woman she had been.

"Buy me a hot dog," she said suddenly, breaking Alex's train of thought.

He looked around and found another cart with a sign reading 'Hot Dogs,' so he excused himself and headed over. Not knowing what a regal and powerful sorceress might want as a condiment, he skipped the piccalilli and just got two plain dogs.

When he made his way back to where Sorsha stood, Alex found her crouched down, staring at the side of the cart.

"Find anything?"

Sorsha stood up and accepted the dog.

"It looks like the source of the magic is the boiler stone he's using to keep the water hot," she said.

Alex peered down into the water, barely able to make out the reddish-black stone at the bottom of the tank.

"Can you fish it out?"

He looked at Sorsha when she didn't answer and found her enjoying her hot dog. Involuntarily, Alex looked around but didn't see anyone with a camera.

Never let anyone take your picture while you're eating, Sorsha had admonished him on one of their dates, *you'll always end up looking ridiculous*.

With no newsies in sight, Alex took a bite as well and turned back to the cart.

"Aww," Sorsha said, obviously aware of why he looked around. "That's sweet of you to make sure nobody had a camera."

"You looked before," Alex accused her.

She didn't reply, just took another bite while waggling her eyebrows at him.

"I don't have my kit," Alex said, "do you think it's safe for me to take the stone out?"

She was still chewing, so she shook her head. Handing him her hot dog, Sorsha reached out above the steaming water rising off the open compartment and closed her fingers while raising her hand. A moment later the stone broke the surface of the water and immediately began to steam in the frigid air.

Now that Alex could see it clearly, its color was wrong. He'd been using a boiler stone to brew coffee in his office for years and he knew that once they heated up, they would glow a dull red color. This one had cracks running all along the surface that pulsed with a sickly yellow color. Alex had the disturbing impression that they were veins.

"That doesn't look right at all," he said.

Sorsha opened her hand and brought it down underneath the hovering stone.

"Give me your handkerchief," she said.

Alex pulled the folded cloth from the pocket of his suit coat, then placed it on Sorsha's upturned hand. She took hold of the corner and opened the fold once, so it was still folded in half along the long axis. Satisfied, she released the tension in her hand and the stone slowly sank down into the handkerchief.

"You'd better hang on to this," she said, folding the handkerchief closed again and handing it to Alex.

"Is it safe to do that?"

"It's calmed down since I took it out of the water," Sorsha said.

That made sense. Boiler stones would heat up when exposed to water, but once they were dry, their magic became dormant.

"Do you know what's wrong with it?" Alex said, accepting the bundle and tucking it in his outermost coat pocket.

"I'd have to study it, but this isn't the place for that. I know it doesn't feel like sorcery."

"If there's a rune on it, that will be easy to find," Alex added. "Is there anything else going on with this cart?"

Sorsha ate the last bite of her hot dog, then walked slowly around the beat-up vendor cart.

"No," she said at last. "Now that the toxic rock is gone, it's lost most of its magic. I still wouldn't eat anything that came out of it, not ever."

"I'll tell Detweiler to have it destroyed."

"Speaking of the lieutenant," Sorsha said, looking around, "shouldn't he be back with our nefarious vendor?"

She was right, Detweiler and Officer Stovall should have returned by now.

"That's not a good sign," he said.

Five minutes later he was proved right when Detweiler returned with the car but without Stovall.

"What happened?" Alex asked, leaning heavily on his cane.

"The little bastard pulled a gun," the lieutenant growled. "Let's just say that he was a bad shot and Officer Stovall is a good one."

Alex sighed. He'd figured it would be something like that when it took Detweiler so long to return.

"Stovall is keeping watch on his body and I called for the coroner and a few more officers. Please tell me you have something."

Alex pulled the handkerchief from his pocket and opened it so the lieutenant could see it.

"Well, if running away wasn't already a sign that our vendor was poisoning people on purpose," Detweiler said, "this clinches it. No one in their right mind would use a boiler stone that looks like that."

"I'd worry it would explode," Alex admitted as he returned the stone to his pocket.

"What can you tell me about it?" Detweiler pressed on.

"We'll have to take it somewhere quieter to examine it," Sorsha said.

"What about this?" the lieutenant said, kicking one of the cart wheels.

"Burn it," Sorsha said. "We have the stone, and the cart isn't useful, but it might still be toxic."

"Actually," Alex interrupted her, "with a little bit of luck and my crime scene kit, I think this wheeled dispensary might actually be useful."

Half an hour later, Alex tapped Detweiler on the shoulder.

"Pull over here," he said.

Squinting through his oculus, Alex swept the street with his multi-lamp looking for any trace of a barely visible brown line hovering in the air. Opening the passenger door of the patrol car, Alex climbed out and limped around the front of the car and headed into the street.

"Be careful," Sorsha called after him, as Alex was forced to step back to avoid an oncoming car.

Alex swung his lamp side to side, but nothing materialized. Unfortunately amberlight was dim even in low light and in the light of the overcast afternoon, it was practically invisible.

"Do we need to go back to the last block?" Detweiler asked from the car.

"Give me a minute," Alex fussed. He'd been looking for that thin amber line from street to street, following it back from the cart, now secured by the police to wherever it was the cart stayed overnight. That would either be the dead man's home or some rented space and, if it was the latter, the landlord would know where the man lived.

Finding nothing, Alex returned to the sidewalk. He could have followed the line left by the cart as its deceased owner pushed it through the streets, but that line was so faint, it was practically invisible. The line pointing back to where the cart spent its nights was much more visible, but it ran in a more-or-less straight line, meaning that Alex had to guess where the line would intersect each block, one at a time.

"Maybe further up," he said, turning in the direction they'd been driving. He'd gotten lucky on the last block and seen the line when they drove through it, but the height of the line varied, seeming to undulate as it went. Alex couldn't count on seeing it inside the patrol car.

Raising the lantern up, he moved up the sidewalk, garnering strange looks from passers-by. Ignoring the onlookers, Alex focused his attention through the lens of his oculus. Painful step by painful step, he made his way up the block until finally he had to turn back. He couldn't be certain of the exact spot where the line would cross this block, but he was sure he'd already gone too far.

"Must have missed it," he grumbled.

This time, he swept the lantern up and down with each step. He'd almost moved on when he saw a thread down low, just above the ground. It looked like a spider's web through his oculus, but when he shined the amberlight right at it, he could see the reflected glow.

"Here it is," he said, motioning for Detweiler to bring up the car. "The line goes through here."

Looking up, Alex found himself confronting a store that sold hardware and tools for builders. Sticking his head through the door, he asked a sales clerk if anyone kept a dog wagon there overnight and was promptly told 'no.'

"Next block," he said, limping up to the car and opening the door.

"This is getting monotonous," Sorsha said, checking her watch.

"Getting?" Detweiler scoffed.

"Do you want to find our poisoner's lair or not?" Alex grumbled right back at them.

"Fine," they both said at the same time in the same begrudging tone.

Detweiler maneuvered back into traffic, turning at the corner of the block and again onto the next street. This one was a bit more industrial than the previous blocks with several large, open carriage doors leading into warehouses, along with a few specialty shops, and a grungy-looking apartment building.

"Yell when you see it," Detweiler said as he began driving slowly down the street.

"I don't have to," Alex said, pointing at a building across the street. "That's going to be it."

"How can you tell?" Sorsha asked.

"It says 'Secure Storage with reasonable rates' on the side," Alex pointed out. "Also, it's right where I expect the thread to be."

Detweiler went past the warehouse and turned around, parking the patrol car near the wooden sidewalk.

"I see several vendor carts inside," Sorsha said as Alex held her door for her. "Good call."

"Save it," Detweiler said as Alex gave Sorsha a salacious grin. "You two get any more lovey-dovey, I'm going to be sick."

The interior of the warehouse was a large open space with a concrete floor. Someone had taken great pains to paint exactly straight lines on the floor, marking out a row of squares about the size of a standard vendor cart. Aisles had also been laid out in such a way as to provide ease of mobility while still being able to pack carts in by the dozen.

"You in charge?" Detweiler said, flashing his gold lieutenant's badge at a bored-looking man in a pair of coveralls.

"Milt Green," he said. "I own this place."

"We're looking for a man who operates a dog wagon," Detweiler said.

Milt chuckled at that.

"Well, you've come to the right place," he said. "I've got almost a hundred of them renting space from me. Who is it you want?"

Alex described the man, but Milt just shrugged.

"Sounds like most of 'em," he said. "Excepting the three or four ladies."

"This guy has shaggy hair and clothes that need repair," the lieutenant explained.

Milt started to answer, but Alex wasn't listening. He turned and shined his light over the empty warehouse. Moving forward, he swept the lamp back and forth until he found the end of the tiny thread he'd been following. In the space marked out for one of the carts stood a ghostly image of the cart Alex sought.

"Here," he called, tuning back to the others. "Who rents this spot?" Alex looked down at the painted square and saw a number stenciled inside it. "D-11," he read.

"Oh," Milt said, his face souring, "him."

"Him who?" Detweiler coaxed.

"That's Timmy Paulson's space," Milt said. "He's a mealy-mouthed little barnacle. What did he do this time?"

"He's dead," Sorsha said. "What we need is his address."

Milt looked shocked, then hesitant, until Detweiler waved his badge in his face.

"I'll have to look it up," he said. "I've got his card in my office."

Alex blew out his multi-lamp as Milt headed through a door into the rear of the warehouse. He'd left his kit bag in the car, so he left the burner inside the multi-lamp and just set it on the cement floor. Peeling off the headband that kept his oculus in place, he dropped the little brass and glass monocle into his jacket pocket.

"How are you doing?" Sorsha asked as he rubbed his eyes.

"I'm tired," he said. "I mean, my foot hurts when I walk, but it's not that bad."

"So what's wrong?" she asked, her hand rubbing the back of his neck.

"I shouldn't be so tired," he said, keeping his voice low.

"You just recovered from a month of being unconscious," Sorsha said.

"Six weeks," Alex corrected, "but I was in pretty good shape."

Sorsha put her arm around his back and snuggled into his chest.

"You just need some training," she said. "You'll be back to normal in no time."

"What if I'm not," he said. "What if my magic wasn't just something I used to write runes? What if it's part of who I am?"

Alex had been worried about that since his first day awake. Part of him felt fine, but there was an emptiness inside he couldn't explain and, if he was honest with himself, he didn't want to think about.

"Of course your magic is part of who you are," Sorsha said, stepping around to look him in the eyes. She put her hands on the sides of his face and pulled him down to her level. "You're not going to feel the same until that rune on your chest has purified all the damage you did to yourself because you just had to be everybody's hero."

Alex scoffed at that and shook his head.

"You mad?" he asked.

"Of course I'm mad," she said, her eyes squeezing into slits. "But your ridiculous need to help everyone, and to win no matter what, is one of the things I love about you. So," she slapped him on his chest, "man up and take your medicine. You barely use your magic to solve cases anyway."

Alex knew that wasn't true, but most of his best tricks were ones that just needed runes. He didn't even have to write them.

Sighing, he looked around at the warehouse. He'd been so focused on finding the cart and learning the name of its owner that he literally hadn't paid attention to anything else.

"Hey," he called to Milt, who had just returned with the information card on Timmy Paulson, "is that sign right?"

Alex pointed to a placard on the wall that advertised services for cart owners including wheel repair, fresh water, boxes of pastries, and other supplies. Most interesting to Alex was the offer of new boiler stones for vendors whose existing ones had lost their magic charge.

"Sure is," Milt said. "My clients can even rent tools from me to make their own repairs."

"Can I see your boiler stones?" Alex asked.

Milt hesitated but Detweiler tapped his badge and the proprietor just shrugged. Placing Paulson's card on the counter for Detweiler, Milt crouched down, then came back up with a box of reddish looking stones. To Alex, they always looked like charcoal, just with a smooth surface.

"Miss Kincaid?" Lieutenant Detweiler said, nodding at the box.

"They're all normal stones," she said after squinting at the box for a long moment.

"Did Timmy ever buy a boiler stone from you?" Alex asked.

Milt scoffed.

"He's a week late with his cart rental," he said. "He drinks, er... drank, not meaning to speak evil of the dead, but it's true."

"That means he got his stone elsewhere," Detweiler said.

"Most people in desperate situations hit up people they know," Alex suggested.

"That's the truth," Milt chimed in. "My sister married a real bum and he's always coming around looking for a handout."

"You think Timmy did that too?" Sorsha asked.

"If he drank away his money, what other choice did he have?" Detweiler observed.

"So now we have to find an alchemist who knew Timmy," Sorsha said.

"That's going to be easier than you think," Alex said. "He's either got one in his family, or he met one at his favorite watering hole." He offered Sorsha his arm. "Would you like to take a tour of seedy gin-mills this evening, Miss Kincaid?"

She rolled her eyes as she put her hand on his forearm.

"You always take me to the nicest places."

28

ON THE TOWN

The man behind the bar was the very textbook definition of 'grizzled.' He was at least a foot shorter than Alex but managed to project an air of both danger and authority in spite of that. His mop of black hair was tied back in a ponytail, the kind Alex had seen favored by sailors and men from the orient. His left eye was closed in a permanent squint, which made his open right eye seem all the larger, and when it swung to the door to appraise the new arrivals, a sneer appeared on his lip, though it seemed to be reserved for the gold badge on Lieutenant Detweiler's suit coat.

"I need to ask you a few questions," the lieutenant said, bellying up to the bar.

"You with him?" the bartender said, leaning around Detweiler to look at Alex and Sorsha.

The bar was definitely a seedy establishment, in the basement of a professional building, with sawdust and peanut shells on the floor. It was still early, so there were only a couple of patrons scattered around the room, but even then, Sorsha stood out like an arc light in the dark room.

"We are," Alex said, putting on his friendly smile, "but that doesn't mean I won't have a drink, bourbon, and make it the good stuff." Alex turned to Sorsha, but she gave him a look that stated clearly that she wouldn't be drinking anything served in such an establishment. "Better make it two," he said, looking back at the bartender.

Alex took off his suit coat and put it over one of the well-worn barstools so Sorsha could sit down. This was the fifth gin mill they'd visited with Detweiler, so the gesture of chivalry wasn't as novel this time around. That said, Sorsha gave Alex a sincere smile and sat down.

"Why did you do that?" Detweiler protested as the man turned away to make the drinks.

"He doesn't like cops," Alex whispered back. "Keep trying to ask him questions and I'll keep interrupting you. He'll talk to me and think he's putting you off."

"You aren't as funny as you think you are," Detweiler growled.

"We're here to get information," Alex said, working hard not to smirk, "so you take a few pretended hits to your ego, hopefully we learn something, and we leave."

"Fine," the lieutenant said as the man turned back to the bar.

The bartender set up two glasses that actually looked clean and poured out two bourbons with the efficiency of a man who'd been doing it for decades.

"Enough," Detweiler said, putting his badge on the bar. "I'm looking for a guy who lives around here, and you're going to tell me if you've seen him."

Alex had picked up the shot glass while Detweiler spoke and he sipped it.

"That's not bad," he interrupted as the bartender got red in the face. Clearly his dislike for cops was about to get the better of him. "Have you been saving that stuff since before Prohibition?"

The little man's color changed and he actually smiled, showing a row of straight, white teeth, with a gap on one side.

"My father bricked up his whole stock in the cellar," he said proudly.

"He was a man of taste," Alex said. "The guy we're looking for is anything but, unfortunately. He does like to drink, though, so maybe you've seen him in here once or twice. Name's Timmy Paulson."

A flash of recognition crossed over the bartender's face and he finally nodded. "He comes in here whenever he's got coin to spend. I used to let him run a tab, but not anymore. Once he paid up, it was strictly cash."

"He paid his tab?" Sorsha said. She'd picked up the bourbon when Alex praised it. "From what we've heard, he spends his money as fast as he makes it."

"He made a friend," the barkeep said. "A guy who comes in here once or twice a month. They struck up a conversation one night and then Timmy starts coming in with money, real money, not the pittance he makes with his dog wagon."

"Who was this friend?" Detweiler demanded, earning an even more squinted glare from the barkeep's left eye.

"We'd really like to know," Alex said, putting his glass back on the bar for a second round.

The man gave Alex a similar squint, but then uncorked the bottle and refilled the glass.

"Rodney Tieg is his name," the man said. "Tall, skinny fellow with an average face."

"Is there anything else you can tell us?" Sorsha said, actually sipping the bourbon.

"I think he's an alchemist."

Detweiler opened his mouth, but Alex cut him off.

"What makes you think that?"

"Well, he never said anything," the barkeep said, rubbing his chin, "but he always had that smell, you know, like an alchemy shop."

Alex knew exactly what he meant; having gotten very close to Jessica, he knew why she always showered before they went out. Alchemists always smelled faintly of chemicals.

"That's it," Detweiler demanded, leaning across the bar. "Buddy, if I think you're holding out on me, I'll start drinking here on the regular. With a few of my cop buddies."

The barman's face was growing red until the lieutenant added that last line, then his face blanched.

"That's all I know," he declared, leaning across the bar to face off with Detweiler. "Now order a drink or get out of my bar."

Detweiler held the man's gaze for a long minute, then, apparently satisfied, turned and headed for the door.

Alex paid for his and Sorsha's drinks, then picked up his coat from the barstool, and escorted Sorsha out.

Once they'd climbed back up to the level of the street, they found Detweiler leaning against the patrol car.

"Did he say anything after I left?"

"No," Sorsha said, "but we do have a name now."

"Rodney Tieg," Detweiler said. "I'll call in to the Central Office and have someone look him up in the permit registry."

"Good," Alex said, steering Sorsha toward the nearest corner of the block.

"Where are we going?" she asked.

Alex nodded in the direction of a five and dime.

"I'll call my alchemist friend, Charles Grier," he said, looking at Detweiler. "Pick us up there."

Detweiler grumbled something inaudible that Alex took to be agreement, and Alex led Sorsha to the corner, limping all the way.

"How's your foot?" she asked.

"I'll never take magic healing for granted again."

"So why are we bothering Charles?" Sorsha said. "The lieutenant is going to have Tieg's address for us shortly."

"Yes," Alex admitted, "but who's going to tell us what Tieg's up to? I probably know more about alchemy than anyone here and I wouldn't know if Tieg was doing something weird. We're going to need an actual alchemist to tell us if that toxic rock was made in Tieg's shop."

Sorsha gave out a little snicker as they crossed the street, squeezing his arm as she did so.

"I love the way your mind works," she said. "What's the other reason?"

"Why must there be another reason?" Alex asked, somewhat defensive.

"Because you told me the first reason so easily," Sorsha said. "You always like to keep something back, just for yourself, so you can reveal it later and show how brilliant you are."

Alex didn't know whether to be impressed or irritated that Sorsha had him so thoroughly figured out. Impressed won in the end. After all, having a brilliant fiancée couldn't hurt his reputation any.

"Alchemy is a fairly tight-knit community," he explained. "If I were a betting man, I'd say that Charles knows Tieg, or has at least heard of him. Anything Charles can tell us will be very useful when we have to deal with the man himself."

"Okay," Sorsha said, elbowing him gently. "That *is* pretty smart."

"Never heard of him," Charles said once Alex finally got hold of him. "Should I have?"

"No," Alex admitted, "he's a suspect in that poisoning case."

"Did you figure out how the poison is being spread?"

Alex took a deep breath and explained about Timmy Paulson and his tainted hot dog water.

"That's actually pretty clever," Charles said when Alex finished. "Do you think the hot dog vendor knew what was going on?"

"When we tried to talk to him, he ran off and eventually pulled a gun on the policeman who was chasing him," Alex explained. "The cop shot him dead. We got lucky, though and I was able to track the cart back to where Paulson kept it at night."

"So now you're looking for this Tieg fellow?"

"Lieutenant Detweiler is on the radio with the Central Office right now, having them look through the licensing book. That'll tell us where to find Tieg's lab."

"So you just wanted to know if I knew him?" Charles asked.

"Well, I doubt Tieg is going to tell us what he's up to," Alex said. "I figured you might want to go through his lab for the cops."

"Alex," Charles protested, "it's almost three o'clock, I've got customers."

"The police will pay you for your time as a consultant," Alex shot back.

"I'd still have to close my shop."

"Why don't you borrow Carmen from Linda? She should be capable enough to hold down the fort."

Carmen Harris was almost one of Paschal Randolph's blood magic victims. She'd been working as a prostitute but had the talent for alchemy so, ever since Alex saved her life, she'd been Linda Kellin's apprentice.

"I suppose that might work," Charles admitted after a long moment. "Give me half an hour to make the arrangements and get Carmen over here, assuming Linda is willing to part with her."

"Detweiler is here," Sorsha said, leaning into the phone booth.

"I've got to go," Alex said, "I'll call you as soon as we find Tieg's lab."

The door at the end of the dirty hallway read Tieg Alchemical in faded silver paint in the center of a pane of glass. At the bottom of the dirty window, office hours had been written in the same silver, but the printing was newer.

Alex took all this in at a glance, but the thing that grabbed his attention was the fact that the door was slightly ajar.

"Get back," Detweiler said, stepping in front of them as he noticed the door.

"Don't be absurd," Sorsha said, quickening her pace and stepping around the lieutenant.

She walked quickly and confidently to the door, conjuring a bright blue ball of energy in her hand. Pausing a moment, Sorsha pushed the door open quickly and stepped inside. The energy ball in her hand burst into half a dozen smaller spheres and flew from her hand to light the room with a brilliant glow.

Sorsha held her hand out for a moment, then relaxed and the light in the room died out.

"He isn't here," she said, stepping inside so Alex and the lieutenant could enter.

Alex looked around the lab. It was shockingly similar to the one where he'd watched Jessica work, and like the one in Charles Grier's basement. Absently he wondered if there was something that could be done to make it easier, better.

Andrew is starting to rub off on you, he thought as a smile graced his lips.

"Looks like our friend left in a hurry," Detweiler said, shoving his .38 back into his shoulder holster.

"He must have found out about Paulson," Sorsha said.

Alex leaned on his cane and let the details of the room soak in. Several of Tieg's brew tables still had potions bubbling away on them, their colorful liquids moving along glass tubes and dripping into beakers. There were several other tables where the glassware had been knocked over, their spoiled contents dripping along the surfaces and onto the floor.

"Something's off," he mumbled to himself.

His eyes came to rest on a table with one of the broken experiments. The glassware was knocked over, most of it broken and scattered around, all except one large, long-necked boiling jar sitting over an active burner. As he watched, tiny bubbles began to form along the bottom, reaching up through the liquid in tiny strings.

"Sorsha," he said as the clear liquid began to turn orange.

He turned to find his fiancée looking through a large book atop a writing desk.

"Yes?" she said, not looking up.

"Sorsha!" he yelled, pointing at the jar where the liquid was turning red.

She whirled, her eyes going wide as they realized what Alex had seen. Reaching out, she opened her hand and a frigid wind blew through the lab, extinguishing the flame on the burner and coating the jar in a sheet of frost.

Alex started to relax but it was short lived as the red liquid shifted to yellow. Before he could do anything, Sorsha pushed her hand out again and the jar flew across the room and out the third story window. It had barely cleared the building when it exploded with enough force to knock Alex down and send paper and bits of broken glass flying around the room. The brew lines that hadn't been disturbed were knocked over and shattered while several of the ignited burners caught the alchemical liquids on fire.

"I'm glad that thing wasn't in here with us when it exploded,"

Detweiler said, letting go of the table he'd used to keep from being blown down.

Sorsha knelt over Alex, offering him her hand. With her magic, she was as strong as she wanted to be, but there were more important things to take care of.

"Put the fires out," he said, pushing himself up into a sitting position.

Sorsha turned and snapped her fingers, causing the growing flames to simply vanish. When she turned back to Alex, he was pulling himself up on one of the sturdy tables.

"Well now what?" Detweiler said, looking around at the destruction. "Everything is destroyed."

"Only the alchemy," Alex said.

"Isn't that the important part, darling?" Sorsha asked. "Did you hit your head when you fell?"

Alex gave her a patronizing look, then shook his head.

"Tieg smashed everything that might have given us a clue what he was up to," he said. "The things that were still burning were the ones he didn't care about."

"So, Tieg is on the run and we're back to square one," Detweiler said.

"No, I don't think so," Alex said, limping over to the sturdy writing desk.

Setting his cane on top of the desk, Alex knelt down, then leaned forward until his cheek was on the floor. Reaching under the desk, he scrabbled around for a moment, then withdrew a sickly looking red boiler stone, shot through with yellow veins.

"I saw this when I was down on the floor earlier," he said, setting the diseased-looking rock on the desk before pulling himself back to his feet. "Now we know for a fact where Timmy Paulson got his toxic boiler stone."

"Can you use one of your finding runes to track him?" Detweiler asked.

"If we can find something in here that's important to him," Alex said.

"What about the stone?" Sorsha offered.

Alex shook his head.

"He didn't bother to retrieve it after it dropped," he said. "I suspect the stones are just a means to an end. We need something personal."

"Maybe at his apartment?" Detweiler said.

"Maybe," Alex conceded, though he rather suspected that Tieg had cleared that out as well.

"Well, then you'd better call Grier and get him over here," Detweiler said, reading the look on Alex's face. "We're going to need an alchemist to make sense of all this."

Alex checked his pocket watch for the fourth time in as many minutes and found that it was still roughly a quarter after four. Charles had arrived an hour ago and still wasn't even halfway through clearing Tieg's lab. Now he knew why Danny and Captain Callahan had been so irritable once he'd finished going over a crime scene.

"Don't fidget," Sorsha said, laying her head on his shoulder. "It's unbecoming."

"Was there a phone at that diner down the street?" he asked.

"You know there was," Sorsha said without looking up. "That's where the lieutenant called Charles from."

Alex hadn't been excited about walking half a block on his sore foot, so he'd sent Detweiler in his stead. Now, however, the prospect of a painful limp down to the phone was looking positively invigorating.

"I need to call Sherry," he declared, then waited for Sorsha to remove herself from his shoulder before standing. He told Detweiler that he needed to check in with his office, then he and Sorsha headed for the stairs.

"You know I can make it so you float," she said, "then I'd just have to push you along and you wouldn't have to use your foot."

"Like a balloon in the Macy's parade?" Alex fussed. "No thank you."

It took almost a quarter of an hour for Alex to reach the diner, and when he did, his foot was aching. He'd rather die than tell Sorsha that, however, so he tried his best not to limp too hard. Once he'd reached the phone booth, he sat down on the little bench and dialed his office.

"Hey, Boss," Sherry said once he'd greeted her. "How's everything going?"

"It's hurry up and wait on this end," he grumbled. "Did anyone call for me?"

"Danny," she replied. "He says he has some news about the Gallagher murder."

That piqued Alex's curiosity, so he finished up with Sherry and called the Central Office.

"I hear you've had a break in the case," Alex said. That wasn't exactly what Sherry said, but it was close enough.

"Yeah," Danny confirmed. "A big one. We know who Adam is."

"Is that good or bad?"

"Both," Danny admitted. "You were right about him being a private detective; his real name is Wade Phillips and he lives in the Bronx. His landlady got suspicious because he hadn't been home in a week, so she called missing persons. As soon as they heard he was a P.I., they called me."

"So what was his part in Ann's murder?"

"According to the notes we found in his office, someone hired him to find Ann. The money was good, so he took the job. Right before Ann was killed, however, his notebook suggests he was suspicious about his client."

"Did he say who hired him?"

"Dan Fischer," Danny said, "but Adam, er, Wade suspected that was an alias. We're running it down, in case it isn't, but I'm not optimistic."

Alex didn't find himself optimistic either.

"Wait a minute," Alex said as a new idea crossed his mind. "Did Wade's note say anything about looking for Liam or any of the other missing mobsters?"

"No," Danny said. "Nothing in his case files mentioned them."

"So, that means there's someone unaccounted for in this case," Alex said.

"You know there isn't," Danny replied, "unless you think Liam is the killer. He's the only one left alive."

"Are you sure about that?"

"I took a drive out to Rikers Island and spoke to some of the remaining crew. They were all motivated to find James and Michael's killer. According to them, there's no one left on the outside."

Alex didn't believe it, but he had no evidence to argue with, so he let it go and bade his friend good day.

"You don't look happy," Sorsha said, offering him a cigarette.

"I'm not," he admitted. "I must be missing something in the Ann Gallagher murder. I mean someone wanted to kill her very badly. Chopping someone up is personal."

"So she probably knew her attacker," Sorsha pointed out.

Alex sat up straight in the narrow phone booth. The files said that Ann had worked as a maid in Aidan Connolly's household. The only people that would have been coming in to meet the head of the family would be high ranking members of the organization. The ones that were either dead or in prison.

She was under the Connollys' thumb the whole time, he thought. *The only time she could have met someone else in the organization was when they came to get her off the...*

"Boat," Alex said.

"What?" Sorsha asked, surprised by his outburst.

Alex checked his watch. It was after four-thirty.

"Sorsha, darling," he said in the voice he used to deliver bad news. "I think I need to take you to another classy place, but we're going to have to teleport."

Sorsha raised an eyebrow at him.

"And where might that be?" she asked.

"Ellis Island," he said.

29

THE OTHER END

Alex sat in Liam Cohan's front room in a surprisingly comfortable easy chair. The room was dark, lit only by the occasional glow of his cigarette. The multiple spent butts in the nearby ashtray gave evidence that Alex had been sitting there for some time.

He'd arrived early, well before the police could release Liam. That didn't make the waiting any more palatable, of course, so Alex crushed out a third cigarette, then tugged his pocket watch clear from his vest pocket. Pushing the crown, he allowed the spring-loaded lid to flip open. There wasn't enough light to read a normal watch, but Alex's pocket watch was not normal. Instantly the runes inside sprang to life, glowing in vibrant greens and blues. Alex couldn't feel them anymore, but that didn't make them useless. The glow revealed the hands, telling him that it was ten minutes after seven.

He stifled a sigh and shut his watch, returning it to his pocket. Waiting was always difficult.

"I should have brought a bottle of Scotch and something to read," he muttered.

"You could engage in conversation," Danny Pak whispered from the couch on the far side of the room, "like telling me what we're actually doing here."

"We're waiting for Ann Gallagher's murderer," Alex said, "and the murderer of James Fahey and Michael Cohan as well, though I have to admit, I don't care so much about that."

"Obviously," Danny said, "we publicly released Liam from protective custody over an hour ago, who else would be coming here?"

"I told you," Alex said, "the murderer."

"Don't waste your breath, Danny," Sorsha said from the other end of the couch. "He's figured it out and he'll be insufferably smug until he gets to reveal it in the most dramatic way possible."

"You wound me, my dear," Alex said, placing his hand over his heart.

"I would have if you hadn't brought me along on this little operation of yours," she said, with no trace of humor in her voice.

"Any idea when we can expect the bad guy?" Danny asked, trying and failing to keep his voice down.

"If I had to guess, I'd say he'll want to be here before Liam gets home, so sometime in the next hour."

Danny sighed and settled back into the couch.

Sorsha just crossed her legs and blew Alex a kiss. She'd wanted Alex to sit on the couch with her, but the chair was the only place visible from the front door.

Twenty minutes later, Alex was fidgeting again. Crossing his legs, he lit another cigarette, but it didn't help. He was just too keyed up. He wanted to get up and pace, but the sound of his tread on the floor would surely be heard by someone outside.

Alex had just tapped off the first bit of ash from his cigarette when he heard a board creak outside.

Alex froze, holding his breath as he listened for confirmation that he had actually heard something. After a long moment, Danny opened his mouth to say something, but Alex held up a warning hand.

Several soft clicks emanated from the door.

It was the sound of lock picks searching for the pins inside the tumbler lock, a noise Alex knew well.

There was a sharp snap of metal on metal as the bolt slid open,

Pound of Flesh

then nothing. Having been on the other end of breaking and entering with a lock pick, Alex understood the intruder's hesitation. When a lock released, it always sounded louder than it really was, especially to the person trying to be quiet.

He's waiting to see if he's been noticed, Alex thought.

The next sound was a soft click as the door was pushed free from the jamb accompanied by a creak as it opened. Outside on the porch, a man stood, silhouetted against the glow of a distant street light. He was a big man, standing at least six feet based on his relation to the door frame. Alex could see thick arms and hands, but not much more.

As soon as the door opened, the man stepped quickly inside, swinging it closed behind him. When Alex heard the lock click closed again, he reached up and turned on the lamp next to his chair.

"Hello, Seamus," Alex said, causing the man to whirl around, "I've been expecting you."

In the light, Alex could see that he was an older man, probably in his late forties, with a haggard face, gray hair, and hard, green eyes. His hands were rough and calloused, and in his right hand he carried a long, twisted stick that resembled a club.

"And just who are you, boyo?" he growled in a thick Irish brogue. "Answer me!" he roared, raising his cudgel.

"I'm the guy with the pistol," Alex said, raising his right hand with the weapon in it. "Now, unless you think your shillelagh there is any match for a .45 caliber bullet, I suggest you drop it."

The man hesitated and Alex could see him gauging whether or not he could cross the room before Alex could shoot him dead. In the end, he decided to drop the cudgel.

"There now," he said, "tell me who you are."

"My name is Alex Lockerby, but that's not really important. What's important is who you are. Michael Cohan and James Fahey didn't see you coming. Did they?"

"They ratted out the family," Seamus growled. "That's why they got off scott free." He took a deep breath, then shouted, "They deserve what they got."

"That's funny," Alex said with no trace of humor in his voice. "Ann was the only one who did know you, wasn't she? She didn't deserve to die; your cousin Aiden didn't care about her at all, and he was the godfather of the Connolly clan."

Alex looked at Seamus as if he was expecting an answer, but the older man didn't speak.

"She mattered to you, though," Alex went on, "didn't she?"

"The little bitch," Seamus spat.

"She was one of yours, wasn't she? One of the poor desperate Irish who came to you for money to travel to America, the land of opportunity. The ones your bastard cousin scooped up to make slaves, to serve in his house, in his gambling parlors, and in his brothels. Like Ann's mother Katherine."

"So what?" Seamus said. "They were nothing. Poor, desperate shreds of human debris who should get on their knees and thank me for saving them from starvation." By the end, he was yelling again.

Alex got the distinct impression he was dangerously unbalanced.

"Is she the one who gave you up?" Alex asked. "There was a note in the police file that the authorities in Ireland had scooped up members of the Connolly mob in their country. The report didn't list any names, but a ten-year prison stint would explain the lateness of your revenge."

Seamus just stood there and glared at Alex.

Time to wrap up this show, Alex thought.

He used his left hand on the armrest of the chair to push himself up to his feet.

"Well," he said, picking up his cane, "I do thank you for confessing to your string of brutal murders, and for," he gestured with his gun to the shillelagh, "bringing the murder weapon with you."

Alex took a step out of the parlor and into the foyer. As he went, his cane skidded on the polished wood and his support went out from under him. The moment the cane moved, so did Seamus. He crouched down and grabbed his cudgel. Alex fell hard and his gun went skittering away.

"You figured me out," Seamus said, advancing on Alex with the shillelagh clasped in both hands, "lucky for me, you'll never live to tell anyone."

He raised the cudgel over his head, and Alex smiled.

"See," he said as Seamus' eyes went wide. "I do need you around."

"You did that on purpose," Sorsha said, coming up behind Seamus.

Danny walked around the other side of the murderous Irishman and gave Alex a hand up. For his part, Seamus' eyes were as wide as saucers as he fought against Sorsha's power.

"You'd better get that club," Alex said as he moved to pick up his cane, "it's evidence."

Sorsha snapped her fingers and Seamus released the club and slowly lowered his arms behind his back. It looked like he was moving casually, but his muscles strained to resist. It was a losing battle.

"All right, Seamus Connolly," Danny said, snapping handcuffs around the paralyzed man's wrists. "You are under arrest."

Sorsha snapped her fingers again and Seamus staggered forward, only to be pulled back by Danny.

"Come sit down, Seamus," he said, pushing the bound man toward the parlor.

"And what would you have done if dear Seamus had gotten your gun?" Sorsha asked as Alex leaned down to pick up the weapon.

"Oh you would have gotten to him before that," he said.

Sorsha looked at him coldly with a raised eyebrow.

"And if I didn't?"

Alex pressed the button that released the slide magazine of his 1911, dropping it out into his hand.

"Let's just say I had it covered," he said, holding up the magazine to reveal it was empty.

"I knew you did that on purpose," Sorsha said, then she slapped him across the face and turned away from him. "I was scared for you."

Alex put the cool body of his gun against his smarting cheek.

"Fine," he said in an exaggeratedly hurt voice. "I won't involve you next time."

Sorsha turned back to him, her eyes narrow. She leaned close and Alex could feel waves of cold coming from her.

"Thank you for including me in your performance," she said. "That was very nice of you."

"Sorry I scared you," he returned.

"Better," she said with a half-smile.

"What do you say I take you to dinner," he said. Sorsha gave him an imperious look. "Somewhere nice," he went on. "I'll even put on my tux."

Sorsha smiled at that.

"I'll need to change as well," she said, looking down at her slacks and vest outfit. "I still smell like sawdust and stale beer from the last place you took me out to."

She smiled at him and the pain of the slap he had heartily deserved vanished.

"I'll go talk to Danny and find out how far away the Jersey cops are," he said, "then once they're here, we can go."

Alex thought he'd be a long time getting into his tuxedo, with his injured foot holding him back, but his foot was feeling better than it had been in a while.

"Probably the result of all the sitting I got to do waiting for Seamus," he observed to himself as he used the bathroom mirror to tie his black bow tie.

His dressing completed, Alex dropped his pocket watch into his left coat pocket, where it wouldn't be too close to his skin, then added the gold lighter to his trouser pocket. His rune book normally went in the inside left pocket of his coat, but since Iggy had warned him off carrying that many runes, Alex tore out a few vault runes and tucked them into his pocket as well.

Satisfied that he was ready for a night out with Sorsha, he picked up his cane and headed into his vault to await her arrival. He looked over at his drafting table at the work he'd left undone. Iggy had taken the Limelight enhanced constructs he'd been working on and put them to work, so there really wasn't much left to be done.

"Runes you can't even use," he muttered, thinking of the improved shield constructs.

Turning away from his desk, Alex focused on his library. He thought of perusing some of his books, but they were mostly books on magic and magical theory, which made them equally unappealing in his current state. Frustrated, he turned away from the library, wanting to pace, but not wanting to put too much strain on his foot.

It was then that he heard the click of an electric light turning on accompanied by the 'ding' of a small bell.

He turned to see a red light above the office hallway blinking on and off. Since sound didn't travel through the cover doors thanks to Iggy's security constructs, Alex had rigged up the light with a wire that went all the way to his office. When the phone on his desk rang, the light would begin pulsing and a bell would ring once. Up to now it was something he'd never actually used, and he felt a thrill of excitement that it actually worked.

Shaking off the moment of inaction caused by his reaction, Alex headed down the little hallway that led to the office's cover door. Tapping the door with his gold key, Alex pushed it open and crossed the hall to his office.

Everything was dark, since Sherry and Mike had gone home hours ago, so Alex crossed to his desk and switched on the light. The glow of the magelight cast a white circle on the desktop, revealing the usual stack of folders and several notes that had been torn from a pad. Most of them were his, reminding himself to do certain things when next he was in.

Alex ignored them and scooped up the receiver from the telephone.

"Lockerby," he said as he held it to the side of his head.

"Alex," Detective Arnold's voice greeted him. "I'm glad I caught you. We've had a bit of a break in the speakeasy case and I wanted to run it by you."

"Why aren't you at home?" Alex demanded.

There was a pause, then Arnold chuckled.

"My wife's sister is in town, so she's making some fancy vegetable stew for dinner tonight," he said.

"Not a fan?"

"No," Arnold admitted. "My wife knows how I feel about it, so I won't get in too much trouble."

"So what's this break in the case?"

"Well, first off, I put a guard on Mrs. Hannover's hospital room," Detective Arnold said. "Just as a precaution."

"Do you think she's in danger?" Alex asked.

"I can't say for certain, but it seemed prudent after what happened to Thelma Rubison."

Alex, who'd been leaning back in his desk chair, sat up at that.

"You found her?" he asked.

"Yes," Arnold said. "Didn't I say that?"

"No," Alex said.

"Wow, I could have sworn I mentioned that," Arnold said. "My wife is always telling me that I would need wood screws to keep my head on, if it wasn't already attached. Anyway," he continued. "I was wondering why she changed her name from Ruby Tomlinson to Thelma Rubison, so I had some of my boys check the records for both names."

"I take it they found something."

"It turns out," Arnold said, "that there's no record of either name, but we did find out that there is someone with the last name of Tomlinson living in the south side mid ring. Garnet Tomlinson."

"Garnet?" Alex asked. "Like the gemstone?"

"Exactly like that," Arnold said. "I don't know about you, but that seemed like quite the coincidence, seeing how we're looking for someone called Ruby Tomlinson."

Alex didn't like coincidences and he said so.

"Well, I'm with you on that one, so I went over to talk to Garnet. She turned out to be a very attractive young woman in her mid-twenties. I was about to leave, though, when I noticed she was wearing black."

"Someone close to her died recently?" Alex guessed.

"When I asked about it, she said her grandmother, Ruby, had been killed two weeks ago by a burglar who strangled her to death."

"Another coincidence," Alex said.

"You know, I didn't want to believe this whole Central Park Butcher story right from the start," Arnold said. "It felt too sensational to be true. Now, I'm starting to believe."

"I know what you mean," Alex said, his mind whirling.

"Any ideas you might have on this would be appreciated."

Alex sighed. If the story of the Butcher was true, it was obvious what the man was doing, he was trying to make sure there were no remaining pictures of him from his days as an employee of the Silken Cushion. If Alex knew who had worked there back in the day, he'd probably find more strangled bodies than just Ruby Tomlinson.

That line of thinking yielded a decent motive for the killer, but Alex wondered why he was striking now, fifteen years after the Silken Cushion closed its doors forever. Had someone threatened to expose him? Was there a policeman or detective digging into the old case?

Something was still missing; he could feel it.

"If Ruby Tomlinson was her real name," Alex asked, "and she owned a house, how come you couldn't find a record of her name?"

"The house was in Garnet's name the whole time," Arnold said. "Garnet didn't know about it until Ruby's death."

"So Ruby went to great lengths to conceal her whereabouts," Alex mused.

That could mean that she was in hiding, Alex thought. *Most likely hiding from the person who ultimately killed her.*

"Let me think about it and get back to you," he said aloud as Sorsha appeared in his open office door. She was clad in a shimmering red gown that hugged her body in all kinds of interesting ways as she leaned against the frame of the open door.

"Call me tomorrow then," Arnold said, then hung up.

"When I heard you in here," Sorsha said, "I thought you wouldn't be ready."

"Nope," Alex said as he stood awkwardly. "Just heard the phone ringing while I waited."

"What was all that about?"

Alex smiled and reached for the little chain that would turn off his desk light.

"I'll tell you about it over dinner," he said.

Just before he tugged the chain, he noticed that one of the notes on his desk did not bear his signature brand of scrawl. Focusing on it, he saw that it was from Sherry, informing him that Director Stevens of the Manhattan FBI Field Office had called and asked Alex to call back.

"Now what?" Sorsha asked when she saw Alex hesitate.

"Just a note to call Director Stevens," Alex said. "I'll call him in the morning."

"Or you could just ask him tonight," Sorsha said. "I was feeling like the Emerald Room, we haven't been dancing there since the time we went to see that Broker fellow."

"What's that got to do with Stevens?" Alex asked.

"It's his favorite place to unwind," Sorsha said. "Five will get you ten that he's there right now."

Alex didn't know if that was likely, but Sorsha seemed confident so he just smiled and went along.

"That sounds fine then, though we'd better leave from your office."

"Why my office?"

"The reason I wanted to talk to Stevens in the first place," Alex said. "Some FBI goons are following me." Alex chuckled as he thought of something. "Or, rather they would be, if I hadn't been using my vault to get all over the city today."

Sorsha gave Alex a wicked smirk.

"No," she said, taking his arm. "Let's get a cab from the brownstone. I'd like to take a look at these G-men who have the unmitigated temerity to follow my fiancé around."

30

A NIGHT TO REMEMBER

Alex resisted the urge to look over his shoulder as the taxi entered the inner-ring, heading for the Emerald Room. He'd seen the men in the surveillance car when he'd walked Sorsha to the cab, and he had no doubt that one of the pairs of headlights back behind them belonged to them.

"Stop worrying," Sorsha said, picking up on his nervousness. "Whoever they are and whatever they're after, they're just here to watch."

"Unless they aren't," Alex said.

"If they aren't, I'll make short work of them."

"You keep your head down," he said, taking her hand. "Something about this stinks and I wouldn't put it past those Federal busybodies to be packing spell breakers. They know we're an item, after all."

Sorsha contemplated that for a moment, then shook her head, sending her platinum hair flying.

"They wouldn't dare," she said. "No sorcerer would stay quiet if the government killed one of us."

"You're assuming anyone knows they're FBI," he said. "I only found out by luck."

"Don't get twitchy until we've talked to Director Stevens," she said as the cab began to decelerate.

"We're here," the cabbie said from the front seat as the car gently rolled to a stop.

"Wish me luck," Alex said, as he got out on the street side of the car and limped around to open Sorsha's door.

She took his offered arm, stepping lightly out onto the sidewalk. There was a short line of people standing in front of the club, but Alex ignored them. He escorted Sorsha right up to where the bouncer waited. He was a big man, at least as tall as Alex with a barrel chest that seemed to be barely contained by his tuxedo coat. His face was flat, with a squashed nose and close-set eyes that reminded Alex of a gorilla.

The perfect man for the door, Alex thought as he walked right up to the man.

In the years that he dated the sorceress, Alex had learned that bouncers at high end clubs were trained to recognize the New York Six as well as sorcerers from important places like Hollywood, Washington, and Chicago.

"Miss Kincaid," the enormous man said as he stepped back from the door so she could pass. "Welcome to the Emerald Room."

To his credit, he didn't seem disturbed by the appearance of a sorceress and simply held the door so they could enter.

As they passed inside, Alex felt a wave of nostalgia. It had been five years since he'd first set foot in this club. In that time, not much had changed. The Emerald Room was still a large, two-story-high space with curved tiers of tables surrounding the dance floor, bandstand, and the long mahogany bar.

The first time he'd been here, he'd worn an illusory tux created by Iggy's magic. Even his money had been a facsimile back then. Now he had more money in his pocket than he'd had in his bank account back then and his tux was of the highest quality without being actual silk.

Back in those days he didn't have a girl on his arm, much less one of the most beautiful and powerful women in the world.

It's been an interesting five years, he thought.

Just like five years ago, the tables were crowded, the band was in full swing, and the dance floor was packed. Unlike back then, however, the club manager was hurrying up the steps to welcome him.

I guess the doorman alerted him, Alex thought.

"Miss Kincaid," he said as he arrived. "I'm Arthur Fredrickson, the manager here. Welcome to the Emerald Room."

"Thank you," Sorsha said, the epitome of grace and polish. "It's been too long since I've gone dancing here."

"Well, I can help with that," Fredrickson said with an ingratiating smile. He was a trim, athletic man of average height with slicked-back hair, brown eyes, and a pencil mustache. "My private table is near the dance floor and you're welcome to use it. Just follow me."

He offered Sorsha his arm and she took it, thanking him for his generous offer and attention. Alex smiled and followed along in their wake, looking around at the crowd as he went. Sure enough, he caught sight of Sorsha's former boss, Adam Stevens, sitting at a table on the upper tier with a woman Alex assumed to be his wife.

"Here we are," Fredrickson said, removing a silver rope that blocked off a table against the wall. It was large enough for maybe four people if they pushed in tight, but it was set for only two. "Will this be satisfactory?"

"Indeed," Sorsha said, giving the man a winsome smile. "Mr. Lockerby and I would like a menu, I think."

"Very good," Fredrickson said, then he snapped his fingers and, as if by magic, an immaculately groomed waiter appeared at his side. "This is Pierre, the head waiter here in the Emerald Room. He will see to you personally. Is there anything else?"

"That will be quite satisfactory," Sorsha said, "Thank you."

"If you need anything more, you have only to call for me," Fredrickson said, then he bowed and stepped back.

He had hardly gone when the head waiter stepped up. In lieu of a menu, he recited the food available from memory and promised to bring Sorsha a martini and Alex an excellent whisky.

"We should probably talk to Adam before our food arrives," Sorsha said, motioning to a cigarette girl. "Did you see where they are?"

"Up there," Alex pointed.

"What do you need?" the cigarette girl asked as she approached with her tray of tobacco products.

"Do you see that man on the top row?" Sorsha asked.

"That's Mr. and Mrs. Stevens," she said. "They're in here at least once a week."

"They're old friends of mine," Sorsha said. "Would you ask someone to invite them down for a moment?"

Alex was ready and passed the girl a five spot.

"Of course, miss," she said with a curtsy. "I'll deliver the message myself."

With that she turned and left, leaving Alex and Sorsha alone for the first time since they arrived.

"This is nice," she said, taking his hand.

"We're practically here on business," Alex said with a chuckle.

"I miss this," Sorsha admitted. "Ever since the FBI dissolved the magical crimes unit, they haven't had much use for me. All I've been able to do is sit in my office and go over reports, or hide away in my lab and enchant steel bars."

"And make money hand over fist," Alex added. "Don't forget that."

"So, you're going to marry me for my money?" she joked.

"It's not high on the list," Alex admitted, "but it's on there."

"Who's getting married?" Director Stevens' voice interrupted Sorsha's reply.

"No one," she said as Alex stood to welcome the director and his wife.

"Director Stevens," Sorsha said, motioning for them to sit. "It's good to see you."

"This is my wife, Leslie," he said indicating the blonde. "Leslie, this is Sorsha Kincaid and Alex Lockerby."

"Charmed," she said in an accent that spoke of southern upbringing.

Stevens held out a chair for his wife, then sat himself.

"I assume this is about my phone call," he said, leaning in so as not to be overheard.

It wasn't much of a worry since they were fairly close to the bandstand.

"What did you find out about the detail following Alex?" Sorsha wondered.

"If they really are FBI, they're off the books," Stevens said. "I called a friend of mine in Washington and he looked through the active case files for New York and New Jersey. Nothing."

"Is it possible the men are here courtesy of your friend, Shultz?" Sorsha asked.

"Maybe," Alex said with a shrug. It was a good thought, Lieutenant Shultz didn't seem like the kind of man to just let things go; after all, Shultz was an officer in Hitler's army. Alex had given the Nazis a bloody nose or two, but he suspected the German army had bigger things to worry about than him.

"I have a theory," Stevens said.

"I'm all ears," Alex replied.

"There's an assistant director out of the New Jersey Field Office," he said. "He's been a thorn in my side for some time. Rumor has it he wants my job."

"Surely you're more important than a lowly assistant director," Sorsha said.

Something clicked in Alex's mind.

"This guy wouldn't be Marcellus Washburn, would he?"

"How did you know that?" Steven asked.

"I had a run in with him when a bunch of German goons shot up the Homestead Brewery," Alex explained. "Apparently our man Washburn had people watching the place. He was very angry when there wasn't anyone he could arrest."

Stevens rubbed a hand across his strong chin.

"When I first heard about Washburn's ambitions," he said, "I looked into him. He was quite the hotshot in the FBI's organized crime unit."

"He told me that he'd been after the Rosonos for years," Alex said, remembering the man's unhinged rant. "He blamed me for helping Tony Casetti go straight."

"Maybe that explains why he's watching you," Sorsha said.

"*If* he's the one doing it," Stevens cautioned. "It is just a hunch after all."

That was a good point. Other than pointing the finger at Washburn, Stevens hadn't really told him much. He was sure there wasn't an active FBI investigation against Alex, but Stevens might have been deceived.

"I think you've talked enough shop," Leslie said, putting her hand on her husband's arm. "I'd like to dance."

Stevens put his hand over his wife's, then nodded at Alex and Sorsha.

"I hope I've been helpful," he said. "Please excuse us."

Alex rose as they got up and waited until they left to return to his seat.

"What are you going to do?" Sorsha asked, once Mr. and Mrs. Stevens were gone.

"Nothing for right now," he said. "There's still too much I don't know. If Washburn really is having me followed, I need to learn why. For right now I'll let them follow me around and keep an eye on them."

Alex had rather more of a plan than that, but he didn't want to let anyone in on it until he'd had a chance to hash it out more thoroughly in his mind.

Before they could talk more about it, their waiter returned with their food and they enjoyed an excellent meal talking about frivolous things. When at last they were done, Sorsha stood and dragged Alex down to the dance floor.

"You can lean on me," she said when he brought up his injured foot.

He decided it didn't really hurt that badly.

"Admit it," Sorsha said as they awkwardly moved through a fast-paced number, "you enjoy this."

Alex laughed at that.

"My foot is loving it too," he said.

"Just a bit longer," Sorsha said, her eyes sparkling.

"I'm just glad Father Harry insisted I learned to dance," Alex replied. "Though you're much spryer than Sister Gwen."

"We should visit his grave," Sorsha declared as the band switched to a slower song. "You know, introduce him to your fiancée."

"I'm sure he'd like that."

Mercifully, Sorsha relented at the end of the next dance and Alex escorted her back to her chair.

"I could use another drink," she said, turning to look for their waiter. She spotted him, but he was busy with another table.

"I'll get it," Alex said. His foot throbbed when he stood up, but with the assistance of the cane, it wasn't so bad.

He limped his way down to the bottom level of the club, then around the dance floor to the bar on the far side.

"Two martinis," Alex told the bartender, deciding he didn't want to make another trip, "and a neat Scotch while I wait."

Alex watched the bartender pour his whiskey, then, picking it up, he turned his back to the bar to watch the dance floor. He raised his eyes up to the entrance, high above and began scanning left and right, looking for any signs of the men who'd been following him. In a place like this, they'd stick out like a sore thumb.

"Assuming they could even get in," he mused. Two men in government approved suits would never make it past the bouncer without flashing their IDs. "If they did that, the bouncer would surely remember them," Alex muttered. That didn't seem likely, but he finished going over the crowd anyway.

"Your cocktails, sir," the bartender said as Alex finished sipping his Scotch.

Alex turned back to the bar and came face to face with someone he recognized.

"You," Malcom Snow sneered as he recognized Alex. "I hear I have you to thank for ruining my triumph."

"I beg your pardon?" Alex said, genuinely confused. As he looked at the man, he saw he was clad in a silk tuxedo with a cocktail of some kind in his hand. Based on how he was weaving with the music, the drink he was holding was not his first.

"I had the whole story," Snow went on, "a nice, brutal murder or two, the cops are baffled, the Mayor is helpless..." He paused and shook his head, looking wistful. "God, what a public relations nightmare." His eyes suddenly focused again and he grabbed Alex's lapels. "I could have ridden that story to victory," he snarled. "The election is just a few days away, and now..." He paused again. "Now I'm back in a dead heat with that idiot Mede."

"That's hardly my fault," Alex said, batting the man's hands away from his coat.

"Of course it's your fault," Snow bellowed. The effect was lost thanks to the brassy music, but Alex could see that the man was genuinely angry. "You had to go and catch the killer, didn't you? And what a killer. Was he some vile madman or homicidal maniac? No." He sighed and shook his head. "Turns out he's just some washed up mobster looking for revenge. It's barely newsworthy and everybody looks good."

Alex stepped back from the man, disgusted by his callousness.

"Look on the bright side," he said. "Maybe that weird disease will get worse."

"You think so?" he said, actually looking hopeful.

Alex shrugged and picked up the martinis.

"Who knows," he said, then realized that with both hands holding martinis, he couldn't hold his cane. Setting one down, he picked up the cane and hung it over his arm before picking up the second martini and limped back to Sorsha.

"What kept you?" she asked with a scowl of disapproval.

"I ran into Malcom Snow," he said, setting both glasses in front of Sorsha.

"Are you trying to get me drunk?" she asked, eyeing the martinis.

"I had a Scotch while I waited for him to make yours, so you're behind," Alex explained.

"Ah," she said, feigning seriousness. Picking up the first glass, she took a sip. "So who is Malcom Snow?"

"He's a candidate to fill Royal Copeland's Senate seat," Alex said. "He was the one flogging those stories about Ann Gallagher's murder in the press. As I understand it, Snow figured if he made the mayor and the cops look bad, he could tout himself as a reformer."

"That's disgusting," Sorsha said.

"That's politics," Alex answered. "At least it looks like his campaign is on the rocks as a result."

Sorsha raised her glass to him in a toast.

"I guess I did my good deed for the day," Alex said, allowing himself a satisfied smile.

"Father Harry would be proud," Sorsha agreed.

Alex ordered another Scotch once Pierre worked his way back to them. Sorsha made small talk while they watched the band and the dance floor. Alex was willing to try another dance, but they had to retreat before the song finished.

"Had enough?" Sorsha said once they'd sat for a while.

"Of your company?" he asked. "Never. I would like to go somewhere where I can hear myself think, though."

"How about my private balcony?" she said.

Alex drained his glass and set it down on the table.

"Let me get the bill, then we'll find somewhere to draw a door."

Sorsha's private balcony was attached to her bedroom and looked out over the Island of Manhattan. Despite the winter cold, the balcony was perfectly comfortable, thanks to her magic. Two chairs stood on either side of an elegant metal table with a stained-glass top.

The wind blew with a ferocious force, but the magic of the castle blunted it down to a gentle breeze.

To Alex, it felt wonderfully still.

"Better?" Sorsha said, coming up behind him and rubbing her hands over his shoulders.

"Much," he said as she worked the tension out of his neck. "You've been holding out on me."

"A girl never reveals all her secrets," she said, an undertone of mirth coloring her voice. "We're best when we're mysterious."

Alex had to agree with that. The more he learned about women, and Sorsha in particular, the less he seemed to know.

It would be interesting, of course, to dig into her business and personal life and find out all her secrets, but she was right, that would ruin the mystery. Still, it was tantalizing, and he was a detective, after all.

Alex sat forward in his chair with a sudden movement, pulling himself out of Sorsha's hands.

"What are you doing?" she demanded, grabbing him and pulling him back.

"I just thought of something I need to look into tomorrow," he said.

Sorsha dug her thumb into the crook of his neck and Alex winced.

"And you're going to tell me all about it," she said, leaning down to whisper in his ear, "right?"

"Of course, darling," Alex said with exaggerated compliance. "Do you have any cigars? This kind of thing goes better with a good cigar."

Sorsha scoffed, then reached into nothingness and handed him a Cuban wrapped in cellophane.

"Now talk," she said, moving around to the other chair to face him.

31

THE LOCKET

Alex Lockerby liked to think of himself as a man who enjoyed many epicurean pleasures; he fancied reading, good whisky, a warm fire, and the taste of a fine cigar. Politics, however, was not among them. He knew people who counted politics as a hobby, and Andrew Barton knew every local politician by name.

In Alex's experience, politicians came in two flavors, the simpering, effete egotists, or the hard-bitten, double-dealing mobsters. The idea of schmoozing either variety made him want to hit someone, ideally the politician in question.

With that idea firmly in mind, Alex entered the ballroom of the Knickerbocker Hotel with Sorsha on his arm. As it always did, her presence caused a stir and before he knew it, Alex found himself sitting in the front row with his famous fiancée.

"When you asked me to come with you," Sorsha said, leaning close to Alex's ear, "I didn't think we were actually going to watch a debate between our Senatorial candidates."

"We have to wait," Alex said with a slight shrug. "You know how these things are."

Sorsha checked her pocket watch then snapped it shut with an audible click.

"This is supposed to start in ten minutes," she said. "In nine minutes, I'm going to powder my nose, and you're on your own."

"Fair enough," Alex replied. Truth be told, Alex was enjoying the chance to sit down for a few minutes. It had been a long day of work and even though his night out with Sorsha at the Emerald Room was only yesterday, it felt like it had lasted a week — to his foot, at least.

Closing his eyes, Alex just sat on the padded chair and reveled in being still. The temptation to lapse into a doze pulled at him, so Alex opened his eyes, focusing on the men who were moving on and around the raised speaking platform. All of them seemed to be involved in some facet of setting up the various bits of sound equipment that would both project the speaker's voice to the live audience and send it out over the airwaves to the state at large.

Alex knew very little about sound systems and how they worked, but he did know they seemed to require an exceptional number of wires.

Danny worked on telephone lines when he was in college, Alex reminded himself. *You ought to have him explain all this to you. It might come in handy someday.*

"You again," the voice of Malcom Snow interrupted his wandering thoughts.

Alex opened his eyes to find the chubby alderman standing over him.

"Mr. Snow," Alex said, pasting a smile on his face, "fancy meeting you here."

"This is where I should be," Snow said, "why are you here?"

"To support the political process," Alex said, with no trace of sarcasm.

"After that buggy ride you sent me on?" Snow growled. "I looked into that strange outbreak the papers mentioned. According to them, the number of sick people has fallen off dramatically."

"I guess that's too bad?" Alex said, phrasing it as a question.

"Yeah," Snow said, sarcasm practically spilling out of him, "imagine that. Better yet, imagine what I learned when I asked a few of my cop buddies about it."

Alex crossed his legs and leaned back in his chair.

"I couldn't possibly guess," he said.

"They told me that the source of that illness had been found and eliminated by Lieutenant Detweiler," Snow said, "with your help."

Alex shrugged at that.

"All I did was lead him to a food cart," he said. "It was the lieutenant's case."

"Sure it was," Snow said. "You told me about that just to waste my time."

"Don't forget making you look like a ghoul," Alex said.

Snow clenched his fists, but mastered himself quickly.

"We'll see how funny you are after the election," he growled, then turned away, storming up to the stand.

"One of these days, you're going to annoy the wrong person," Sorsha said, leaning into his side.

Alex wanted to answer her, but a man emerged from behind the stage and started addressing the crowd. True to her word, Sorsha excused herself and Alex didn't see her for the entirety of the debate.

Having never seen a political debate, Alex paid attention to the first bit. The moderator would ask a question, something relevant to current events, and each man would get the opportunity to speak and then to rebut their opponent, which usually devolved into a shouting match.

Alex had a headache after ten minutes, and after fifteen, he got up and went back out to the lobby to find Sorsha.

Nearly an hour later, the debate ended and people began to stream out of the ballroom. Some were excited, but most just looked bored. Alex could sympathize; he'd worn a look like that when he'd fled the debate earlier. Now, of course, all traces of boredom and apathy had been stripped from his face and he eagerly stood and started moving against the crowd.

"Wait for me," Sorsha said, rushing up to take his arm.

With Sorsha, Alex found the going much easier as most people made an effort to step around her. Eventually the crowd thinned and the two made their way up to the front where the stage stood. Each candidate was there, talking with a small group of their supporters and Alex walked right up to Malcom Snow.

"I'm sorry folks," he said in a loud, confident voice, "Mr. Snow isn't going to be able to keep talking right now, he has another appointment."

"Shut up, Lockerby," Snow snarled. "I've had all the nonsense I'm going to take from you."

"Oh, if only it were nonsense," Alex said. "Unfortunately, I'm talking about the crimes of Herman Franks, the Central Park Butcher."

At the name, several people gasped, the ones old enough to remember the story.

"Who?" Snow asked, looking bored.

"Herman Franks," Alex repeated. "According to the police, he kidnapped and murdered over 30 people between nineteen twenty-two and nineteen twenty-four. He was careful, but the police eventually caught on to him when they found bodies buried in the flowerbeds in Central Park. Later they found more bodies and personal effects in the reservoir."

Some of the crowd were beginning to listen to Alex's story with rapt attention, while others grumbled that he should leave.

"What's the point of all this?" Snow asked.

"Don't worry," Alex assured him, "we're getting there. Now where was I?"

"Clothing in the reservoir," Sorsha suggested.

"Right. One of the missing children was a fourteen-year-old girl named Karena Grimaldi," Alex continued. "That's important because her mother, Lisa, was a seamstress and sewed labels in all of Karena's clothing. Once the police were sure that the bodies they were finding were, in fact, those of the missing people, they began a manhunt. Eventually, suspicion fell on a man named Herman Franks, but before the police could arrest him, Franks disappeared. When the police searched the apartment where he lived, they found bloodstains and some clothing Franks hadn't gotten around to disposing of."

The crowd gasped almost as one and Alex suppressed a smile.

"So why are you telling us this?" Snow asked again. "These people aren't here to listen to you talk about an old crime."

"I should have thought it was obvious," Alex said, giving Snow an incredulous look. "I'm here because you are Herman Franks."

This time the gasp from the crowd was total. For his part, Snow just shook his head and laughed.

"That's simply not true," he said. "On top of that, you couldn't prove it even if it were true. You're just making another attempt to disrupt my candidacy." He stepped up, close to Alex. "This time, however, you're going to pay for making baseless accusations against me. Everyone here is a witness that you slandered me in a detestable fashion and you will be hearing from my attorney."

Alex matched his predatory grin.

"Oh, I don't think so," he said. "Your attorney is going to be far too busy defending you to worry about me."

"How do you figure that?" Snow asked, his smile turning from anger to amusement.

"Easy," Alex said. "You see, you couldn't run for office if there were any evidence that you were Herman Franks, so you set about eliminating anyone who knew you from back then."

"I couldn't run for office?" Snow said with a laugh. "I've been an alderman for five years."

"True," Alex said, "but aldermen don't get their pictures in the paper unless they're involved in some scandal. The same can't be said for Senators. Alderman gave you a taste of power, but you wanted more."

"Wanting to serve my state and its people doesn't even make me unique," Snow said. "Lots of people want that. It certainly doesn't make me a killer."

"It does if you are, in fact, Herman Franks," Alex countered.

Snow laughed again.

"A wild, unsubstantiated slander," he said.

"It would have been," Alex said, "if you hadn't killed Ruby Tomlinson."

Snow just shook his head and turned to the crowd.

"I'm sorry, folks," he said. "I don't know what this lunatic is up to, but I'm certain I'm not going to stand here and listen to any more. Let's move to the lobby and I can continue answering your questions."

"I think I'd like to hear a bit more," the voice of Detective Arnold rose from the back of the crowd. He walked forward, parting the crowd like Moses with the Red Sea. Five uniformed officers came along in Arnold's wake, all looking serious.

"What is the meaning of this?" Snow protested. "First I have to endure baseless accusations from the police department's lackey, and now it's your turn?"

"Mr. Snow," Detective Arnold said, "if the allegations that Mr. Lockerby is making aren't factual, well then I think you're right. You've got a solid foundation for a slander suit."

"Well then," Snow said, an easy smile creeping onto his face, "why don't you take this fraud out of here," he indicated Alex, "and I'll file charges in the morning."

"Yes, sir," Arnold said, though he held up a placating hand, "that would definitely be the thing to do if Mr. Lockerby is, in fact, lying. In order to determine that, though, I think we should hear him out."

"That's absurd," Snow said and turned to walk away only to find himself blocked by the uniforms.

"Just another minute, sir," Arnold said, "and I'm sure we can have this whole thing cleared up." He turned to Alex and motioned for him to continue. "I believe you said something about the murder of Ruby Tomlinson, a woman who owned a fancy speakeasy during Prohibition."

"That she did," Alex said, picking up the story, "and because she catered to the rich and famous, the police never raided her establishment. Except once. It was on October ninth of twenty-four."

"How did the police get permission to raid the kind of place the Mayor might have frequented?" Detective Arnold asked.

"I'm glad you asked; it seems that one of Herman Franks' neighbors remembered him bragging that he tended bar in a high-class place called the Silken Cushion. Ruby Tomlinson's place."

"Well if the cops raided the place, then they got their man," Arnold said. "Why are you accusing Mr. Snow of being Franks?"

"Franks had an inside man at the police department," Alex said.

Pound of Flesh

"According to the police file his coworkers testified that he never missed a day of work...until October ninth."

A ripple of astonished muttering went through the crowd and Alex noticed that they'd drawn in more people from the foyer.

"After that, Herman Franks disappears," Alex said, raising his voice to better be heard. "But then Ruby is strangled in her own home two weeks ago and, a few days later, Mrs. Melissa Hannover hears what she thinks is a ghost haunting her house. It turned out to be someone in the secret speakeasy in the basement that Melissa didn't even know existed."

Alex turned to look around at his audience, ending with Malcom Snow.

"Would it surprise you to learn that the person who built the house with the secret speakeasy was none other than Ruby Tomlinson? How about if I told you that whoever broke in there, knew it was there, and they were going through all the photographs still left hanging on the walls?"

"Why would anyone care about old photos?" someone in the crowd yelled.

"Because," Alex explained, "there's bound to be an old photo of the original Silken Cushion, the one the police raided. If such a picture exists, it would have Herman Franks in it."

"Why didn't the cops take that photo when they raided the original speakeasy?" another person called out.

"They did," Alex said. "It's listed in the police report but, alas, it's currently missing from evidence."

Detective Arnold cleared his throat before more of the peanut gallery could chime in.

"You think it was stolen from evidence by Franks' inside man?" he said.

"That's exactly what I think," Alex said.

Snow sighed and shook his head.

"This has all been terribly interesting," he said. "There was even a moment when I started to believe Lockerby's tale, but that's ridiculous since I'm not this Franks fellow. From the sound of it, there's nothing more to do until I file my lawsuit in the morning, because, unless you have that old photograph you mentioned, there's no way you can tie anyone to these crimes, least of all me."

He turned to leave but the uniformed officers stopped him again.

"I'm glad you said that, sir," Detective Arnold said, reaching under his rumpled overcoat and bringing out an oblong photograph in a wooden frame. He turned it around, then held it up and slowly moved it from left to right so everyone could see.

The photo showed eleven people standing around a long wooden bar with a sign hanging behind them that read, 'The Silken Cushion.' Clearly visible in the back, wearing a bartender's apron, was a younger version of Malcom Snow.

"Is this the photograph you were talking about, Alex?" the detective asked.

"Looks like it," Alex replied. He turned to Snow and raised an eyebrow. "Isn't that you? Right there in the back?"

"No," Snow said in a calm, even voice. "That isn't me."

"Are you sure, sir?" Arnold said, tuning the photo so he could see it, "because I could swear that's the spitting image of you."

"That photograph is what, fifteen years old?" Snow said. "That could be anyone. Not to mention that it's probably a fake, cooked up by this one." He jerked his finger at Alex.

"Well, it is true that Mr. Lockerby found this photograph," Arnold said.

"I was suspicious when I found out that Ruby Tomlinson, a woman who spent upwards of fifty thousand dollars to have her new speakeasy built, under an unassuming house, was living in the south side mid ring," Alex declared. "A woman of means wouldn't be living there, right?"

"You see, Alex pointed that out to me, and I agreed that it was strange," Arnold said.

"Spare me," Snow said, rolling his eyes. "Now you've just admitted that you two cooked up this outrageous lie together."

"I went to see Ruby's granddaughter," Alex said. "She told me that Ruby didn't have a will. Now, a woman who once ran one of the most prestigious speakeasies in New York has money somewhere, so I asked her if I could look."

Alex held up his hand, dangling a key ring from his index finger.

"This was tucked into the space behind a sliding bit of wainscoting," he explained. "It's the key to a bank deposit box."

"That's where I took over," Detective Arnold said. "With Ruby's granddaughter, Garnet, we went to Ruby's bank and found her will, a memoir she wrote but never got to publish, and a passbook for a secret account with a rather large sum of money in it. And, of course," he added, "this photograph."

Snow shook his head and clapped.

"I'm sure the young Miss Rubison will be thrilled that her grandmother left her such a large inheritance," he said, "but nothing in your entertaining story ties me to it in any way. No jury is going to believe an old photograph, and if you have the stones to take this before a jury, I'll sue the entire department for harassment."

"Let me see if I understand," Detective Arnold said. "You're saying that this isn't you in this photograph?"

"No," Snow said, "it is not."

"So your real name isn't Herman Franks either?" Arnold persisted.

"No."

"And you never knew a girl named Karena Grimaldi?"

"Of course not," Snow scoffed.

Detective Arnold took a deep breath, then he sighed.

"I'm glad to hear you say that, sir," he said. "I really am."

"And why is that, Detective?" Snow asked.

"Well, there's this doctor over at Bellevue Hospital," Arnold began, "he's a psychiatrist named Dawson. Anyway, he comes by the Central Office every so often and briefs us on the new things they discover about criminal psychology. The other day he talked about mass killers."

"Fascinating," Snow sighed.

"It really is," Arnold shot back. "You see, what Dr. Dawson told us is that people who commit multiple murders, well, they like to hold on to things that remind them of their crimes. Keepsakes if you will."

Detective Arnold reached into his pocket and pulled out a tiny silver chain with an oval locket on it.

"This belonged to Karena Grimaldi," he said, holding it up so the locket dangled down. "I know that, because in the file it says that

Karena was wearing an oval silver locket when she went missing, and inside were her birth date and a picture of her mother."

Arnold grabbed the locket and popped it open with his thumbnail.

"Miss Kincaid," he said, holding the locket out, "would you read the inscription under the cover?"

Sorsha took the locket in her pale hand and leaned closer to it.

"It says, May nineteenth, nineteen oh-nine," she said. "And there's a picture of a woman on the right side, though I can't say if it's Karena's mother."

"May nineteenth," Arnold said, holding the open locket up again. "There's no doubt about it, this is Karena Grimaldi's locket."

"Or it's one you had made this morning," Snow said.

"You know, Alex here," the detective pointed to Alex, "he said you'd say something like that. So, after we found the photograph," he held that up in his other hand, "We got a warrant to search your home."

"That's outrageous!" Snow shouted. "You planted that and you know it."

"No sir," Arnold said in a sad voice, "we didn't. And to make sure that you couldn't make any claims like that, Alex and I were accompanied by Captain Callahan and Chief Montgomery of the New York Police, as well as the District Attorney and Billy Tasker, who is a member of the press." Arnold held up the locket again. "We found this, and a great many other things in a lock box hidden under a stone slab in your basement."

Snow moved like he intended to rush the little man, but the policemen grabbed him almost instantly.

"If you never met Karena Grimaldi, like you claim," Arnold said, dangling the locket in front of Snow, "then how did a locket, that we know belonged to her, end up in your house? That would be one hell of a coincidence."

Alex, who had been holding in a predatory grin, finally let it out. For his part, Snow wisely decided to clam up and said nothing as he was led from the room by the police.

"Alex," Detective Arnold said after he returned the locket to the inside pocket of his coat, "I really appreciate your help on this one."

"Are you kidding?" Alex said. "It was worth it just to see the look on Snow's face when you showed him that locket."

"Don't be so modest," Sorsha said, bumping him with her hip, "a lot of people will finally be able to put their ghosts to rest."

Alex hadn't really thought of that. He knew that Snow, or rather Franks, had killed somewhere around thirty people, mostly kids, but he'd been working on that as a problem to solve. Now that it was done with, the reality of it hit him. He simply couldn't imagine what those parents must have gone through, or rather he could, but for the sake of his own sanity, he chose not to.

"I'm hungry," he said, taking Sorsha's arm. "I think Iggy would love to see us for dinner."

"And I've got a mountain of paperwork to do," Arnold said, then wished them good evening and headed out after the policemen.

"I'm proud of you," Sorsha said as they made their way toward the foyer.

"Well, I did solve a fifteen-year-old case," he said.

Sorsha gave him an unamused look.

"I meant that you held your tongue admirably and let that nice detective have all the credit. There were a couple of times I thought you were going to explode."

Alex laughed. He and Detective Arnold had worked out their story ahead of time, but Alex still wanted to just blurt it all out.

"I guess I did good on that too," he said, giving Sorsha a sly smile. "You really are a lucky girl being engaged to a brilliant fellow like me. I'm a catch."

Sorsha let out an exasperated noise, but couldn't hold it and burst out laughing. Alex joined her as they made their way down to the street level to find a cab.

32

CURSES

Alex wiped the last of the dishes dry, then returned it to the china hutch and hung up the towel to dry. He and Sorsha had joined Iggy for dinner after leaving the Knickerbocker Hotel, and this time Alex had been able to pick out the car the people watching him were using as it followed their cab. Since they were returning to the brownstone, there wasn't any need to try to shake them. After all, as Iggy had pointed out, they already knew where he lived.

Crossing the kitchen, Alex headed for the library where Iggy had made up the fire and was sitting in his overstuffed chair. Since Sorsha had been joining them at least four times a week, they had made a change to their usual set up. A third chair now stood to the left of the fireplace and far enough out from the shelves so Alex could walk behind it to get to his book-safe or to the Monograph. This was for Sorsha and came with its own side table and reading lamp.

When Alex arrived, Iggy was trimming the end off a cigar and Sorsha had her long, black cigarette holder in her hand. The liquor cabinet on the far side of the fireplace was open and both Iggy and Sorsha had thick tumblers beside them on their respective tables. As usual, Iggy's glass contained a red liquid that Alex knew to be port, and Sorsha's glass contained green Chartreuse.

Since everyone was picking their favorite, Alex poured himself two fingers of twelve-year-old, single-malt Scotch. When he finished, he replaced the bottle, picked up the tumbler, and shut the cabinet doors. The liquor cabinet was in the corner of the room, next to the right-most bookshelf and the window that ran along the front of the building. As Alex turned to take his usual seat, he caught sight of the black sedan parked across the street.

"Are your friends still out there?" Iggy said, as Alex moved the gauzy curtain aside for a moment.

"Yep," Alex said, releasing the curtain and heading for his seat.

The first floor of the brownstone was five feet above the street level, so there was no chance the surveillance team could see into the room, even with the semi-transparent curtains. There were a pair of heavy drapes designed to keep the heat in, but Iggy had put runes on the glass that prevented them from letting the heat out, and he preferred to leave the drapes open, that being the case.

Alex sat down in his chair and propped his injured foot up on the ottoman. He took a sip from his glass, then set it on the side table. He didn't get the chance to have Scotch on the rocks much, but he did prefer it to room temperature. A thought came to his mind to ask Sorsha to cool down his drink, but she'd probably stick her finger in it just to tease him. Not that it would matter, since Scotch was alcohol and would sterilize her finger.

He smirked at that image and Sorsha raised an eyebrow at him.

"What's so funny?" she said in a good-natured tone.

"Oh, just remembering the look on Malcom Snow's face," he lied.

"Yes," Iggy said before Sorsha could respond. "I've had quite a bit of fun reading young Mr. Tasker's take on your exploits with that Irish mobster, so I can't wait to see what he says about this evening's festivities."

Sorsha smirked at the idea, but covered it by sipping her Chartreuse.

"From what you've told me," Iggy went on, "it was masterfully done, getting Snow to admit his crimes in the presence of a police lieutenant."

"I imagine Detective Arnold will get an award from the mayor," Alex said, sipping his Scotch again. "Maybe a nice plaque to hang on his wall."

"Well he certainly deserves it," Sorsha said. "Putting up with you is positively heroic."

Alex gave her a beaming smile, then went back to his warm Scotch.

Maybe I can get an insulated bowl with a lid, he thought, *put one of Sorsha's cold disks at the bottom and keep ice right in the liquor cabinet.*

"I must confess," Iggy went on, not noticing Alex's distraction, "if half of what you said is true, you and Detective Arnold really pulled a fast one on the alderman."

"He was too slick," Alex said. "We knew we'd need to catch him in a public lie, then all his details about not being Herman Franks would be suspect."

"What about the necklace and the other things you found in his basement?" Sorsha asked. "Don't they have his fingerprints on them?"

"No, actually," Alex said. "Not on them or the box they were stored in. Whenever Snow handled them, he must have worn gloves. That's why we needed to expose him as a liar."

"Yes," Iggy nodded sagely. "He might have been able to convince a jury that the box of keepsakes from his victims wasn't his, that he was just an innocent bystander."

"But not now," Sorsha agreed. "Now any jury will doubt anything he says."

"He still might get off," Iggy observed.

"Not likely," Alex said. "Billy is going to be digging up all the old dirt about the Butcher of Central Park. By the time Snow goes to trial, the public will be howling for him to get the chair."

"Isn't that jury tampering?" Sorsha asked with a smirk.

Alex sipped his Scotch and shrugged.

"I can live with that," he said.

"As can I," Iggy added, puffing his cigar.

"Sorsha," Alex said, eyeing his glass. "Can you get steel that looks like rocks?"

"Of course," she said. "Steel is poured into all kinds of useful shapes. You didn't think those bars I enchant were dug out of the ground that way?"

Alex mentally chided himself for not thinking his idea all the way through so he could spot obvious things like that.

"What if," he said, pointing to his glass, "you got some steel cubes or balls and enchanted them."

"That would be a very laborious thing to do," Sorsha said. "The only reason I'm able to do so many disks is that I enchant the entire bar and someone else cuts them into disks."

Alex remembered how Waverly Radio used large boards with interconnected slots to enchant their special receivers.

"I might be able to help with that," he said.

"Fantastic," she said, "but you still haven't told me why I would want to do that."

"Ice," he said, holding up his drink. "I was thinking that I really prefer Scotch on the rocks."

"Ah," Iggy said, catching on to Alex's train of thought. "Steel balls wouldn't need to be refrigerated, and they wouldn't melt and water down your drink."

Sorsha looked up at the ceiling for a long moment, then smiled.

"If we can get past the duplication problem, that might work," she said. "I could market them to bars and nightclubs everywhere. We'll paint them blue and call them Heavy Ice."

"Bloody good idea," Iggy said, sipping his port. "Though I would never drink port over ice, no matter what it's made of."

"What?" Alex asked as Sorsha fixed him with a suspicious stare.

"Based on your deals with Andrew and that gangster Casetti, you're going to want a cut of this idea, aren't you?" she said.

Just like those other two deals, Alex had been thinking nothing of the sort and he said so.

"No need for anything like that," he went on. "After we're married, it won't matter."

"When are you two going to tie the knot?" Iggy asked.

"Why Iggy," Alex said with mock offense, "I didn't know you were trying to get rid of me."

"Rid of you?" Iggy scoffed. "I'm looking forward to a nice suite in that flying castle. You know, a father-in-law apartment."

Alex wasn't sure if the old man meant it or not, but Sorsha found it very funny and laughed so hard she almost dropped her cigarette.

"You know you could have that right now," she said. "I've got some space I'm not using that would make a lovely apartment. There's even room for your greenhouse."

"Sounds lovely," Iggy said, "but I couldn't move in until you two are official; what would people say?"

Iggy's tone was so comical that everyone laughed this time.

Alex hadn't really thought about it, but him marrying Sorsha would cause a fair amount of upheaval in his life. Of course that was marriage in general, which was why he'd avoided it for so long. He'd had offers, he'd even talked about it with Jessica, though she always put him off and now he knew why.

"Pensive, my love?" Sorsha asked as Alex grew quiet.

"Just thinking through the logistics," he said.

"Well, we've got time to prepare," she said. "Sorcerers are expected to be cautious and deliberate. We won't be able to get married for at least a year."

"We've been dating longer than that," he said, not sure how her timeline worked out.

"Yes, but we'll have to announce our engagement officially," she said. "Then we have to give the press and the public time to get used to the idea."

"Better make him a partner in your Blue Ice business," Iggy said. "That'll go a long way toward explaining why a great lady such as yourself is taking up with a private detective."

"Thanks," Alex said to Iggy, as sarcastically as he could.

"No, Ignatius is right," Sorsha said, tilting her head in the adorable way she did when she was thinking. "If we were business partners, in a wildly successful enterprise, our engagement would practically be expected."

Alex resisted the urge to roll his eyes. He had a job, a job he liked very much, why was everyone always trying to give him another one?

Before he could protest, the phone in the kitchen began to ring.

"I'll get it," he said, rising painfully to his feet, then pointed his finger between Sorsha and Iggy. "Don't set my wedding date while I'm gone."

Grumbling under his breath, Alex ignored his cane and just limped to the kitchen.

"Hello?" he said, picking up the earpiece from the hook on the wall.

"Alex," Charles Grier's voice came over the wire. "What have you gotten me into?"

He was breathing heavily and trying to keep his voice low at the same time.

"What are you talking about?" Alex asked, pressing the earpiece to his head to try to hear better.

"They came for me," he gasped. "I was analyzing that stone you gave me, but I needed some ingredients to make a proper Solution of Revelation, I was out of—"

"Focus," Alex interrupted.

"When I got back to my shop, there were men there destroying everything, they were looking for the stone, I'm sure of it."

"You have it with you?"

"Of course," Charles said. "I would never leave something important unattended, I brought it with me."

"What happened then?" Alex said.

"I ran off before anyone saw me, but they burned my shop, Alex. They burned it."

Alex's mind raced. He knew Rodney Tieg was up to something, but this seemed way beyond the machinations of a back street alchemist and a dog wagon jockey.

"Where are you?"

"Down the street from my former office," Charles said, "at the five and dime on the corner."

Having been to Charles' office many times, Alex knew right where the alchemist was and it wasn't far enough away from the now-burning shop to suit his liking.

"Hang on," he said, then leaned around the door frame to look into the library. "Sorsha," he called, waving the sorceress over with an urgent motion.

"What is it?" she asked as she rose from her chair.

"That trick you do," he began, "where you teleport to the location of someone on the phone, can you do it in reverse?"

"What?" she demanded, not understanding.

"Can you listen to someone's voice and then teleport them here?"

Sorsha thought about that for a moment, then nodded.

"Not while the wards are up," Iggy interjected from his chair. "What do you intend to do?"

Alex quickly explained about Charles, then handed the phone to Sorsha.

"Better open the front door," Iggy said. "That will provide a window in the brownstone's protection big enough to allow the teleport."

Alex moved to the vestibule, then took hold of the front door. From the inside, all anyone had to do to leave was to turn the door handle; it was only from the outside that a rune key was required. Turning the handle, Alex pushed the door open a foot, then turned back toward the kitchen.

"I'll keep watch here," Iggy said, stepping into the vestibule.

Alex thanked him and moved back to the kitchen.

"Charles?" Sorsha demanded in an urgent voice. "Hold on."

She closed her eyes and gritted her teeth as her magic reached out, seeking the alchemist. A moment later, Charles Grier appeared on the floor, wide-eyed and gasping. Alex started to smile and relax, but something was definitely wrong. From under the little man's suit coat, a red stain was spreading across his white shirt.

"There was a gunshot," Sorsha said, dropping the phone's earpiece.

"Iggy!" Alex shouted, kneeling down to grab his friend's hand. "Hang on," he said. "We'll get you patched up."

"Alex," Charles gasped, grasping Alex's shirt front. "It's a curse stone," he gasped. "Alchemy and runes combined together."

"What?" Alex said.

"During the Inquisition," he managed, then slumped back down to the floor as the last of his breath escaped his body.

THE END

You Know the Drill.

Thanks so much for reading my book, it really means a lot to me. This is the part where I ask you to please leave this book a review over on Amazon. It really helps me out since Amazon favors books with lots of reviews. That means I can share these books with more people, and that keeps me writing more books.

So leave a review by going to the Pound of Flesh book page on Amazon. It doesn't have to be anything fancy, just a quick note saying whether or not you liked the book.

Thanks so much. You Rock!

I love talking to my readers, so please drop me a line at dan@danwillisauthor.com — I read every one. Or join the discussion on the Arcane Casebook Facebook Group. Just search for Arcane Casebook and ask to join.

And Look for Alex's continuing adventures in "Equal and Opposite." Arcane Casebook #11 coming later this year. You can preorder Equal and Opposite from the Arcane Casebook series page on Amazon.

ACKNOWLEDGMENTS

Special thanks to my amazing beta readers, they really took this book to the next level.

Bob Brown
Virginia Carper
RJ Carvalho
Dawn Clemons
Mark Denman
Mike Dunkle Sr.
Ann Engel
Pam Faye
Michelle Gawe
Tan Ho
James Hodges

ALSO BY DAN WILLIS

Arcane Casebook Series:

Dead Letter - Prequel

Get Dead Letter free at www.danwillisauthor.com

Available on Amazon and Audible.

In Plain Sight - Book 1

Ghost of a Chance - Book 2

The Long Chain - Book 3

Mind Games - Book 4

Limelight - Book 5

Blood Relation - Book 6

Capital Murder - Book 7

Hostile Takeover - Book 8

Hidden Voices - Book 9

Dragons of the Confederacy Series:

A steampunk Civil War story with NYT Bestseller, Tracy Hickman.

These books are currently unavailable, but I will be putting them back on the market in 2022

Lincoln's Wizard

The Georgia Alchemist

Other books:

The Flux Engine

In a Steampunk Wild West, fifteen-year-old John Porter wants nothing more than to find his missing family. Unfortunately a legendary lawman, a talented thief, and a homicidal madman have other plans, and now John will need his wits, his pistol, and a lot of luck if he's going to survive.

Get The Flux Engine at Amazon.

ABOUT THE AUTHOR

Dan Willis wrote for the long-running DragonLance series. He is the author of the Arcane Casebook series and the Dragons of the Confederacy series.

For more information:
www.danwillisauthor.com
dan@danwillisauthor.com

facebook.com/danwillisauthor
tiktok.com/@danwillisauthor
x.com/WDanWillis
instagram.com/danwillisauthor

Made in the USA
Columbia, SC
11 July 2025